SHE WAS THEIR TARGET

ALSO BY P.D. WORKMAN

Zachary Goldman Mysteries

She Wore Mourning

His Hands Were Quiet

She Was Dying Anyway

He Was Walking Alone

They Thought He was Safe

He Was Not There

Her Work Was Everything

She Told a Lie

He Never Forgot

She Was At Risk

He Drowned in Memory

Their Walls Were Empty

They Came for Him

They Sought Vengeance

She Was Their Target

His Fear Was Real (Coming Soon)

And more at pdworkman.com

SHE WAS THEIR TARGET

ZACHARY GOLDMAN MYSTERIES #15

P.D. Workman

ISBN: 9781774685341 (KDP Paperback)

ISBN: 9781774685365 (KDP Hardcover)

ISBN: 9781774685372 (Large Print)

ISBN: 9781774685389 (Lulu Paperback)

ISBN: 9781774685358 (ePub)

ISBN: 9781774685396 (Accessible Audio)

To those who crave acceptance

And those willing to accept

CHAPTER 1

Zachary stared at the screen on his phone after the call ended, frowning and thinking about what the woman had said.

Jennifer. She had been Jennifer Olson when he had known her, but he couldn't remember what she had just told him her married name was. He looked down at the notes he had scribbled while she was talking. Kristin Jones. That was her daughter. So she was Jennifer Jones now. A common name. One of those ones that was really fun to trace when he was trying to track someone down. But he didn't have to track Jennifer down. He had her phone number and a time and place to meet with her.

Kenzie crossed his line of vision and said something to him. It was like she was far away or underwater. He knew she had spoken to him, but wasn't sure what she'd said. Zachary rubbed his temples and focused on her, trying to pull his brain away from the woman on the phone. He was sitting on the couch in the living room, where he had been working on his laptop, and Kenzie had come in from the kitchen.

"Sorry, what?"

Kenzie raised her brows and shook her head, sending her dark curls bouncing. He wondered how many times she had repeated herself already. She didn't look pleased about having to do it again.

"Where are you?" she asked. "Who was that on the phone?"

"Uh... a new client. Maybe. A woman I went to school with."

"Oh...?" Kenzie sounded interested. Zachary rarely talked about school or his years in foster care. She knew the overall shape of his life before he had turned eighteen and aged out of the system, but he didn't talk about it a lot. Didn't mention specifics. He avoided even thinking about it if he could help it. Talking about it was the last thing he wanted to do. So when Kenzie learned something about his past, it was usually just one tidbit, or maybe something that came up in couple's therapy. Where he still did his best to avoid diving too deeply into it. “What is her name?”

That part was easy. “Jennifer.” He looked for something else to tell Kenzie about her, to show that he was willing to share. “She was... in high school with me, I guess. I don’t remember very much about her. She was older. A couple of grades ahead of me.”

“So you probably didn’t know each other very well. Kids tend to stick with their own grades at that age.”

Zachary cupped his hands over his eyes. “We were... she was very nice. Not a lot of people in high school were nice.”

Kenzie made a sympathetic noise. “It’s a tough age, even without all the stuff that you had to go through.” She paused, waiting for him to say anything in response. “Are you going to help with supper?” she asked eventually. “Tyrrell will be here before long.”

"Oh. Yeah, of course." Zachary rubbed his eyes briskly and got to his feet. That was probably what she'd been asking him.

It wasn't like he was making the meal. Kenzie was handling most of that. But Zachary tried to help out—setting the table, making a salad, and getting out anything else she needed. He was happy to give her a hand with anything she needed him to do in the kitchen, but she didn't usually trust him to do the actual cooking. That might have something to do with his ADHD and several meals in the past either put into the stove still wrapped in plastic, left in until they burned, or left sitting for an hour in a cold oven because he had forgotten to turn it on. That, and the fact that coordinating several dishes at once so that nothing burned and everything was finished at the same time required a level of concentration and executive function that he just didn't have most days. He could manage a salad or a sandwich, which wouldn't be ruined if he left them out or they sat on the counter for a while.

Waking up from his reverie about Jennifer, Zachary could smell the hearty scents of tomato sauce and cheese coming from the oven. And garlic. Hopefully, she had made garlic bread to go along with whatever else she had made—a favorite of Zachary's and Tyrrell's.

"Sorry, I should have come in earlier."

Kenzie shrugged. "You were on the phone."

Zachary moved around the bright, cheerful kitchen, getting out the plates, glasses, and cutlery. He was determined to stay focused on the job and not forget anything because he was thinking about Jennifer. He didn't want to think about Jennifer. He would distract himself with the dinner preparations and then with the conversation with Tyrrell and Kenzie over dinner.

His younger brother Tyrrell was doing well with his job at Kenzie's family foundation. He had been there a few months, and all indications were positive. But that could end at any time. Tyrrell was an alcoholic and had been unable to stay sober for more than a year or two since he was a teenager. While Zachary hoped that the latest treatment program had made a difference and Tyrrell could maintain his sobriety, he was alert for any signs that Tyrrell had started drinking secretly.

The doorbell rang. “There he is,” Kenzie said unnecessarily.

Zachary left what he was doing and went to the front door to let Tyrrell in and punch his code into the burglar alarm keypad so the alarm wouldn’t be triggered. They didn’t need security guards showing up for their dinner party.

“Zachary!” Tyrrell grinned at his big brother and threw his arms around him in a quick man-hug, pounding him on the back. “How’s it going, bro?”

“Pretty good,” Zachary told him, and stepped back to allow him in. “How’s everything with you?”

They started walking toward the kitchen.

“Alarm,” Kenzie called out.

Zachary looked back at the keypad. “I did it, didn’t I?”

Tyrrell shook his head and stepped back to punch the code in himself. There was an answering beep as the system cleared.

They joined Kenzie in the kitchen again. Tyrrell looked around. “Anything I can help with?”

Kenzie shook her head. “I think everything is done. Have a seat and tell us how it’s going.”

Zachary went over to the stove to help take out the hot dishes and get things to the table, but Kenzie frowned, making him retreat instead to sit down with their guest.

“It’s going great. Hillary says I have become ‘indispensable,’” Tyrrell bragged.

“Good for you.” Kenzie approved. “She’s so capable; I never thought she would let anyone else help out with the important stuff. I’m glad she has you to backstop her now.”

“Filing is up to date. The database is current. Mostly. I have some research to do on some organizations that we might consider supporting. She says it’s nice not to be behind on all the administrative stuff.”

“I’m sure it is.” Kenzie placed hot pads on the counter and transferred dishes from the oven. “I think we’ll just serve up buffet style, so we don’t have to try to pass around the hot dishes or reach across to get everything.”

She opened up the tinfoil-wrapped garlic bread and Tyrrell and Zachary salivated, watching her slice the crusty loaf. Kenzie paused to look at them. “You guys are two peas in a pod. You’d better eat your veggies!”

“Yes, ma’am,” Tyrrell and Zachary responded in unison, then laughed.

Zachary felt a warm flush of affection for his brother. Looking at them, someone who didn't know them would think that they had grown up together. But Tyrrell had only been eight when they had been placed into foster care, and Zachary had not seen him until decades later. A year and a half ago. They shared the same dark hair and eyes, some similar facial features, and memories of their family before the fire, but that was all. Zachary had spent eight years in foster care without any contact with his biological family and, when he aged out, he had been alone.

He was lucky to have his siblings back in his life again.

It was best to focus on the present.

CHAPTER 2

So, tell us about this friend of yours who called," Kenzie told Zachary, after Tyrrell had finished talking about what was going on in his life and at the foundation.

Zachary stopped chewing and looked at her. He had already said he didn't remember Jennifer very well, so he hadn't expected Kenzie to pursue it. He strained to swallow the lump of garlic bread still in his mouth.

"Uh... I don't know how much there is to tell," he waffled.

Tyrrell and Kenzie were both looking at him with interest. He supposed he would have to tell them something.

"You said she was an old friend from high school?" Kenzie prompted.

"I didn't think you were in contact with anyone from that far back." Tyrrell took a huge bite of the crusty garlic bread himself and spoke around it. "Other than Mr. Peterson."

Zachary had been in and out of various families and facilities for years, and the only person he had kept in contact with was his old foster father, Lorne Peterson. It was Mr. Peterson who had sparked Zachary's interest in photography and set him on the path to becoming a private investigator, even though, by that time, Zachary had long since moved on to other families and facilities. Along with his partner Patrick Parker, Mr. Peterson had provided Zachary with a sense of stability and family that he had not gotten anywhere else.

"We haven't been in touch. This is the first time I've heard from her in years. Since she moved away. That's why..." Zachary shrugged, "I don't know much about her. It was a long time ago."

"And she just reached out and called you?" Tyrrell asked. "Maybe she has some old romantic feelings for you." He waggled his eyebrows. "Wants to rekindle things."

Zachary's face burned. "It was never anything like that!" He glanced at Kenzie, hoping she didn't suspect Zachary's motives. “She’s a potential client. That’s all. Needed a private investigator, and I guess she heard about one of my other cases...”

He’d had a few big cases that had hit the media and spread his name around, so some people who called him now were interested in hiring him specifically, rather than just a random name they had picked out of an internet search.

Jennifer hadn’t said which case she’d heard about. Zachary had recently investigated the death of a man who the medical examiner had initially said died of natural causes when, in fact, he had been poisoned. It had made a small splash in the Vermont papers but had not gone national like a couple of Zachary’s other cases.

“Oh, I see.” Tyrrell nodded. But he was still using his teasing voice. “A potential client.”

“She is.”

“What kind of case?” Kenzie asked, trying to rescue Zachary.

Zachary rubbed his forehead. He was starting to get a headache. “Her daughter. She died suddenly and Jennifer wants it investigated.”

“Oh, dear,” Kenzie shook her head at this. “How old was she?”

“A teenager. I’m not sure how old. Do you remember a Kristin Jones?”

“No.” Kenzie’s forehead creased as she thought about it. “I don’t remember the name and haven’t had any teenage girls through recently. Are you sure she went through the Roxboro medical examiner’s office?”

“No. She didn’t say. It might have been one of the bigger hospitals.”

“Yeah. Probably.”

Having Kenzie as a contact in the local medical examiner’s office was handy, but Zachary was not disappointed that

Jennifer's daughter hadn't been autopsied by Kenzie or Dr. Wiltshire. He didn't want to challenge another one of their cases quite so soon.

"By 'died suddenly,' do you mean she committed suicide?" Kenzie asked.

"No. Jennifer said it was in the middle of a medical procedure."

"Oh." Kenzie nodded. "Well, that does happen," she admitted. "Sometimes there are unexpected complications."

"I don't know the details yet. We're going to get together tomorrow, and then I'll know more."

"Don't raise her hopes," Kenzie warned. "If it was in the middle of a medical procedure, the cause of death could be unknown, but they're usually pretty thorough investigating cases of potential doctor error."

"I'll tell her that."

“What was she like?” Tyrrell asked. “Back when you knew her?”

Even though he remembered Jennifer being nice to him, Zachary wasn’t looking forward to meeting and reconnecting with her, especially under such tragic circumstances. It would not be a joyful reunion. And he wanted the past to remain in the past. His chest tightened and his heart beat painfully hard just thinking about it. How would he feel the next day when he had to face her in person?

“I don’t know,” Zachary told Tyrrell testily. “I don’t remember.”

Tyrrell sat back in his chair, looking at Zachary speculatively. “Okay, bro... sorry...”

“Zachary said that she was kind,” Kenzie told him. “But it was a long time ago.” She looked at Zachary. “A lo-o-ong time ago,” she drew the word out, teasing him.

“I’m not that much older than you.” Zachary shook his head and picked up his crust of garlic bread. He appreciated her trying to shift the conversation away from him, but wasn't in the mood for teasing and joking.

"He must be at least ten years older than you," Tyrrell studied Kenzie. "I mean... look at him. And look at you."

Kenzie's red lips curved into a smile.

Zachary was no catch physically. He'd lived a hard life and had plenty of scars to show it. And while he'd put on weight and looked pretty good now, he was usually underweight during a depressive cycle and looked worn and gaunt. Right now, he was on the upswing, the hollows in his cheeks filled in and his eyes not sunken.

But Kenzie definitely looked better.

"Only three years," Kenzie laughed. "He's no cradle robber."

* * *

Later, Tyrrell had gone home and Zachary was sitting in bed, watching Kenzie spread moisturizing cream on her face. One of those things that kept her looking young and fresh, he supposed. It had never occurred to him that he should take better care of his skin. There were much higher-level things he had to be concerned with. His mental health. Not taking on cases involving dangerous people. Getting enough sleep and, before his last med change, forcing himself to eat enough despite the nausea caused by his prescriptions.

"Are you okay?" Kenzie asked, looking at him.

He tore his eyes away from her, realizing she probably thought he was staring at her, when he was actually lost inside his own head. "Yeah, I'm good. Sorry."

She continued dotting the moisturizer on her face and rubbing it in. "It's just that... you've seemed distracted. A bit... out of sorts, maybe. You're usually relaxed when Tyrrell is here. But you seemed like you had something else on your mind today."

"Just thinking about this new case."

She looked at him, waiting for more information.

"There's not anything to tell yet." Zachary looked down at his phone to check for messages or emails. "I won't know anything until I've had a chance to meet with her."

"But you're not looking forward to it, are you?"

"No."

"I thought you would be excited about seeing an old friend. It would be different if she were someone who didn't treat you very well. I can see you putting her off and saying you have too much on your plate. But if she was good to you..."

Zachary tried to think of the best way to explain it. He knew he should be happy to see Jennifer.

"She was good. But with the rest of the stuff going on around then... it was a pretty dark time. I don't want to think about it, and I can't separate Jennifer out and only think about her. It's all woven together."

Kenzie screwed the lid onto her face cream and put it on her side table.

“Sure, I can understand that. Sorry for pressing you. I’m not trying to be intrusive.”

“It’s okay.” He scrolled down the endless timeline on one of the social media apps, not looking at her. “I know it sounds backward. That meeting someone who was nice would bring back bad feelings and memories. But that’s the way it is. I’ve tried to leave all of that behind me. I don’t want it coming back up.”

She knew only too well how he had repressed other memories. But they hadn’t stayed where he had buried them. They had come bubbling back up again, and he’d had to deal with them instead of being able to compartmentalize and push them down again. He still wasn’t finished dealing with them. It had been over a year and had been the subject of many therapy sessions.

"You're strong enough to deal with it," Kenzie assured him. "Maybe you weren't when you were a teenager, but you've grown a lot since then. You've learned a lot about yourself and dealt with a lot of hard stuff. You can deal with this too."

"I'd rather not."

Kenzie chuckled. "I'm sure you would. But we don't always get the luxury of choice."

She'd been dealing with traumatic stuff lately too, and he was proud of her for it. He put his hand down in the space between them, and Kenzie interlaced her fingers with his and held his hand firmly.

"For tonight, let's focus on the present."

Zachary wholeheartedly agreed.

CHAPTER 3

Zachary checked the address of the building before getting out of his car. He wasn't sure what Jennifer did professionally, but it was a nice building. And she was in Burlington, not Roxboro, so it would cost a lot more there.

He often met with clients in coffee shops or similar places the first time. A neutral location. Never his home—which was actually Kenzie's house—and rarely at the client's home or office. He was wary of being ambushed by someone who didn't appreciate his work on a case. Whether he had done background on them that meant they didn't get a job they wanted, or he had caught them cheating on their spouse or on an insurance claim. Or something worse—like discovering their part in a crime for which they had never been prosecuted. While most clients were completely innocent and came to him for help with their real-life problems, some wanted to contact him for other reasons.

But he knew Jennifer. He recognized her voice, even so many years later. She didn't still sound like a schoolgirl, but he recognized the cadences and the way she mouthed her words. It was as distinct in his brain as a voiceprint. He didn't need independent verification. He knew Jennifer. How many hours had she spent showing him how to do his homework, talking him through it patiently, and showing him over and over again how to complete it?

She had spent a lot of time helping him. Now it was his opportunity to return the favor.

Pulling his laptop bag onto his shoulder, Zachary stood out of his car. He shut and locked the door, tried the handle, and pushed the lock button a couple of times on the key fob. He looked around, eyes sharp for anyone who might have followed him or be paying too much attention to him. He could never be too careful. He didn't want to put himself or his family or friends at risk because he had been too distracted by the upcoming appointment.

No one appeared to be paying too much attention to him. No suspicious cars were pulling up and looking for a parking spot nearby. He hadn't seen anyone when he'd been out on the highway. He pushed the key fob button one more time.

Eventually, deciding that there were no threats awaiting him, Zachary went into the building and pushed the button for the elevator. The floor he stepped out onto was pleasant and bright. The color scheme was pink and silver, with clean, polished surfaces and the company's name on the wall behind the receptionist in chrome script.

Zachary cleared his throat nervously and stepped up to the reception desk. His feet sank into the thick carpeting. Not what he would have expected to find in an office building.

"I'm looking for Jennifer Olson. Jones, I mean. Jennifer Jones."

The receptionist, a black woman with wavy hair, nodded pleasantly. "Is she expecting you?"

“Yes. I have an appointment.”

“And your name is?”

“Zachary. Goldman.”

He wiped his sweating hands on his pants and waited for her to call Jennifer and announce him. She nodded when she hung up the phone. “If you want to sit down, she’ll be out in a few minutes.”

He hadn’t expected Jennifer to make him wait, but he supposed that when he saw the well-appointed office, he should have known that she could be bogged down with important business. He was surprised that she was working so soon after her daughter’s death. Was that because her employer was a jerk or because she wanted to keep herself busy and not think about it?

He walked over to the chairs in the waiting area, then back across the space, pretending to be looking critically at the artwork decorating the wall. Really, he was pacing. He didn’t want to sit down and wait for Jennifer. He needed to keep moving to keep the anxiety at bay. To keep the memories from pushing their way to the surface.

It was only a minute before Jennifer came out to greet him. Apparently, she wasn't weighed down too heavily with work, she just needed time to get out to the front.

"We'll be in the boardroom," Jennifer told the receptionist. She looked at Zachary, pressing her lips together while she examined him. She gave a little nod and a tentative smile. "Zachary?"

Zachary nodded. She stretched out her hand to shake. Zachary took it, and she pulled him in for a hug. He wasn't expecting it and stumbled awkwardly into her arms. Jennifer held on to him for a few seconds. He wanted to pull away from her, but gritted his teeth and stayed still. She gave him a squeeze and then released him. There were tears in her eyes.

"Come on," she invited. "It's so good to see you." She smiled broadly, and he saw her swallow, trying to keep her emotions at bay.

She had always been the strong one. The one who protected him when he was vulnerable.

Zachary followed her to the boardroom, where she shut the door and adjusted the horizontal blinds across the large windows, so they were not clearly visible to anyone walking by in the hallway. She squeezed his arm and motioned to the chair at the head of the large table.

"Have a seat. Can I get you coffee? Water?"

"Coffee."

There was a carafe on a counter at the side of the room. Zachary assumed it was full and fresh. Jennifer nodded and got them each a mug, then sat down around the corner of the table from Zachary and looked at him.

Her face was lined. He could still see the girl that she had been. The young woman he had known. But she had aged, and the lines on her face spoke of profound grief. It had been pressed into her features, and he wasn't sure whether anything would ever erase it. She had dark hair and eyes and her hairstyle was short but seemed unkempt. Like she might have remembered to run a comb through it after her morning shower, but nothing else. Or she might have styled it earlier but then run her fingers through it all day as she mourned for her lost daughter, unable to keep her hands still.

"It's so nice to see you again," Jennifer said. "I've often wondered what happened to you since I left… Then I saw you on the news. That you'd become this big-time private investigator. Wow. I never saw that coming. Good for you."

"Not big time," Zachary said in embarrassment. "I've had a few cases that have become well known, but I'm still… just a little fish. Just one man, doing what I can to help others and put bread on the table."

"You never did have a lot of confidence in yourself. But you've done well. You should be proud."

"I am. I'm glad to be able to do this. I enjoy it. I have the freedom to do things the way I want to. It's good."

"Good." She nodded her approval. She stared off into space for a few seconds. Swallowing again, several times. Trying to stay in control. Zachary was anxious for her. He found actual tears easier to handle. Jennifer's silent distress was difficult to watch. "So I told you on the phone… that I recently lost my daughter. It was so sudden. So unbelievable. I still can't believe that this nightmare is real. But every morning I wake up and…" She choked and took a few seconds to continue. "And it's still true."

Zachary nodded. "I'm so sorry."

She nodded her acknowledgment.

“Can you tell me how it happened?” Zachary suggested. “Just start wherever you like, whatever is easiest.”

CHAPTER 4

Jennifer sighed and stared off into space, her eyes swimming in tears. But she didn't shed them.

"She had dental surgery. I mean, you hear about things happening. People being allergic to the anesthetic; not waking up afterward. I had to sign a waiver but never thought anything would happen to her." She shook her head, pressing her lips together. "They came out and said there had been some complications, and took me into an office to talk to me privately. And told me... that her heart had just stopped."

"And... do they know why?"

"They couldn't explain it. They said there were several possibilities, and the medical examiner would have to do an autopsy and see if he could find the cause. I didn't want them to—but I did, too. I wanted to know what had happened. How we could have prevented it. I don't know why that matters. It isn't like I can go back in time and change the choices we made. Decide not to have the surgery or not to do something else… something we did wrong the first time. But to have them come back and say they still don't know why. That her heart just stopped and they can't explain it. How could that be? How could they not know why a healthy girl just died like that?"

"I don't know. They gave you some possibilities? Like the anesthetic?" Zachary pressed gently for some details.

"Yes. And the medical examiner couldn't say whether it was the anesthetic or something else. But she'd had anesthetic as a baby. She had a few procedures when she was really little. Why would something that didn't bother her when she was tiny be a problem now, when she was grown up?"

"I don't know. I guess sometimes these things develop over time. Like suddenly becoming allergic to shellfish or peanuts."

"They said she might have had a heart condition. Maybe some kind of arrhythmia that was affected by the anesthetic."

"And were those the only two things they suggested?"

Jennifer rubbed her eyes and looked back at Zachary. "I don't know. What if they did something wrong? What if they... injected her with something? Or nicked an artery and couldn't stop her from bleeding out? Maybe they just didn't want to tell me. They were afraid of getting sued because they did something wrong."

"It does happen," Zachary admitted. "But that would have shown up in the autopsy. That would have been obvious to the medical examiner."

"Maybe he is in on it too. I need you to follow up and see. He could be corrupt. He could be covering it up, just like the dental surgeon."

"A cover-up is unlikely. Especially with the medical examiner's office. They have quite a bit of oversight."

"Things can still happen. They can still get things wrong."

"I know. I have reinvestigated a few cases that the medical examiner originally put down as natural or accidental death. They don't always get it right. I'm just saying that the chances of them being in on some conspiracy… are pretty low."

She sighed. "I know. I'm just grasping at straws. I need it to be something that I can understand. I need it to be logical. And… being told that they just don't know… it isn't enough for me."

"There's no guarantee that I will find out anything different."

"I still want you to look into it. Find out."

Zachary took a deep breath and let it out again. "Okay," he agreed. He pulled out a card with his rates on it. "These are my rates. I'll need an initial deposit."

Maybe he shouldn't charge her, since she was his friend. Or maybe he should give her a discount rate. Or to proceed without the initial retainer. But he needed to know that she was serious about it and wasn't just going to call it off after she'd slept on it.

Jennifer glanced at the rate card and nodded. "That's not a problem." She met his eyes. "I do want to hire you, Zachary; I'm not asking for a favor."

"Okay. I will do what I can." Zachary pulled out his notepad and wrote down a few brief notes in his chicken scratch. Jennifer watched his pen move. She could remember, he was sure, how bad his handwriting had been in high school. It had not improved much. He could print neatly if he knew that someone else needed to be able to read it, but that took a long time. When he was just writing for himself, he was as quick and brief as he could be and still keep it legible. He didn't always succeed; sometimes he was baffled himself, with no idea what it was he had written down.

He glanced up at her. "It's still just as bad as it ever was."

She smiled slightly, though all the lines on her face still pointed down. “I thought maybe I had remembered it wrong. Exaggerated it.” She chuckled. “But I didn’t.”

Zachary nodded his agreement.

“I need you to give me as much background on Kristin as possible.”

“Medical history?”

“Well, if she had anything significant in her history, I should know about it, yes. But I was thinking more generally, too. What kind of person she was. What her life was like. Where she had difficulties. Just... the shape of her life before this happened.”

Jennifer blinked several times, but the tears still didn’t fall. Maybe she was all cried out. She must have shed many tears since she had received the news that Kristin had died during the procedure.

"She had a couple of surgeries when she was little, for birth defects. A hole in her heart. An intestinal thing. When she was twelve, she had appendicitis and they removed her appendix. She never had any trouble with anesthetic, so I didn't think of it being a problem with her dental surgery. I wish I had known... I wish I had at least... told her I loved her before she went under. It didn't seem like a big deal. I thought I would be seeing her again in an hour. I didn't know... it would be the last time."

Zachary nodded. "There was no way that you could know. I'm sure that she knew you loved her. And she wasn't afraid, going into the surgery. She knew that she had been okay before."

"No." Jennifer agreed with Zachary's assessment. "She wasn't afraid of it. She was just going to sleep. She said if she did anything goofy when she woke up, I should video it. So I could show her later."

Zachary smiled. He could imagine a teenager wanting to document everything. To play it to her friends on her social networks or private chats. Kids lived their lives online.

“What was she having done?”

“Wisdom teeth. The dentist said that we didn’t have to do it. They weren’t causing her any problems. But they could cause crowding later. And all of her friends were having it done. It’s just the thing to do these days. No one even thinks about it twice. When you get your wisdom teeth in, you get them pulled, because our jaws aren’t large enough to accommodate them anymore.”

“Right. How clear are your recollections of what the dental surgeon told you when they informed you that there had been complications?”

She sniffled, staring past him at the wall. “Pretty clear.”

“Did he say that she might have reacted to the anesthetic? Did he give you any... timeline or progression of what had happened? When they noticed she stopped breathing, was it partway into the surgery or right at the beginning or end? Had there been any problems like... her choking? Taking longer to put under?"

Jennifer shook her head slowly. "They said that her heart stopped. They were monitoring her, and it just stopped."

"Did they try to do CPR? Did they have one of those defib machines?"

"I don't know... they said they did everything they could. But her heart had just stopped."

"Did they call an ambulance? How do they handle something like that?"

"Well... because she was under a doctor's care, and he had her on the monitors and already declared her dead, they just called the medical examiner's office. There weren't any police or anything like that, because it wasn't an unattended death. But they said the medical examiner still had to look into it."

"So the morgue attendants just came and transported her body?"

Jennifer nodded. She bit her knuckle, her face and body rigid as she wrestled with the memory. Zachary could only imagine how devastated she must have been watching them take the body away. She had come for a routine surgery and then watched them take her baby away in a body bag.

CHAPTER 5

Let's talk about Kristin's life," Zachary said, putting his hand over Jennifer's other hand on the boardroom table. "What was she like?"

Jennifer forced a smile and a few deep breaths. "She was lovely. I know that there is a lot of talk about moms and teenage girls and how they can never get along. But it wasn't like that with us. Not at all. I wasn't her best friend and confidante, I'll admit that, but that wasn't what I was trying to be. I just wanted to be a good mom and take care of her, raise her to be a healthy, happy adult."

She stopped, swallowing and breathing, trying to get past the fact that she would never see her lovely daughter grow into a happy and healthy adult. Zachary stood up and went over to the counter where there were a few water bottles and glasses, and he poured a glass of water for Jennifer. The bottles were cold, but not icy. He returned to the table and handed it to her.

Jennifer nodded her thanks and took a sip. After a few minutes, she was able to go on.

“We didn’t have the fights and rebellion that a lot of moms and daughters do. She was a thoughtful girl, and reasoned things out rather than just following the crowd or trying to rush into the dating scene. I told her the high school stuff you see on TV is just fiction. Most kids go through high school without a serious boyfriend or girlfriend. Maybe a few dates, going out to a dance or party, but not like the serious intimate relationships you see on TV dramas. And she was okay with that. She wanted to date and do some of the fun social things, but she wasn’t looking for Mr. Right. Or to get serious with a boy.”

Zachary nodded. He wrote down a few words and doodled. Jennifer might or might not know what her daughter had been thinking and what she had wanted. A lot of parents thought that their kids had no interest in the opposite sex and were shocked to discover they had been intimate with multiple partners. Teens weren't always the same person at school or the mall or a friend's party as parents saw at the dinner table.

"So she dated a little?"

Jennifer looked down. She fidgeted with the glass, turning it in circles on a coaster.

"She wanted to. She was interested in boys and the social scene. But... she wasn't very popular."

"Ah."

"You remember what it was like." Jennifer looked at Zachary, meeting his eyes. "The cliques. The bullies. How the... less popular kids... were harassed."

Zachary swallowed. He shook his head slightly, not wanting to be drawn into memories about their high school days. "Yes, I remember."

"Kristin was... heavy. She was a nice-looking girl, and so friendly and outgoing. But people didn't see that. They just saw her weight and judged her by her body. Teenagers are so focused on outward appearances. The right clothes, makeup, body shape…"

"Are they still?" Zachary couldn't help asking. With such a high percentage of the population being overweight, it seemed like the ideals should have shifted. What was considered fat when he went to school was normal now. "Was there a lot of fat-shaming? Even when so many of the other kids are overweight?"

Unless Kristin was extremely overweight, so that she stood out from the crowd. Or if only the skinniest girls were allowed to be part of the "in" crowd.

"It's just the same as it ever was. Or worse. I know you would think that we should be past that now. All of the stuff that is preached on tolerance and inclusivity and diversity. Trying to shed all of those old prejudices. But weight is still an issue—a big one. There is still a lot of shaming going on. And high school is one of the worst environments."

Zachary remembered the hell that had been high school. It seemed like there had been predators on every side. That nowhere was safe. People that he thought would be nice were not. There was no way to avoid the bullies, to become invisible. When he had known Jennifer, he had been in a bad place emotionally. He remembered a suicide attempt and hospital stay, followed by an outpatient halfway house before being placed in Ptarmigan House, the group home where he and Jennifer had met. Everyone at school seemed to know about his attempted suicide, which just took the bullying to the next level, with both boys and girls telling him he should kill himself, and get it right this time.

They had taken him off all his meds while he'd been in the hospital, saying that they needed to get a baseline and see what he needed. To find something that would work for his depression. Off of his antidepressants, ADHD meds, and sleep aids, he had been a complete mess. Anxious and jittery all the time, hypervigilant, and still depressed, though he tried to pretend that he was holding things together and wouldn't attempt suicide again. He promised them, even signing an agreement when he left outpatient care, that he would not attempt suicide again, but would instead reach out to his doctor, helpline, or caregiver at Ptarmigan House if he were having suicidal thoughts. But the suicidal thoughts hadn't gone away. How was he supposed to overcome his depression while on a med holiday?

And the teachers... some of them had been the worst bullies of all.

"How did she do in school?" Zachary asked, forcing his brain to turn back to the case. To Kristin and what had happened to her. "Marks? Teachers? Favorite and least favorite classes?"

"Well, phys ed, obviously. They were supposed to be sensitive to all kids' abilities and body types, but she got a lot of harassment in gym. She felt like she was targeted by the teachers as well as the other kids. I'm sure they just meant to help her. To encourage her to get into shape and to find physical activities that she enjoyed. But it just came off as disapproval and more shaming. Calling her out in front of the class. Expecting her to be able to keep up with the jocks and cheerleaders. Of course she couldn't. There was no way she could run as fast as them, do push-ups, lift her own body weight... I'll never understand why they would force heavy kids into activities like that. Couldn't they start with... I don't know... yoga or tai chi? Walking? Just getting them to move their bodies in a comfortable environment..."

Zachary remembered skipping most of his phys ed classes. Unless a teacher or guidance counselor actually walked him to the gym. And when he did go, he still got in trouble. He remembered one incident where he had lost control in wrestling practice. Trying to defend himself against a bigger, stronger boy. How they'd had to pull him off of that other boy and reported him to the supervisors at Ptarmigan House, who had disciplined Zachary in their own way.

A shudder ran through his body at the memory. Jennifer either saw it or felt the vibration through the table. She put her hand on Zachary's arm. Strengthening. Steadying.

"It's okay. That's all over now." Her voice was so filled with sorrow. Not that Zachary was no longer under the boots of those who had terrorized him as a teen, but that Kristin's troubles had ended. She no longer had to worry about bullies, children or adults.

CHAPTER 6

She didn't hate school," Jennifer said. "In spite of gym and the kids who bullied her. She had a lot of friends. Kids who banded together, like you and me. I told her just to find the good ones and not worry about everybody else. She did well in her classes. Didn't get top marks, but she wasn't dumb. She understood the work and studied for her tests, and she was always in the upper part of her classes." Jennifer rubbed at the corners of her eyes, even though no tears had leaked out that Zachary could see. "She wouldn't have had any trouble applying for college. Not Ivy League, but any of the colleges around here would have taken her."

"Did the school have any concerns? Want to talk to you about anything happening at the school?"

"No. Kristin wasn't the kind of girl who attracted a lot of attention. She got along. Did what she was told. Turned in her homework. Didn't dress in provocative fashions. Just a quiet girl who blended into the background, I think."

"And did she have any health issues?"

"Well... her weight, like I said." Jennifer hesitated, then pulled out her phone and thumbed through it for a minute to find a picture for Zachary.

Kristin had a round, pleasant face, but was looking down and to the side, looking sad and like she just wanted to fade out of the pictures. She was more than just a little pudgy. Obese. But so was a significant portion of the population. She didn't look grotesque. She was clean and well-groomed and her clothes were tailored to her body rather than either draping her like a tent or being pulled tight. Her blond hair fell beside her face in waves.

"She's very pretty," Zachary told Jennifer.

"I always thought so. But I'm the mom, so I know I'm sort of biased! She was such a sweetheart. We got along so well and I was lucky to have her. I knew that I was. So many of my friends are always fighting with their kids about something. Breaking rules, drinking, getting in trouble at school. Kristin was just a nice, friendly, well-rounded person."

Her face flushed, and it took Zachary a moment to realize that she was embarrassed by her use of "well-rounded," considering her body shape.

"She was lucky to have you," Zachary told her. "You were always good to me in school."

His mouth was dry and his tongue stuck to the roof of his mouth as he tried to figure out what else to say to her. He couldn't talk about those days. It was just too hard.

"Thanks." Jennifer rubbed her forehead, looking like she had a headache. She probably did; fatigued, worn out by crying, mourning the loss of the little girl she had loved and cared about so much. "I don't know how any of this is going to help you, though."

"You never know what might be relevant or help to point me in the right direction. Was there anything else about her health? You mentioned her weight. Her wisdom teeth. The surgeries she had when she was little. Was there anything else recently?"

"She had asthma. I think that went along with being overweight. It was just really hard for her to get around sometimes, carrying that much weight. But she was working hard and she was losing lately. I didn't ask her how much or draw any attention to it, but she was definitely slimming down."

"Dieting?"

"Not on any extreme diets, if that's what you mean. She was trying to eat more healthily. More vegetables, smaller portion sizes. And to get out and get some exercise. She had taken up walking, and I think that was probably the biggest influence. She'd be gone for an hour or two every day, walking around the neighborhood. I don't know how far she got or how many steps; I was just really proud of her for putting in the effort. We both knew that her weight was the biggest risk to her health."

Except it hadn't been. Unless her weight had contributed to her death. The biggest risk had been hidden, something that they never even saw coming. That even now, they couldn't be sure of.

"What did the medical examiner say was the cause of death?"

"Sudden cardiac death. Cause unknown. But he said it was natural causes. I don't understand how it can be natural causes when they don't know the cause."

"Well... it just means it wasn't homicide or an accident. He could have said undetermined, I suppose."

"That would have been more honest, don't you think?"

"It sounds like it. We'll have to see what details the medical examiner's report gives when we get it."

She shrugged dispiritedly. She put both hands over her face and held them there momentarily, before drawing them down. She looked exhausted.

“Are you getting any sleep?”

“Not really. I fall asleep now and then when I don’t expect to. But when I try… I just lie there thinking about Kristin and what happened to her. About how much I miss her and how quiet the house is. Only it isn’t quiet. There are all kinds of noises that I never noticed before. Almost like she is haunting it.”

“Do you live alone? You don’t have any other children? A spouse or boyfriend?”

“I spent too much time at work,” Jennifer confessed. “My husband eventually got tired of it. We’re still on good terms, but it is a few years since he left. And he has custody of our son. Clark is younger than Kristin. Younger than Kristin was. Fourteen. He’s skinny. Really into computers. He kind of reminds me of you in ways.”

Zachary laughed. "I use computers, but I wouldn't say I'm any kind of an expert. I still need someone to come and fix it for me if something goes wrong."

"Well, we didn't have computers when we knew each other either. I just meant... I don't know. He's like you in other ways. Introverted. Does his own thing. He isn't one of the mean kids; I can't remember him ever saying anything rude to Kristin about her weight or anything else. A lot of teenage boys would have taken every opportunity."

Zachary doubted Clark was anything like he was. Shy and geeky, maybe, but that hadn't been Zachary's problem. PTSD, ADHD, learning disabilities, depression, being adrift without any support system. Clark hadn't had to deal with any of those things, from the little Jennifer had said. But she meant it as a compliment. Comparing Zachary to her son was her way of bringing him closer to her family and showing him that he wasn't as distant as he thought, despite the silence of years.

"Did you have Clark very often? Do you, I mean? Does he come to see you on weekends or holidays? Did he spend any time with Kristin?"

"They got along. They had very different interests, of course, so they didn't spend a lot of time together, but when we were together for anything, they got along well enough."

She hadn't answered the question of how often she had Clark over. Less often than she would like would be his guess. Had Clark chosen to be with his father instead of his mother? Or had it been the courts? They might have decided that Jennifer was too busy with her career to give him the attention a younger child needed. "A few years" since the breakup probably meant at least three. The needs of a ten or eleven-year-old were quite a bit higher than those of a fourteen-year-old.

Zachary decided not to press the issue. It wasn't his place to pry into Jennifer's personal life. He needed to focus on Kristin and finding out what had caused her sudden death.

CHAPTER 7

I'll look at the medical examiner's report in detail," Zachary told Jennifer. "I have a friend who will help me with that. Give me some ideas on anything that might have been missed or wasn't filled out the right way... if anything looks wrong... But my expertise isn't in the medical stuff. It's in private investigation. Talking to people. Figuring out if something was going on in her life that she wasn't telling you. Or maybe symptoms she was having that no one recognized at the time. Even changes in behavior can indicate that there was something going on. Something medical."

Jennifer opened her mouth and then shut it. Zachary watched her, waiting for her to think about whatever she had been about to say.

"What do you mean, changes in behavior?" Jennifer asked finally.

“Anything that you might have noticed. If she was more irritable. Angry or sad. Or maybe not. Maybe she seemed... flat. Or maybe she was even happier, or experiencing more extreme mood changes. Doing things impulsively like shopping for stuff she couldn’t afford or engaging in risky behavior.”

“Are you trying to imply that she was taking drugs?”

“No. I’m not. I don’t have any idea what she might or might not have been doing. You’re her mother; you’re the one who had the opportunity to see those things. I didn’t. I have to rely on what people tell me. But sometimes... those things can mean that there was something else going on. Something under the surface. My ex-wife... she was walking into things. Getting angry all the time. Having more extreme mood swings. It turned out that it was Huntington’s disease. No one had suspected it.”

This seemed to mollify Jennifer slightly—a good, concrete example. “So Kristin could have had something. Some disease that was making her act differently. And that might have had something to do with her death."

"I don't know. Was she acting differently lately? Had you noticed something?"

Jennifer chewed on her lip. She looked away from Zachary. "There were things. She was having headaches. What you said about spending money... I didn't know it then, but all the money she had been putting away for college is gone. I don't know where it went. I don't know what she bought with it. She didn't have new clothes or jewelry, or a car. Nothing like that. Her last report card at school... She wasn't doing great. I told you that she got good marks, and she always has, but on her last report card, her marks were down. I thought it was just because the work was getting harder. They expected more from her."

"Did you talk to her teachers about it?"

"No. Kristin said she would do better next term. She didn't want me to talk to them. She said she'd straighten it out and her marks would be back where they were supposed to be the next time." She shook her head at Zachary. "Do you think she had a brain tumor? Or Huntington's disease? Or some other medical problem? Did I not see it?"

"We'll see what the autopsy showed. And we'll ask more questions. After I have talked to some of the people she knew. If she'd had some behavioral changes, then it's worth looking at. With headaches and a drop off in her marks..."

Jennifer gave a little gasp. "I should have known. I should have seen it. How could I not realize that was a warning sign? That there was something going on with her physical health? When she started to lose weight, I thought it was a good thing. That she was finally getting her eating and exercise under control. But what if... what if she was being eaten up by cancer?"

“Those could also be signs of stress,” Zachary told her reassuringly. “Maybe it was just her classes getting harder. She was studying harder, giving herself a headache. Maybe she needed glasses. If she was struggling to keep up and maintain her marks, she might have been eating less because she was worried, or she was burning more calories off with anxiety. It might have just been normal teenage stuff.”

“How will I know? How will you figure that out?” Jennifer rubbed her face. The lines deepened rather than relaxing. “I thought I was a good mom. I thought we had a good relationship. How could I not know what was going on in her life?”

“We don’t know anything yet. We can’t answer questions like that without more information. We don’t know whether there was anything for you to see. Anything that you should have noticed.”

"There was. I failed her. I let my baby die, because I was too wrapped up in my work and I thought she would tell me if something was wrong."

* * *

Zachary was glad to get out of the building and into the fresh air. He should probably have felt uncomfortable going from the carefully climate-controlled, air-conditioned office to the heat and the dust and the exhaust of Burlington. But he was glad to get away from the oppressive atmosphere. He hadn't been comfortable since he had walked into the building. Jennifer had done her best to make him feel comfortable there, but he hadn't.

Once, he and Jennifer had shared something. Their lives had been on a similar path. But he should have known how things would turn out. How she would become successful in what she did and have a family, and he would still be struggling with trauma and mental health issues. If he had known when he was fourteen that he would never get over his depression, would he have had the strength to carry on?

She had given him hope back then. She'd made plans, told him how they could overcome their challenges, and encouraged him to plan for a future he couldn't see. She had told him that they didn't have to be defined by the fact that they lived in a group home. It was just one stop along the way and things could change. They could get better.

As Zachary got back into his car, his phone rang. He looked down at it and saw Kenzie's picture on the screen. Her head thrown back in a laugh, curly hair wild. He'd taken that picture of her, and was both proud of himself and grateful to have her in his life whenever he looked at it.

"Hi, Kenzie." He put the phone into the dashboard mount and started the engine. There was a pause while the car connected to the phone's Bluetooth before Kenzie's voice sounded over the speakers.

"... Just wondering how you were doing. I know you had that meeting with your friend today."

She didn't sound upset or jealous about it. He'd been worried that she might feel threatened by Jennifer's reappearance in his life. He and Kenzie had a good relationship, but that didn't mean she was always happy about his meeting with another woman.

"I just got out." Zachary pulled away from the curb. "It was... pretty tough."

"I expect so," Kenzie agreed. "Losing a teenager would be devastating. Almost as bad as losing a young child."

He was reminded of the case he had been working on when they had first met. Isabella Hildebrandt, who had just lost her five-year-old son. She had been deep in mourning and her mother had been concerned for her safety. With good reason.

"She is... I can tell she isn't herself. It's terrible."

"Well, you know how to get me if you need any help on the case. Did you find out which medical examiner did the autopsy?"

"Burlington. I don't know the doctor's name yet. Jennifer has already requested a copy of the report, so it shouldn't take too long before I've got something we can dig our teeth into."

"Good. I hope there's something I can help with. Bring her some peace."

"The cause was apparently given as sudden cardiac death."

"That's a tough one. It can be really hard to tell what made someone's heart stop. Without a lot of outside information and a medical history that points to previous problems... sometimes it's impossible to tell just by looking at the body."

"She had a hole in her heart repaired when she was a baby. Could that have anything to do with it?"

"I doubt it. They would have told her if there were any ongoing problems. It's a pretty common procedure. They didn't have any trouble with it?"

"Doesn't sound like it. She also had some intestinal problem. And appendicitis a few years ago."

"None of that sounds like any particular syndrome. Heart problems can show up in teenagers without any warning. Even athletes. You've seen some of the games where a player just suddenly goes down on the field. An arrhythmia. Even if they've had an EKG done before."

"She wasn't an athlete. She was quite overweight."

"Well, that could definitely contribute. She might have had blocked arteries."

"A teenager? Someone that young?"

"Yes, it's a possibility. They are finding out that heart disease starts a lot earlier than we ever thought. And with how people eat now, especially teenagers, it's not like when everyone was living on the farm and eating fresh, whole foods. The average person eats a huge number of calories, fat, sugar, salt. Nothing like what our grandparents or great-grandparents ate. And we're still learning what that lifestyle can do to our bodies."

Zachary thought guiltily of the number of times they ordered in or ate fast food. And even when they ate at home, they weren't focused on vegetables and whole grains. He knew he ate way too much cheese. And bread slathered with garlic butter.

"Hmm." He cleared his throat. "Now you've got me worried."

"Well, considering we can barely keep the weight on you, I don't think you have too much to worry about. But my jeans are getting more than a little tight these days."

"That's probably my fault. You're cooking for me."

"I cook for myself too," she brushed his comment away. "I could eat better if I put my mind to it. Make more salads. Take my lunch to work. Meal prep ahead of time so we aren't ordering in several times a week."

"I can help more with meals. I don't do enough."

"Well..." She didn't sound too keen on letting him loose in the kitchen. Which was understandable, since it was her kitchen, and she had already seen what kind of havoc he could wreak when he got distracted. "We'll talk about it. See what we can arrange."

"Okay. I'll help out more. I can put something in the oven while you're still at work. Or keep an eye on a Crockpot."

"Yeah. We'll see. Are you on your way home, then?"

Zachary looked at the time. He hadn't set up any other appointments to take care of while in Burlington. But he would have a lot of interviews to do there looking into Kristin's case. It seemed like a waste of time to drive all the way home and then cram more into each of the following days as he tried to see everyone.

"I think I may stop in at her school. I can at least get started. You don't need me at home for a few more hours."

"Okay. You're not too tired? You sound like your meeting with Jennifer might have worn you out."

"I'm tired... but I think it will pass. Just wrung out. Lots of emotion. I let it affect me."

"Your compassion is one of the reasons you're such a great detective, Zachary. Don't run yourself down."

He smiled at her tone. She loved seeing his soft side. So much for the hard-boiled PI persona.

"I'll make sure I'm home in time for supper," he promised.

"See you then."

CHAPTER 8

Zachary had gathered all the information he could about the neighborhood Jennifer lived in, who they knew, and what school Kristin had attended. He wasn't sure he could figure out anything about Kristin's health that her mother didn't know. Still, Jennifer had retained his services, so he was going to do his best to find out and, if possible, bring her some peace in knowing that she hadn't done anything wrong and could not have predicted what was going to happen when she took Kristin in for that routine dental surgery.

The school was a private school that ran year-round in three trimesters. Uniforms, high tuition fees, good teachers; a good program that was supposed to help to prepare their students for the college of their choosing. As Zachary parked his car in a visitor slot and walked to the administrative office, he couldn't help contrasting it to the school he and Jennifer had attended.

It hadn't been the worst school. It had been a public school, but it wasn't ghetto. He and Jennifer were the exception rather than the rule, living in a group home instead of with their families, too poor to buy their own clothes or have anything but cast-offs or donations that the public made to the less fortunate. Everything smelled like cigarette smoke even though neither of them smoked. They were mainstreamed, but a number of the other kids in the home were in alternative programs—apprenticeships or recovery programs, job training, programs that tried to keep kids off the street. Tyson, Zachary's case worker, said that he was too smart for those programs, and that if he just "applied himself," he would be able to succeed in the mainstream school. Zachary recognized that those other programs mostly led to dead ends so, even though he wished he could get away with goofing off and only going to school a couple of days a week, he applied himself and tried to bring his marks up.

Jennifer had helped him out. He didn't know why she had decided to take him under her wing. She was a couple of years older than he was, and in an accelerated track that would have her finishing school early. She was made fun of for her clothes and the fact that she lived in a group home, Zachary knew, but other than that, people seemed to tolerate her and treat her like a normal person.

She probably hung around him because she wanted to be with someone familiar. He was the only one in the group home who went to the same school. They could walk home together and Zachary didn't judge her by her appearance or the smells that clung to her clothes. He admired her and looked up to her. It couldn't have hurt her ego to have an adoring fan to walk home with. So she helped him with his work. She didn't give him the answers to his homework, but tried to teach it to him, to help him to break down and understand what was in his textbooks.

It couldn't have been easy for her. She had spent a lot of time with him, as he remembered it. He had struggled for hours with the work, both in school and out of it. Being off of his

ADHD meds meant that he was no longer "rebounding" when he was trying to do his homework, but also that he didn't have that aid to help him to focus on the work and keep moving forward instead of staring at the same page for hours and taking nothing in. Or forgetting to even take his books home with him.

He reached the office and stood at the counter, waiting for assistance. A woman came out of one of the back rooms carrying a stack of papers. She had wavy blond hair, a lined face, and was significantly overweight. She was dressed in a well-tailored skirt suit. Probably required dress at a school like this.

"Yes? Can I help you, sir?"

"My name is Zachary Goldman," Zachary introduced himself and flashed one of his business cards with a yellow crest on it. Intended to look like law enforcement unless someone actually looked at it and read it, which no one ever did. “I am looking into the unfortunate death of one of your students.”

“Oh,” her face fell into the appropriately solemn expression. “Kristin Jones.”

“Yes. I guess you heard about it.”

“Well, yes, of course. Everyone heard about it. That poor girl. And Mrs. Jones. She was always very involved with Kristin’s education. Made donations to the school.” That would be the school’s loss. Jennifer wasn’t likely to continue making donations after Kristin’s death. “Education was very important to her.”

“I wonder whether I could talk to some people who knew her. A couple of teachers. Maybe her friends, if they have free time or when classes let out…”

“Oh, I wouldn’t want to interrupt any classes…”

"Are all of her teachers busy right now? No one in the staff room?"

"Well..." the woman glanced back the way she had come. "There might be someone..."

Zachary nodded and waited. He didn't need to press her; she decided to take the initiative and talk to whoever she had seen in the staff room.

"Wait here for just one minute. I'll see."

In another five, Zachary had been installed in a small meeting room with Mr. Bryce, a math and science teacher.

"We were very sorry to hear about Kristin," Mr. Bryce told him, his long face grave. "So sudden. So tragic. We forget how fragile life is. Think that we will all be here tomorrow. But... that's not how life works. Any one of us could be gone tomorrow. Just like that."

Zachary nodded. His stomach was tight at the thought. He struggled with his depression, keeping himself alive when his thoughts turned to suicide. And as Mr. Bryce said, it could all be for nothing. His life could blink out like a light switched off in an instant. Hit by a bus. A cardiac event. Some bizarre accident. He didn't like to think about it.

"It has been quite a shock to Mrs. Jones, as I'm sure you can understand," he told Mr. Bryce, trying to keep his own feelings masked and to act as businesslike as possible. "She didn't have any warning, and she is still trying to understand what happened to Kristin and to find meaning in it."

Bryce nodded solemnly. "But… it was just one of those tragic, unpredictable things. She reacted to the anesthetic…?"

"We're trying to sort that out. I wonder if you can tell me about Kristin. What kind of a student was she?"

"Well…" Bryce frowned, his brows drawing together. "I don't know what to tell you. I can't see anything relevant to…

whatever it is you're trying to do. She was… sort of a mousy student. Didn't have much to say. Stayed quiet unless she was called upon. Didn't offer answers, but knew them if you pinned her down. She was a fair to good student as far as grades went. We're pretty tough here, so getting a good mark here would probably mean excellent marks at another school. It's a demanding program, but we turn out some really fantastic graduates who go on to become doctors, lawyers, senators…"

Zachary didn't need the commercial. He nodded, trying not to show his impatience. "And she was keeping her marks up? Nothing had changed?"

"Ah… well, we saw a dip in her grades the last term. I'm sure Mrs. Jones probably told you that. I couldn't tell you why. It seemed like she just wasn't trying as hard. Maybe she had an outside interest that was taking her attention, distracting her from her schoolwork? She handed in a few assignments late, which wasn't like her. I thought maybe… problems at home, a boyfriend…" He shrugged expressively. "She never said anything in class. We had no relationship outside of class where she might confide in me. I don't know if she ever talked to her guidance counselor about whatever was going on. If there was something going on. Maybe she was just finding the work harder."

"Did you teach her in more than one subject?"

"Yes, advanced math and science."

"And was it one or the other that her marks went down in?"

"It was both. And I did take the opportunity to look at her other marks on the computer. Her grades in other classes were faltering too."

"So it was across the board, not just one subject."

He nodded. "Yes, that was definitely the case."

"Then it wasn't just one concept she was struggling with."

"I would agree with that."

"Was there anything else you noticed? Any changes in her behavior...?"

Bryce scratched his jaw, thinking about it. "As I said, she had missed a few assignments or handed them in late. That was new. I had wondered if she was ill."

CHAPTER 9

You did?" Zachary leaned forward, hyper focused now. "What made you wonder if she was sick? Other than handing in assignments late?"

"Her appearance had changed. Her face... her pallor. And I think she had lost weight. I know there were a couple of times when she had to leave class, claiming a migraine or stomach upset. Since she wasn't the type to make trouble or take advantage, I assumed she was telling the truth and not just off to meet someone or ditch class. As I said... she was pale, lost some of the healthy color she used to have. Maybe she was on a diet, losing weight and not getting as much water or vitamins. I'm not an expert in nutrition."

"Dieting could cause any of those symptoms," Zachary agreed. "Her mom noticed that she was losing weight too. Thought that she had started eating healthier."

Bryce grimaced. “I don’t think so. Just my opinion, but someone who is eating healthy shouldn’t look like that.”

Zachary wrote a few notes down in his notebook—migraines, stomach, weight loss, and pale. Kenzie might be able to help him sort out whether it was some illness or likely just to be dieting. And whether that could have triggered some problem with the surgery.

Bryce was staring at Zachary’s notepad.

“Sorry,” Zachary said, “you don’t mind if I take notes, do you? I need to keep track of any issues she might have had and any questions I have to follow up on.”

“Is that some kind of shorthand?”

Zachary’s face warmed. He could say yes, that it was shorthand or his own personal code. “No, it’s just my chicken scratch. Although Kenzie says that calling it chicken scratch is an insult to chickens.”

He chuckled. “I would be inclined to agree.”

“I can read it. Usually.” Zachary finished jotting down the words that would later serve as a memory aid.

“Did nobody ever teach you how to write? Your pencil grip looks painful. You must fatigue very fast.”

“I know. It’s a learning disability. It’s the only way that works for me.”

“You should have had occupational therapy.”

Zachary shrugged. “I had a little in school. But they didn’t do as much of that kind of thing then, and I didn’t practice at home like I should have.”

Bryce nodded his understanding. “Kids hate it, I know. It’s torture to get them to practice, but it’s the only way to reprogram their brains so that they learn to do it properly.”

“Too late for me. I’ll just keep doing my chicken scratch. I don’t do a lot of writing, I type when I’m at home, and that’s much easier.”

“How about texting? If you’re good with the onscreen keyboard, you could take notes on your phone. That would be easier to read later and would be backed up to the cloud.”

Zachary nodded slowly. “I don’t like to rely too much on technology, since it sometimes fails, and then I could lose everything. But maybe I should consider it.”

“We encourage our students to use modern technology as an assistive device whenever possible. You’ll see kids with their phones out during class, and I know that most schools won’t allow that but, if that’s the easiest way for them to get their thoughts down, then why not? If they’re texting to each other or posting selfies and miss what’s being said in class, that’s their loss. Our kids are dedicated. They want to succeed. That won’t happen if they use their phones for entertainment during class instead of as a tool. You can use it to make recordings too," Bryce was warming to the subject; obviously it was something he had strong feelings about. "You could record your interviews and then play it back and make notes when you're back at your keyboard. Then you could be sure not to miss anything."

"I could," Zachary agreed. "They really are amazing little devices. Who would have thought when we were kids—" he corrected himself, realizing that Bryce was younger than he was, "—when I was a kid that something like this would be possible. A phone and computer in the palm of your hand. Take it anywhere with you. Calculator, recorder, phone, notebook, calendar, camera... we would never have believed it. It would have been like something out of Star Trek."

"Us older people," Bryce generously included himself as part of Zachary's generation, "need to learn how to use them to our best benefit. Too many are afraid of technology or not willing to learn new things."

"Well... I appreciate your suggestions. And thank you for talking to me about Kristin. You've been very helpful. I will need as many perspectives as possible to figure out whether her death was foreseeable or preventable."

Bryce shook his head sadly. "I'm sorry I didn't do anything when I thought she was sick... called her mother to discuss it or looped in her guidance counselor. I should have known that there was something wrong. But I didn't know it was that serious."

CHAPTER 10

None of the adults Zachary talked to at the school seemed to have much more to say than Mr. Bryce. Most had failed to notice any difference in Kristin, unless it was that her marks had fallen, and they expected that to change before the next report cards were issued. Kids' marks did that, they went up and down and when kids realized there was a problem, they corrected their course. Or parents took a firm hand and enforced homework, study time, and tracked assignments to ensure they were completed and submitted on time.

When classes were a few minutes from dismissal, Kristin's two closest friends were called out to see if they would talk to Zachary. Ala and Rain were like inverse images of each other. Rain was white with long, straight blond hair and Ala with dark skin and features that suggested Indian descent, her wavy hair cut in a short bob. Ala smiled at Zachary and looked friendly, while Rain looked sullen and standoffish.

“I’m a friend of Kristin’s mom,” Zachary told them when he introduced himself. “She’s asked me to... ask some questions about how Kristin was before she... passed away. She’s afraid that the doctors may have missed something they should have been aware of.”

“I don’t know of anything,” Rain said, and looked away. “You know, we’ve got things to do. We’re on the field hockey team and we’ll get in trouble if we miss practice or show up late.”

“If I could just spend a few minutes with each of you separately,” Zachary said. “It would be a big help to Kristin’s mom. She said that you were Kristin’s best friends.”

The two girls exchanged looks that Zachary couldn’t interpret. They were friends with her? Or they weren’t, but didn’t want Jennifer to know that? Maybe they had been friends in younger grades but had drifted apart. Or maybe there had been a big blow-up that Jennifer didn’t know about.

“We can’t stay,” Ala agreed. “They’ll want us on the field.”

"I'm sure your coaches would understand that you just lost your friend and want to help her mom out in any way you can."

They looked at each other again.

"You must feel pretty bad about her death," Zachary tried. "It must have been a huge shock to you too."

"Yeah," Ala admitted. "When my mom told me... I couldn't believe it. I thought there had to be some kind of mistake. People don't just die like that, having their wisdom teeth out." Her voice was plaintive and she shook her head. "No one had a chance to say goodbye or anything. We were supposed to do everything together. You know, school, prom, college... we had plans. And now..." She spread her hands in a gesture of hopelessness.

"Let's see if we can find anything out about why it happened. It will only take a few minutes, and I think it would be helpful for you to come to terms with things. Give you some sense of closure. That you've done everything you could to understand it and to help her mom."

It was all nonsense. A sense of closure? Zachary wasn't any kind of therapist. And he didn't imagine that they would feel much better after talking to him than they did before. He couldn't give them back that future they had planned together. He couldn't do anything to help them feel better about it. Maybe he could help Jennifer. But even that was doubtful. What did he have to take back to her? So far, nothing except what she had already told Zachary. That Kristin's grades had been faltering and she had been losing weight.

Finally, Ala nodded. She looked at Rain, who rolled her eyes and gave Zachary the biggest attitude of contempt that she could manage. But she didn't object or walk away from them.

"I appreciate it," Zachary told them, as if both had agreed enthusiastically. "This means a lot to her mom."

Rain looked at her phone with a practiced flick of her wrist. “Talking to us separately is going to take twice as long. You can talk to us both at the same time. We’re both going to tell you the same thing anyway.”

Ala looked like she would object to this, but when Rain gave her a frown, she nodded her agreement.

“Yeah. You’d better take both of us together,” she agreed. “We really do need to get to field hockey. We’re in the semi-finals. It’s really important.”

Zachary sighed and conceded. He’d run into the same thing when interviewing teenagers before. It was all or nothing. They stood together. And he wasn’t the police, he didn’t have any kind of authority.

“Did Kristin play field hockey too?” he asked as he showed them to the room the principal was allowing him to use.

"Kristin?" Rain said in a tone of disbelief. "No way. She couldn't run."

"She was working on getting into better shape, wasn't she?"

Rain folded her arms and shook her head. "She wasn't interested in field hockey or any sports. She couldn't run. Couldn't do anything strenuous because of her... asthma. She had to use her rescue inhaler every phys ed period. You can't do team sports with a condition like that."

"That would be pretty hard," Zachary admitted. "I didn't realize her asthma was that bad." He took out his notepad and made a quick note. Maybe it had contributed to her death. If her airways were that narrow...

"She didn't like sports anyway," Ala said.

Zachary nodded. He'd been pretty averse to sports in school too. He should have liked a class where he could actually move around and work his energy off instead of being expected to sit still all the time. Still, the bullying from the jocks and his clumsiness and skinny build had ruined any hope of his ever enjoying any team sport at school.

“Did Kristin get bullied? In gym or if she signed up for any teams?”

“She didn’t sign up for any teams,” Rain rolled her eyes dramatically.

“And she didn’t go to gym if she could find a way out of it?” Zachary guessed.

“Well, yeah. Of course.” Rain moved forward in her seat, her gaze on Zachary intense. “We protected her, you know. We didn’t let anyone bully her.”

Jennifer had done the same, standing up for Zachary when she was around. Defending him if she could. But she had still just been a teenager and was vulnerable herself. She wasn’t always successful. It was only fitting that someone had stepped in and defended her daughter, completing the circle.

"I'm glad you did that. Good for you."

"They tell you the school has zero tolerance for bullying," Rain said. She looked over at Ala. "But that just means they look the other way. If they don't see the bullying, it doesn't exist."

There was no way that a school could ever end the bullying. Students would take advantage of teachers' backs being turned, the privacy of restrooms and showers, and activities that happened on the school grounds after classes had let out and the teachers were no longer paying attention. They could do their best to provide a good learning environment, but they could never eliminate all the bullying.

And some of it came from the adults themselves. Teachers and staff who figured that being in a position of authority over the students meant that they could do whatever they wanted to. Sometimes using those same isolated corners, or offices with locking doors, or sometimes verbally abusing students right in the open, in front of thirty other students. What could they do about it?

CHAPTER 11

Did Kristin have trouble with anyone in particular?"

Ala shook her head. "What does that have to do with anything? With her dying at the dentist?"

"You never know what might be connected. If she was having problems at school, she might have been stressed out. She might have been depressed. Taking pills. Starving herself. Any of those things could affect her health and her heart."

The girls were silent, neither one giving anything away.

"Her marks were dropping. Her mother and the teachers both noticed that she was struggling at school. Is that the only thing she was having trouble with, or was there something else going on?"

"She didn't talk about her marks." Ala shook her head and shrugged. "She never said anything to me about them being bad."

Zachary looked at Rain to see what she thought about this, and she didn't disagree.

"I don't know if they were bad," Zachary clarified, "but they were dropping. She was having trouble with something. Mr. Bryce said that she was missing deadlines. Forgetting to hand in assignments or getting them in late."

"She'd been kind of absentminded," Ala ventured. "I know she was having headaches. Got to school late sometimes. Maybe it was just stress."

"It might have been. You don't know anything specific? If she was having trouble with a teacher or a bully? If she was drinking or trying out a diet that wasn't giving her enough calories to get her through the day?"

They both shook their heads. Zachary watched their faces and their body language for tells. They might be good at keeping their faces still, but there were other signs. Swallowing, blinking, licking their lips. They were holding back, which didn't surprise him at all. Why would they tell a stranger Kristin's secrets? She was gone now. They wanted to keep her name unsullied.

"Was she drinking? Is that why she was having trouble with deadlines and getting to class on time?"

"No." Rain's nose wrinkled. "Kristin wouldn't do that. She was too smart to start drinking."

"Taking pills? Something that was supposed to help her to relax?"

"No. I never saw her taking any pills," Rain declared, shaking her head.

"She'd been sick lately." Zachary watched them for their reactions. "Those migraines. Leaving class sick. Losing weight. She wasn't looking good. Her skin was pale. So what was going on with her? Did she see a doctor?"

"It wasn't anything," Ala declared.

Rain gave her a quelling look. One that clearly meant not to say anything. But Ala was on the verge of explaining it to Zachary, telling him why it wasn't anything to worry about. Just a new diet she was trying, or something that her doctor would take care of.

“Do you think you're protecting her mom by not telling me what you know? She wants to know the truth. If Kristin was sick, then her mom deserves to know that.”

“She doesn't need to know anything,” Rain said firmly. “It was just a weird thing. One of those random things... People collapse. They seem perfectly fine one minute, and then are passed out cold.”

“My mom had to sign all kinds of papers when I got my wisdom teeth out,” Ala contributed. “I remember—this big, long list of risks, medical history, and all of that. Sometimes things happen. That's why the doctors make you sign all that stuff.”

“Did she have a medical condition that her mother didn’t know about? It sounded like her asthma was worse than her mom told me. Maybe she was keeping it a secret because she didn’t want her mom to worry. Sometimes kids do that.”

“There was nothing wrong with Kristin,” Rain insisted. “Nothing at all.”

* * *

He watched them as they hurried down the hallway to the locker room, so they could change and get out to the field where their team was waiting. There were voices coming from around the corner, and Zachary stopped, listening to them.

A girl’s voice: “Did you hear about it? The police said that it was a heart attack. Like, right? We didn’t already know that? Too many Twinkies!”

“Or too many Big Macs,” another voice chimed in. “Like, she was as big as a whale! It’s no wonder she died.”

"Did you ever see her try to run?" the first voice asked with a giggle. "That waddle, waddle, waddle of her fat butt, and crying and looking for her inhaler. She was so pathetic. She couldn't even do a fast walk!"

"My mom said maybe it was a glandular problem. Like, her thyroid or something that she couldn't help."

"So? Then she should get whatever meds it took to fix her. Can you imagine walking around looking like that? They had to make her uniforms special. They didn't carry any that would fit her."

"She was nice, though. She never—"

"Nice girls finish last. Haven't you ever heard that? If you want to get ahead in this world—if you want to get to an Ivy League school—you have to take the bull by the horns. You have to take it. She wasn't anything. She just sat around like a houseplant, waiting for the teachers to water her or turn her toward the sun. She never did a thing to get ahead. Never volunteered for anything or joined any clubs or teams. You have to do those things, get it on your resume. Schools don't take you based just on your marks anymore. You need to have the full package. And Kristin Jones did not have that package. It's probably a good thing she died when she did. She was a waste of skin. A lot of skin. If I was her, I would have killed myself."

Zachary leaned on the wall with one hand, trying to control his visceral reaction to the mean girl's criticisms and strident voice.

Why don't you kill yourself? Why don't you get it right next time? You're a waste of space, Goldman.

He tried to feel the coolness of the wall under his hand, the rough texture of the paint. He was not in school anymore. It wasn't his school. He had left that scene behind long ago. They were just silly, ignorant girls who had been threatened by someone who was nice and smart and looked different from them. Just like those who were different were made fun of all over the world by ignorant people.

CHAPTER 12

Zachary checked back in at the office to let them know that he had finished and was leaving. He didn't want them to be concerned about a stranger hanging around the school. Then they wouldn't have to look for him to ensure they could lock up safely. He checked the time and decided he should probably head back to Roxboro if he wanted to be home in good time for supper. Maybe he would even have time to start on it before Kenzie got home. He was sure that she would appreciate it. Even if it just meant that he set the table, got out a salad and side dishes, and left the main course to her.

It was a quick drive from Burlington to Roxboro—a nice drive on the highway, which helped him unwind after the school interviews. As much as he tried to tell himself that his high school experience was over and he had left those days long behind him, the words he had overheard and Rain's and Ala's comments about bullying at the school had gotten under his skin. His brain seemed to think he was back there again, in danger, constantly having to be vigilant.

The hypnotic effect of the highway helped to counteract that, bringing him into a calmer, more meditative state. He stopped for gas when he hit the outskirts of town, where it was cheapest. As he filled the tank, he remembered being there and running into Bridget. She had been angry to see him there, sure he was following her. But he hadn't been. She was paranoid because of her Huntington's disease, though they hadn't known it then. She was also in the early stages of her pregnancy with the twins, and had been very pale and suffering from severe morning sickness. Bad enough that she'd had to go to the hospital a couple of times due to dehydration.

Remembering how she had looked that day, so pale and vulnerable, he longed to see her again and to be able to protect her. He was with Kenzie now, and he didn't have any right to think about another woman, especially one who had treated him like Bridget had. He was still coming to terms with the fact that she had been abusive, that he had sought out and been most comfortable with someone like his mother, someone who would bully and berate him for anything she saw as failings. And Zachary had a lot of failings.

He needed to just put his life with Bridget behind him. He had tried very hard to move on with his life and it baffled him how he longed to go back to her and to have that relationship again, when he was in a much happier and more equal relationship now. Was it because Bridget and Gordon had committed to each other in a way that Zachary and Kenzie hadn't? He had thought that he and Bridget would have children together even though she had told him from the start that she didn't want children. But that had been a lie. She hadn't wanted children with Zachary. Gordon was another story.

Seeing her with the twins broke his heart. It was his life Gordon was living. His wife, the children who should have been his, the happiness and fidelity that he had expected to have when they had married.

When he got into the car after gassing up, he fully intended to go straight home. Kenzie would expect him to be there when she returned from the morgue. He had work to do and wanted to start dinner by the time she got home.

But the car seemed to drive itself of its own accord to Bridget's house, and he pulled over on the street and stared at it.

Gordon could give Bridget everything she wanted. He gave her a mansion to live in and the staff to run it and do whatever she needed help with. There were maids, cooks, and nannies to ensure Bridget didn't overtax her strength. He had given her the twins, two perfect little girls Zachary had protected from harm more than once.

It wasn't just his own imagination and paranoia that they had been in danger. Gordon had not been able to protect them.

Only Zachary had. And which was more important? Providing Bridget with a big, beautiful home or keeping her children safe?

But he was not allowed to be there. Bridget had threatened more than once to take out a protective order against him if she ever saw him at the house again. Yet Gordon had called Zachary back. When the stakes had been so high, it was Zachary he called. Gordon had known that Zachary was the only one who could keep Bridget and the babies safe, and he had shown it through his actions.

Zachary opened his laptop case and pulled out a pad of paper. Not one of his little pocket notebooks, but a letter-sized tablet that gave him plenty of space to write. He tried to make his letters and words as legible as possible and to keep them running across the page in neat, horizontal lines. He didn't know how some people could do it. Even with the blue lines guiding him, his sentences moved up or down the page like a seesaw.

He wrote out everything he could think of. Dr. B had given him assignments like this before. Write a letter to Bridget. Explain your feelings. Think of everything you would tell her if you could.

And then burn it, shred it, or throw it out.

Acknowledge the feelings and then destroy the letter so that no one else would ever see it. Come to terms with his feelings, acknowledge them, and then he would be able to rid himself of them.

But the feelings were all still there, raw and unresolved. Just like his school experiences. Those experiences and feelings were still there, just under the surface. He hadn't been healed by the therapy and all the exercises he had completed that were supposed to help him deal with the past.

He folded the finished letter carefully into thirds. He wished that he could give it to Bridget. Maybe if he had the chance to express his feelings to her instead of being shut down and told to leave, he could get over it.

If he just felt like he had been heard.

* * *

It was much later than he had intended when he got home. His chest and stomach muscles hurt like he'd been doing heavy lifting or a sport he wasn't accustomed to. He had been holding himself so tense for the past few hours.

Zachary was exhausted.

He picked up his laptop bag and climbed out of the car, enervated. Almost as bad as he would have been from a panic attack. He locked the door, checked the handle, and locked it again. He walked around the car, checking each handle to make sure that they had all locked. He pressed down on the trunk to ensure it was still secured in place. He pushed the button on his key fob once more to ensure the security system was armed.

Zachary entered the house and cleared the burglar alarm, mentally congratulating himself for remembering it even when he was exhausted. He could hear Kenzie talking on the phone in the kitchen and looked in on her.

"Oh, here he is," Kenzie said, when she saw him in the doorway. "Thanks for letting me know."

She lowered the phone and pressed the hang-up button.

CHAPTER 13

Who was that?" Zachary asked, as it was evident that it was someone who knew them both and had possibly called Kenzie to give him a message or get information from him. He hadn't looked at his own phone since he had left the gas station, even though he knew it had rung and blinked alerts at him a couple of times.

Kenzie slid her phone into her pocket, pressing her red lipsticked lips together hard, so they flattened out and disappeared. Zachary swallowed. It wasn't good news. Something had happened. He wasn't sure he could take anything else.

"That was Gordon."

Zachary's heart sank. He scratched the back of his head, trying to think of something to say. There was no way to explain or excuse himself. He had known there was a danger in even driving past Bridget's house or anywhere he knew that she would be. Running into her accidentally at the mall or the gas station was one thing. Showing up anywhere that was on her regular schedule was a big no-no.

“Do you want to tell me about it?” Kenzie asked. She motioned to the table, inviting Zachary to sit down.

“I… I don’t know why I did that.”

He couldn’t help wondering how much she knew and how much Gordon knew. Had Gordon just seen him or caught him on a surveillance camera? Or was it worse than that?

“Why you did what?” Kenzie drilled. Just like a foster mom or group home supervisor who wouldn’t let him get away with fudging an answer in hopes that they didn’t know the full extent of his transgressions.

“Why I… went by Bridget’s house.”

“Went by it?”

Zachary cleared his throat and licked dry lips. "I... stopped there," he admitted.

"And...?"

"I just wanted to see it... to make sure that everyone was safe."

Kenzie opened her mouth to object, and Zachary rushed to fill in more details before she could argue against his statement.

"I had to make sure that there wasn't anyone watching the house. That there weren't any dangers that they were unaware of. I couldn't let anything happen to Bridget or the babies."

"They aren't in danger anymore. Anyone who intended them harm has been put behind bars."

"We don't know that," Zachary pointed out. "We just know of the ones we are aware of. Gordon is still running a business that could make him enemies. The way that he works, the way he treats his employees, the things that he does... he could have hurt or offended a lot of people, not just the ones we know of."

"But that isn't your job. It's Gordon's job to ensure they have the security they need and that his wife and his children are protected. It's not your job."

"I know," Zachary admitted miserably. "I just... can't help feeling that they are in danger and I am the only one who can help, like before."

"I told him not to call you." Kenzie shook her head. Her cheeks were red. "I told him not to call you again, and he did anyway. This is on him too."

Zachary swallowed. While he agreed, he couldn't fault Gordon for calling him when they needed his services. Zachary had come through and the children had been returned unhurt. That was what mattered. He would never have forgiven Gordon if he had called someone else and the twins had come to harm. Zachary's life was intertwined with Bridget's and he didn't think anyone would ever be able to untangle them, no matter how much he sometimes wanted to.

"I'm sorry," he told Kenzie, looking down at the shiny tile floor. "I've been trying, but..."

"But this is escalating," Kenzie said flatly. "We're not just talking about driving by the house or stopping to make sure there is no one else hanging around."

"I..." Zachary trailed off and shook his head, unsure what to say. Unsure how much she knew.

"If you don't want to talk to me about it, maybe you'd better call Dr. B and talk to her. Maybe set up a couple of extra sessions."

Zachary rejected this immediately. "We can handle it in my regular sessions. I don't need to change anything."

"You need to change something."

"I know that, I mean, I don't have to change my schedule. My sessions with her. We were able to get it under control before."

"With just one session a week?" Kenzie challenged.

They hadn't been a couple yet then. Zachary knew Kenzie and they dated or went out to meals occasionally, but they hadn't been boyfriend and girlfriend yet. Kenzie didn't know the extent of the treatment Zachary had been through at that time.

"More for a while. But I was stable on just one session per week."

For a while. Until Gordon had hired him to surveil Bridget to find out if she was seeing someone else. That had pushed him back over the edge. Even so, he had thought that he was back on track. The new medication protocol and his hospital stay had reset things and he was able to stay away from Bridget's house.

Mostly.

And then the twins had been kidnapped.

And now he couldn't get them out of his mind. With everything he did, he still had Bridget and the twins in the back of his mind, worrying over whether they were okay. Feeling the constant pull to check on them.

"And you were doing group support for a while," Kenzie added. "When did you stop doing that?"

"I was... it was... I don't think it was helping that much. I kind of let it fade after a few months."

"Well, if it helped initially, then maybe you should go back to it. Until you're doing better again."

Zachary sat down at the kitchen table. He put his face in his hands, elbows on the table. He was wrung out and exhausted. He didn't have the mental energy for the conversation.

"I'll get it worked out. It's just going to take a little time."

"Does Dr. B know you've been leaving notes for Bridget?"

CHAPTER 14

Zachary groaned. He had hoped Gordon had not told Kenzie that part. That Bridget was putting the notes somewhere safe and not telling Gordon or Kenzie. Or that Gordon or a staff member was disposing of them without Bridget seeing them, which was probably more likely.

But Gordon had called Kenzie, and Gordon knew that Zachary had left a note in the mailbox for Bridget. At least once.

"Does Dr. B know?" Kenzie repeated.

"No."

"How do you expect her to help if you're not giving her all of the information?"

"I will."

"You need help, Zachary." He could hear the sadness and frustration in her voice. How many times was she going to put up with his relapsing before she told him it was time to clear out? There had to be a point at which it got to be too much and she decided she wasn't going to put up with his failings anymore.

"I know."

"You need your meds reviewed. I had high hopes for this protocol, but I just don't think it's working. You're having side effects. You can't get your... obsessions under control. I really think you need to do something proactive. Get your meds changed. Increase your number of sessions with Dr. B. Start going to a support group. Or get a referral to an effective program..."

"I'll talk to Dr. B," Zachary repeated. "We'll work out a plan."

"There's got to be something that you can take that will be more effective without a lot of side effects."

Zachary shook his head. He pulled his hands down from his face and looked at her. "I've been on pretty much everything that's out there. There's no such thing as a drug that doesn't have side effects. Not for me."

"There's got to be something."

"This is a good protocol. It's been working."

"You're still stalking Bridget, and it's going to land you in jail. That's not working. And with the misophonia, obsessive thoughts, headaches, and inability to sleep..."

"The sleep aid works."

"When you take it! But most of the time, you won't, so what good is it?"

"If I need it, I take it."

Kenzie shook her head and made a gesture as if pushing it all away. "Fine. That's your business. It's your body and you can make the choices you please. It's got nothing to do with me."

There was a hard lump in Zachary's throat. He knew where this would lead. "I'll do it," he promised. "I'll talk to Dr. B and we'll increase my sessions... increase my dosages and see if that will help. I'll find an OCD Anonymous group. I'll take the sleep aid every night." His eyes were hot with tears. He was going to fall to pieces if she kicked him out. It was worth doing whatever she asked him to do.

Kenzie stopped talking and just looked at him.

"I don't want to force you into anything," she said in a quieter tone. "This is for you, not for me. Do you want to live like this?"

"I don't want to lose you," Zachary choked out. His vision blurred and it was a struggle to keep his composure.

"You're not going to lose me. I'm not going anywhere. But I want you to be the best you can. You don't want to keep going back to Bridget. I know you don't. And I know you know there is no future with her. It's a problem with your brain. But there are ways to deal with it. Things that might help."

"I will. I'll get help."

Kenzie bit her lip. "I know you don't want to live like this," she repeated.

Zachary nodded. He wished that it was as easy as she made it sound. Get more therapy, take more drugs, and it would naturally go away. He wouldn't feel the pull toward Bridget anymore. He would be able to just drop the obsession and go on with his life with Kenzie without another hiccup. But there was no "off" switch for his brain.

Neither of them said anything for several long minutes. Kenzie turned away from the table and started to prepare dinner.

Zachary had intended to help. But now he felt like a lump of dough that had been dropped there. Unable to move or get up. Too drained to do those things that sounded so easy. Make a salad. Get out of the chair and set the table. His limbs were sodden and heavy.

For a while, he just sat there, putting his hands over his face again, propped up by his elbows on the table. Thinking about what he had to do and trying to avoid thinking about it all at the same time.

Avoiding it won out. That part of Zachary's brain just shut down and, instead, he started to think again about Kristin. He wouldn't let his personal demons get in the way of solving the case. He would bring Jennifer some kind of consolation. He didn't know what, but he would find something.

"All drugs have side effects," he said aloud to Kenzie.

He could feel her looking at him for a moment before answering.

"Well... yes, all drugs have side effects. But not everyone gets all of the side effects. Some people only feel the benefit of the drug, and don't have any negative effects."

Must be nice to be someone like that.

"I know that you say that you've tried pretty much everything out there," Kenzie started, "but—"

"I was thinking about this new client," Zachary told her, cutting across any attempt to tell him about new drugs or combinations that he should try. "What if she was taking something that interacted with the anesthetic she was given? Or something else. Even just Tylenol or that gel they put on your gums. What if she didn't tell anyone she was taking something that might be contraindicated?"

"Well, okay, yes," Kenzie said slowly. "That's a possibility. But her mother should have talked to the dental surgeon and anesthetist about anything she was on."

"But what if her mother didn't know?"

"How could she not know?"

Zachary pulled his hands away from his face and looked at her. "Did your mother know everything you did as a teenager?"

"No, but she knew if I was taking any medications."

"Kids take all kinds of things without their parents knowing about it. They smoke, drink, do street drugs, take contraceptives, pop Adderall for an all-nighter..."

"Well, yes," Kenzie admitted.

Zachary was sure Kenzie had seen more than one teen through the morgue who had been taking stuff their parents never knew or suspected. For some, it might be the first time they had taken something. For others, it was late in the game and their parents had been in the dark for years.

"So do you think that this girl might have taken something?" Kenzie asked. "How likely is that?"

"With how available everything is today... I wouldn't say it's unlikely. I haven't talked to a lot of people yet, but her mom, teachers, and friends all say she was losing weight, having migraines, and experiencing other symptoms."

"Do you have a drug in mind?"

"I don't know. Most weight-loss pills are amphetamines, aren't they?"

"Older ones, maybe. They're more careful today. A lot of them are appetite suppressants, diuretics, fiber supplements."

"But those wouldn't cause migraines."

Kenzie shrugged. "They might. Diuretics especially. Dehydration is a common cause of headaches."

"And stomach problems, gastrointestinal, that could be from any kind of pill. Or a supplement or change in diet."

"Sure. It's a very common symptom."

Kenzie continued to face him rather than turning back to the stove right away. "What else? Was there anything else that might make it easier to figure out what she was taking, if she was taking something?"

"I don't know. Her marks were down. She missed turning some assignments in or turned them in late. Her mother responded when I said there might have been a change in her mood, but didn't say she was more depressed or anxious. But there was some kind of response there."

Kenzie pursed her lips. "Hmm. Hard to tell from that. It's all pretty vague."

"Weight loss. Pale skin."

"Did she have an eating disorder? Did she need to lose weight? You said on the phone that she was somewhat overweight."

Zachary had downloaded a few pictures onto his phone from Kristin's social media and the school website. He flipped through them and handed his phone to Kenzie with one representative picture on the screen.

"Okay, yes," Kenzie acknowledged. "She's obese. She might have been severely restricting calories. Her mother might not have been able to see how much weight she had lost. Or she might be binging and purging, which can be very hard on the body."

"But you still can't guess what she might have been taking."

"No. I can look at some of the literature, see what is popular with kids these days. We might get lucky."

Zachary nodded. "Yeah. If you could do that, it might help."

CHAPTER 15

Kenzie happened to be walking down the hallway toward the bedroom when Zachary was taking his nighttime meds in the bathroom, the door partway open. She paused to talk to him and watched while he opened up the pill bottles for each of his night meds and swallowed them, her eyes sharp.

Zachary took the sleep aid as he had told her he would. She gave a slight nod.

"I was hoping that you would call Dr. B tonight, talk to her about... what's been going on," Kenzie said tentatively.

"Tomorrow is Wednesday," Zachary pointed out. "I'll just talk to her during my regular session."

"And you'll set up a more intensive therapy plan?"

Zachary swallowed another pill. "I'll see what she suggests."

"Maybe there is someone she could recommend who would be better at the OCD stuff. She's really good at trauma, but maybe someone else could do more about the compulsions."

Zachary looked at her, thinking not of his issues, but hers.

"What?" Kenzie asked, taking a small step back.

"Nothing." He turned toward the mirror and got out his toothbrush and toothpaste.

She didn't move. She had obviously seen something in his eyes and wanted to know what it was.

"It's nothing," he repeated.

"You looked like you were going to say something."

Zachary squirted a small amount of toothpaste onto his toothbrush. "Just that... I thought Dr. B was going to give you a referral. Someone for you to talk about... what happened to you."

Kenzie drew in her breath.

It wasn't so easy when the shoe was on the other foot.

"Yeah… I got some names from her. I just need to follow up."

"Are you going to?"

"I think… things have been going better lately. Maybe I'm past it. I wasn't convinced from the start that I needed to see someone about it. I just needed some time to recover."

Zachary nodded slowly. "Well… that's good. I'm glad you're feeling better."

Kenzie gave Zachary a look that told him to back off. But he hadn't said anything. He wasn't being sarcastic. Of course he was happy if she had been able to get over her traumatic experience.

But he knew she was still hypervigilant whenever they went out somewhere. Even with him along, she still jumped at every little thing. She still had nightmares that he had to wake her up from. She still looked at her father with suspicion, worrying about what he might be involved in.

She wasn't over it by any means.

* * *

But it wasn't Kenzie who had a nightmare that night. Even though Zachary had taken his sleep aid, or maybe because he had taken it, his sleep took on a different quality. He didn't lie awake worrying about everything, as he often did when he laid down to sleep. He was able to get to sleep fairly quickly, but he awoke to Kenzie shaking him and was disoriented, unable to remember where he was or to picture the room around him.

"What is it? What's wrong?" he demanded, heart pounding. He sat bolt upright and looked around, immediately on the alert for danger. The smell of smoke? An intruder? An unidentified sound?

“Nothing, it’s okay,” Kenzie assured him. “You were having a dream. You were calling out.”

His throat hurt like he’d been yelling or crying. Zachary felt his face and wiped away tears. Usually, he remembered what he had been dreaming. But the meds messed that up. He felt removed from the scene, like he wasn’t even there but was watching it from above, floating several inches from the ceiling. He rubbed his eyes, trying to get a better look at everything around him.

“Can I turn on the light?”

She groaned. “I’d rather you didn’t. How about the flashlight on your phone?”

Zachary was willing to compromise. He felt on his side table for the phone and pulled it from the charging cord. Even the tiny LED light made the room too bright, and Kenzie groaned again and covered her face with her hands.

Zachary slowly swept the room, moving his phone back and forth to shift the shadows and to allow him to see into the corners, the closet, all of the shadowy places.

“What was I dreaming?”

“I don’t know.” Kenzie’s voice was muffled by her hands. “I couldn’t tell what you were saying. I don’t know if you even were saying anything or just cry—calling out.”

However much Zachary tried to recall it, he was unable to bring any images, however fleeting, to his mind.

“Go back to sleep,” Kenzie advised.

“I just need to go check...” Zachary slid his feet off of the edge of the bed and stood up.

Kenzie said something else, but Zachary wasn’t sure what it was or if it was anything coherent. He had woken her up, so there was no guarantee that anything she said or remembered would make any sense either. She might just as easily have been having a nightmare herself, dreaming that Zachary was screaming or calling out to her. She might not be fully awake, but talking in her sleep.

He turned off the flashlight app as he walked out of the bedroom, letting his eyes adjust to the dimness of the house. Streetlights shone through the living room's large windows, filling it with a silvery light.

Zachary paced to the front door, then to the back door that led into the garage. He checked the locks and the burglar alarm panels. There was no sign that anyone else had been there. Nothing tampered with. No alert on the burglar alarm panel screen that a door or window had been opened. Zachary paced back to the front door. He unlocked and opened the front door, and the alarm beeped out an initial warning. It was still armed and working. Zachary stepped out onto the front steps and reached over to the mailbox, opening the lid and feeling inside for a note. His fingers encountered a piece of paper, and he pulled it out, knowing it would be another threat.

Maybe to Kenzie. Maybe to the twins. Maybe to him.

He stepped quickly back into the house and shut and locked the door, then cleared the alert. Kenzie did not need to wake up to the burglar alarm sounding its klaxon in the middle of the night because Zachary was disoriented and unable to get back to sleep.

He looked down at the paper in his hand.

It was a printed flyer and coupon for one of the local pizza eateries. He let his breath out slowly. He turned it over to ensure nothing threatening was printed on the back. There was not.

He walked to the back door and checked it again. There was no mailbox to check there. He went to the fridge and got himself a drink of cold water. He was parched. That was probably what had woken him up or given him nightmares. He was just thirsty. He'd been sleeping with his mouth open—one of the side effects of the sleep aid. In the morning, he would have to put up with the fuzzy, disoriented, half-asleep feeling that it would leave him with for several hours before it faded.

Unless he stayed up and didn't go back to sleep. That might be a better idea.

CHAPTER 16

Kenzie went off to work in the morning as usual, without any more discussion about Zachary's visit to Bridget the day before. He was relieved not to have to talk about it but, at the same time, couldn't ignore the fact that it was still hanging over their heads, the big elephant in the room. Or sitting on his chest. He knew that things had not been resolved. He had made promises to Kenzie, but he would still have to prove himself. Show that he could follow through on them. He needed to get his life back under control. Maybe the measures they had discussed would help, and maybe they would not.

He felt like he couldn't catch his breath all morning while pretending everything was normal and waiting for Kenzie to leave. He thought that once she was gone, he would feel better, but he just felt a combination of emptiness and anxiety.

He found it hard to concentrate on his morning routine. Checking his email and reviewing the task list that Heather helped him to maintain. Trying to map his day out. He had to follow up on a few administrative issues that Heather had been bugging him about, to review the invoices she had drafted and ensure that everything was in line with what he had promised his clients so they could be sent out. He couldn't collect if he didn't send out his bills. And there were several emails in his inbox that he wanted to deal with, but he knew they were lower priority and he shouldn't waste his time on them.

He was distracted by everything. He couldn't stay focused on one task and kept jumping from one thing to another, hoping to land on something that could hold his attention. But thinking about Jennifer and her loss, the memories she had stirred up, and his inability to stay away from Bridget, his attention was completely shot. He eventually took one of his ADHD meds, even though he didn't like to, and again trolled through the emails still languishing in his inbox waiting for it to kick in.

By the time his therapy appointment rolled around, he had basically wasted the entire day. Hopefully, Heather had managed to get through some of the skip traces and other background work on their list so that he could at least say that they had accomplished something.

He was aware that the nurse receptionist at Dr. B's office was watching him as he paced around the waiting room, too anxious to settle in one place. He was usually pretty good about sitting down and waiting for his appointment. It was part of his routine, and he no longer had to fight himself to see her as he used to do. But knowing that he had to talk to her about his re-emerging problem with Bridget, he wanted to be anywhere else. He had managed to get himself to the office, but his heart was pounding, running a mile a minute, and his legs wanted to walk him right back out the door. He didn't want to see the disappointment on her face.

Dr. B was at the door between the waiting room and her treatment rooms, looking at him with a mildly concerned expression.

"Zachary?"

"Oh. Hi."

"Come on in."

She led the way to her office, where they usually met, and Dr. B gestured to the chairs for him to have a seat.

"Uh, I need to move around today."

She nodded. "Whatever you need," she agreed, and sat down behind her desk. She didn't ask him what the problem was or why he was so agitated today.

"Did Kenzie call you?" Zachary wanted to know.

Dr. B shook her head. "About what?"

"About me. About what happened. Or about her therapy. Did you give her a referral to another therapist for her PTSD?"

“No, I haven’t talked to Kenzie since your last couple’s session. What’s wrong? Is she having problems?”

“No, it’s not that.”

“What happened, then, that you thought she might have called me about?”

“Nothing happened. She’s been doing okay. She says she’s doing better and maybe doesn’t need anything for the PTSD, but she’s still... really jumpy. Easily triggered.”

“We can discuss it next week if you are concerned.”

Zachary shrugged. He knew that Kenzie’s PTSD and her need for therapy were not the issue. He had wanted to know whether Kenzie had called Dr. B about him and Bridget. She usually told him if she were going to, keeping the communication between the two of them open, but she might have called without telling him.

It might have been easier if he didn't have to introduce the topic himself. His therapist would already know what he needed to talk about and they could dive into it without the difficulty of breaking the news.

"So, what is it?" Dr. B persisted. "What made you think that Kenzie might have called me?"

"It wasn't about her; it was about me... I... have been having some problems that we haven't talked about."

"Well, I'm glad you're bringing it up. We can't deal with it if I don't know what's happening, can we?"

Zachary breathed in and out, focusing on his belly, trying to take nice long, soothing breaths that would ease the tension in his muscles and the writhing of his guts. He walked across the room and back again.

"I've been worried about Bridget and the twins."

"Mmm-hmm?"

Dr. B sat still, waiting for him. She didn't push or act shocked and disappointed; she just sat waiting. Zachary supposed that after how much he and Dr. B had already talked about Bridget, it wasn't a surprise to her that Zachary would bring her up again.

"I've been... well, you know that they were snatched. The babies. And that I helped to get them back again."

"Yes. You might have mentioned that," Dr. B agreed wryly.

Of course it had been the subject of several other sessions. How Zachary had dealt with it at the time. Whether he had made the right choices for the twins and his own mental health. How he was dealing with things after the babies had been returned to Bridget and everything was back to "normal" again.

"I've been having a lot of thoughts about her."

Dr. B nodded. "Yes. That was to be expected. She is your 'drug,' and I had no doubt that being exposed to her again would cause some problems. Do we need to increase your meds?"

Zachary swallowed and nodded. "Yeah. I told Kenzie I would talk to you about it."

"So she thinks your meds should be increased."

"Yes."

"And what do you think?"

"I told her I would."

Dr. B waited. Zachary knew he hadn't actually answered the question. He cleared his throat and looked for a way to answer without admitting his failings. It wasn't fair that Gordon called him in to deal with the kidnapping of the twins and then that Zachary should suffer the consequences. That he should have to increase his sessions and his meds to comply with other people's dictates because of something Gordon had done.

"I think... I need extra help," he admitted, his stomach cramping hard.

"Okay. Let's talk about what extra help you might need."

"I told Kenzie I'd get an increase on my meds and more sessions."

She made a note in the file in front of her. "It sounds like the two of you think this is pretty serious."

Zachary ground his teeth. He knew it was serious, but he hated breaking the news to her. He shouldn't care about what she thought. She'd seen him at his worst and was there to help him. But he didn't like to disappoint her. Even though she never acted shocked or criticized him, he knew he had disappointed her. That she had hoped he would do better. It was the same feeling he'd had when he'd gotten in trouble at school or done something else to disappoint a foster parent or social worker. And some of them reacted much worse than Dr. B ever would. He knew that, but he still had that fear in his stomach that she would reject him, react violently, and tell him that he would have to find another therapist because she was done with him.

She didn't ask again or speculate on what might have happened. She just waited for him to tell her what had happened.

"I went by Bridget's house."

"By it?"

"To it," Zachary amended. He hadn't just driven past it, as his words had implied. "I stopped there. Watched the house."

"Did you talk to her? Did she see you there?"

"No. But... I did something stupid."

She nodded.

"I... I wrote her a note. About my feelings. About her, and our relationship, and our marriage."

"I see."

"Like the exercises you've had me do. Writing out what I feel, getting it all down on paper."

"Yes."

"But then... I didn't throw it out. I left it there for her."

"Where?"

"In her mailbox."

Dr. B nodded. "I see. And did she get it? Did she contact you?"

"Gordon called Kenzie. I guess he saw it. I don't know if Bridget saw it or not." He paused. "I don't think so."

She would have called him if she had. She would have freaked out. Screamed at him. Started an application for a protection order to keep him away from the house.

“Well, it’s probably a good thing that Gordon took care of it.”

“Yeah. Keeps me out of jail.”

“I imagine Gordon feels some sense of responsibility for having brought you back in again.”

“I understand why he did. And... I’m glad he did. But I wish he hadn’t.”

Dr. B chuckled. “Yes. Exactly.”

Zachary put his hands on the back of the chair that he should have been sitting in. He looked up at the ceiling, trying to keep his emotions under control.

“It wasn’t the first time.”

"You've left other notes?"

He swallowed hard. "Yes."

She picked up a water bottle from the shelf under her window and put it on the desk between them. Zachary cracked it open and took a drink. Dr. B made some notes in the file.

CHAPTER 17

This has been going on since the kidnapping?"

"Yes."

He knew she was disappointed in him for not bringing it up before. For not being honest with her about how it had affected him.

"But this is the first time Gordon has called Kenzie about it?"

"Yes. As far as I know."

"Is that because it is escalating?"

"No," Zachary protested immediately. If anything, he was doing better. He was pulling back, not leaving them as often.

"Is Gordon concerned about what you have written?"

"Umm... I didn't talk to him. You'd have to ask Kenzie. Or him."

"Was there anything in the last note that you think pushed him to call Kenzie?"

"No. It was... all pretty much the same."

Dr. B studied him. She held his gaze. "You didn't make any threats?"

"No."

"To yourself or Bridget? Or anyone else?"

"No."

She held eye contact with him for a few more seconds, then nodded.

"Why do you think he called this time, then?"

"I don't know. I guess... he just got fed up with it. Decided that Kenzie should know. She's told him not to call me, so he called her..."

"Okay. So this has been going on long enough to cause concern, and you have not been able to pull back. So I think you are right; you need some further intervention."

Zachary nodded.

"And this is probably affecting your professional and personal life as well."

He rubbed his forehead. "I've got a new case. I really need to work on it, but I've been so distracted today."

"Just today?"

He thought about the number of times he had been by Bridget's house lately. Not just the times he'd stopped and taken the time to write her a note and leave it for her. But the times that he had just driven by, too, that he had just checked to make sure everything was okay. Sometimes several times a day.

"Not just today."

"Let's discuss how we can attack this problem."

Zachary had one eye on the clock and knew they had already gone over his allotted time when Dr. Boyle leaned back in her chair with a sigh, putting down her pen.

"And is there anything else going on? You're more agitated than you have been since the kidnapping. Is that just because of Kenzie finding out?"

"Well..." Zachary let his mind go over the events of the past few days. "I have a new client... she's a girl I went to school with."

"Oh, really." The therapist leaned forward again, studying Zachary's face as she picked up her pen. "You don't normally have anything to do with anyone you knew as a teenager. Other than Mr. Peterson. How has that affected you?"

"Just remembering stuff that was going on when I knew her... I don't want to remember. I don't want to bring it all back to the surface."

"No. You know it can be difficult to integrate the past, so I understand you have some trepidation about it. This girl... she was a friend?"

"Yeah."

"Not someone who was manipulative? Who might have taken advantage?"

"No, no, nothing like that. She helped me with homework. Stood up for me. She was nice."

"Your age? Older? Younger?"

"Older."

"And that was the extent of your relationship? School friends?"

Zachary hesitated. Dr. B waited. “We were at the same group home.”

“Ah. That’s how you knew each other, then.”

Zachary shrugged. He looked at his hands. “Yeah.”

“And she had some issues too. Mental illness? Addiction?”

“No, none of that. Jennifer was really smart and she wouldn’t get into drugs. She was a runaway. Her mom had remarried and she wouldn’t have anything to do with her stepfather. Whenever the police took her home, she’d run again, so she ended up in a shelter and then the group home.”

“The stepfather was abusive? Or they just didn’t get along?”

“She never said.”

Dr. Boyle shook her head. “Come on, Zachary. You know.”

Zachary closed his eyes, which didn’t block the images out. He didn’t know. She had never told him any of the details of her relationship with her stepfather. He had never seen any interaction between the two of them or even seen her parents.

But Dr. B was right. He didn't need to be told. He had enough abuse in his own background to recognize it. He didn't need her to tell him anything about it to visualize a dozen different scenarios.

"He was abusive."

"So you have this new person in your life who is stirring up memories of a very dark time, someone who may have suffered some of the same abuses as you did. Maybe this is not a good time to take this case on."

"I need to. Her daughter died. She needs to know what happened."

"Someone else can help her. How did her daughter die? Please don't tell me that was the result of an abusive relationship."

"No. She died suddenly during surgery."

Dr. Boyle tapped her pen on her notes. "Our time is past, and I do need to get on to my next patient. We are going to meet again on Saturday."

Zachary nodded.

"Get your new prescriptions filled. Go to an OCDA meeting. Be prepared to talk to me about your old friend and how you're feeling about how things are proceeding."

"Okay."

"We don't have to talk specifics about your shared experiences when you were kids or the memories that might stir up. But I want to know how you are feeling. Pay attention to what's going on inside and let's keep that out in the open. The rest... will follow when you are ready."

Zachary felt like he might be able to manage that. He breathed in and let out a long, slow breath. "Okay."

CHAPTER 18

It was a relief to sit down in the solitude of his car once more. He appreciated the extra time Dr. Boyle had spent with him and how much she and Kenzie wanted to help, but he also just wanted to push all of his feelings and the issues with Bridget away. And his feelings about Jennifer and their shared past.

He covered his face with both hands and massaged it. So many tense muscles. So many feelings trying to come out. It took so much effort to stay in control, even in his therapist's office, where he knew it was safe to let it all out.

But he also felt lighter. He was no longer struggling with his feelings toward Bridget on his own. Kenzie knew what was going on and so did Dr. B. They would help him to get through it. He didn't have to bear the whole burden alone or to continue to keep it a secret.

He had three days to focus on the investigation to see if he could move it forward. Maybe by the time he saw Dr. Boyle again, he would have reviewed the medical examiner's report, finished his interviews, and given Jennifer an answer, even if it wasn't the one she wanted.

He straightened up, wiped his sweating face on his sleeve, and started the engine.

Zachary had fully intended to go home. To take care of whatever else he could before Kenzie got home, help with supper, and spend a quiet evening with her recovering from his difficult day. Get a better sleep, one that wasn't interrupted by nightmares, and start the next day fresh.

But he didn't end up in front of Bridget's house, either.

Zachary sat there for a few minutes looking at the house, wondering if he should just turn around and go back home. But eventually, he decided that he was there for a reason and got out of the car.

After going through the process of checking the lock and car alarm system several times, he walked up to the house and rang the doorbell. An older black woman opened the door. Her face brightened when she saw him.

"Zachary! How nice of you to stop by. Did Rhys know you were coming?"

Zachary shook his head. "I was just in the area. Thought I'd take a chance that he was in."

"Well, you're in luck. Come on in." Vera Salter motioned for Zachary to enter and put her hand on his back as he stepped through the door, warmly encouraging him. "Rhys! You have a visitor."

It was a minute or two before Rhys showed his face. Zachary couldn't believe how much Rhys matured between visits. His gangly teenage build was starting to fill out, his face more angular and defined. The sadness that had been so profound when Zachary had first met him was still there. His mouth pointed down when he wasn't conscious of it. But on seeing Zachary, Rhys gave a grin and reached out. He pounded

Zachary on the back in a bro hug. Zachary nearly had the wind knocked out of him. Rhys was definitely growing up.

“Hey, Rhys, good to see you. How have you been?”

Rhys gave Zachary a thumbs-up, one eye on his grandmother. He motioned for Zachary to follow him and led him back to his bedroom.

He had a study desk, which he hadn’t had the last time Zachary had been there, and a proper office chair. Vera had probably decided that doing his homework hunched over a laptop on the bed was not good for his posture. Zachary spun the chair to face the room instead of the desk and sat down. Rhys flopped down on the bed and spread his hands apart in a “what’s up?” gesture.

“I just... thought it’s been a while since I saw you, and it would be good to see you again, if you were home. And... you are.”

Rhys rolled his eyes.

Zachary looked around the room for anything new or any sign that Rhys was depressed or anxious about anything. Everything looked pretty much the same as before, other than the new desk and chair. Schoolbooks, sports equipment, and other teen detritus scattered on all surfaces, including the floor. The scents of mingled teen sweat and air freshener.

“So, how are you really?” he asked.

Rhys held his hand up in a horizontal position and wobbled it back and forth.

So-so.

Zachary nodded. That was expected. Rhys had not led an easy life and struggled with his speech. His mother was in prison, thanks to Zachary, And Rhys was dealing with other issues that he did not want shared with his grandmother. Being a normal teenager was hard enough. Rhys had not exactly won the lottery.

"School okay?"

Rhys gave him wide eyes and raised brows, which Zachary interpreted as What do you think?

"Can't be too easy," Zachary commiserated. "Do you have... friends you can talk to?"

Rhys pointed to his throat.

Zachary shook his head. "Not talk talk. But... communicate with. Share with."

Rhys pulled out his phone and pointed at the screen. Like with most teenagers, texting and other messaging apps were second nature to him. Unlike with most teenagers, his texting often consisted of mostly gifs and a typed word here and there, rather than predominantly text. It could be challenging to interpret his symbols at the best of times. Zachary preferred face-to-face interactions when he could manage them. It was much quicker and easier to figure out if he was on the right path or missing Rhys's signals.

"Yeah. Do you have a lot of people that you communicate with?"

Rhys nodded.

Zachary thought about Jennifer and school. They had not had the luxury of texting with friends. Kids hadn't even had their own phones. They hadn't been allowed to use the phone at the group home for anything but contacting their social workers or for emergencies. When he went home at the end of the day, he was cut off from everyone at school. Except for Jennifer, if she were home. It was good not to have to deal with the bullies and baddies at school, but he probably would have had more friends if he'd at least been able to communicate outside of school time by some means other than using his feet to walk to someone's house.

Rhys made a throat-clearing noise and waved at Zachary.

"Sorry. Just thinking of when I went to school. No phones."

Rhys gave him an open-mouthed look of horror.

"It's true," Zachary told him. "Way back in the dark ages."

Rhys shook his head slowly as if in disbelief.

"I went to... I just met someone I went to school with." Zachary shifted on the chair. He liked that it was a swivel chair and he could move around a bit on it instead of being forced to sit still. Though if he tried to spin while carrying on a conversation, it might cause some difficulties. Slightly distracting.

CHAPTER 19

Rhys turned his palm up, encouraging Zachary to go on.

"It's... a sad case. She wants me to look into her daughter's death. Your age. A teenager."

Rhys nodded, his mouth returning to his usual solemn, sad expression.

"She was a good friend to me, but we never kept in touch. I should have, I guess, but the way I was moved around, I didn't really have that option. I never knew where she went when she left the house. And I had my own stuff to deal with."

Rhys traced a heart shape on his chest and raised his brows.

"No." Zachary shook his head. "Not a girlfriend. Just... someone who helped look out for me. And I... never returned the favor."

They were both silent for a while. Silences weren't awkward with Rhys like they were with everyone else. Neither of them expected the spaces to be filled immediately.

"Her daughter..." Zachary wondered how much he should tell Rhys. Unlike Zachary, Rhys was plugged in to teen culture. He knew much more than Zachary did about most aspects of the modern teenager's world. Maybe not about trafficking and some of the uglier issues that Zachary had dealt with as part of his investigations, but he would know a lot more about current trends and popular issues. "It might just have been an accident. A freak reaction to the anesthetic when she was having her wisdom teeth pulled."

Too late, he wondered whether Rhys had had his pulled or whether this story would freak him out and make him refuse to have his done. He mentally pushed the issue away. There was nothing he could do now that he'd said it. He couldn't unsay it.

Rhys nodded seriously, waiting for more details.

"It might have just been a freak accident," Zachary reiterated. "But I'm looking into whether it could be something else. Maybe she had a medical condition that had never been diagnosed. Or maybe she was taking medications that her mom didn't know about that shouldn't have been mixed with something the doctor gave her."

Rhys made a motion toward the door.

It took a moment for Zachary to understand. "Like your grandma, when Gloria—when her meds were messed up. She was so confused and forgetful."

Rhys pointed at him. You got it.

"Yeah. Sometimes doctors even prescribe medications that shouldn't be taken together. I've had that happen. They don't always look them all up. Or some people are just more likely to react."

Zachary tried to put everything he knew so far into a coherent picture.

"She had lost weight, her grades were going down, and some of the adults said she had been sick or was pale."

Rhys formed the familiar ASL sign for "friend" with two forefingers hooked together and raised his brows.

"Her friends aren't saying very much. I wish I could get them on my side but, so far, they aren't even telling me as much as the adults in Kristin's life. And of course... the adults don't really know what the kids are into, do they?"

Rhys let out a chuckle. He played with his phone, thumbing it on and flashing it toward Zachary.

"Her phone? Yeah... I was going to do some social network snooping, but her name is pretty common. And she probably didn't use her real name on most of them, right?"

Rhys nodded his agreement. He touched and flicked his screen and reached his phone toward Zachary. Zachary stood up and took it from him briefly. He saw the avatar of a bobblehead basset hound and the name BanjoBass5405. He had seen Rhys use dog gifs a number of times to express his feelings, especially the droopy-faced basset hounds that always looked sad.

“Is this you? One of your usernames?”

Rhys nodded.

He was wise not to use his own picture for the avatar. Zachary often tracked people’s alternate user accounts with a facial recognition search. By not using any form of his name or his face, Rhys made his account much more secure from snoops like Zachary. Although he had a few other tricks up his sleeve as well.

“If I get Kristin’s phone, I might be able to find out what other accounts she had. What she was really doing online.”

Rhys nodded and pointed at him.

"Is there somewhere teen girls are more likely to connect?" Zachary asked. He knew the most popular social media platforms, including those that were gaining in popularity and those that were falling out of favor with kids. "Especially if they were talking about things like weight loss or dieting that they didn't want to share with the whole world?"

Rhys thought about this. He tapped something into his phone and thumbed through a number of screens rapidly. Zachary could catch the beginning notes of songs or the first syllable or two of someone's speech, but Rhys's phone volume was turned down and he didn't stop long enough for Zachary to tell what the videos were talking about.

Rhys tried a few different searches before he looked satisfied. He passed the phone to Zachary. Zachary tapped the triangle in the middle of the screen to play the first video. A blond cheerleader type gazed into the camera, speaking rapidly with a high, affected voice. The captions at the bottom of the screen didn't do much to help Zachary sort out what she was saying, they flew by so fast. He swiped to the next video, another girl talking seriously. Then another bouncing around the screen. He started to see and hear the pattern of the videos. Have you taken the challenge? and What were your results? were common refrains. They talked about dropping pounds in days, about having to look just right for a dance or event in the one perfect dress that they found that looked just like the one some celebrity had worn. Five pounds, ten pounds, twenty pounds, in days or weeks.

"What are they doing?" Zachary asked, sitting on the edge of the bed so that Rhys could also see. "What are they talking about?"

Rhys pointed at the hashtags in the video that was playing: #weightlosschallenge #Rx4Fx #SlaythePounds.

Zachary watched a few more, noting the hashtags being used. He wrote them down in his notepad and tucked it back away.

“Do they private message through this app too?” he asked, “Or is it all public?”

Rhys shrugged. Either.

Zachary investigated a little further, watching the videos associated with Rhys’s search but being careful not to go into any of his friends or history pages. He wasn’t there to intrude on Rhys’s privacy. Though he wouldn’t mind knowing whether Rhys was still in contact with Luke. Luke’s history and the organization he once belonged to did not make him a safe person for a vulnerable young man to be in contact with. Zachary had to assume they were still corresponding with each other, though both Rhys and Luke had lied to keep their continuing relationship a secret before.

“This is really helpful,” Zachary said, and handed the phone back to Rhys. “I’ll know some things to look for now if I can get my hands on her phone. What about... drinking and drugs? Anything hot out there right now? Something a girl your age or a little older might have gotten into without her mother figuring it out?”

Rhys rolled his eyes and made a wide gesture. Anything.

CHAPTER 20

Jennifer resisted the idea of Zachary searching Kristin's room or her phone. He had met her at home this time and hoped she would just nod and direct him to her daughter's room. But she kept him in the living room, arguing that searching her room was unnecessary.

There was a plush pink carpet. The walls and the brick surrounding a small fireplace were white. There were brass fittings around the fireplace, which looked like it had never been used. The logs inside were the decorative variety, making the room feel cold despite the warm summer temperatures. There were pictures across the mantel. Mostly Kristin, with a couple of a boy that Zachary assumed was Jennifer's son. The one she didn't have custody of.

"I don't know what you think you're going to find," she protested, the lines of grief etched deeply on her face. "You're supposed to be investigating those doctors. Finding out what happened in their operating room. You should be looking into their backgrounds, finding out if they have malpractice suits against them or something."

"I am," Zachary assured her. He had already passed the names on to Heather for investigation. He didn't need to go to the dental office to find out if they were facing any lawsuits. And they weren't likely to tell him whether any of the doctors there were struggling with alcoholism or dementia. Something like that was more likely to appear on the rate-your-doctor sites. Heather would be checking the reviews for any patterns. If the dental surgeon or someone else in his office had been making a lot of mistakes, it would probably show up there first. Heather would also check their social media, looking for any red flags or bad behavior. "That's already in the works. But I need to look into Kristin's life too. See whether she was hiding anything. Or whether she had any symptoms that she didn't even recognize. We need to come at this from multiple directions."

"They killed my baby," Jennifer insisted. "I want you to figure out who is responsible and make sure that it never happens again!"

"If one of the doctors has a history of making careless mistakes, we'll find out," Zachary promised. "I'm looking into that. But you need to remember that there may be nothing to find. It might have just been a freak thing. Something totally unpredictable."

"I don't believe that."

"I know. And I will do my best to find out the truth for you. But to do that, I need access to Kristin's life. Her room, her phone, her computer. Anyone she might have confided in."

"Fine." Jennifer sighed. She just sat on the couch for a few more seconds, looking very lost and alone, all by herself in her beautiful home. Eventually, she moved, pushing herself up from the couch as if she were ninety years old. "I'll take you to her room."

Zachary could have found his way, but she apparently didn't want him wandering around the house alone. Did she have something to hide? Something she didn't want Zachary to see? Or was she just being a gracious hostess, even when it brought her pain?

Kristin's room seemed like the typical teenager's. The walls were painted a deep rose, except for one paneled in white—a feature wall. But of course, most of the walls were covered with posters, pictures from childhood, school projects, and other memorabilia Kristin wanted to keep around her, making it her own space.

It was a stark contrast to the rooms Zachary had slept in as a teenager. They always had rules that nothing could be mounted on the wall. No tape, pins, or nails allowed. Not even that sticky tack putty that wasn't supposed to mar surfaces. His belongings fit in a drawer or crate. Sometimes a box he had scrounged himself to try to protect them from dust and vermin. A couple of changes of clothes. His camera. A few toiletries, books from school, pens and pencils. But his camera never went in the drawer or box. He always kept that around his neck, at school and everywhere else. Hidden under his jacket or in a pocket when necessary. But always there, its weight reassuring him of its presence. The one thing of value that he owned.

Jennifer stood in the doorway, waiting.

“This will take a little while,” Zachary told her. “It would probably be easier on you if you didn’t have to watch me touching her things.”

She didn’t move at first, her mouth set in a firm, unhappy line. Zachary ignored her and began his search, looking through the items on top of her dresser and then opening each drawer to look through the contents. After a few minutes of watching him, she withdrew, apparently deciding he was right. Or that Zachary would not make a mess of things and she could trust him to stay there alone.

His heart ached for Jennifer. She was in such pain. Zachary knew how painful it was to lose a family member. Not through death, as she had, but he had been cut off from the rest of his family just as abruptly as she had been from her daughter, and he had mourned that loss for years.

Was there really any chance that he was going to find anything in Kristin's room that would help him figure out what had happened to her? Was any explanation going to make Jennifer feel better?

Somehow, he doubted that his investigation was going to bring her any peace.

CHAPTER 21

Zachary found a hard-backed notebook under the folded clothes in the bottom drawer. He opened it and stood flipping through the pages. He had thought at first that it might be a journal. The type of thing that girls on TV wrote in, pondering their lives, baring their souls about all of their crushes, the ups and downs of school, fights with parents, and secret hopes and dreams. But while it was dated, there were no long recountings of Kristin's daily life or aspirations. The dates were followed by numbers and a few brief words. A data log. If he weren't mistaken, a weight loss diary. He could see one number going down every day or every few days, some other numbers that were not weights, but some other measurement. Heart rate? Respiration? Dosages?

He set it to the side and kept looking. He didn't find any pills. The daily log did not include any notes of what she had eaten. Maybe one of the numbers was calorie intake. Or workout tracking. Jennifer had said that Kristin had been walking, one of the few activities she could do. Maybe one of the series of numbers was minutes walked or calories burned.

Under Kristin's Bluetooth speaker, he found a folded piece of paper with a name and phone number on it. Ares. Someone from school? A boy she had a crush on? It was the only evidence of a possible romantic interest in Kristin's life. Zachary took a picture and left it where it was. There was no photo anywhere to go along with it.

Like Rhys, Kristin had a study desk. Her laptop sat alone on the top, and he would come back to that. There was a single deep drawer at the side, the right size for letter-size file folders, with a rail to hang them on. But the mass of papers thrown haphazardly into the drawer did not seem to be organized in any way. Zachary pulled them out in layers, looking for dates that would indicate how old they were.

There was a tidy stack of file folders at the very bottom of the drawer, with school assignments from the previous school term neatly sorted. But everything from the current term seemed to have just been thrown on top without regard for subject or date. The older filed materials had been completed carefully, and each had a few pen notations and a grade at the top. Some had been prepared on the computer and printed out, and others were handwritten. Printed, because kids were not taught cursive like they used to be. Kristin's printing was small and regular. Zachary would have said that he didn't remember anything about Jennifer's writing, but when he looked at Kristin's, a strong wave of nostalgia washed over him. He could remember watching Jennifer write, marveling at her neat cursive and printing. At how effortlessly the letters and words flowed from her pen. That was what it was like for normal people. The words just came, almost unconsciously.

But the papers from the top half of the drawer, the current term's materials, were markedly different. Kristin's printing was uneven, frequently scratched out or overwritten, full of errors in spelling. Most of them did not have any teacher's markings on them, but those that did were covered with red marks, and the grades at the top were far from being the good grades

Jennifer had claimed Kristin was making. Jennifer and Kristin's teachers had admitted that Kristin's grades had dropped, but had said that she was a good student who needed a little time or tutoring to boost her marks.

No one had even implied that Kristin was failing. But last term's A's and B's had turned into D's and F's. More than a student who was just distracted or struggling with new material. More like the plunge of a teen who was on drugs or had been through a serious trauma.

He didn't have time to sort through everything or log all of the papers, so Zachary satisfied himself by taking pictures of a representative sample from the current term and the previous one.

As he put the stacks of paper back into the drawer as they had been, a smaller paper fluttered out from between some of the school assignments. A receipt. For a prescription.

* * *

After Zachary had finished the search, He showed Jennifer the receipt. She shook her head. “The only prescription Kristin had was for her inhaler. For her asthma. I don’t know what that is.” She shook her head. “It must be... Kristin had an infection a few months ago. It must be for that.”

“She was prescribed antibiotics?” Zachary looked at the name of the drug. It wasn’t any antibiotic that he had ever been prescribed.

“Yes. Or antifungal. I don’t remember what kind of infection it was. Something she picked up in the school locker room, probably. You know how kids share everything.” She shook her head. “I told her not to share towels or water bottles. That’s just gross.”

Zachary nodded. “I see. So the only other prescription she had was for her inhaler?”

"Yes. Or sometimes other things to control her asthma. She had tried some pills that were supposed to help. Steroids, maybe? I don't remember. I remember she didn't like them."

"The taste?"

"No. Side effects. Hair loss, weight gain... she didn't need that."

Weight gain was something Kristin definitely did not need to be dealing with. Physically and socially, it would have added a big burden.

"So she was managing her asthma without them?"

Jennifer nodded. "She'd been dealing with asthma for a long time. She did okay."

"From what her friends said, it was pretty bad."

Jennifer frowned. "Who said that?"

"I don't remember which one it was. But they said that any physical activity was a problem."

"Well... except for walking. She was doing a lot more walking. I think that was why she was losing weight. She was really committed to it. And once she got down to a healthier weight, she would be able to be more active and her asthma would be less of a problem. They always said that the best way for her to improve her asthma was to drop the weight."

As if that were something she could just decide to do. As if the only reason that she was overweight was that she wasn't committed enough to being healthy.

"So, as far as you know, this prescription was probably for her infection a few months ago."

"Yes. I'm sure that must be it. She hasn't had anything else, other than the steroids." Jennifer looked at the piece of paper again. "And I don't think the timing was right for the steroids, so that must be what it was."

CHAPTER 22

Did Kristin have a boyfriend?"

"No." Jennifer was definite on this point. "I told you; she would have liked to have socialized a bit more with the boys, but it wasn't in the cards. She wasn't very popular. You know how that is. You can't just break into the popular crowd. Even if you do all of the right things, have the same interests, wear the right clothes, you don't get in if the gatekeepers don't let you in."

Zachary hadn't ever even wanted to be part of the popular crowd. He would have been happy just to be invisible. To be ignored. While he had sometimes wished that he had friends, even one best friend, like the kids on TV always did, he would settle for being left alone. It had been a nice change, when Jennifer had come along, to have an older girl pay attention to him and not be mean. She talked to him like he was a real person and helped him out. He knew it was just because they were in the group home together, but it didn't matter. Jennifer could have hung out with any of the other kids at the home. Any of them would probably have been happy to be friends with a pretty, kind, normal girl. But she had aligned herself with Zachary.

"Did Kristin have any boys that were friends? Had she ever mentioned anyone she had a crush on?"

"She would mention a name now and then, just in passing. People in her classes or that she'd been paired up with for a group project. But no one special." Jennifer shrugged. "No names doodled on her notebooks. She had friends home sometimes, but I didn't hear them talking about anyone special. You know how girls get together and giggle..."

Zachary couldn't picture either Ana or Rain getting giggly over boys. Or the sad-looking girl he had seen in the in the pictures of Kristin. But he supposed he hadn't seen Ala and Rain at their best. It was a sad time. They were mourning her death, even if their faces didn't show it as clearly as Jennifer's.

"Did she ever mention the name Ares?"

"Ares?" Jennifer's brow wrinkled as she thought about it. She knew that Zachary wasn't just making names up. That he must have gotten that name somewhere. "No... did someone say something to you about him? I don't remember Kristin ever mentioning him."

"Just a name I saw."

She looked doubtful. Zachary couldn't blame her. He was keeping the details back from her, but he didn't know anything so far. He didn't know that they were friends. They might have been texting each other or she might have been working up the courage to call him. Or just fantasizing.

"Are you finished in here?"

Zachary looked slowly around the bedroom for anything he might have missed. He hadn't checked all of the usual hiding places. Under the mattress, behind drawers, behind the posters. But Jennifer was eager for him to be out of there, and he had found a few things that might be helpful. “Can I take her computer and phone?”

“What do you think you’re going to find on them?”

He tried to be patient, even though he had already gone over it several times. Jennifer wasn’t stupid. He remembered her as being much smarter than he was. But she was emotionally distraught. She couldn’t accept that Kristin might have done something that had contributed to her death. As far as Jennifer was concerned, it could only be one of the doctors. Negligence during the surgery for one reason or another. A mistake made. Something that explained what had happened to Kristin and yet didn’t reflect on anything Kristin or Jennifer had done or could have done to prevent it.

“I would just like to be sure that there was nothing going on that you don’t know of. Anything that might have caused a problem.”

"But there wasn't. How could there be? This wasn't something that another kid did. It wasn't suicide. She didn't even die in her bed at night. She died in a doctor's office. In a surgery. That's what killed her."

"I know. I'm just looking for any contributing factors."

Zachary picked up Kristin's laptop. He slid the logbook under it, trying to keep it out of sight. "Do you have her phone?"

"I don't want you to... it has all her pictures on it. I need those."

"I won't delete anything. I won't mess around with anything at all. I just want to look through her social networks, make sure there isn't any spyware on the phone, and take a little look around to see what else might have been happening in her life. That's all."

Jennifer sighed heavily and patted her pockets. "Okay, but only for a few hours. I want it back today."

That was going to make things difficult. But Zachary could probably negotiate once he had it in his possession. Let her know that he needed it for just a bit longer so that he could finish examining it. Or clone it onto his hard drive and use an emulator program to explore the data. Once it was in his possession, he had the choice.

Jennifer handed the slim phone to Zachary. The case was faded in places, rubbed by Kristin's fingers for hundreds of hours until the color had started to wear away. Like with most kids, it was not just a communication tool. It was her life, her friend, her confidante, her entertainment. And for Zachary, it would be a window to that life. A way to reconstruct her last few days.

"Do you know her passcode?"

Jennifer gave him a six-digit number. He tapped them on the screen and it unlocked. "Great, thanks."

So Kristin had trusted her mother enough to give her the unlock code. That either meant that she trusted her mother not to go snooping where she wasn't wanted—which was doubtful—or she had hidden the apps, conversations, and data she had not wanted her mother to see.

"What's that?" Jennifer demanded, as Zachary shifted everything to slide them into his laptop bag. "What's that book?"

Zachary pressed his lips together. He had been hoping to get out of there without Jennifer noticing it. He displayed the hardcover notebook to her. "It seems to be a weight loss log. I wanted to review it for any information relevant to her... physical condition."

Jennifer stared at it. "She was keeping a journal?"

Zachary opened the book to display one of the spreads. Date down the left column, groups of digits and words in the line following. Jennifer leaned in closer for a look. “What is all of this?”

“I know a doctor. I’ll work with her to determine what each number represents. I don’t think it will be too hard to figure out. It isn’t code, just shorthand.”

Jennifer’s eyes worked across the page and then down it. She shook her head slowly, blinking, bright reflections from tears in her eyes once again. “That’s... I didn’t realize she’d lost so much. She was looking better. But I didn’t know how much.”

“She didn’t tell you. And she was probably wearing the same clothes. Hiding her weight loss so it wasn’t so obvious.”

“You think she had an eating disorder? That she was anorexic?”

“No. I think she just didn’t want to be asked about it. She didn’t want to have to explain to anyone what she was doing or why she was losing weight. If people started commenting on the huge amount of weight that she had lost, it would just make her feel bad. Like she was so awful before."

Jennifer seemed to accept this. It was more palatable than the idea that Kristin was intentionally keeping things from her mother or suffering from an eating disorder that had weakened her heart and contributed to her death.

"I don't like you taking it away. Taking any of this stuff away. Can't you just look at it here? It will only take a few minutes."

"It will take longer than that. I'll want to do a pretty deep dive. And that's easiest to do at home, where I have all the proper equipment."

He would probably have to just copy everything and return the equipment and notebook to her.

"I'll get it back to you as soon as I can. But you want me to do everything possible. You want as much information as you can get, don't you?"

"I don't know. Yes, of course." But her initial answer was probably the more accurate. She wasn't sure what she wanted to discover. She probably didn't want to know about everything that was going on in her daughter's life, all of her thoughts and feelings and secret shames. Jennifer just wanted to know the good stuff. To have happy, innocent memories of her daughter and know she had done everything she could to protect her.

CHAPTER 23

Zachary considered the information he had found so far while cloning the hard drive on Kristin's laptop. Usually, he got his computer guy, Gerry, to do such tasks, but Gerry had walked him through it a couple of times, and everything seemed to be working as it should. He looked at the prescription receipt and shook his head. He had a feeling that it wasn't an antiviral or antifungal, and Jennifer had already said that she didn't think it was the steroid prescription Kristin had been given. And it wasn't her inhaler.

He considered for a few minutes, then decided to try Kenzie. If she were too busy to talk to him, he'd ask her in the evening. But it was nice to talk to her partway through the day, and he didn't want just to sit there staring at the computer while the data was transferred. He should be making progress on other fronts at the same time.

“Medical Examiner’s Office,” Kenzie answered briskly, then saw who was calling. “Zachary. Hi.” Her tone was cautious, as if she thought he was calling about something negative.

“I just wanted to run some ideas past you,” Zachary said. “But if you’re too busy, it can wait.”

“Some ideas about your case? Sure. Have you received the medical examiner’s report?”

“Not yet. Hopefully tomorrow.”

“What did you find out, then?”

“I wondered about the possible side effects of birth control pills. I’ve heard that there are risks in taking them.”

“Sure. Quite a number of possible side effects, some of them pretty dangerous.”

Zachary thumped the table in front of him. “Hah. I thought so. So if she was taking birth control pills and didn’t tell her mother or the dental surgeon, is it possible that a side effect from that prescription could have resulted in her death?"

"I don't know if it creates any additional risks during surgery, but for sure they can cause clots, strokes, heart attacks. And a lot of less serious side effects."

"Birth control pills could give her a heart attack?"

"Or put her at a higher risk for a heart attack. Yes."

"What about some of the other things she was having? Migraines, stomach problems, difficulty concentrating?"

"Any of those, sure. They're hormones. Headaches are common. They can cause all kinds of mental issues. Problems with concentration or memory, depression and other mood issues. Think about the issues that women have with PMS or pregnancy. All of those areas can be affected."

"I'll bet that's what Kristin was on."

"Do you know for sure? What did her mother say?"

"Her mother said that it was a prescription for an infection. She thinks. She can't remember for sure. I think that Kristin probably went out and got them prescribed without her mother knowing about it. Suddenly she's having all of these issues..."

"And weight loss."

"Right. Could contraceptives have caused that too?"

"No... the opposite. They tend to cause weight gain. One of the things that women hate about them the most."

Zachary thought the other side effects should have been hated at least as much. But he wasn't plugged in to the women's network. Who knew what things were talked about when no men were around?

"What does the prescription say?" Kenzie asked. "Is it a brand name? Progesterone?"

“No.” Zachary studied the multi-syllabic word on the printed receipt and did his best to read it to Kenzie.

She didn’t say anything.

“Are you still there? Did you get that? I’m probably massacring the word. Do you want me to text it to you?”

“That’s not a birth control prescription.”

“It’s not?” Zachary blew out his breath. “Here I thought I had it all figured out. She has a new boyfriend her mother doesn’t know about, a prescription she doesn’t know about...”

“It’s a good guess,” Kenzie admitted. “I might have gone there too. But that isn’t a contraceptive.”

“What is it?”

“I’m not sure. It’s not something I’m familiar with.”

"I probably didn't pronounce it right. Do you want me to message it to you?"

"I'd better get back to my work here. You can show it to me when I get home. I won't be too much longer, I just need to tie up a few loose ends."

"Okay. Talk to you later, then."

Kenzie hung up. Zachary looked at the computer to see how the data transfer was progressing. He considered whether to search the name of the prescription to find out what it was on his own, but decided against it. He had plenty of other tasks that he should be doing, and discussing the medical aspects of his cases was one of the things that he and Kenzie enjoyed doing together. If he looked it up before she came home, there would be no point in her looking at it. He could search what it was for and what the side effects were, but that would ruin their fun.

He unlocked Kristin's phone and looked through it for hidden apps. There was no point in going to her readily apparent social apps with their plain vanilla messages if she were using something else to communicate with people and the mainstream stuff was just for her mother's benefit.

He was distracted by the beep of his computer, indicating that he had mail from Heather. He had been falling down on a number of tasks that Heather had already reminded him about more than once. He needed to focus and get a few of them done.

* * *

When Kenzie got home, Zachary looked around at the equipment and papers scattered around him on the couch, laptop desk, and carpet. It was disorganized and distracting. He would just keep jumping from one unfinished task to another if he didn't corral it and take control.

"You okay?" Kenzie asked with a laugh.

“Yeah. I just didn’t realize I’d gotten snowed under…”

“That looks like quite the project.”

“Yeah.” Zachary shook his head, embarrassed by his ability to generate a mess in such a short time. A talent that more than one foster mother had not appreciated. “Just give me a minute and I’ll get this picked up.”

The laptop hard drive was finished cloning. The phone was nearly dead and would have to be charged before he could do anything more. There were at least a dozen more emails in his inbox than the last time he checked. Kristin’s logbook, Zachary’s notes, and other materials he had meant to scan or file were jumbled together. The prescription receipt was buried somewhere.

Zachary worked through the piles of paper in an effort to get everything organized. His own work was as disorganized as Kristin’s schoolwork in her desk drawer, everything just thrown together in a jumble. For Zachary, that was the normal state of affairs and he needed to work at it to keep things organized better. Or get help from someone who was naturally organized. But it was evident from Kristin's previous term's work and neatly labeled file folders that it was not normal for her. Something had happened in the past few weeks or months that had caused that to change. If not the brain fog from a hormonal contraceptive, then what?

Zachary took some of the papers into the home office where they were supposed to be filed and grabbed a box to corral everything to do with Jennifer's case. Kenzie looked out through the kitchen doorway as he finished putting everything away.

"That looks better."

Zachary joined her. "You'd think someone had set off a bomb in there. I don't know how I can manage to create that much of a mess in such a short time."

"Neither do I, to tell the truth," she told him with a laugh. "Did you make any headway after we talked?"

"Well... I got a few things done. Or partway done. But I didn't really move the case forward. But I did save the medical stuff to discuss with you."

"Oh, good." Kenzie's tone was genuinely pleased, not sarcastic. Zachary might expect her to be tired of dealing with death and the medical field after spending hours on it every day, but she was always happy to discuss whatever questions he brought to her.

She already knew about the prescription, and Zachary filled her in on the weight loss log as they worked together on dinner preparations.

"Now, are you sure it is a weight loss log," Kenzie asked with a teasing smile, "and not something else? There are a lot of different things that she might have been tracking."

"You'll have to take a look at it. I'm... ninety-five percent sure, and that's what her mother seemed to think too. But we could both be wrong."

"We'll see!"

CHAPTER 24

Kenzie looked at the notebook when she sat down at the table before starting to dish up. While they liked to discuss files over dinner, it was best not to have too much paper at the table where it could be damaged by spills. Zachary intended to return everything to Jennifer in the same condition he had received it.

Kenzie's eyes ran across the entries. "Date, weight, it looks like some symptoms she was tracking, dosages, heart rate and blood pressure." Kenzie sipped her water, gazing at it and seeing whether she could squeeze any more information out of the records. "This one looks like a running total of her weight loss. Over fifty pounds, that's nothing to sneeze at. She was doing really well."

"Her mom said that she was walking a lot. She didn't know anything else. Even that Kristin was keeping this log."

"Well, I would expect her to have noticed this. Kristin was a big girl, but fifty pounds shows, even off of someone who is grossly obese."

"She did notice… but she didn't know it was that much. And she thought that Kristin was doing it healthily."

"Considering the fact that she died… I wouldn't count on it. Dieters can be really hard on their bodies. If she was also purging or severely restricting calories or taking drugs that were harmful to her system, her heart and other organs would be at risk. Something like anesthetic could cause a problem."

"Because of what she was doing, not because she was allergic to it?"

"An allergy is always possible too, even if she'd had the same anesthetic without incident before. Sometimes allergies can develop quite suddenly. There's no way to know without more information."

“If the doctors had known what she was doing, would they have done anything differently?”

“No guarantees. I assume they monitored her heart rhythm and blood pressure while administering the anesthetic. But subtle shifts in rhythm can be missed. Or her heart might have just stopped without any warning.”

“But they wouldn’t have said it was too risky to do the surgery?”

Kenzie considered. “No, I don’t think so. There were risks, but unless they knew she was taking something that had a known conflict with the anesthetic, I don’t think they would have been that concerned.”

She handed Zachary the logbook and he took it back into the living room to put it with the rest of the items related to the investigation.

"And what was the prescription?" Kenzie asked. "Do you have that out there too?"

"Oh, yeah." Zachary pulled out the receipt and handed it to her when he returned to the table.

Kenzie looked at the name of the drug for a minute and shook her head. "I'm not familiar with this."

She pulled out her phone and carefully tapped out the drug's name. She scrolled through the results with her thumb.

"It is a weight loss drug. Prescribed for people with type 2 diabetes, to help stabilize blood sugar, delay stomach emptying, and suppress appetite." She nodded slowly. "Was Kristin diagnosed with diabetes?"

"Not that Jennifer said, no. But then... she has downplayed a few things. Kristin's weight loss. Her poor marks at school this term. The severity of her asthma."

"Maybe Kristin was diagnosed, but Jennifer didn't want to tell you because she was afraid that would be the end of your investigation. You would just tell her it was a complication of Kristin's diabetes. Or because she had not told the surgeon that Kristin was diabetic."

"It's possible," Zachary admitted. There was a knot in his stomach at the thought of Jennifer lying to him. That was going beyond forgetting to give him information or shading the truth. He had shown her the prescription, and she had brushed it off as being an antibiotic. But she must have known the truth. "Kristin wouldn't have been able to get the prescription without a parent, would she? She's a minor."

"It's hard to say. Some doctors would feel obligated to tell her parents and others wouldn't. Did Kristin have the ability to pay for it? Without whatever medical insurance her mother carried?"

"Jennifer said that Kristin's bank account was empty. That all of the money she had put away for college was gone, and she didn't have anything to show for it. No new clothes, car, or anything else you might expect a teenager to buy."

"She did have something to show for it. Her weight loss."

"I guess." Zachary poked at the casserole on his plate. "You think she might have done it without Jennifer's knowledge, then?"

"If she paid for it out of her own bank account. It sounds like it."

"I'll have to follow up with the doctor." Zachary nodded to the prescription receipt. "Did she just go to her family doctor? Jennifer didn't say anything about not recognizing his name."

Kenzie tapped his name into her phone. "He is a specialist. Bariatrician."

Zachary had never heard the word before. He shook his head. "Specializing in...?"

"Weight loss. From the looks of his website... he specializes in LipoSlayerRx."

"LipoSlayerRx?"

Kenzie indicated the prescription receipt. "The brand name for that."

"LipoSlayerRx. It sounds very..." Zachary tried to put the feeling into words. "Very... commercial?"

"Yeah, I would agree with that. I've seen this before. I didn't recognize the drug name, but I've heard the branding before. Advertisements on the internet. In my inbox, videos, social media timelines. I've seen it around quite a bit lately."

Zachary didn't think that he had. But Kenzie was probably closer to the target demographic than he was. A female professional with a good income. And she'd complained a number of times in his hearing about having gained weight the past few months. With all of the electronic eavesdropping built into home automation systems and monitoring search engines and social media discussions online, it wouldn't take long for one of them to pick up on her interest in weight loss.

"Is it new? Or just a new label for something old?"

"Pretty new. This whole class of drugs. They seem to be very effective for weight loss. Without the side effects that we've seen in the past from amphetamines."

"But it does have side effects."

"Looking at her weight loss log, I would say so."

"Could this have caused all of her problems? Digestion, headaches, the drop in her marks?"

"I'd have to look at the reported side effects from their drug trials. It's possible. Although the drop in her marks..." Kenzie grimaced and shook her head. "I would think that was more likely to be some kind of distraction at school. Certain drugs do cause mental impairment... brain fog, dementia, forgetfulness... but I wouldn't expect that from something that stabilizes blood sugar. I'd expect the opposite. Better focus and ability to concentrate."

"Unless she had a migraine. Or upset stomach."

"Well... I guess so. If she wasn't feeling well, it could impact her schoolwork."

"She had to leave classes a few times because she wasn't feeling well. So it was more than just a bit of nausea."

CHAPTER 25

Zachary was no longer hungry. Maybe the talk about weight loss was affecting him. Or maybe it was the thought that Jennifer had lied to him or intentionally not told him things that might have a bearing on his investigation. He pushed food around on his plate without much interest. Kenzie was nearly finished eating her meal and Zachary's plate was still basically untouched. She eyed it, opening her mouth to comment.

Zachary's phone rang. It was lying on the table next to him, and he looked at it surreptitiously. They had a rule against answering calls at the dinner table. But Kenzie was finished and Zachary didn't think he was going to eat any more. And the caller ID on his phone showed that it was Jennifer.

"This is her. Do you mind if I...?"

Kenzie nodded. "Sure. Go ahead."

Zachary stood up and walked away from the table before swiping the call and putting the phone up to his ear. “Hi, Jennifer. I was going to call you.”

He suspected she was calling to see if he were finished with Kristin’s phone and computer. She was worried she wouldn’t get them back, or Zachary would do something to damage them or erase data.

“Oh?” Jennifer’s voice cracked. “Does that mean that you found something?”

“I found out that she was on a weight loss prescription drug,” Zachary told her. “What you told me was an antibiotic.”

“A weight loss prescription?” Jennifer sounded doubtful rather than guilty at being caught in a lie. “She wasn’t ever on a weight loss prescription. I didn’t want her to be stigmatized by her weight…”

“Then she got the prescription without your knowledge?”

"I don't think you could be right. She was just walking more, getting in better shape."

"She had a prescription. In her name. For LipoSlayerRx."

"LipoSlayerRx? That crap? I remember her asking about it once, and I told her to stay away from it. It's so hyped up. I don't trust anything that hits the media like that."

"Like what?"

"Have you been living under a rock? You never heard of it?"

"I haven't... but I'm not exactly their target demographic."

"You're pretty thin," Jennifer admitted, as if she thought it was a bad thing.

And she hadn't seen him at his worst. Before his last hospital stay and the change in his prescriptions, his weight had been a significant concern. It always dropped when he was in a depressive cycle, and the previous drug cocktail had made him nauseated so much of the time that it was a real struggle to eat enough calories to maintain his weight.

"So you had no idea that she was on LipoSlayerRx."

"No. If I had... I would have strongly discouraged it."

"She was having success losing weight with it."

"That was just because she was putting in the work. You know that none of these quack medicines really work."

"You think it was snake oil?"

"Of course I do. None of those weight loss medicines do anything. And then half the time, they end up being pulled off the market a year later because they cause heart problems." Jennifer cleared her throat. "You don't think... that's what happened, do you? That it damaged her heart?"

"There's no evidence to support that yet, but we'll look into it. But it isn't an amphetamine."

"I worked so hard to keep her from worrying about her weight. From being defined by it. There were so many great things about her. She was smart, funny, and kind... why was it the only thing people cared about was that she was overweight?"

"I wish I had an answer for you. But kids—people—bullies are good at identifying weaknesses, especially the ones that cause you the most distress. And they dig away at them..."

"Yeah," Jennifer agreed, her voice hoarse. There were a few seconds of silence. Zachary didn't know what else to say to her. She hadn't asked for Kristin's possessions back like he had thought she would.

"Was there something else?" Zachary asked eventually, when she didn't say anything.

"I got the autopsy report."

"Oh." He didn't know whether to give his condolences for this or to act like it was good news. He had no idea what the correct response was to such an announcement. "Well, I'm glad it came through. Did you get a hard copy or an electronic copy? Should I come and get it?"

"They sent it by email. So I can forward it on to you."

"That would be great. I can look at it tonight and sort things out. We'll see if anything is new to us or if they overlooked anything."

"Okay. I'll send it to you."

"I'm sorry, Jennifer..." Zachary felt like condolences were definitely required. Jennifer sounded stunned, like she had just found out about Kristin's death. Like it had just hit her again. "Is there anything else I can do? Is there someone who could be with you?"

"No. I'll be fine. If you can find anything out... I want you looking at the report, not patting my hand and telling me it will all be okay. Nothing is ever going to be normal and okay again. Never."

"Someone should sit with you."

"No. I'll have a drink and go to bed. I don't feel like being around people right now."

"Not too much."

"Not too much what? Oh," she gave a bleak bleat of laughter. "Don't drink too much? I won't. Never could hold my liquor. Just a glass of wine. It will put me to sleep."

"Okay. I want to make sure that you're all right."

"If you can get me any answers... that's what I need the most."

"Did you look at the report?"

"I opened it," she admitted. "I thought I wanted to read it. But seeing her talked about as 'the deceased' and the pictures... I couldn't." She swore. "I had no idea how awful it would be. I thought it would be dry and clinical and that would keep me from being emotional about it. But that just made it more horrifying."

"You shouldn't have read it." Zachary took a deep breath and held it for a moment. "I'll get on it as soon as I receive it."

"Thank you, Zachary. I owe you."

"No, you don't." He thought of all the times she had helped him and intervened on his behalf that semester that they'd been in Ptarmigan House together. And on top of that, she was paying him for his work. "You don't owe me anything."

CHAPTER 26

Kenzie saw Zachary go to his laptop and open the lid.

"Are you working tonight?"

Normally, the evening was reserved for time together, unless Zachary had surveillance or a job that couldn't be done during the day.

"Actually... you are too," he told her. "The autopsy report came in."

"Oh, okay. Let's have a look at it, then. You want to print off a couple of copies?"

"I'll print you off one. I'll read it on the screen."

He knew she preferred hard copies and would dog-ear pages, highlight passages, and write notes in the margins. Zachary, on the other hand, would use the computer's text-to-speech function to read passages to him, which was much easier than trying to decode each of the medical words and construct the sentences in a way that made sense to him. It was much easier to understand if he could hear it.

He found Jennifer's email, downloaded the report, and opened it. He sent a copy to the printer and started by browsing through the file to look at each of the photographs and figures. Jennifer should not have looked at it. Zachary had a hard enough time keeping a professional distance from the subject. There was no way a mother should see her child like that. He hoped the wine would help her to forget.

Kenzie went down the hall to get her copy as it came out of the printer in the home office, starting her reading in there as she waited for it to spit out each page.

She returned to the living room while Zachary was reading each heading and the descriptions of the photos and graphs of test results. Then he would drill down to reading some of the longer passages and discussing them with Kenzie.

"The medical examiner didn't know that she was taking LipoSlayerRx," Kenzie told him.

Zachary looked up at her. "Since Jennifer didn't know, I guess nobody told him. He couldn't tell that she was taking it? From the tox screens or whatever other tests?"

Kenzie shook her head. "It isn't like you see on TV where they can identify any poison or chemical present in the body. Tox screens won't pull up things like LipoSlayerRx." Kenzie made a face. "I'm just going to call it Rx, okay? I hate the name."

Zachary nodded in agreement.

"The medical examiner noted the injection marks on her belly. But he assumed they were from insulin."

"Then she was diabetic?"

"Being so overweight, I would be surprised if her pancreas could keep up with the insulin production she needed. But the blood tests show pretty good glucose levels. So the Rx was doing its job. The medical examiner just didn't know it was Rx rather than insulin."

"Right. Okay." Zachary had already seen the picture of the needle marks on her stomach. "Is that a normal place to inject? Not into a vein?"

"We aren't talking about recreational drugs you want to get into the bloodstream. Insulin and drugs like Rx work best injected into the fatty areas."

"I thought the prescription would be a pill. I can't imagine a teenager having to give herself a shot in the belly." He shuddered at the thought. Some people committed suicide by injecting drugs. Zachary could never go that way. He wasn't afraid of needles, but he couldn't imagine using one on himself.

"Some diabetic six-year-olds give themselves injections," Kenzie told him, amused.

“Sheesh. That’s awful.”

“It’s not a nice disease. Kristin was certainly old enough to handle her own injections if she wanted to. And the autoinjectors that Rx comes in make it easy. Like an Epi-pen.”

“Still. In the stomach.”

“Yes,” Kenzie nodded. “In the stomach.”

Zachary looked down at his computer. “There were no needles in her room. I didn’t do a thorough search—they could still have been hidden in a hoodie pocket or a box in the closet—but they weren’t obvious.”

“She wouldn’t have wanted her mom to find them if the prescription was a secret.”

“No. Maybe she kept them in her locker.”

"Might have. But I would expect her locker to have been cleared out and everything sent to her mom. There would have been a pretty big to-do if they'd found needles."

* * *

Kenzie was still studying the medical examiner's report, and Zachary planned to go back to it after Kenzie had milked everything out of it that she could but, in the meantime, he decided to work on her phone. Jennifer wanted it back soon, so he might as well be ready for her.

He had already sorted out which apps and social media Kristin actually used—as opposed to the public ones her mother saw—so he was able to get straight into it. There were no saved chats or posted videos, no screenshots of conversations that Kristin had engaged in. The app had done everything it was supposed to, wiping the trail behind her so that whatever interactions she'd had with her friends and communities on social media had remained private.

He got out his notepad and started searching the hashtags he'd copied from the posts Rhys had found for him—#weightlosschallenge #Rx4Fx #SlaythePounds.

He immediately found himself immersed in the world of LipoSlayerRx. Now that he knew about the drug and what to look for, he saw it was everywhere. Though it was rarely called by its full name, "Rx" and "Slay" were peppered everywhere. There were apparently social media challenges to see who could lose the most weight with it. There was storyline after storyline of celebrities rumored to be taking Rx, even though it was only supposed to be for grossly obese people with diabetes. Men and women alike used it to shed pounds before a walk down the red carpet or a photo shoot.

It was no wonder that Kristin had asked her mother about the drug and had been interested enough to get a prescription without her mother's permission. It was the new miracle drug—a cure for the obesity epidemic. The hype wasn't just limited to social media and supermarket tabloids. Major news outlets were onboard, the results of drug trials were quoted, and everyone seemed to have an opinion. Jennifer was right to ask what rock Zachary had been hiding under. He had no idea how he had missed all of the chatter about the drug.

CHAPTER 27

Zachary was not able to get in to talk to the principal, but the vice-principal, Mr. Cortez, agreed to help him. Cortez looked Zachary over, and then his eyes drifted away, bored. He had better things to do than babysit some private investigator. Zachary didn't have any place in the school. They had only indulged him because of how shocking and sudden Kristin's death had been. Cortez looked at the clock on the wall.

"Students are in classes right now. What can we help you with, Mr. Goldman?"

"You know that I'm here about Kristin Jones."

"I am aware, yes. Though I'm not sure why. She died in a doctor's office. It was nothing to do with school. And you've already been here asking questions once before. I think it's appropriate for us to ask when exactly this is going to be over. Our students need to get back to normal life. Distractions like this are not good for students who should be focusing on their studies."

"I imagine they'll be distracted by Kristin's death whether I'm asking questions about it or not."

"I think that if you were not here causing a disruption, they could get back to their work. You are creating a distraction. So what can we do about that?"

"Did you clear out Kristin's locker? To give her personal items to her mother?"

"Yes. I was involved in collecting her things."

"How long after her death did that take place?"

Cortez rolled his eyes and thought about it. "The next day, I would say. It isn't like there was a rush. Mrs. Jones would not have wanted us racing over there with our little box of odds and ends. She needed time to grieve and adjust to the fact that her daughter had just died. That's a pretty shocking position to be put into. She didn't have any warning that her daughter had any health problems."

"Well... she knew some of her health problems," Zachary corrected. "Her asthma, for one thing. And her weight. I imagine there were other issues that she didn't think were as serious. And she knew that Kristin was failing this term."

"Not failing," Cortez objected. "She was still above a failing grade. But her marks had gone down."

"She was failing. It was only because of her higher marks at the beginning of the term that it averaged out to a passing grade."

Cortez looked like he would argue the point.

"She had F's on all of her recent assignments," Zachary said. "The ones that she had managed to hand in."

"That... may be. I'm not sure of every student's marks."

“So the school and Mrs. Jones did know that there were some things wrong.”

“But that isn’t why you are here,” Cortez argued impatiently.

“What kinds of things did you find in her locker?”

“The same things I would have found in anyone else’s locker. Textbooks, notebooks, other school supplies. A jacket and some other clothing or personal items.”

“No needles?”

“Needles?” Cortez’s brows drew together. “Certainly not. Why would there have been needles? You think that Kristin Jones was mainlining drugs? The idea is ridiculous.”

“No. Not mainlining. And not street drugs. She was injecting a weight loss prescription. Like insulin.” Zachary wasn’t sure how much like insulin Rx was, but he figured that if he framed it as a legitimate diabetes prescription, Cortez would be a lot less likely to fight back against the idea.

"Oh." Cortez looked taken aback. "Well, of course, if she needed to take medications, she might have had them in her locker. But no, I checked her locker out myself. Worked with her locker partner to identify which things were hers. And there were no prescriptions. No needles."

"Then I need to talk to her locker partner and her close friends so that we can find out what happened to her medication and needles."

"You don't think another student could be using the needles for... something, do you?"

"I think that whoever took them did it so that Kristin's mother wouldn't find out about the prescription she was on. Because she wouldn't have approved. I think she was just honoring what she thought Kristin would have wanted."

"Her mother didn't know about this medication?" Cortez demanded.

"No. She didn't know that Kristin was taking anything but her asthma inhaler. But she was."

"You're sure of that?"

"The medical examiner was."

"Oh. Well, we can find out from her friends who might have removed the rest of Kristin's personal items from the locker."

Zachary nodded. "Good. Who was her partner? Who did she share the locker with?"

"Ala Singh. I'll find out what class she is in. She and another girl were Kristin's best friends."

"Rain Murdoch."

Cortez raised his brows, then nodded.

"I talked to them both before," Zachary said. "I would like to talk to them again, since they were holding back information the first time. Now that I know Kristin was on this prescription, it might be easier for me to get to the full truth."

"They're a pretty tight-knit group," Cortez said slowly. "I wouldn't count on being able to get anything out of them that they don't feel like sharing. Especially if they think they are protecting Kristin's reputation. There isn't much else they can do for her now. Just staying loyal to her memory."

"I'll see if I can get anything out of them."

Cortez just looked at Zachary for a moment as if trying to think of a way to get rid of him. But Zachary was not going anywhere. Cortez could ask him to leave, but he would be back. Until he got what he wanted. He could try to contact the girls at their homes or follow them once they got off of the school property, but he would prefer not to get arrested.

"I'll call them in and have a chat with them," Cortez said firmly. "I don't know about letting you talk to them again. I'm surprised you were allowed to the first time, to tell the truth.

Their parents might have objections to them talking to… a stranger."

"Neither of them said they wanted their parents there."

"I don't imagine so," the vice principal agreed dryly.

What teenager would want their parents there supervising? Hearing about what they did with their friends and any other private business. No, they wouldn't want parents in on that.

Zachary stood waiting at the reception counter while Cortez looked up the girls' information and had them called to the office. It was a few minutes before Ala and Rain showed up together. They saw their vice principal and Zachary there waiting and exchanged concerned looks. But their faces, when they turned to Zachary, were flat and expressionless.

"Let's meet somewhere private," Zachary suggested, not allowing Cortez to take control of the conversation. It would be harder for Cortez to take over once Zachary made it clear that it was his interview and he had asked the vice principal for his help.

Cortez scowled at Zachary for an instant, then nodded to the girls. “Come around here.” He motioned them past the reception desk. Zachary stepped forward quickly and led the way. They were taken to a larger room than they had been in the first time, which was fine with Zachary. If Mr. Cortez was staying, the smaller meeting room would have been claustrophobically close.

“I gather you know Mr. Goldman,” Cortez nodded toward Zachary.

“Yes.” Both girls nodded their agreement.

“Mr. Goldman—”

“Zachary,” he interposed.

Cortez glared at him. “Mr. Goldman has made some serious allegations that I think you would like to address.”

Ala looked at Rain, the anxiety now written clearly on her face. Serious allegations?

“I know the two of you were just trying to protect your friend,” Zachary said slowly. “You wanted to keep her mother from discovering things she hadn’t wanted to share in life.”

Neither girl said anything or made any sign.

“You kept denying that anything was going on with Kristin. You were hiding the fact that she had been taking LipoSlayerRx to lose weight.”

Rain’s shoulders rose and fell in an unconcerned shrug. “Why would that matter to anyone?”

“I asked you about her health and if she was taking anything.”

“But it’s not really any of your business, is it?” Rain asked caustically.

“I have been hired by her mother to find out what happened to her. What all of the contributing factors were for her death.

And you hid the fact that she had been taking a medication that might have had a significant effect—did have a significant effect—on her health."

"She was fine. She was just fine."

Zachary looked at Ala. "Did you remove the needles from the locker to keep them from her mother? Or did Rain do that?"

Ala's eyes were wide. She shook her head but could not seem to find her voice.

"Which of you took her prescription?" Cortez asked sternly.

They looked at each other. Rain shook her head at Ala. But Ala was the weak link. She looked at Zachary, swallowing. She preferred to engage with him, not the vice principal. Zachary would go away and she would never have to face him again. She might have to deal with Cortez for several more years.

"You took the needles?" Zachary asked her. "The autoinjectors?"

“I didn’t use them or sell them,” Ala protested. “I just... got rid of them.”

“So the two of you knew Kristin was on Rx.”

They didn’t deny it.

“And you knew that it was affecting her.”

“She’d lost a lot of weight,” Ala said. “She’d never been able to do that before. She said it was a lifesaver. That it was the only thing that had ever worked for her. She’d never seen the numbers on the scale go down before, only up.”

“And that was really important to her.”

“Of course it was,” Rain snapped. “She didn’t want to go around looking like that any more than anyone else. It was just the body she was born with. And then she got the right prescription. She could finally lose it. Take control of her life.”

“But it was also making her sick.”

"So what? Some headaches and nausea? It was worth it to start feeling better about herself."

"What about her failing grades? Weren't they an issue?"

"Kristin said she just needed to study harder. She'd get back on track with her schoolwork."

"Did you notice other changes in her behavior? Her attention, memory, mood?"

"Rx was the best thing that ever happened to her," Rain insisted. "She wouldn't do anything to jeopardize that."

"Maybe it was just all of the hype around Rx. A placebo effect."

"A placebo made her drop fifty pounds when nothing else ever helped? Who cares? If it was just a placebo, then so what? It was what she wanted."

CHAPTER 28

She wanted to lose weight at the expense of everything else?" Zachary challenged. "Her schoolwork, her health, her relationship with her mother? Ultimately her life?"

"Rx didn't kill her. She died during surgery. The anesthetic or something," Rain asserted.

"Adults don't get it," Ala said in a small voice. "You all forget what it was like. Or maybe things weren't so bad when you went to school. Back before the internet and cell phones. You don't know what it's like to have something like a weight problem when you're going to school. Something that is so important you would give anything to fix it."

Zachary rubbed his thumb against the arm of the chair he was sitting in, feeling the combination of rough and smooth surfaces, trying to focus on physical sensations to keep him anchored in the present and not to think about what it had been like when he went to school. When he would have sacrificed anything to be like everyone else. To have a brain that worked properly and his own family to go home to every day, to be indistinguishable from everyone else.

“I’m sure it wasn’t as bad as that,” Cortez said smoothly, dismissing the idea. “We have a no-bullying policy. We have a very tolerant school community and accept all body types.”

Ala’s eyes flicked to Zachary to see his reaction to that. Zachary couldn’t even pretend that he believed Cortez’s words. He rolled his eyes and shook his head.

“No school is without bullying.”

“We do everything we can to nip it in the bud and ensure our school is a safe and nurturing environment for all students. We have an excellent record.”

“Record?”

“Our incidents of bullying are very low, and they are dealt with immediately. I challenge you to find anyone who claims to be bullied and hasn't had their case heard if they brought it forward to the administration."

"Having a low level of incidents reported does not mean bullying is not taking place," Zachary told him. "It may just mean that students know they won't be taken seriously or be dealt with effectively, so they don't bother to report it."

"Our students know that we will address any reports of bullying. Don't they?" Cortez addressed the question to Ala and Rain.

They both just stared back at him. Cortez made a gesture as if demonstrating that they had confirmed his words. The girls looked at Zachary. They knew there was no point in arguing with Cortez about it, but Zachary understood there was a difference between no reporting and no bullying.

"Do you still have Kristin's prescription?" he asked Ala. "Her autoinjectors?"

Ala shook her head. “No. I... got rid of them.”

“What did you do? Throw them out?”

“Yes.” Her eyes went back and forth as she tried to compose her lie. “In the big dumpster behind the school.”

Cortez shook his head. “The garbage is collected every Tuesday. So... you won’t be able to find them. They should have been disposed of properly,” he told Ala sternly. “Needles are only supposed to go in designated containers. Not in the garbage bin with everything else.”

“Well, I didn’t know where else to put them. I don’t know where you’re supposed to get rid of needles.”

Cortez looked at Zachary. “I think we’ve gotten everything out of these girls that we are going to. I’m very disappointed in you,” he told them. “Lying about what happened. Hiding the needles and throwing them out. Not being open and honest with their mother and the school administration. That’s not how members of this school behave. You signed an honor code when you started here, promising to be honest and to report anything to the administration that did not align with the school policies. I have a good mind to talk to your parents."

"What good is that going to do?" Rain demanded. "You think that they're going to be happy to hear that? That it will stop anyone from breaking the honor code in the future? You may as well keep quiet and just take their fees and donations."

"Miss Murdoch, I would advise you to change your attitude. Attending this school is a privilege. If you were to be expelled, you would not be happy being put into the public school system."

"And do you have a nice fat donor to replace my father?"

"That is not the issue."

But Zachary could see that Cortez was already recalculating, knowing he needed to stay in Mr. Murdoch's good graces if he could. The school fees and voluntary donations must have been pretty high.

And Jennifer must have been making pretty good money to afford to enroll her daughter in the school.

There was a tap on the door, and a woman stuck her head in.

"I'm sorry, Mr. Cortez, but there's been an incident..."

He stood up quickly. "We're done here." He gave each of the girls a stern look. "I'd better not have any more trouble from the two of you. I am going to make a note on your files, and if something else happens..."

Neither of them said anything. They just sat there looking at him.

"Good," Cortez declared. "Now, you get to class. Mr. Goldman, I assume you're on your way out?"

Zachary didn't bother to answer either. Mr. Cortez apparently preferred to put his own interpretation on things. He could take Zachary's silence to mean what he liked.

Cortez left the room to take care of the "incident," whatever it was. Zachary looked at Ala and Rain, and they looked back at him.

"I hope I'm not quite as bad as that," Zachary said, shaking his head.

Ala giggled.

"It might be a long time since I went to school," he went on, "but I remember a lot more than I would like to. I understand how bad things must have been for Kristin to make weight loss more important to her than anything else. I'm sorry for whatever she had to go through here. And if you are dealing with bullying..."

"There will always be bullies," Rain said in a hard voice. "No matter what. We deal with it."

"I hope it isn't too bad... like with Kristin."

"Kristin was a big target." Rain stopped and her cheeks got pink as she realized what she had said. "An easy target, I mean. For a lot of people. We did our best to protect her, but sometimes... stuff still happened."

Zachary nodded. No matter how diligent they were in trying to stay with her and keep her from being bullied or even assaulted, they couldn't be with her every minute of the school day. There would still be opportunities for people to say or do things to her.

"You did your best. I'm sure she was grateful for that, and her mother is too."

Rain showed softening for the first time. Her eyes glistened and her lips twitched. She dropped her gaze to the table and swallowed. “She was our friend. We stuck together.”

“Thank you for that.”

They didn’t say anything else. Zachary pushed his chair back slightly as if he were about to leave.

“Oh. By the way, who is Ares?”

The eyes of both girls widened in shock. Ala looked at Rain for reassurance. Rain’s mouth was open, but she didn’t seem to know how to respond to this.

“Ares, at…” Zachary looked at the photo on his phone and read off the number. He paused, waiting to see what they had to offer. “I am a private investigator, you know. I will find out.”

They still didn’t offer it up. “Was he Kristin’s boyfriend?”

Still silence. Ala was clearly uncomfortable, looking at the door and measuring the route to safety.

“Does he go to school here?” Zachary asked. “Should I ask Mr. Cortez about him?”

“He’ll think we told you something,” Ala protested.

Zachary wasn’t sure whether “he” meant Mr. Cortez or Ares. Which one of them was she concerned would think she was a snitch? He waited, watching both of them and hoping that the silence would make his argument for him.

“Ares goes to school here,” Rain said finally, delicately, as if picking out a safe path through a minefield. “He wasn’t her boyfriend.”

“Why would she have his number? Did she have a crush on him? Did she have his number because she wanted to get together with him?”

They both shook their heads.

“So I should ask Mr. Cortez? Maybe I can get Ares pulled out of class too.”

“Don’t,” Rain said explosively. “You don’t know what you’re dealing with here.”

“Then maybe you’d better tell me.”

CHAPTER 29

School let out early on a Friday, so Zachary didn't have too long to wait. He took up a post and watched the corner from a distance, waiting for Ares to make his appearance. It wasn't long before the boy showed up, as Rain and Ala had said he would. He arrived in a small group to begin with, but each of the other boys broke off and went in different directions. Going home or staged nearby as lookouts in case there was any trouble?

Zachary waited until Ares was alone, and watched him for a few minutes. Then he got out of his car and approached.

He was only a few feet from Ares when the boy realized Zachary wasn't just a pedestrian walking by but wanted to talk to him. He took a step back and looked around quickly. His guards, if that's what they were, were not in sight.

Zachary was not much of a threat, a small man with a slight build, even if he had filled out since Christmas. He was several inches taller than Ares, but probably not much heavier. Ares was a pleasant-looking young man, dressed in his school uniform. His facial features and dark hair suggested he was perhaps Middle Eastern, though the name was Greek. Did he look Greek? Zachary wasn't sure what Greeks typically looked like.

"Who are you?" Ares demanded. His accent suggested he had been born in the US. Maybe shades of New York.

"My name is Zachary. I wanted to ask you about Kristin Jones."

Ares looked surprised, but masked it immediately. "Jones. I don't know any Kristin Jones."

"I'm sure you must have heard about the girl who died."

"Oh, was that her?" He shrugged and shook his head. "Don't think I ever met her."

"She knew you. She had your phone number."

"Lots of people could have my phone number. Doesn't mean that I know them."

"But I think you did, didn't you? She was a customer."

"Customer?" Ares spread his hands, smiling pleasantly. He had a very innocent, boyish face. A mask. "A customer for what? Do I look like the corner store?"

"Do you really think I don't know what I'm talking about?" Zachary challenged. "What's the point in this charade? I'd rather get down to details and forget about all of this... posturing."

"You don't have anything on me."

"Who said I was looking for something on you? I said that I wanted to talk about Kristin."

Ares considered him seriously. Zachary saw his muscles tense an instant before he decided to make a break for it. He grabbed the loop on the back of Ares's backpack and held on tightly, jerking Ares back when he tried to run. Ares could have just slipped his arms out of the backpack if he thought that Zachary was a danger to him. But he was clearly more concerned about leaving his backpack behind than escaping. He tried to jerk away, and looked at Zachary, his jaw set angrily. Confrontational now instead of the pleasant boy he had been pretending to be.

"What's your problem?" he demanded. "You a cop? You don't have anything on me. And you don't have the right to search or seize anything of mine."

Zachary looked at the backpack. Nice and roomy. Certainly there was something in there other than just a few notebooks or a slim laptop. Rather than trying to pull it off of Ares's back, he unzipped the main section and checked inside.

"Hey! You can't do that!" Ares protested. "That's illegal search and seizure!"

"I'm not a cop."

"You still can't do that!" Ares jerked away, but Zachary had already reached into the backpack and pulled out a handful of injectors and packages of pills.

"What's this?" he demanded. He was surprised that Ares still didn't run, but the boy seemed unwilling to leave any merchandise behind.

"Give that back," he insisted, grabbing at the drugs. His face was red, suffused with blood.

Zachary held them up high and behind him so that Ares couldn't reach them.

"Who do you think you are?" Ares demanded. "That's mine. Give it back or I'm gonna call the cops!"

Zachary laughed. He looked at the packets of pills in his hand. "Are you telling me these aren't controlled substances?" He recognized a number of the identifying shapes, colors, and imprints. "Adderall, opiates, benzos... You really want the cops coming around to restore your stolen property to you? You want to go to prison?"

"I wouldn't go to prison. I'm just a kid."

"Even on your first offense, with this much merchandise...?"

Ares stopped trying to grab them from Zachary and stared him in the face. "Who are you?"

"I'm someone who asked you nicely about Kristin Jones. Only, you decided to lie to me."

The boy folded his arms across his chest. "What do you care about Kristin? She died in some operating room."

"And I care. Maybe you don't. Maybe no one else cares about the truth, but I do."

"Why?"

"Because her mother does. And she doesn't think this was just a matter of reacting to a medication they gave her for her surgery. She thinks there is something else going on."

Ares shrugged. "So what? Why should I care?"

"Because if the drugs you sold her contributed to her death, the police could come around here asking you questions. And you could easily end up behind bars until you're an old man."

Zachary knew that if Ares did go to prison, it wouldn't be for long. But to a teenager, someone in their thirties was old. Maybe even someone in their mid-twenties. So he figured he could be forgiven for the exaggeration.

"I didn't have anything to do with her death."

"Then you shouldn't mind talking to me about what you sold her."

CHAPTER 30

Ares surveyed Zachary, his jaw tight and his arms rigid across his chest. “Who says I sold her anything?”

“What does that matter? All that I care about is that you did.” Zachary looked at the items clutched in his hand. He removed an autoinjector with his other hand and looked at the name and branding on it. “So this is what LipoSlayerRx looks like? Or is this counterfeit?”

Ares looked offended. “It’s the real deal! I don’t sell junk.”

“Really. How much for one shot?”

Ares shook his head and didn’t answer.

“If you’re selling it at knock-off prices, then it must not be the real deal. You’re making money, so you must have a supplier that sells it on the cheap, or else you’re mixing your own and just labeling it as Rx.”

"There are ways to get it cheap."

"Yeah? Like what?"

Ares shrugged. "Maybe it's getting close to the expiry date and has to be used up. Or someone lost the shipping documents."

"Because it 'fell off' of a truck?"

Ares smiled and nodded. "Maybe you know something about the business."

"So you're selling expired or stolen product."

"I didn't say that."

Zachary ran his eyes over the injector, looking for any sign that it had been tampered with. Something to indicate that it had been opened up or that a new label had been applied.

"And you probably open them up and dilute them. Add something to... extend their life. Make them more potent."

Ares seemed to think this was funny. “Look, man, when people are desperate for a product… someone has got to sell it to them. Why should it be some other guy? Why not me?”

“Because it’s illegal. Because when you adulterate it with something else, you’re putting lives at risk. Because you’re a kid and should be studying instead of selling drugs.”

“I’m not selling drugs. I’m providing a service. There’s no crack or meth here. Nothing that is going to kill you. Just a few meds a person needs to make it through their day. What should it matter? They need the product; I can supply it.”

“How long have you been doing this?” Zachary shook his head. The boy looked about eleven. But he knew that saying so would just make Ares less likely to talk to him.

“Long time. I know my business. And you don’t have any right to come around here and steal my product and tell me how I should be running my business. So why don’t you give that back and get off of my corner? If you stay around here, you're going to attract trouble."

"I'm not ready to go home yet."

"Come on, man!"

"Talk to me about Kristin."

Ares rolled his eyes. "What's there to tell? The girl needed Rx. But it was getting too expensive for her to buy it through the pharmacy. And there were shortages. It's skyrocketing in price because of the celebs. Suddenly, it's not available anymore for the people who really need it, because the stars are buying it up and everyone who watches them stream wants to get in on it too. They're inflating the market. Suddenly, it's not for folks like Kristin Jones anymore. It's for the beautiful people who want to be more beautiful. Who want an easy solution. And they take it out of the hands of people like her, who really need it."

"So you're just providing a service. You're her knight in shining armor."

"That's right." He smirked. "That's what I'm telling you."

"And you only sell to people like her, who really need it. You don't sell it to any of the 'beautiful people' at your school."

Ares's eyes narrowed. "My business practices are my own business. I'm providing a necessary service. If it wasn't me, it would be someone else."

"How long before Kristin's death were you selling it to her?"

"Who knows? A few weeks."

"You know. So how long was it?"

"I didn't keep track. Three, four weeks. She bought twice a week."

“And you didn’t overcharge her or sell her an adulterated product.”

“That’s right. She paid less to me than she did to the pharmacy. It’s highway robbery, what they charge.”

“Where did Kristin get her money?”

“Not my business.”

“Where?”

“I don’t know. Her bank account. Her college fund. Her mom’s purse. That was her own business, not mine. I just needed the money, not its history.”

“And she didn’t swap it for services?”

“I only accept cold hard cash. What services?” Ares looked at Zachary and got it. He looked revolted. “Kristin Jones? Are you kidding me? I’m not pimping her out or accepting services. Who would want that fatso?”

"She didn't show you her appreciation?"

"She showed me her green. That's all I cared about. I have no interest in anything else."

"Turn around."

Ares scowled at him. "What?"

Zachary motioned for Ares to twirl. "Turn around."

Ares slowly turned his back on Zachary, wary that he would steal the rest of what remained in his backpack. Zachary tucked the handful of injectors and pill packages back into the main section. Ares looked over his shoulder anxiously a couple of times, but then relaxed when he saw his goods were being returned to him.

Zachary kept a few items back, shoved into his pocket out of sight.

“Thanks,” Ares said with a sigh of relief. “You’re a gentleman. I don’t know who you are, but you’re all right in my books.”

Zachary smiled at him. It felt fake and forced, and he was sure that the boy would be able to see that he wasn’t sincere. “I just want to be able to reassure Kristin’s mom. She needs to know what happened.”

“You think she’s going to be happier if she finds out Kristin was taking Rx? How is that going to help?”

“The truth. That’s what sets us free.”

“You’re crazy, man. The truth is just an inconvenience. Mom’s better off believing that God just took Kristin early because she was too perfect to stay here on the earth.”

Some parents may have believed that, but Jennifer was not the type. She hadn’t believed in God or fate back when she and Zachary had been going to school, and he hadn’t seen any sign that she had changed her mind since then. She only wanted the truth, however painful it might be.

CHAPTER 31

Zachary had looked up the address of the doctor who had written Kristin's prescription for Rx. With Ares on hand, it might have been a few weeks since she had picked up a real prescription, but she had gone to the effort to get it legitimately. She had seen a doctor, even though her mother didn't approve. As Ares had pointed out, Kristin was the kind of person that LipoSlayerRx had been made for. Someone who was struggling with obesity, had tried everything else, and needed a little bit of help. She was exactly the type of person the drug had been designed for. Jennifer might not have approved, but she couldn't deny that Kristin was severely overweight and needed more than a walk or another diet to achieve her goals.

The clinic was bright and clean, everyone professional and helpful. Zachary felt a little awkward sitting in the waiting room of a bariatric clinic considering his slight build, but not everyone there was obese or even noticeably overweight. As

Ares had observed, the beautiful people wanted in on Rx too. They wanted to be even more beautiful.

Eventually, Zachary was shown to the doctor's office. Westley Race looked very much like Zachary had expected him to. His dark hair, neatly trimmed and moussed, was beginning to show hints of gray at his temples. His face had a few small wrinkles around his eyes but, otherwise, he looked young and vibrant. He observed Zachary with an amused glint in his intelligent eyes, giving Zachary a sense of unease.

"Well." He folded his hands on top of his desk. "I take it you are not coming to me because you want to lose weight."

Zachary smiled. "No. You would be right about that. I have more trouble in the other direction. Putting it on."

"I'm afraid I'm not much help for you there. Eat more calories. Splurge a little. Eat out more."

"I'm actually here to ask about a former patient of yours." Zachary emphasized the word "former." "Kristin Jones."

"You must know that I am not able to talk about my patients. There are privacy laws. Very strict ones."

"Well, you don't need to worry about Kristin's privacy. She's passed away. And I was hired by her mother, her only next of kin. So you have permission to tell me everything you know."

"It doesn't actually work that way."

"I could get a court order, but that seems like a lot of unnecessary bother."

"Without one, my hands are bound."

"I see." Zachary nodded. "Well, maybe you could answer some questions for a patient who might come see you. A friend of mine who is interested in losing some weight."

"I'm always happy to talk to new clients." He smiled. "What does your friend want to know?"

"When I looked you up online, it looks like you're a big promoter of LipoSlayerRx."

"Rx is revolutionary. There hasn't been anything like it on the market before. And it's effective. It helps people who have been struggling with their weight for years. Who have done everything, including bariatric surgery. They get on Rx, and the pounds just melt away. Why would I not be behind a miracle cure like that?"

"There have been miracles in the past... that have later been shown to be dangerous. That end up causing damage to the heart or the liver, or suicidal thoughts, or severe birth defects. You know that a 'miracle' is pretty rare. That there are almost always drawbacks."

"I know Rx. I have been dealing with it for months. Your friend would have nothing to be concerned about."

"What would you say to someone who was experiencing side effects?"

"The side effects are generally mild. Gastrointestinal discomfort. Headaches. Really... people go through much worse with dieting."

"What about mental problems? Concentration, mood, memory?"

"It's possible. But most people don't have any problems with it. And if you do find the side effects to be too troubling, then you stop taking it. No permanent harm done."

"Except for Kristin Jones, who is dead."

Dr. Race glared at him. "You're blaming Rx for her death? That's ridiculous. Where is your evidence?"

"I'm still gathering it. But she was taking Rx before she died."

"So was the woman who was walking across the street and got hit by a bus," Race said flippantly. "One has nothing to do with the other."

Zachary leaned back in his chair. "What about minors?" he asked. "Would you recommend it for younger patients?"

"Absolutely." Dr. Race nodded emphatically. "There's nothing that says it is contraindicated in children. And in our society today, just look around you at how many overweight and obese schoolchildren there are. Do we really want to wait until they're adults before we start treating them? This epidemic has hit children just as hard as adults, and the results are devastating. Think about how they are treated in school, their self-esteem, the wear and tear that the extra weight puts on their joints and heart. They're practically crippled by the time they are adults. Do you know how many young patients I've had to recommend to specialists for joint replacement?"

Zachary hadn't even thought of that aspect of it. While he'd had to deal with the same bullying and ostracism that overweight children had, he had never had to worry about the physical side effects. Other than potential physical abuse. As an adult, he wasn't in great shape physically, but he could get around without much pain. He was sometimes bothered by old injuries, his broken bones and scars, and he often felt awkward about his gait since he had suffered a spinal injury, but as long as he wasn't trying to rush or go up or down stairs, he was usually just fine. He had been assured that no one watching him could tell the difference.

"But is it safe for children? You must have some cut-off that you would recommend."

"It's absolutely safe for children. And if you had ever dealt with a one hundred pound three-year-old, you would know there is no cut-off. If a child is obese, even as a toddler, you need to deal with it. Before it becomes a bigger issue." He chuckled. "Literally."

Zachary thought that was in poor taste, but he brushed it off. "So you wouldn't have any problem prescribing it to a teenager."

"No. Not at all. I would do it without a second thought."

"What if they had a parent who was against it? What if a child came to you without their parent and wanted you to prescribe it to them without parental approval?"

Dr. Race sat back, putting his fingertips together as he considered his answer. Zachary didn't think that he had any trouble with the answer, just with phrasing it. Race raised his brows. "I wouldn't ask what their parents thought about it. I don't need parental approval to write a prescription. If an overweight or obese teen came to me for a prescription, I would have no problem writing it. Don't underestimate the damage that the obesity epidemic is doing to our society. It will self-destruct if we do not get it under control. Our society will collapse under its own weight, so to speak. Rx is the first real hope we have of overcoming it. There will be other drugs developed, whether they use the same mechanism or others, but Rx is the first drug I can see actually having any effect on obesity in our society. Including our children. Without it, we are doomed."

"You don't think that's an exaggeration?"

"No. Do you? How far do you think you can walk out that door," Race pointed to the door of his office, "before you run into someone who is suffering from being overweight? Who is putting a strain of the resources of our society? Think of the medical bills for preventable diseases. Lifestyle diseases can be overcome. But not just by willpower. We need to acknowledge that. Science has replaced the foods that our great-grandparents ate with something completely different. It would be unrecognizable to them. And science is the only thing that can save us. No amount of diets and infomercials will make any difference."

Zachary looked at the door. “I wouldn’t get any farther than the waiting room,” he pointed out, “considering this is a bariatric clinic.”

“Smart guy,” Race said with disgust, shaking his head. “You really need to think this through. We are not living in the same world as it was when you were a kid. How many obese kids would there have been in your school classes?”

“I don’t know.” Zachary thought back to the wide array of school classes he had attended. “Maybe one. Not even one per class, but one per grade, depending on how large the school was.”

“It’s one in five now,” Race said succinctly. “That means in a class of thirty, six of them are obese. And one in three are overweight. Ten kids in that class are overweight or obese. And when you or I went to school? Being overweight was unusual. The gross obesity that you see now was unheard of. You just didn’t see it.”

Zachary nodded slowly. He knew things had changed, but it had been a gradual process and he hadn't been completely aware of it. He especially hadn't thought about how it affected children.

"And all of the studies say that Rx is safe?" he asked Race. "There are no concerns? No demographics that are considered to be high risk?"

"I've read all of the studies. That's my job. I'm sure you know that it has become a very popular weight loss aid, not just in the obese, but for those who are only looking to drop a few pounds, to have a more svelte figure. I would not tell anyone that it was unsafe for them to take Rx. I have no qualms. And anyone who keeps their obese child from taking it? That should be considered neglect or abuse."

CHAPTER 32

It was Friday night. Date night. Zachary had suggested that they go out for dinner. There were Friday nights when date night did not work out, because he was surveilling other people who were out on date night. A remarkable number of spouses "worked late" Fridays, or had to go on an overnight trip, or had something planned "with the boys." And Zachary followed them, reporting back to their spouses on what they were really doing.

But this time, he didn't have any adultery cases to look into. They were not his favorite and he tried not to take too many on. On top of the fact that he didn't like to be the one providing the proof that would break couples up, he was afraid that it would make him cynical and suspicious of his own relationships, never able to take his own partner at her word.

He hadn't exactly been jealous with Bridget. He'd been amazed that she was with him at all, to begin with. Waiting for the other shoe to drop. Thinking that there must be another side to the story. Some kind of punchline to a joke that would break his heart. But he had followed her, tracked her vehicle, and kept a log of her schedule. He had made notes of the things that she said that turned out not to be true, whether they were lies that she told him or someone else. He had told himself that he was just looking out for her. He'd been trying to protect himself. He didn't want to be the spouse who didn't know that his wife was seeing someone else until it was over.

Had Bridget been seeing Gordon before she had kicked Zachary out? He didn't think so. He'd been watching her pretty carefully. There hadn't been a lot of opportunities for her to carry on an affair. And Gordon was a busy person. He couldn't just take off in the middle of the day for a rendezvous with his girlfriend whenever he wanted to. He had a business to run. But Zachary still doubted himself. He wondered whether she had played him for a fool after all.

"Hey, come back here," Kenzie prompted, touching Zachary's hand.

"What?" He looked at her and glanced around to reorient himself to their surroundings. The buffet restaurant. One of their favorite date locations. He loved the many options, the warm, nourishing smells, and the happy chatter that filled the dining area. "Oh, sorry. I was just thinking..."

"About your case?"

"Mmm." Zachary gave a slight nod. "Do you think it is negligence to not give someone a medication they need?"

"Well..." Kenzie stabbed a fork at her salad. "Yes, I do. Depending on what it is and why they need it, it could cause sickness, distress, or death. Negligence isn't just withholding food. Withholding needed medication would be as well."

Zachary thought about Kristin. How desperate she must have been to get her hands on a medication that would work. With so much in her life out of her control, with how she was undoubtedly treated by not just the other kids, but the teachers and people who didn't even know who she was. It wasn't like it was a matter of life and death, like if she had type 1 diabetes and Jennifer withheld insulin. But was it wrong for Jennifer to decide that Kristin couldn't have a medication that might turn her life around, make her healthier, and help her feel better about herself?

"You look like you don't like my answer," Kenzie said, smiling.

"No, it's just... where is the line? How do you decide if a medication is necessary or not? Obviously, if withholding it will kill them, then that would be negligence. But what it if is not a condition that will kill them? What if it's just...?"

"Like a mental illness, for example?" Kenzie suggested. "What about when you were in foster care and they would force you to go on a med holiday? Was that negligence?"

He nodded slowly. "They said that they needed to take me off of everything to get a baseline and figure out what I really needed. Because they thought I was on too many meds. So they thought it was medically necessary."

"And was it?"

Zachary shook his head. "It was terrible. I couldn't sleep. Couldn't focus on anything at school unless I was in the resource room, away from everybody else. I was so jumpy and hypervigilant; I couldn't relax for a minute."

"And did they eventually put you back on everything they had withdrawn?"

"Pretty much, yeah. They tweaked some of them a little bit, but there weren't any significant changes. I needed them."

"What I find hard to believe is that they took you off of your antidepressants after you attempted suicide. That seems like... I can't imagine what they were thinking."

"Some antidepressants cause suicidal thoughts, especially in teens." Zachary shrugged. "I guess they had to take me off of them to find out whether I was suicidal because I was depressed or because of the antidepressants."

"Terrible idea. They could have switched out for a different class of antidepressants instead of just removing everything."

"Yeah. That probably would have been better. But everybody thought that they had the answers. That they could fix me by trying something different."

"So, does that answer your question about withholding meds?"

Zachary grimaced. "Not really. What about something like Rx? Refusing to give your child a weight loss drug?"

"Hmm." Kenzie didn't answer for a few minutes, working her way through a large green salad. Zachary stared down at it. Usually when they went to the buffet, Kenzie had a few small portions of the entrees and side dishes, not just the salad.

"That one is a lot tougher," Kenzie admitted. "A prescription like Rx could make a world of difference for a girl like Kristin. Her physical health, as well as social position and mental health. Obesity can lead to heart disease, diabetes, cancer, and other lifestyle diseases, as well as contributing to depression."

Zachary nodded his agreement. He scooped up a forkful of chocolate pudding, savoring the act of having dessert in the middle of his main course as much as the pudding itself.

"But on the other hand..." Kenzie put her fork down on her plate. "This is a new drug. There haven't been any long-term studies because it hasn't been around long enough. Are people going to be able to go off of Rx when they reach their goal weight? Or will they have to stay on it forever to maintain a healthy weight? And if they do... what are the effects of being on it for ten, twenty, or thirty years? Does it eventually stop working? Cause organ failure? Infertility? And it is so hyped, being advertised so aggressively and discussed on social media, people taking challenges to see how much weight they can drop quickly. That's risky behavior."

"Jennifer said that it was snake oil."

"And if that's her opinion, then she's not really negligent if she won't let her daughter take it. In her mind, she's protecting her."

"And she didn't know Kristin would just go ahead and take it on the sly anyway."

"Which is more dangerous," Kenzie agreed. "Because if she's hiding it from her mother, then she is not getting the necessary monitoring and support. Mom doesn't know if Kristin's health is suffering. Or whether her focus or mental health are compromised by the side effects." Kenzie sipped her drink, staring down at her meal. "I don't think I could call it negligence. Not when it is such a new, overhyped drug."

"Insulin must have been a big deal when it was first discovered."

"Yes, it certainly was. But the benefits were dramatically visible. There was no doubt that it was saving children from death. Reviving them from comas. You can't get much more obvious. Rx shows dramatic results, but not that dramatic."

Zachary went back to a thick, pink slice of roast beef. "Talk to me about the autopsy results."

"I think we've already covered everything. Kristin was obese. She had heart disease and a number of medical issues related to her weight. She had injection marks on her belly from injecting Rx. Her blood glucose levels were good. She had lost weight recently."

"Could Rx have caused some kind of reaction to the anesthetic she was given, resulting in her death?"

"Unknown. As I said, there isn't enough history. We have no idea how Rx might interact with other drugs."

"Could her glucose have been too low?"

"It wasn't."

"Several people said she was pale and didn't look good. She'd been having headaches and digestive problems."

"Rx is known for giving people a white or gray pallor. That's common knowledge on social media. The headaches and digestive issues too, and they are not something that necessarily indicates serious issues. The medical examiner in Burlington didn't find any evidence of any pathology in her brain. Some precancerous polyps in her gut, but that's not likely related."

"Those weren't caused by Rx?"

"I doubt it. Being overweight and inactive are risk factors. They can also be familial. Inherited."

"The doctor who prescribed the LipoSlayerRx said that there are no contraindications. That all of the studies show that it is safe."

Kenzie shrugged. "It would depend on what kind of studies they've done. I haven't had a chance to look at them yet. If they kept them small, they might not have a good representative sample. And frequently, they only test on adult males, not women or children. I'll look at the tests, but I'm not sure how extensive they have been or if they followed proper scientific principles."

"The FDA would require them to, wouldn't they? You can't go to market with a drug without a certain level of testing."

Kenzie raised her brows. "From what I understand of the FDA approval process... they are hand in glove with the pharmaceutical industry. There have been a lot of accusations thrown around that since they are funded by the pharma industry, it's actually pharma that decides what goes through. And particularly what is fast-tracked without the level of... safety information that you would expect."

"They are funded by the companies they are supposed to be regulating?"

"Yes." Kenzie pushed her plate away. "Sorry, I need something better than this."

Zachary grinned. "You can eat salad at home. When we go out, you should get something you don't have at home."

She looked at his plate as he went for another bite of chocolate pudding. "Like roast beef with chocolate pudding?"

"Like everything with chocolate pudding."

Kenzie chuckled and went to get herself another plate at the buffet.

CHAPTER 33

When they got home, Zachary was rummaging through his laptop bag to find a thumb drive that Mr. Peterson had given him with some photography on it the last time they had been over for a visit. He came across the autoinjector and pills that he had kept from Ares's merchandise.

"Oh, I forgot." He held them up for Kenzie to see. "I wondered whether you could get these tested."

She looked at the drugs dubiously. "Where did you get these and why do they need to be tested?"

"I got them from Kristin's dealer." At Kenzie's surprised look, he went on. "She went to him when the Rx got to be too expensive. As we know, she had pretty much cleaned out her bank account paying for it, but she still needed a supply, so she went somewhere cheaper."

"And how did this guy get it cheaper? I doubt he was a wholesaler."

"Yeah, I don't think so. I think they're probably stolen goods. But maybe also diluted so that it would go farther."

"So you want to see whether it is the real thing. Or whether it has been tampered with or replaced."

"Yeah."

She shook her head. "I can't do that. I can't just take random evidence to the medical examiner's office, assign it a file number, and have it tested. We need to actually have a case that it's related to."

"Kristin Jones's."

"Her case is with the Burlington medical examiner's office. Not Roxboro."

"Well, yeah, I guess so."

"You'll need to talk to the cops here and get them to open a case and order the tests, or take it to the police in Burlington and have them send it to the lab for testing."

Zachary rolled his eyes. He had been hoping to avoid the police on this case. Kenzie had the facilities to order the tests. But he supposed she had a point. They would have to be associated with a file. Proper procedures and audits being what they were, she couldn't afford to push something through that wasn't properly authorized.

"I guess I'll call someone," he agreed.

"Maybe Campbell," Kenzie suggested. "He could point you in the right direction."

Zachary suspected that mostly Kenzie just didn't want him to go to Detective Garcia, who he had worked with on a recent case. Garcia was too attractive and friendly for Kenzie's tastes. She didn't like another beautiful woman having anything to do with him. He should feel flattered that Kenzie felt so possessive of him. But half the time, he felt resentful that she didn't trust him to work with Garcia without being swept off his feet by her.

"I haven't talked to him for a while," Zachary agreed. "I guess I'll reach out to him."

Campbell had always been good to Zachary. He hadn't given him a hard time like some of the other cops did, and had occasionally given him a nudge in the right direction when he could.

Zachary had also given him good tips or evidence in the past that had allowed him to close some cases.

But it was going to take some explaining.

* * *

Kenzie decided that a bath was in order before bed and, when they separated, Zachary went back to his computer bag rather than going straight for the shower himself. He would have a quick scrub and shave before bed to ensure he was ready for anything else Kenzie had in mind, but that wouldn't take nearly as long as Kenzie's bath and before-bed pampering. She could easily take an hour.

With Kristin's phone open beside him, Zachary set up new profiles on the same social networks she had been using, picking names that had no connection to him and creating a few new faces or avatars to go with them. It only took a few minutes to create each one. Once they were set up, he did a few searches about weight loss and LipoSlayerRx, on each, watching and liking videos and other posts. He stalked a few of the non-celebrities who were talking about taking Rx. He asked them whether they'd had any side effects associated with the prescription, trying to sound like a teenager who was interested in starting on the prescription.

He was startled when the door between Kenzie's bedroom and the en suite bathroom opened, and he realized that he had misjudged or lost track of time. He put both phones away and stood up. It wasn't quite as late as he had thought; Kenzie hadn't taken an hour. But he still should have been well into his bedtime ritual if he wanted to spend some unhurried private time with her before they went to sleep. Kenzie didn't have to be at work early, but she usually put in a couple of hours on a Saturday morning to tie up loose ends and ensure she was ready for the coming week. And Zachary had a list of things he hoped to do on Saturday while she was out.

"I'm just hopping into the shower," he called out to Kenzie. "You'll be up for a few more minutes?"

"A few."

She sounded annoyed. Of course she did. When she'd told him that she was going to have a bath, she had expected him to coordinate his schedule with hers, not to lose track of time. It was their couple's time, and he was supposed to be focused on her, not work.

Zachary started the shower and stripped so quickly that it wasn't even warm by the time he stepped in. He lathered up and rinsed off in a rush, but then forced himself to slow down and take a few minutes to enjoy the warmth of the water and the soothing background of white noise that filled the bathroom. Kenzie wouldn't expect him only to be thirty seconds in the shower. And he wanted to be relaxed when he joined her, not all wound up and anxious because he was in a rush.

So he also shampooed his short-cropped hair and massaged his scalp as he rinsed it out. When he finished the shower and dried off, he spent a few minutes shaving and clipping his nails. Once he was finished, he looked thoroughly presentable instead of like someone who might be homeless.

He joined Kenzie in bed. She was putting some cream on her feet, and rubbed it in briskly once he came in. She leaned over to hug him and inhaled deeply, her breath tickling the soft skin around his ear and throat. “Mmm. I love the smell of your shaving cream.”

He tried not to react to her teasing and pull away, but he couldn’t help himself. His skin was all pleasurable goosebumps. The strawberry scent of her shampoo was delicious, and he pressed his face into her hair.

For the first time since Jennifer had called, Zachary wasn’t thinking about school and Kristin, not even briefly on the edge of his consciousness.

CHAPTER 34

In a perfect world, falling asleep early and peacefully with his arms around Kenzie would mean that Zachary slept through the night without any nightmares or awakenings. But it didn't. He slept well for the first little while, relaxed and unencumbered by any worries about his case or anything else. The investigation could wait. Thinking about Bridget could wait. Worrying about how Jennifer would feel about the results of his investigation could wait. It was night and no one could expect him to be working.

But he awoke with a start, and the first thought that entered his consciousness was that someone else was there. An intruder. He sat up and grabbed his phone, activating the flashlight mode and sweeping the light around the room, looking for a dark figure, a large shadow just waiting to be noticed. But if there was an intruder, he was not in the bedroom.

Kenzie rolled over and asked a question in sleep talk that Zachary could not make out. He knew that he was probably imagining things and shouldn't bother her about his conviction that someone else was in the house. He was wrong. He would search the house, as usual, and would find out, as usual, that there was no one else there.

He slipped silently out of bed and walked around the house, looking for some sign that there was someone else in the house. Or that there was something out of place. Even just an explanation for what had woken him up. The tapping of a branch against the house in the wind, loud motorcycle engines outside, or neighbors having a loud argument. But everything was still. No sign of anyone else in the house or anything outside that might have woken him up.

He looked out the windows but couldn't see any sign of life. It was too late for partiers and too early for runners and dog walkers.

Eventually, Zachary gave up on finding anything that would explain his alarm and sudden wakefulness. He sat down with his computer and the two phones and went to work, checking various forums where people were talking about Rx, shooting video about Rx, or reporting on celebrities rumored to be taking Rx.

* * *

"You been up for long?" Kenzie asked, having her first sip of coffee. She seemed relaxed, like she'd had a great night followed by a sound sleep. Zachary had enjoyed the evening, but was resigned to the fact that he would never get more than a few hours of sleep without a sleep aid, even if he were totally relaxed and at peace.

"A while," he said, not bothering to quantify it. She probably had a pretty good idea of how long he had been up anyway. She hadn't woken up all the way or gotten up in the night to check on him, but they'd been living in the same house for long enough for her to know that even on a good night, he was unlikely to sleep for long. Which was one of the reasons she was always urging him to take his sleeping pills.

“You have your session with Dr. Boyle today. Don’t forget.”

Zachary was confused for a moment. His sessions were on Wednesdays, and it was Saturday. Then his chest tightened as he remembered. He had set up extra sessions with Dr. B because of his continuing problems with Bridget.

“Right. It’s on my schedule,” Zachary agreed, keeping his voice casual and upbeat. No need for her to know that he was anxious about having another session or irritated by the fact that he had to. It wasn’t her fault, after all. He was the one with the problem. She was trying to help him to stay on track.

“I’ll be at the office,” Kenzie said. “May as well be out at the same time so we can be home at the same time.”

“Sure. Good plan.”

Zachary closed the lid of his computer, then closed his eyes for a few seconds to rest them. Too much time staring at the computer screen. But not as bad as sometimes, when they got so gritty and inflamed that he couldn't blink without pain.

"Eye drops," Kenzie advised when she saw him blinking, trying to irrigate them with his own tears. "Don't you think it would make more sense to keep them by your computer than in the bathroom? Then they'd be there right when you need them."

"Yeah," Zachary agreed. "That's a good idea."

He went into the kitchen to help himself to a cup of coffee. "Do you want your toast yet?" Kenzie wasn't dressed for work, but still wore the shorts and t-shirt she'd pulled on before falling asleep.

"Sure, why not? I'll be decadent and eat breakfast in my pajamas. I don't have to be at work early."

He put a piece of bread in the toaster for her and opened the fridge to find a yogurt cup for himself. He caught Kenzie's frown.

"Mixing things up this morning," he told her lightly.

No need to tell her that he couldn't even stand the thought of opening a granola wrapper today. Maybe he'd want one later in the morning. He put butter and marmalade on the table for Kenzie. In a few minutes, they were sitting down to eat.

"I've started to gather information on side effects of Rx people are reporting on social networks," Zachary informed her.

"Already? Who have you been talking to?"

"People on these social platforms are all around the world, so even if it's late at night for most of the patients in the United States, they're awake on the other side of the world."

"They have that much reach? I guess I didn't think about them being in other parts of the world. Everyone talks about the obesity epidemic in America, not the rest of the world, so I didn't think about it being distributed that widely."

"It might not be as popular in other countries, but it seems to be prescribed all over the place. And there are a lot of celebs or ex-pats in other countries too. People with the kind of money you need to make to afford Rx."

"Celebrities." Kenzie sounded depressed at the idea. "Of course everyone has to jump on the bandwagon. And the more celebrities who take it, the more everyone else—kids especially—will want to take it."

"Yeah. And so far, the celebs are all saying it's the best thing since sliced bread. But there are a few people who complain about side effects."

"Anything concerning?"

"Hard to say yet. The headaches and digestive problems that I expected. Some complaints about brain fog, memory, depression. One woman complaining about chest pain. A man who had a stroke. Too early to tell whether they are related or not."

"Well, keep track of what you find. People will probably report unrelated symptoms. Just like the placebo effect, you have the nocebo effect. People having negative symptoms because they expect to."

Zachary didn't know that was a thing. But it made sense. If he took a new med and developed a symptom he hadn't had before, he assumed it was from the medication. Even though it might be something he had eaten or been in contact with, or just a coincidence. That was one of the reasons that they did drug trials. To see which symptoms were common and, therefore, attributable to the drug.

"Okay. I'll wait until something shows up repeatedly before assuming that it's actually related."

Kenzie nodded. “I really hope that Rx is not causing any serious problems. We need an effective weight loss solution in today’s society.”

Her hand strayed to her waistband, but it appeared to be an unconscious gesture. Zachary did not jump in and tell her she didn’t need to worry about her weight. He couldn’t claim to know women’s minds well, but he was pretty sure that telling a woman unbidden that she didn’t need to lose weight was tantamount to telling her that she did. Noticing her weight would be enough to upset her. Even if he weren’t noticing her weight, but just her own concern with her weight.

“How is your day going to go today?” he asked, changing the subject. “Not too much you have to get done at the office, I hope?”

“No, things have been pretty quiet. Just tidying up a little. Making sure all of my ducks are in a row. Just a couple of hours.”

CHAPTER 35

It was an effort to go to Dr. Boyle's office on a Saturday. Zachary was used to going every Wednesday during his regular time slot and, other than the days that he lost track of time, his brain was ready for it. But going on a different day for an additional session was much harder. He wanted to have the day to work on his investigations, spend time with Kenzie, and do whatever else he wanted.

Not only that, but Dr. B hadn't been able to fit him into an afternoon slot, so he had to go in the morning. And he was really not ready to do therapy in the morning. It felt like a punishment. Like having to go to school on a Saturday to paint the fences or pick up garbage. And maybe it was his punishment for giving in to his compulsions and writing to Bridget. It was fitting that he should have to do some kind of retribution.

“How are you today?” Dr. B asked pleasantly. “Are you enjoying your weekend?”

Zachary looked around him at the office. “Well... no. Not yet. This isn’t exactly where I wanted to be. No offense.”

She laughed. “None taken.”

Did she resent having to be there on a Saturday to deal with him and whoever else she’d had to schedule for the weekend? She must want the time off too. She had a picture of a little girl on her desk that Zachary assumed was her daughter. She must want to be home to play with her daughter when it wasn’t a school day.

“Sorry about this,” he apologized. “I didn’t think about how much of your time this takes.”

“Don’t worry about it. We’ll get you through this, and you can go back to the regular schedule. But for now, let’s focus on getting back the ground you’ve lost.”

"I haven't been back there since I saw you last." He swallowed and licked his dry lips. "I've been busy with an investigation and have stayed focused on that. At least for a few days."

"And I hope you can maintain that focus so that the compulsions will fade. It's perfectly understandable that you've regressed on this. What happened to Bridget's twins was awful. But she is okay, and so are they, and you don't have to be the one to protect them. They have a protector in their lives. And the police and whatever other community and law enforcement resources they need. They will be safe."

"I hope so," Zachary agreed. Life was easier when he hadn't been over there. He could act like he was stronger than he was. How long would he be able to hold out this time? A few more days? Weeks? Months? Until when? Until he heard that one of the little girls had fallen and scraped her knee? And then he would be back at their sides, making sure nothing else could harm them?

“How have you done on the other goals that you made?” Dr. B asked, looking down at the file on the desk in front of her. “Did you get to your OCDA group?”

“Oh… no, not yet.”

“It was Thursday night, I believe.”

“Yeah, I think it was… I forgot about it. I’ve been very busy with this case.”

“Busy-ness is good when it keeps you from falling back on your compulsions. But it won’t last. You need to be working with your community, developing relationships with people who understand and can give you support and suggestions in your journey. You can’t do this by yourself.”

“Well… I have you and Kenzie.”

“That’s not a wide enough network. You need more.”

"Okay. Yeah. I promised I would go, and I will. Getting used to a new schedule will take me a while."

"Have you put it on your phone calendar?"

"No." Zachary pulled his phone out of his pocket and entered the OCDA meeting into his phone as a repeating appointment while she watched. "There. Now it is."

"Good. You've been taking the higher doses of meds that we ordered? Got all of your prescriptions updated?"

"Yes."

"How is that working?"

"Okay. I'm not sure how much of a difference there is, but it's only been a few days. It will take time."

"Any increase in side effects? New symptoms?"

"Yes... an increase. But nothing new."

“Anything that I need to know about?” Dr. B met his eyes and waited.

“No. I can manage it.”

“Good. And you have been taking your sleep aid and other meds every day?”

Zachary shifted uncomfortably. He had forgotten that he had promised to take the sleep aid every night. That he had promised to take everything every day. Usually, he only took the ADHD meds if he had a lot of reading to do or needed to be able to focus on something boring for some other reason. And he only took the anxiety meds if he was extra stressed and needed them. Kenzie didn’t like him picking and choosing which he needed daily, but Dr. B and the rest of his medical team said that he was the best judge of what he needed. Kenzie didn’t have to take a whole raft of meds every day. She didn’t know what it was like.

“Zachary?” Dr. B prompted.

"No. I haven't been taking them every day."

"I thought that was part of your agreement with Kenzie. What you had resolved to do to work on the situation with Bridget."

"Yes... it was. But I forgot about that. I just went back to normal. With the increased meds, I mean, but just taking the sleep aid if I need it."

"And you haven't needed it?"

"No."

"You've gotten a full eight hours of sleep every night?"

Zachary nearly laughed at that. Even taking the sleep aid, he couldn't manage eight hours. Sometimes seven, but that always made him feel groggy and depressed. More likely, the sleep aid would give him five or six hours. Unless he was so overwhelmed by stress and flashbacks that he couldn't do anything but crawl into bed and sleep the day away. And he didn't want to go back into that dark hole.

“Not eight hours. But... enough.”

“You’re looking pretty good, but you still have shadows under your eyes, which tells me that your ‘good enough’ is probably not good enough for your body’s needs.”

“I try. I do the best I can.”

“I know that. But you made promises to Kenzie.” She looked at her file notes. “Your next couple’s session is Wednesday. I think then we’d better talk about what is reasonable and what you can follow through on. Unless you want to renegotiate it with her before that.”

“Uh... no.”

Not if he could help it.

One thing he could say for couple’s therapy was that Dr. Boyle was a good mediator and had helped guide them through several sticky situations that would probably have ended up in a blow-up and hurt feelings if they had tried to discuss them at home.

“Okay. That will be our focus on Wednesday, then. Are you going to take sleep aids every night until then? All of your pills?”

He knew the answer she was waiting for was yes, but he wasn’t sure he could give it. He could try to take the sleep aids until then, but he didn’t want to waste so much time sleeping, especially when he was on an active investigation.

“I’ll... try to take one tonight.”

“Okay, tonight. I would like to hear from you Monday morning. Let me know how you are doing with that. Just a phone call. You can leave me a message if I’m in a session.”

Zachary nodded. “Sure.”

“Are you going to remember that?”

Zachary dutifully added it to his calendar.

"Good. We want to stay on top of this, Zachary. I know that you don't want to be controlled by your impulses any more than any of us want you to be in trouble or distress. Use your support network. And that includes going to meetings."

"I won't forget the next one. It's on my calendar."

CHAPTER 36

One of the problems with going to see Dr. B, especially for an extra session that made him feel like a failure in life and disrupted his usual daily and weekly flow, was that he spent so much time thinking and talking about strategies to resist the compulsion to see Bridget that he was focused on Bridget when he left. And that was not a good situation. He was emotionally exhausted early in the day. He had been thinking about Bridget, about the possibility of driving by her house, leaving her a note, or crossing paths with her somewhere else in town. No one could blame him for an accidental encounter.

So the urge to see her was high.

He sat in the car and pulled out his phone. He brought up the built-in friend tracking app and touched the screen, zeroing in on one of the triangles. Not Bridget, but Kenzie. They had both agreed that using the tracking app was okay. Zachary could reassure himself that Kenzie was safe and, if she were out running errands, estimate how long it would be until she was home. She could see where he was so that if he were on an investigation and got into trouble, someone would know where to find him. And if she got home and he wasn't there, she could check whether he was on surveillance, running an errand, or sitting in front of Bridget's house. It was a way for him to be accountable to her.

Of course, if he planned ahead, he temporarily turned off his location tracking so she couldn't see where he was. But usually, he didn't do that. He wanted her to know where he was so that she wouldn't be anxious and so that they both knew how serious his compulsions were. Sometimes he hoped that she would see him at Bridget's house so that she would get angry and tell him to stop, which would help him stay away. Or else she might force him to increase his meds and see Dr. B more often, which was a relief even though he didn't want to do it. The "good" half of his brain knew that he needed to do these things, even though the other half just wanted to keep feeding his addiction.

Kenzie's location triangle was over the police department building. So she was in the basement at the morgue, where he expected her to be. He liked that Kenzie was reliable, and that when she told him she would be somewhere, she was. Early in their relationship, when he had tracked her car without her permission, she had been pretty steamed. And he knew that was stalker behavior rather than normal behavior. He liked it that they could trust each other now and she didn't mind his checking on her location via the friends app. A phone app where they both shared their own locations was normal. Socially acceptable. Not like putting a tracking device under the car of a girl he had only been out with once.

He could not track Bridget through the friends app, because she had never shared her location with him. And he knew she never would. He had also tracked Bridget without her permission and, when she had found tracking devices on or inside her car, she had been more than a little bit upset.

But he remembered Gordon's words when Bridget had disappeared and they were worried that she had been kidnapped. He had said that he wished Zachary had put a tracking device on Bridget or her car so they could find her. If Zachary had been tracking her—maybe her phone or a bug in her purse—it would not have taken him so long to find her. It had been a close thing. Another day, and she probably would have been dead.

Gordon's words had reassured him that it was a good thing to track Bridget, even if she didn't agree to it.

* * *

His next errand was to see Sergeant Joshua Campbell to drop off the drugs he had removed from Ares for safekeeping and, hopefully, lab testing. He wasn't sure whether Campbell would be in his office on a Saturday morning. More likely, he was out fishing or doing yard work or golf. He pictured Campbell doing something physical and outdoorsy in his time off. Maybe because he'd only ever seen him stuck behind a desk or on a crime scene. He wanted Campbell to have an escape from that life.

The desk sergeant confirmed that Campbell was in and, after talking to him on the phone, escorted Zachary to his office, though Zachary knew the way.

It looked about the same. A slightly messy desk. Pictures of family members he had never told Zachary about. A squeaky desk chair and a couple of guest chairs where Zachary could sit down to discuss this new case.

“Zachary,” Campbell greeted, standing up to shake his hand. “You’re the last person I was expecting to see.”

He held Zachary’s hand for a second too long, and Zachary tried to process the words to figure out what he was talking about. Zachary pulled back slowly and sat, holding the laptop bag in his lap.

“Uh... good to see you too.”

Campbell settled back into his chair, which let out a loud squeal of protest. “I was just talking about you.”

“Oh. With who...?”

“With Gordon Drake.”

Zachary tried to swallow the lump that immediately swelled up in his throat. His cheeks burned. “Oh.”

“He’s inquiring about how to get an order of protection against you. Discreetly. Or if there is anything else he can do to keep you away from Bridget.”

“I...” Zachary looked down at his hands and couldn’t think of what to say. He could protest loudly that Gordon just had it out for Zachary and that he hadn’t been over there to see Bridget. He could say that they had run into each other in town, as two people who knew each other and lived in a small community could expect to. But Gordon probably had the proof. There wasn’t any point.

"I don't understand you, Zachary." Campbell stared at him. "You have a wonderful girlfriend. She's a great partner for you and puts up with your... idiosyncrasies. You're better matched with her than you ever were with Bridget. So why are you doing this? Just focus on Kenzie and forget all about Bridget."

"It's not that easy."

"It is. Would you rather end up behind bars?"

"No. But... after what we had together... and the trials she's had the last few years... I need to see her and know that she's okay. And to protect her from... anything that could happen."

"You need to get your head on straight. Because they are this close," Campbell held up his fingers, pinched so close together that they were almost touching, "to filing an order against you."

Bridget had threatened it before, but she had never done it. Zachary had come to think that she never would. That it was just words. Something that Bridget said to make herself feel better, more in control. But if Gordon was pursuing it, Zachary was in a lot more trouble than he had realized.

"I'll stop," he promised, gulping again. "I've increased my meds. My therapy sessions. I'm going to an OCD Anonymous group." That was a stretch, considering how long it had been since he had gone to one of the meetings. "It's just my brain. I was doing well, but when the twins were kidnapped… it triggered everything again. I can't shake the anxiety. The worry that something terrible is going to happen to her."

"You need to know what a risky position you are in. Your PI license could be pulled. You could end up in jail. What is going to happen to your livelihood if one or both of those things happens?"

Zachary nodded. "I know."

Campbell sighed and leaned back in his chair, ignoring the squeaks and squeals that made it sound like it would fall apart at any moment.

"So, that's not what you came here to talk to me about. Why are you here?"

CHAPTER 37

To turn in some evidence in a case that I'm investigating. And maybe... it would be a good idea to run some lab tests..."

"What have you got?"

Zachary dug into the laptop bag and pulled out the injectors and small packets of pills. Campbell leaned forward again to study them.

"You dealing drugs now?"

"Not mine. A school kid, selling them to other kids."

"He must have pretty good connections."

Zachary looked at the pile, assessing it. Thinking about how much merchandise Ares had been carrying in his backpack.

"Yeah. It was a pretty good haul. This is just... a small sample."

"Everybody wants to grow up to be a drug dealer these days." Campbell pushed around the bags, separating them to look at the pills. Like Zachary, he knew many of them on sight. "It looks like school stuff. No crack or heroin. Surprisingly, not even a bud of weed. This stuff all looks like it came straight out of a pharmacy."

"He suggested that it might have fallen off the back of a truck. Maybe expired lots. It doesn't look like anything that he cooked up at home. But what I wondered was whether the LipoSlayerRx has been diluted. Or adulterated."

Campbell picked up the autoinjector and examined it, as Zachary had, for any signs that it had been tampered with since it came from the factory. "Why this in particular?"

"That's what my client's daughter was on when she died."

"A death case. I haven't heard anything about bad lots of Rx. Seems like everyone is taking it these days, and I haven't heard anything about any problems."

"You're familiar with it?"

"With how popular it has become? Yes. There is a lot of counterfeiting going on because it is so expensive. The company has asked us to keep an eye out for illegitimate sources. If this is counterfeit... it's a good one."

"If my client's daughter got ahold of one that wasn't actually Rx, but was something else, or was contaminated with something else, then that might have contributed to her death. If it was pure Rx..." Zachary nodded toward the injector, "If this source is selling a legitimate product, then it's possible that Rx contributed to her death."

"Well, every drug has its risks," Campbell admitted. "But as I said, I haven't heard of any deaths attributed to it. We don't have a lot of parents coming in here worried that their kids are hooked on the stuff. They want to know if the stuff they are getting at discount rates is Rx. Different problem altogether."

"You're seeing a lot of counterfeits?"

"Yes, but you can usually tell. It has a different brand name. Misspellings or uneven coloring on the sticker. Or whoever has been taking it is talking about the rush they get from it. Real Rx shouldn't give you a rush. That's more likely to be amphetamines. It will still help you to lose weight, but..."

Zachary shook his head. "But you don't want to be on that stuff."

"No. If you're having a lot of side effects—did your girl have a lot of side effects?"

"Some. We're still trying to sort it out. She was keeping a log, and we've been talking to people she went to school with. Her teachers and mom, though they are less helpful."

"Teens don't usually confide in their parents."

"No. I wish Kristin had, in this case. Then Jennifer wouldn't feel so guilty now, wondering if it was because Kristin was taking this stuff that she died. If Jennifer had known and had told the doctors, would anything have happened differently?"

"Did she overdose? What happened?"

"She had surgery. Wisdom teeth. Died on the table."

Zachary didn't know whether there was an actual operating table in a dental surgery. Maybe just a reclined dental chair. He'd never seen one done.

"So it might not have been anything to do with Rx," Campbell pointed out. He didn't look as concerned as he had. A teenager dying during surgery was tragic, but probably not anything he had to be worried about.

"It might not have had anything to do with it," Zachary agreed. "But it is a risk factor that the mother did not know about, and the doctors did not know about, and maybe it was. Kenzie says that since it's a pretty new drug, we might not know all of the contraindications yet. Whether it is safe to use with general anesthetic. What the long-term consequences are. And, of course," Zachary indicated the injector. "Whether what she was taking the last few weeks was Rx."

"Well, I don't envy you trying to unwind all that. I'm not sure that it can be done."

"Will you have the injector tested? Make sure it isn't laced with Fentanyl or something?"

Campbell nodded. "You have the name of the kid you took it off of?"

"He goes by Ares. No idea if that's his real name or a street name. Hangs out on a corner near a school in Burlington."

"Burlington," Campbell stopped with his pen poised above his paper. "This isn't even from Roxboro?"

"No. Kristin's death was in Burlington. That's where the autopsy was done. She went to school there. Bought her replacement Rx there."

“Why don’t you take this crap to them?”

“I don’t know the police in Burlington as well as here. And none of them are you.”

Campbell laughed. “No. Lucky them.”

“I hoped you could still test it, even though it came from Burlington.”

“I can. But I’ll have to interface with their drug department and see what they know. If this Ares character is known to them. What their counterfeit Rx trade is like. I can’t just pass it off to one of my detectives.”

“Sorry about that.”

Campbell shook his head slowly. “You’re causing me all kinds of trouble today.”

“Uh... yeah. Sorry about that too.”

"You stay away from Bridget. Apologize to Gordon. Tell him you understand and you'll stay away. Maybe he won't file against you."

"I'm... not actually supposed to talk to him."

"He doesn't have a protective order against you yet."

"No. I'm just not supposed to. Kenzie has kind of... taken up a mediation position between us. Doesn't want us to have anything to do with each other."

"She's a smart cookie. Though I don't know that I'd want to be trying to keep you in compliance. You have a real problem."

"I know. I'm working on it."

"I hope it doesn't take a stay in the county jail to convince you to stay away."

"No."

Campbell nodded briskly. “All right, then. Get out of my office. I’ve got real work to do. And you should be out there enjoying the weather on a nice summer day. It’s Saturday. You shouldn’t be working.”

“You are.”

“Yeah, well, you know how it goes. People expect the police to enforce the law every day of the week.”

Zachary nodded. He headed for the door.

“Oh, and one more thing,” Campbell called after him.

Zachary stopped and turned.

“Be careful. These big pharma companies… they have a long reach. You want to be careful who you cross.”

CHAPTER 38

Zachary's phone rang. He looked at it and swiped to answer Kenzie's call. "Hey! How are you doing? I was just—"

"My phone says you're here. Are you coming down to see me?"

"I was actually in to talk to Campbell. Do you want me to come to see you?" He was always mindful of giving her space when she was at work. He didn't want to just show up and expect to be able to visit with her or take her out for lunch. She was a busy person and had a lot of responsibility. He didn't want to get on Dr. Wiltshire's wrong side by distracting Kenzie from her work or monopolizing her time. But it was a Saturday, and Dr. Wiltshire shouldn't even be there. And since it was a Saturday, Zachary didn't have to worry about Kenzie working certain hours. She wasn't supposed to be there either, so she could take as much or as little time as she liked.

"Yeah, why don't you come down?" Kenzie agreed. "I came across some interesting stuff."

Zachary was always interested in anything unusual Kenzie encountered in the medical examiner's office. He had never considered becoming a doctor, but he had always been interested in medical stuff. Maybe because he had seen so many doctors during his formative teen years.

"I'll be right there," Zachary agreed.

He was carded by a guard at the elevator. They knew him, but always insisted on checking his ID anyway. Zachary wasn't upset about it. He was glad there was some security to ensure that Kenzie wasn't harassed or at risk, especially when she was alone during the off hours.

He took the elevator to the basement and walked down the long corridor to get to Kenzie's desk at the entrance to the medical examiner's office.

"Hi, Kenz." Zachary glanced around before he leaned across the desk to give her a quick kiss. "Here by yourself?"

"Yes. Nice and quiet, so I can actually get something done."

"And you found something interesting?" He leaned his elbows on the high counter of her desk, getting comfortable.

"I was pulling studies that have been done on Rx. To see what we really know about it and when it is safe to use."

Zachary nodded. "Great."

"I've only glanced at those so far. They look pretty benign. Nothing that jumped out at me. Except for one thing..."

Zachary waited.

"They do real-time patient monitoring."

"Real-time?"

"As in, they get telemetry every few minutes. Heart rhythm, blood pressure, respiration, all of that."

“How do they do that? Do they have some kind of implant? I didn’t see anything about that in the medical examiner’s report.”

“No, no implant. With all of the technological advances these days, we don’t need an implant. Just a wristwatch.”

“Really? One of those smartwatches? Like the fitness ones?”

Kenzie nodded. “Exactly. Many mainstream watches can monitor your heart and warn you if it speeds up or slows down too much or if you have an irregular rhythm.”

“I’ve heard that. There was an article in the paper. ‘Lives saved because of this simple consumer technology.’ And they were talking about modern pacemakers too. How they can be programmed and tracked and send out reports over the air.”

“Yeah. It’s pretty amazing what they can do now.”

“So we need to find Kristin’s watch. Find out what the data was in the hours before she died.”

"Her prescribing doctor should have access to it too."

Zachary really didn't want to talk to Dr. Race again if he could help it. If the doctor knew he had all of that information, then he should have offered that information to Zachary when he'd been there asking questions.

"Right. I can check with him too. But first, I'll see if Jennifer has the watch."

Kenzie nodded. She looked pleased with having provided Zachary with this information. And she was right; it could be critical to establishing what had happened to Kristin.

"That's really helpful, Kenzie. Are you going to be here much longer?"

"No. Not a lot. But long enough, you don't want to be hanging out here waiting for me. You can get done whatever else you need to, and I'll be home within..." She looked at the time on her computer, considering what she still needed to do. "About an hour."

"Great, I'll see you then."

Kenzie nodded. She held his gaze for an instant, and Zachary was uncomfortable, feeling something unsaid between them. Something that he needed to know. But that she had changed her mind about and decided not to say.

"What...?"

"Nothing, just..." She trailed off and looked uncertain. "Just... wondering how things went with Dr. B this morning."

"Good. Good. I went. Had my session. You don't need to worry about that. You can call her if you want to, verify that I was there."

"No. I don't need to. It's just that..."

Zachary saw the truth before she could finish the thought.

She knew that he had been to Bridget's. She had either seen it on her tracking app, or Gordon had called her too. He cleared his throat and looked away.

"You were there again," Kenzie said quietly.

"I'm sorry."

"Right after your session, you went straight over there. How could you do that?"

"Because... we had just spent an hour discussing her. I didn't want to..."

"But you did. You did want to, and that's exactly what you did."

"You know how... how when you have a scab, and it itches, and you want to scratch it or peel it off? And you know you shouldn't, because it will hurt and will probably open it up and make it bleed again...?"

Kenzie nodded.

"It just... itches. I didn't want to do it. I didn't want to go there and upset her or Gordon, or hurt you, or defy Dr. B. I just... I was going crazy with the itching. And it was the wrong thing to do. I have been doing so well this last week, since Gordon called you and I increased my meds and stepped everything up. I just couldn't stay away. I had to..."

"Scratch your itch."

"Yeah."

"Well, you know what the consequences are going to be. Gordon is not going to put up with it forever. They'll file a protective order, and then you'll have to stay away or end up in jail."

Zachary swallowed and nodded. "I'll do better," he promised.

Kenzie just shook her head sadly and went back to her work.

CHAPTER 39

Zachary was in bad shape going home. Depressed? Despondent? He was so angry with himself. With his stupid brain for not working the right way, but making him repeatedly do the things that he knew he shouldn't. For how weak he was in resisting the compulsions. He would never do anything to harm Bridget or the twins, but to keep going back there like some psycho stalker, making Bridget and Gordon worry about what Zachary might do next. Escalate? Go into the house? Try to stop Bridget on the street? Touch or try to take one of the girls? TV always portrayed people with obsessive thoughts or stalker behavior as being bad, truly mad and evil. But that wasn't what Zachary was like.

He was so upset that it took him a while to notice the car tailing him. He was checking his mirrors and watching his surroundings just as he always did. Constantly vigilant about who or what might be going on around him.

But his distraction had nearly made him miss it this time.

A dark car, black or blue, keeping a few cars back from him but making all of the same turns. Just a coincidence? He didn't think so. If it was a coincidence, it would have ended up behind him at some point. Not always back a few cars. And while the driver might have been just going in the same direction or headed to the same neighborhood as Zachary, he thought it was unlikely they would be sticking with him for so long.

He turned right twice in a row, effectively doubling back the way he had come. He watched behind him. No car. He drove for a couple of blocks, breathing slowly and evenly, trying to keep his heart rate down. If he'd had a smartwatch, it would be sending all kinds of alerts out now. Maybe he would get one in the future. It could be set to notify Kenzie or Dr. B if he had a panic attack. Though he wasn't sure what they would do when they got the message. Kenzie could look at the friends app, find out where he was, and then come to him if she wanted to.

But if they weren't together when he had the panic attack, the chances were, it would be over by the time she got there. They might seem like they lasted an eternity, but it was usually only a few minutes. And then he didn't want to talk about it. He wanted to take a pill and go to sleep.

He was sure that he had lost the car and that he had imagined things. Someone had just been going in the same direction as he was. Just a coincidence. But then he saw the car pull in a couple of blocks behind him. Staying well back so as not to attract his attention or be noticeable. But it was there, and it was the same car.

Zachary swallowed and looked around, assessing his surroundings.

They had picked him up at the police station. So were they cops? Did Campbell send them out at Gordon's request to see what Zachary would do after their meeting? Whether he would go straight back over to Bridget's again and leave another note? He hadn't left a note that morning. He hadn't even stopped. Not for very long. He had just driven by, looking at the house, trying to reassure himself that all was well and he didn't need to keep checking in on them.

But Gordon had obviously looked out the window and seen him, or had reviewed a surveillance camera and found Zachary on the video. He'd put money into upgraded security systems after the kidnapping. Even though the twins hadn't been kidnapped from their home, and there wasn't much they could do about making sure that they weren't snatched from a parking lot again, other than sending a couple of bodyguards along with Bridget whenever she went out.

Zachary pressed his foot down on the gas. He gently raised his speed, forcing the following car to do the same if they wanted to keep up with him. They would have to close the distance, or he would get away from them at the higher speed. He decided to take the highway. That would force them to either close in enough that he would be able to identify them, or to drop back and let him go.

Or maybe he would get pulled over for speeding, for once, and they would have to abandon the chase because of the traffic cops. He took the next opportunity to turn off toward the main street and, in a few minutes, he had worked his way over to the nearest freeway exit.

After merging, he pressed his foot to the floor and shot forward.

When Kenzie was in the car with him, he had to be careful how fast he drove. Despite the fact that Kenzie drove a hot little sports car, she was cautious about breaking the speed limit by more than a few miles per hour. When Zachary was on his own, he moved a lot faster. He didn't weave in and out of traffic, but he definitely got into a lane that he could move quickly in and went as fast as the flow of traffic would allow.

Today was different. He wasn't just moving as quickly as his lane would allow. He pressed the gas pedal to the floor whenever he had empty lane in front of him and, when he ran out, he quickly switched to the lane with the best traffic flow without signaling, only dropping his speed as much as necessary to make a safe lane change. There were a few honks from irritated drivers who felt like he had cut them off or was moving too quickly but, generally, by the time anyone could hit the horn, he was long gone, the noise way behind him.

To begin with, the dark car tried to keep up. They didn't close the distance enough for Zachary to get a good look at the driver, license plate, or any identifying features from the car.

After a few minutes, they were lagging far enough behind him that he could barely make out their position in his rearview mirror. He kept going and, eventually, he couldn't see them anymore. He dropped his speed and watched for them to reappear in his mirror, but they did not. He timed another ten minutes just going with the traffic flow and waiting for them to pop up again, but they did not. He took the next exit and doubled back toward Roxboro.

He frowned as he continued to watch for them. They might have taken an exit before him and be traveling back toward home or sitting on the shoulder waiting for him, knowing that he had to go back to Roxboro sooner or later. But he didn't see them.

Were they cops? If they were, he would have expected them to do a better job keeping up. And maybe even to pull him over to give him a ticket or a stern warning. But there was no sign of the police on the highway. Who, then? Had Gordon hired another PI to tail Zachary? So that they would know where Zachary was and what he was doing, and could assess better how often he was showing up at the house, what he was doing there, and if he was a threat to Bridget.

That was probably it. Gordon had decided to quit waiting around and take action. No longer satisfied with just passively checking his security cameras to ensure that Zachary wasn't near the house, he had called Campbell to give him a heads-up, had called Kenzie to put her on notice, and had put a tail on Zachary.

In which case, it was nothing to be concerned about. He could come and go as usual and not put himself or Kenzie in danger. Maybe if he knew that someone was watching him, just waiting for him to show up at Bridget's house again, it would be a deterrent. He would be able to convince his malfunctioning brain that going back there was not only wrong, but dangerous, and that he would have to give up watching her and take up a new hobby.

Back in Roxboro, he continued to watch for the tail car. Since he didn't know for sure who it was, he didn't want to lead them back home. He didn't want anyone showing up there, threatening him or Kenzie. Leaving notes in the mailbox. But the Godfrey case was closed. Those characters would not be bothering him anymore. And Gordon would not threaten harm, just to file a protective order against Zachary.

After stopping at the house, Zachary watched the cars and sidewalks around him, watching for anyone who was watching him or lying in wait. Home was a safe place. He needed to keep it that way.

CHAPTER 40

Even after sitting outside to reassure himself that no one was surveilling him, Zachary was still anxious after entering the house. He kept looking out the windows, trying to identify anyone or anything unusual. Were there cars on the street that he didn't recognize? Someone out walking a dog while actually casing out the house? Anyone looking at the house numbers trying to identify which one was his?

He saw a couple of school-age kids walking down the other side of the street. One of his neighbors got home from the grocery store and walked up to their door with bags of groceries. All normal Saturday activities.

His phone rang, making Zachary jump. He checked the caller ID. Jennifer. He swiped to answer the call.

"Jennifer? Everything okay?"

She sighed heavily and didn't answer. Of course everything was not okay. "I was just... wondering what you have found so far. It's been a while since you told me anything."

"Uh, sure. Sorry about that. I have been occupied with the case, not something else. I just don't have any conclusions yet, and I didn't want to bother you with anything unimportant or undeveloped."

"So you have some leads?"

"I have a few things I'm looking at. I was wondering... about Kristin's watch."

"Her watch?"

"She had a new watch, didn't she?"

"Yes. She got it a couple of months ago and loved it."

"And I was just wondering if you have that. If I could look at it."

"You have her laptop and her phone. I'm sure there's a lot more information on those. I doubt if there's anything at all on the watch."

"It was a smartwatch. It stored and transmitted... certain information."

"What kind of information?"

"Information about her health. Heart rhythm, breathing, blood pressure. Stuff like that."

"Oh. I didn't know it could do all that. How do you know that?"

"Apparently, anyone on Rx was put on real-time monitoring. So if we could get her watch, we could see what her heart health was like before she went into surgery and, if she was still wearing it, get more information about what happened before she died."

"Why wasn't that in the medical examiner's report? Shouldn't they have pulled all of that information?"

“They might not have realized what kind of watch it was or that it was recording any of that information. I’m sure if they had known, they would have included that information in their report.”

“I guess it would be in the bag of personal items they gave me when they... released her. Can you hold on for a minute, and I’ll get it?”

“Sure,” Zachary agreed.

He watched out the window while she put down the phone and looked for the watch. Still no suspicious behavior that he could see outside. He could relax. No one had followed him.

Eventually, Jennifer returned to the phone. “I can’t find it.”

“It wasn’t with her personal effects?”

“No. I’ve looked through everything in the bag and I shook out the clothes to make sure that it didn’t get caught on something. They must still have it.”

“That doesn’t seem likely… but I guess it could have been mislabeled or put in the wrong place. Can you call the medical examiner’s office and see if they can find it? I wouldn’t think it would take them too long to realize they had a watch that hadn’t been properly accounted for.”

Jennifer hemmed and hawed, obviously not wanting to do that.

“This is important information,” Zachary urged her. “Vital. If you want to know what happened to Jennifer, it could provide a lot of the answers.”

“Can’t you call them?”

“They won’t talk to me. Only to you. And if you’re going to call them to give them permission to talk to me, you may as well ask them about the watch.”

Jennifer growled something under her breath. Zachary didn’t ask her what she had said.

“You’ll call them, then?”

"I suppose so. But not right now. I'm..." Jennifer hesitated. Zachary had a sneaking suspicion she was casting around for a good reason why she couldn't call the medical examiner's office now. "I have a stack of other jobs I need to do, including several other phone calls. I have a demanding job."

"Okay. Let me know what you find out."

* * *

Zachary sat down with his computer to go through the social networks he had posted to about Rx and any side effects people might be experiencing with it. There were disappointingly few answers, and a lot of rants about how he was trying to smear the name of a good product. A lifesaving product.

He tried a few searches on the various platforms for any negative messages about Rx. There weren't a lot of them. Either everybody thought that the product was wonderful, or the company was shutting down any negative publicity as soon as it appeared. He imagined that threatened lawsuits would get most of them taken down quickly. By the platform, if not by the person who had posted them.

There were a couple of recent messages from BombshellBlake. Frowning, Zachary tapped one of them and a video began to play. It was a face that was familiar to him. Brittany “the Bombshell” Blake had stayed at the same vacation resort as he and Kenzie had before Thanksgiving. They had ended up snowed in, and a series of unexpected events had resulted in their getting to know Brittany much better than expected. While Zachary had thought initially that the social influencer was just a spoiled rich girl, he had learned that she worked hard to get what she had, and was otherwise a pretty normal, nice person.

And her fans had been the ones to break through the snow to get them out of there. They had saved Brittany’s life, and maybe several others in the process.

He listened to Brittany—perfect, fit Brittany, who worked out every day to stay slim for the cameras and was extra careful about what she ate—talk about being "body positive." She encouraged her followers to be happy with their bodies and not to give in to the messages of companies like TrimProGenix, the makers of LipoSlayerRx, and think that there was a shortcut to achieving the perfect body. There wasn't any such thing as a perfect body, and people should accept and be happy with the bodies they had, wherever they were at in life.

Brittany expounded on how all races, colors, weights, and shapes were equally beautiful. Pictures flashed across the screen of Brittany hugging larger women, taking selfies with singles or groups of people with different cultural backgrounds, disabilities, and body shapes. Brittany the Bombshell apparently loved and approved of everyone and didn't want anyone listening to the toxic propaganda from companies like TrimProGenix.

He watched the second video, which was similar to the first. Both videos had a number of positive comments from people who approved of her message. But they also had a lot of detractors. People who couldn't accept such a message coming from a skinny girl. Or who were "tired of all of the Rx bashing." Even though Zachary hadn't seen any as he had searched through messages about the drug. Even when he had asked about side effects, he wasn't getting very many responses. He had to wonder what had happened to everyone who had previously spoken out about Rx.

As he watched, the videos posted by Brittany disappeared and were replaced by error messages that the content could not be found. Zachary refreshed the screen and searched for any messages posted by Brittany. There were a few older ones, but the two recent videos were gone. And so was anything else with any reference to Rx.

Even with her millions of followers and her influence over social media, the Bombshell was being shut down.

"Crazy," Zachary muttered under his breath and shook his head.

He tapped Brittany's name and the command to direct message her. He obviously wasn't going to have any success posting to her publicly on the Rx issue. Whatever they said would be taken down. And he would probably be banned. Brittany might be able to get away with speaking out about Rx and staying on the platform, but a newbie account that had just been opened the day before? He would be kicked out before he could say two words against the drug.

It took a while to decide what to say to Brittany in the message and, even after he had thumb-typed it, he wasn't happy with it. But his exact words didn't matter. He needed to reach Brittany and see if she could be of any help to him. She was obviously familiar with Rx and what TrimProGenix was doing. Maybe she could help him figure out what to do next.

He switched apps and tapped Kenzie's name to call her. She didn't pick up. So she was probably too busy at the morgue to answer, or she was in her car on the way home already. He got her voicemail greeting and waited to leave a message.

“Hey, Kenz. You’ll never guess who I just ran into online. And who is against Rx. I’ll tell you when I see you!”

With that tease, he hung up, smiling to himself. She would go crazy trying to guess. But never in a million years would she hit on Brittany Blake’s name.

CHAPTER 41

His phone rang, and he immediately swiped without looking to see who it was, expecting it to be Kenzie. She probably hadn't even had time to listen to his message. She had just seen his caller ID and was calling him back.

"Hey!"

"Zach?" It was Jennifer's tentative voice, confused at his greeting.

"Oh—I thought it was Kenzie. Sorry."

"I did it. I talked to the medical examiner's office to ask them about the watch."

"Good," Zachary approved. "Do they know where it is?"

"No, they said they don't know what I'm talking about. That she wasn't wearing a watch when they got her body. It must have been removed at the dentist's office, or she wasn't wearing it that day." Jennifer's voice strengthened. "They never saw it, Zachary!"

"Do you remember her wearing it that day? Would she have left it at home when she went to have her teeth pulled?"

"No. You know these kids with their technology. She'd be more likely to leave her wrist at home than her smartwatch. Of course she had it on."

And now that information was gone. Where had it disappeared to? Had it been lost at the dental office? Would they have taken it off to put in an IV or do something else? Maybe she had to do some testing and couldn't wear any metal or jewelry. He tried to think of any other reason the dentist would require her to take it off. Hygiene, he supposed. It wasn't sterile. But then, he didn't know if they worried about that as much for extracting teeth as in an actual surgery at the hospital.

Or at the morgue? From what he had seen of Kenzie's office, the technicians were pretty careful about cataloging and properly storing everything that came in. If Kristin had been wearing the watch when she came in, then had someone pocketed it because they wanted it? Had it been put down on a counter and forgotten? Fallen back behind a shelf? Had it been stored with the wrong person's personal effects?

"Okay," he said to Jennifer at last. "I guess there's nothing we can do if it was lost. We can't force anyone to find it and give it back. Unless it is trackable from Kristin's phone. Do you know if you can do that? Search for it from the watch app?"

"I don't have a clue. It makes sense that you might be able to. But Kristin never lost it. She was always wearing it."

"Of course," Zachary agreed. Probably the only time Kristin took the watch off was for a shower or to charge it.

"You've got her phone. So, if you can find a way to do it..." Jennifer trailed off. Zachary could picture her expressive shrug.

"I'll see what I can do. Thanks for calling back and letting me know."

"Yeah, you're welcome." Jennifer sighed. "I just hope you can find something before too long. This is getting really… I feel stretched out thin. Ready to snap like a rubber band."

"I'm sorry. Try to get some rest. You shouldn't be working all the time."

"I have to work. It's the only way to put it out of my mind. The only way I can move forward."

Zachary was silent for a moment. She didn't say anything either.

"Take care, Jennifer. You know I'll do everything I can."

"Thank you, Zachary."

She terminated the call. Zachary stared at his phone, unable to move on to the next task.

Somehow he had to help Jennifer. There had to be something that he could tell her that would bring her some peace. But he didn't know what it was. She was the one who had started down this path. But she couldn't control the direction the investigation led.

A banner message flashed across his screen while he was staring at it. Too fast for him to read. He swiped and tapped to freeze it in the middle of his screen.

* * *

Brittany had tagged him. Not on the same app as he had sent her a message through. It was a vague, general message that everyone would overlook except the people tagged in it.

reaching out to my old friends Zachary and Kenzie. It's nice to hear from you again.

He looked at the message for a moment but could glean no more from it than was apparent at first glance.

He returned to the private message he had sent her and was met with reply with an enthusiastic streak of emoji hugs and kisses.

we've got to do something about this, she had messaged, be careful what you post here, even in private messages. I have reason to think it is not secure

She was probably right. It tended to be incredibly easy to hack social networking sites. People did it all the time.

let's talk/meet in private he suggested.

Brittany agreed, and they exchanged several messages back and forth to make suitable arrangements.

* * *

A call had come through from Kenzie while he had been messaging Brittany, but he assumed she was returning his call and he could get back to her after he finished talking with Brittany. She was probably going crazy trying to figure out who he had seen, and he didn't mind drawing out the tension a bit more to tease her further.

But then a text message pushed its way onto the screen.

CALL ME

That wasn't like Kenzie at all. Zachary tapped her name and initiated a call. It was answered almost immediately.

"Zachary? Are you okay?"

"Yes." His heart thumped at the anxious note in her voice. "I'm fine. What happened?"

"I'm on my way home."

"Wait. Slow down. What are you upset about? Should you even be driving?"

"I need to get home. How else am I going to do it?"

"You could catch a cab or ride share. Or wait for me and I'll come pick you up." He picked up his keys from the laptop table. "Are you still at the morgue? I can be right over."

"No. Don't come. I'll be home soon. I'll come to you."

He couldn't ask again whether she was in any condition to drive. She was going to do it no matter what he said, so he might as well not have an argument with her about it.

"Can you tell me what's going on?"

"No."

She hung up the phone. Zachary stared at the screen, shaking his head.

Something had set her off. But he had no idea whether it was a real or perceived threat. She did overreact to things. Despite her reassurance that her PTSD was improving on its own, he hadn't seen a decrease in her symptoms. And that wasn't the way it worked. It wouldn't just disappear on its own.

But he would have to wait a few minutes until she got home. It was a small town, it would only be a few minutes, and then she could explain it to him, and he could decide how concerned he should be. Until then, he would set judgment aside and just wait.

Though he couldn't, of course. His heart was still thumping and he wouldn't be able to relax until she was home safe and sound. His brain was going through all sorts of horrible things that might have happened to upset her. He paced back and forth, trying to calm himself down and to think of what she might need.

CHAPTER 42

Despite his anxiety and panic attacks, Zachary was actually good in a real emergency. That's where his hypervigilant and ADHD brain really paid off. He saw and processed the dangers quickly, went through a hundred different scenarios to see what the results of each decision were, and appeared to be calm and confident.

Unlike when he had a flashback or a panic attack over something that was not a real danger at all, and could collapse in the middle of the floor—or the street—over Christmas candles or an accusation by Bridget.

So he was thinking about what things he could do to calm Kenzie down, from food to soft music and a warm bath or shower. Girding up his loins to support her in whatever she needed him to do. Thinking about how he would help her to sleep and call Dr. B to discuss issues if it were something he couldn't handle. He had the phone numbers for her mother and father if it was a family issue or he needed input from them. He didn't have Dr. Wiltshire's personal number, but he knew the number to the morgue and could have a message passed on to Dr. Wiltshire if it were something to do with work.

Whatever she needed him to do, he was there for her. He would do it.

Finally he heard the big garage door open and her car pull in. The engine sounded fine. Nothing wrong with the car, as far as he could tell. He stood in the kitchen waiting for her. She wouldn't want him jumping all over her the instant she came in the door. Or poking his head into the garage before she had a chance to exit, demanding to know what the problem was. He could be solid and reliable, waiting for her to confide in him.

The door opened and Kenzie stepped into the kitchen. She saw him there and nodded without saying anything. She kicked off her shoes and hung up her purse. She cleared the door open code on the burglar alarm and walked over to him. She wrapped her arms around him and held him tightly. Zachary put his arms firmly around her and held on, waiting.

She took several deep breaths, but he could feel her shaking. Could feel that fluttering movement of her stomach as she shuddered with each breath. He kissed her cheek.

“I’m here,” he assured her.

Kenzie shook her head and at first she couldn’t say anything, couldn’t put what she was feeling into words.

“Do you want to sit down?” Zachary pulled back a little, but she stuck to him. “Have a glass of water?”

“In a minute.”

“Okay.” He could wait.

Several minutes passed. Zachary could hear the clock on the wall ticking. Eventually, Kenzie released him. She went to her chair and sat down carefully, as if she didn’t know if that was her place. Zachary went to the fridge and poured her a glass of cold water. He didn't add ice to it.

"Here you go."

Kenzie took it. He studied her as she sipped. She was quite pale, her red lipstick and black hair standing out in stark contrast to her face. Her curly hair, often wild if she drove with the top down, was still neatly arranged, which meant that she had not enjoyed the summer breeze as she usually did. She had been in a hurry to get home.

He still didn't demand to know what had happened, but merely waited. After making sure she didn't need anything else, he sat down in his chair and watched her.

"There was a man," Kenzie started.

Zachary nodded, waiting. A man in the morgue? A patient? Or a man she had run into somewhere else? Maybe just a man she had known once that something had made her think of.

"He was at the entrance to the parking garage. His car stopped behind the barrier. Trying to use his access card to get into the garage, but it wasn't working."

"Okay. Not someone you knew?"

"No. But there are a lot of people who work there on a different floor or are only there now and then, who don't come and go at the same times as I do, so, unless we had a file together, I wouldn't know them. There are a lot of people there I don't know."

"Yeah, makes sense."

"He was standing there, obviously having problems with the card reader, and he waved me over like he needed help. Sometimes the readers are really flaky, but I'm usually pretty good at getting them to work. So I stopped to talk to him, to give him a few tips."

Zachary tried to read her face. Tried to anticipate what was coming next.

"So he came closer to hear me, so I didn't have to shout across at him."

"Sure."

Zachary could see it in his mind's eye. He knew the location, and he could picture Kenzie stopping to help the man who was having such a difficult time.

"And he got close to me, and he grabbed me! My arm. And he twisted it..."

Zachary looked down at her arm. He should have caught the redness earlier. "Do you need ice? Is it okay?"

"It's okay. No permanent damage. It just hurt, and he twisted it, so my wrist felt like it was going to break. And my shoulder. I was trying to stop him, to keep him from twisting, but he was so strong."

A couple of tears escaped her eyes. Zachary shook his head, not understanding the scenario.

"What did he want? He was the car owner, not some homeless guy?"

She sniffled. "A homeless guy could still own a car. But... it was a really nice car. Late model Mercedes. He wasn't homeless. He didn't look out of place. Or he did, because he looked too fancy, and that place is full of cops, not millionaires. But he could have been someone's lawyer."

Zachary nodded. "Did he say anything?"

"He said..." Kenzie swallowed hard and spoke in a tight, restrained voice. "That I should get my nose out of things that were not my business. I've got plenty of my own files and should stick to those."

Zachary nodded, frowning. He opened his mouth to ask her a question, but didn't get it out.

"It was about Rx, Zachary!" Her eyes were wide and bewildered. "About LipoSlayerRx and Kristin and your friend Jennifer. Telling me to stay away from the case."

Zachary tried to protest that Kristin Jones was his file, not Kenzie's, so if there was anyone to warn off, they should be warning Zachary off. And they hadn't. But he thought about the dark car that had followed him from the police station. They had never caught back up to him. The car hadn't been a late-model Mercedes, but they might have had more than one vehicle. More than one person there to warn them off. Both him and Kenzie. One car had followed Zachary away and one had stayed behind to get to Kenzie. But why? To tell them to stay out of the Kristin Jones case? It wasn't like they were about to have someone arrested. They couldn't prove wrongdoing on anyone's part yet. The medical examiner's report was unchanged. Until it was changed from natural death to homicide, the police were not likely to have anything to do with it.

Zachary had turned the drugs in to Campbell, but did the people who had been watching him know that? They couldn't know exactly why Zachary was there unless they had the house bugged, and he swept it at least weekly for electronic monitoring. Accomplished in covertly monitoring people, he knew how easy it was. How the devices could be practically invisible.

But they knew he was working on the file and that he had seen fit to go to the police about something. And they had followed him to warn him off as well. Only he had shaken them on the highway and they couldn't. Not unless they knew where he lived. Zachary turned in his seat to look out the front window again. Plenty of time had passed. Plenty of time in which to figure out where he lived. Or to follow Kenzie, who would have been oblivious to a tail, back home. He still didn't see any cars that didn't belong on the street. No one was sitting surveilling the house from nearby. No late model Mercedes.

“Did you… make sure that he couldn’t follow you home? Did you watch for anyone behind you?”

Kenzie nodded. “I did the best I could. I’m no professional, but… I didn’t see him or his car again. I pulled over partway.” She breathed hard and her eyes were shiny with tears. “Because I couldn’t drive and I needed to make sure that no one was following me. I just pulled over on the main road, put my flashers on, and watched. That’s when I called you.”

Zachary nodded. “Good. That was a good idea. He would have had to make himself visible.”

“But he didn’t. And I watched. I didn’t see anyone following.”

“Good.” Zachary put his hand over hers, trying to reassure her. “You’re safe here.”

CHAPTER 43

I don't understand it," Kenzie said, shaking her head. "I don't even understand how anyone could know I'd looked at anything concerning Kristin, Rx, or your investigation. That was just between you and me. Unless you told someone else about it."

Zachary shook his head. "No. I haven't told anyone you knew anything about it. I never do. I just say that I know someone with a medical background or something like that. I don't ever say your name or that you're my partner or that you work with the medical examiner's office."

"Then how would anyone know?"

Zachary shook his head slowly, thinking it through. How would anyone know that Kenzie was involved in the investigation? There weren't even that many people who knew that Zachary was. Jennifer, a few of Kristin's friends and other people at the school, and Joshua Campbell. Who else even knew that he was looking into it?

“Someone followed me when I left your building. I thought that Campbell put someone on to me or Gordon was having me tailed to make sure I stayed away. But... it could be Rx. Campbell warned me that these big pharma companies can be dangerous.”

“As if we didn’t already know that,” Kenzie said, rolling her eyes.

They’d had enough experience with that in the past.

“You talked to her doctor,” Kenzie pointed out. “What did you tell him?”

“I told him that I was looking into Kristin’s death. I didn’t say anything about you.”

“But he knows that you’re investigating it. Investigating Rx. And prescribing Rx is practically all he does.”

Zachary's stomach was in knots at the thought that anything he had done could have put Kenzie in danger.

"He's making all kinds of money pimping the stuff. He probably has contacts within the company and gets a lot of kickbacks."

Kenzie nodded. "Yeah. I would guess so."

"And the minute I left there, I'll bet he was on the phone with them, telling them I was making trouble."

"That puts you on their radar. But what about me? Would they look into your background and find out that we were together and just assume that you would involve me in the investigation?"

"Maybe. I don't know. From what you described, it sounded like he knew you were involved in the investigation."

Kenzie nodded. "Yes. He acted like he knew I had been sticking my nose where it did not belong."

Zachary rubbed the back of his neck, thinking about it. It had all been happening at the same time as Brittany had been posting about him and Kenzie on social media. Too fast for her words to have gotten back to TrimProGenix that Kenzie was involved and to warn her off. Kenzie had been threatened right around the time that Brittany had been posting. But he figured he'd better bring her up to speed anyway.

"Brittany is taking on Rx?" Kenzie asked in disbelief when he told her about it. "She's the last person I would expect to talk negatively about a weight loss prescription."

"She's very passionate about the whole 'body positive' thing. She's taken a stand, even though she knows that her posts will be deleted minutes after she publishes them."

"Why would the social media platforms delete them?"

Zachary shrugged. "You said that you saw a lot of advertising about Rx. That means they're putting a lot of money out there.

Paying all of the social media platforms for advertising. If someone is threatening a major source of income…"

"But Brittany is a big social media influencer herself."

"So TrimProGenix must generate a lot more money for them than she does."

"I guess." Kenzie rubbed the crease between her eyebrows, looking fatigued. "This is crazy. How does a company get so much influence over everything we see and read? I mean, they are everywhere. All over my feeds, even if I tell them I am not interested in Rx. They just keep going. With kids who are vulnerable, like Kristin—teens who are being teased and bullied about their weight, and who would give anything just to be able to shed the pounds like Rx's advertising says you can… can you imagine how many kids are taking or trying to get their hands on Rx? And its effects haven't even been studied on children."

Zachary blinked at this news. He pulled his notebook out of his pocket. “You had a chance to look at the studies?”

Kenzie nodded. She took a sip of her water and slowly and deliberately put her glass down again. “I’ve pulled everything I could on their trials to see how comprehensive they were. And... to be blunt, they were not. They pushed things through so fast it is hard to believe that they weren’t paying off the FDA and anyone else who had to approve their applications to get this drug to market. The studies that were done were small and short. Too few participants to say that they know the side effects and interactions of the drug. And too short to know any of the long-term consequences.”

“And they weren’t tested on children. Teenagers.” Zachary closed his eyes, remembering Dr. Race’s words. “The doctor said he wouldn’t hesitate to prescribe it for an obese three-year-old.”

“What?”

"That's what he said."

"I thought it was bad enough to prescribe it to someone as young as Kristin. That's crazy."

"I guess he figured that the consequences of obesity are so bad, it doesn't matter how young the patient is. It is best to start when they are young than to let it develop."

"That's pretty much the same thing as they said about the drug trials. That Rx is such an effective weapon against obesity that it was important to get it to the market as quickly as possible. To save lives. Delaying the release of Rx would result in deaths."

CHAPTER 44

What were the side effects that were found in the trials?"

"Very mild stuff. Headaches, constipation, tiredness."

"Nothing psychological? Or related to the heart?"

"They said that the incidence of depression, mood disorders, or behaviors was too small to be significant. And there was an increased rate of cardiac events, but that was because they were actually monitoring for them. If people hadn't been in the drug trial, they wouldn't have been monitored, and minor cardiac events would not have been documented."

"This is things like heart attacks? I know you hear about how people go into the hospital for a heart attack, and when the hospital runs tests, they find that the person has actually had several heart attacks before, they were just not serious enough to make them go to the hospital."

“Yes. Stuff like that. Or problematic heart rhythms. The person hasn’t had a heart attack, but they are experiencing arrhythmias that could be dangerous.”

“The kind of thing where they could drop dead without any warning, because their heart stopped?”

“Because their heart was not beating the way it needs to to sustain life,” Kenzie agreed.

Zachary looked at her for a minute, then shrugged.

“I need to find out what Kristin’s monitoring showed.”

“Did you find her watch?”

He shook his head. “Not yet. I talked to Jennifer, and she looked for it, but doesn’t have it. She called the Burlington medical examiner’s office to look for it because they had not returned it to her with Kristin’s personal effects, but they said they didn’t have it.”

He walked into the living room and picked up Kristin's phone. He returned and sat down at the table with Kenzie. He glanced over at her quickly, evaluating how she was feeling. She was a lot more relaxed. Still angry or upset by the incident outside the parking garage, but no longer panicked.

"Kristin's phone?" Kenzie asked.

"Yes. I'm hoping it tracks the location of her watch."

"If the battery isn't dead."

"And if it is, it should still show the last location it was recorded at, which should be the medical examiner's office in Burlington. Or the dentist's office."

Kenzie nodded. She had a couple of swallows of water, watching Zachary with interest to see what he would find. Zachary found the tracking app and opened it up.

Under devices, it had tracked Kristin's earphones, but not her watch. Another dead end. Who had taken her watch? Or where had it been misplaced?

He put it down on the table and just stared at it, trying to come up with something new.

"It was a good idea," Kenzie told him.

"Yeah. If it had worked."

"We'll think of something else."

He smiled at her. "You still want to have anything to do with this case? I thought you wouldn't want to be anywhere near it. Not after being threatened."

Kenzie rubbed at the red mark on her arm. "Just the opposite. They've got me mad now. If they thought I was interfering before... they'd better think again."

Zachary chuckled. TrimProGenix might just have shot themselves in the foot.

“We should have something to eat,” Kenzie commented.

“Let’s order something in. I don’t want to make you do any work after what you just went through and, if I do it, you’ll just be crawling up the walls when I put the cheese in your sandwich without taking it out of the wrapper first or something inconsequential like that.”

Kenzie laughed. “That’s just extra roughage, is that it?”

“Exactly. You get used to it.”

“We can order something.”

Zachary was still staring at the phone. Kenzie’s voice washed over him, but he didn’t hear what she said.

“Zachary?”

He pulled the phone toward him and zoomed in on one of Kristin's friend locations. His heart started to thump louder and faster. He couldn't hear anything else.

"Zachary, what is it?"

Kenzie put her hand on his arm and had to shake it a few times before he broke free from his thoughts and looked at her. He still couldn't process what she had said.

"What's going on?" Kenzie asked. "Did you find something?"

Zachary turned the phone around and slid it across the table to her. Kenzie looked down at it.

"Rain is one of Kristin's friends?"

"Yes. One of the girls that I talked to at the school. A couple of times."

"And what is—" Kenzie broke off and Zachary saw understanding flood her features.

CHAPTER 45

Zachary was pretty sure that they had ended up ordering pizza, but he couldn't remember if he had eaten any. Kenzie would probably have brought him a slice while he worked on the computer and insisted that he eat it, but he couldn't remember doing so. He was too involved in his research project, focused on uncovering as much as he could before confronting Rain.

He left the house early so that he could be at the school before the students arrived. He had already dealt with the administration twice and didn't think they would be happy to see him again. He preferred to talk to Rain away from her teachers and school administration this time. He thought it would be more effective if he could confront her face-to-face and say what he wanted to without worrying about whether someone thought he was being too hard on her or wanted to bring the police or her father into it.

And he suspected Rain would speak more freely if no other adults were around.

He knew Rain's address and therefore the direction she was likely to be coming from, so that he could position himself with a good vantage point of the door she was most likely to enter by. Of course, he could be wrong. Sometimes schools had rules about who was allowed to go in what doors, either for security or just for better traffic flow. So he still had to keep an eye out in every direction, but stayed focused on that one door.

Rain did not appear to have any before-school clubs or activities, so Zachary stood there for quite some time before she showed up.

He spotted Rain, walking alone rather than with friends, and homed in on her. She was lost in thought and didn't notice him until they were only a few feet apart. She stopped short and rocked backward, then looked around her to assess all routes of escape. Zachary stood there and didn't say anything to alarm her.

"What are you doing here?" Rain demanded.

"I have some more questions for you."

"Don't you think you've done enough? You keep coming here, making trouble for us, making the administration think that we've done something wrong. And we haven't. We were just good friends with Kristin. So why do you keep harassing us?"

"I'm not harassing you. I'm trying to get answers to my questions and find out what happened to Kristin."

"You know what happened to Kristin."

"I only know part of the story. And I think you can help me to find out the rest. But you've been keeping secrets."

She rolled her eyes and looked away from him, full of teenage attitude.

"I have to get to school, you know? Classes start in ten minutes and I have to go to my locker before that."

"Maybe you'll be late today."

Her eyes widened at the idea of an adult suggesting she could be late for school. "They'll call home, and I'll have to get a note, and detention." She shook her head. "Why would I want to do that?"

"Because Kristin was your friend and you want justice for her."

"She was my friend," Rain asserted. "You don't know what it's like, going to school here, not having many friends." She shook her head. "And now she's gone. It's like... why would I even want to live. You have no idea what that's like."

Zachary nodded. "I might know better than you think."

"Adults don't know anything about what it's like at school."

"I did go to school myself once, you know."

“It wasn’t the same. And if it was, you don’t remember. Adults all have amnesia and think that going to school was the best time of their lives. Like it is on TV or something. How everybody has a best friend and a boy they like, and school is just one big social club.”

“If school had been the best time of my life... I wouldn’t still be here.”

“What do you mean? Where would you be?”

“I would have killed myself.”

Rain just stared at him in disbelief.

“Trust me,” Zachary said, “things get better after high school. Even being homeless once I turned eighteen was better than going to school.”

She looked at him for a long moment. Her shoulders relaxed. “Really?”

"Really. My only friend was Kristin's mom, and she didn't die, but she left, and I didn't see her again. One day she was there and then she was gone. And I was on my own again. She had been helping me... with homework, staying away from the wrong people... just getting through the day. And then nothing. Then it was just me again."

Rain sat down on the concrete stair and motioned to Zachary to sit down, too. "It got better?"

"Once I was out of here. Yes." He motioned to the school, even though that hadn't been the school he had attended. "Out of group homes and foster homes. Away from all of the bullies—especially the teachers. There are still bullies when you're an adult. People who still get a kick out of making you squirm or cry. But they're not nearly as bad as in school."

Neither of them said anything for a while.

"Now cyberbullying," Zachary said, "that's almost as bad. People trying to humiliate you. Telling you to kill yourself. Not having to be face-to-face with the victim makes it easier for them to indulge their inner fifteen-year-old."

Rain laughed sharply.

"But there are things you can do. I can help you if you're having trouble with anyone like that. You can protect yourself from most of the cyberbullying."

"Most of it?"

He nodded. "Most of it."

She sighed. "I looked you up, you know. I guess... you're kind of a crusader. Someone who's not afraid to point out when you see something wrong, to go after it, even if you don't know if you can change anything."

He hadn't ever had someone say something like that to him before, but he supposed it was the truth. Once he got firmly ahold of an issue, he was like a pit bull. He couldn't let go even if he wanted to. He had to see it through to the end.

"Like this business with Rx?" he asked. "I looked you up too, you know."

"Yeah?" Her shoulders lifted and fell in a shrug. "Don't imagine you found anything interesting. I'm just a kid. Just puttin' in my time and trying to survive."

"Were you the one who got Kristin interested in LipoSlayerRx? Or who told her where to get it?"

"It's everywhere, all the time. I didn't have to point her toward it."

The school bell rang. Rain didn't move.

CHAPTER 46

Zachary watched a few stragglers run into the school. Outside, it was quiet, with just the sounds of the traffic driving by on the road in front of the school.

"Where's your phone?" Zachary asked.

Rain's lips tightened, pressing together. Her eyes blazed. Zachary hadn't seen her so angry before, and he had pushed some buttons.

"It's my phone," she told him sullenly. "I paid for it with my own money."

"But your dad took it away because you broke the rules?"

"He's a jerk."

Zachary supposed he was lucky she wasn't using much more colorful language. He waited, figuring he would get more out of

Rain if he let her wind herself up and speak in her own time than if he pushed her.

“He said it was distracting me from my schoolwork and keeping me from getting done what I was supposed to. That I was spending too much time chatting with my friends and messing around and it was bringing my grades down. My grades are just fine. He’s the one who had a problem.”

“What do you think his problem is?”

“That he’s a control freak and can’t stand not knowing exactly what I’m doing every day. Not knowing what I’m talking about and whether I’m saying anything about him.”

Zachary nodded. He let her words stand by themselves for a few minutes before saying anything further.

“He took it to work with him.”

She nodded. “If he’d left it at the house, I would have gotten it back. Even if I had to break into the safe.”

"I could see your phone's location on Kristin's friends app."

"You have Kristin's phone?"

"For now. Her mom wants it back, so probably not for much longer."

She looked away, biting her lip and not saying anything.

"She mostly deleted your conversations, or you guys used apps that expired them automatically."

Rain nodded.

"You could help me," Zachary suggested.

"Why would I do that?"

"Because you were Kristin's friend and I'm just trying to help prove what happened to her and bring her mom some peace. Her mom, who helped me through one of my toughest years in school."

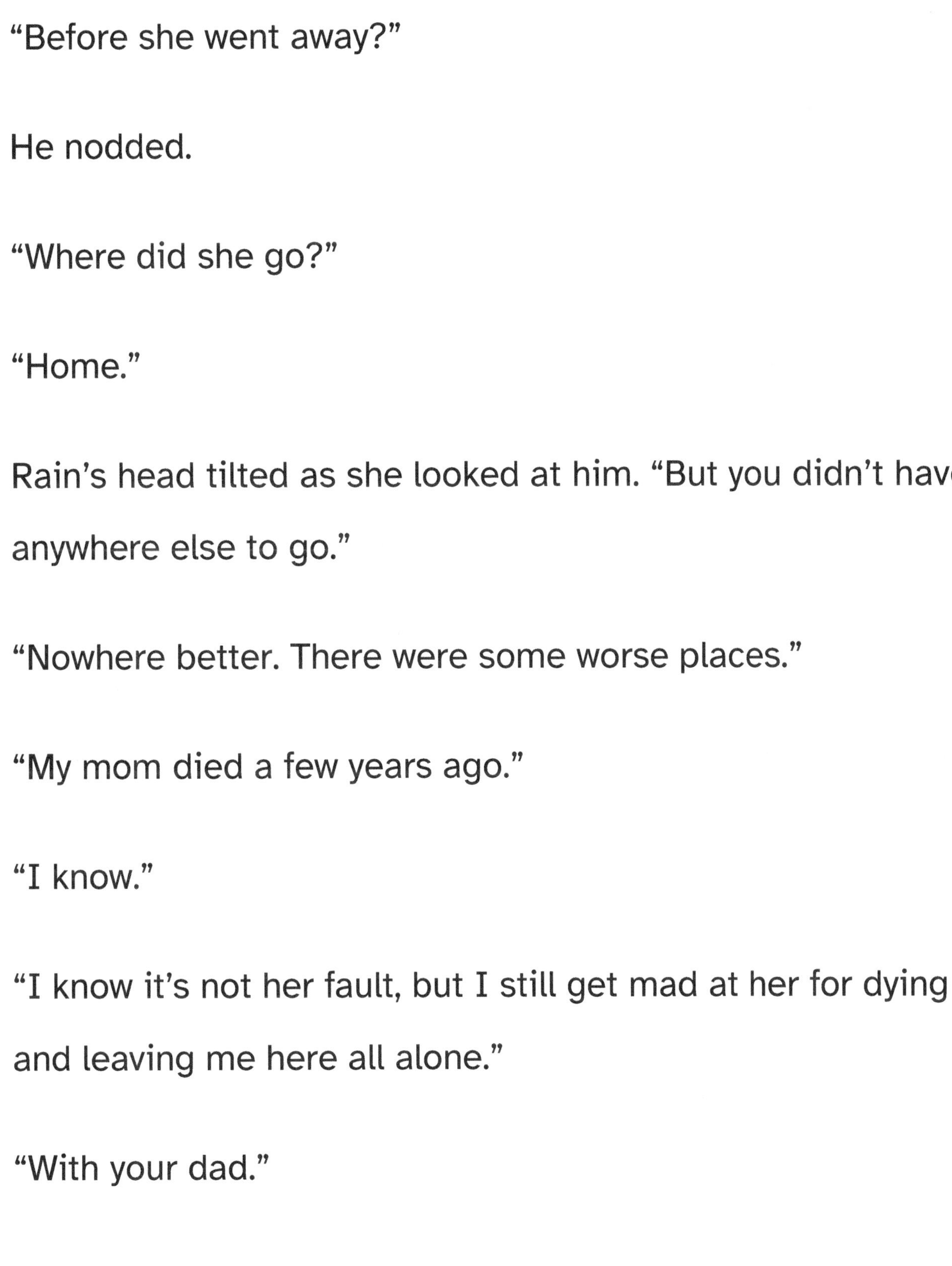

“Before she went away?”

He nodded.

“Where did she go?”

“Home.”

Rain’s head tilted as she looked at him. “But you didn’t have anywhere else to go.”

“Nowhere better. There were some worse places.”

“My mom died a few years ago.”

“I know.”

“I know it’s not her fault, but I still get mad at her for dying and leaving me here all alone.”

“With your dad.”

"Yeah." She sighed. "But he's never there. And when he is... he's like..." She trailed off, searching for words. "He isn't like he used to be."

"He must have been pretty excited when his company came out with LipoSlayerRx."

"Yeah." Rain looked up at the sky. It was a cloudless day, sunny and bright, the sky a pure, clear blue. "For a couple of years, that's all he could think about. He would come home and talk about it. How he was going to change the world. They were going to change the face—and body—of America. They were going to end the obesity epidemic once and for all. Everyone would be better off for it."

"Did he get you excited about it?"

"Yeah. Sure. I could see how bad it was for kids my age, like Kristin, who were fat. I knew it's bad for their hearts and causes cancer and other things. He could really talk it up." She shrugged. “But I guess you know that. You’ve seen the advertising.”

“It’s everywhere,” Zachary said, repeating what she and Kenzie had said. “TrimProGenix has really nailed the marketing. They’ve told a story, they’ve used social media, and they have product placement everywhere. It’s really amazing. Must cost millions of dollars.”

He’d seen the prospectuses they had filed with the SEC. He knew it had cost millions of dollars.

“Yeah. And now he’s part of this hugely successful company... and he’s happy.”

“Is he?”

“Wouldn’t you be? Do you know how much money he made last year? How many magazines he was on the cover of? He loves it. And he loves the fact that he’s making so many people thin. He’s saving the world, one pound at a time.”

“But he lost his wife. And he’s losing his daughter.”

“He doesn’t even know he is.”

“Will you help me?”

“How?”

“I need to get in there. I need to get into TrimProGenix to find the data on Kristin. Someone managed to get ahold of her smartwatch and all the data it held. I need that data for her mom.”

“You think it was the Rx.”

“I don’t know yet. It could be.”

But Zachary knew in his heart that it was. And even if she cooperated with him, there was no guarantee that he could prove it. Kristin’s medical data might show that everything was completely normal and that what had happened to her was just a fluke. One of those crazy things that happens without warning. Nothing that Jennifer could have done about it.

Nothing the doctor could have done. No matter how closely Jennifer had been paying attention to what was happening in her daughter's life, she could not have saved her.

"It's a miracle." Rain bit her lip. "That's what he says. There is no such thing as a miracle cure. But there is. Because Rx isn't like any drug that has ever gone to market before."

"What if they didn't test it properly? What if they are giving it to thousands of kids who are at risk of dying suddenly, like Kristin."

"It was the surgery. The anesthetic."

"Or it wasn't. Or it was the interaction of the anesthetic with the Rx. We don't know because they haven't tested it. They never tested it on kids, Rain. They don't know that it's safe."

Rain rubbed her face tiredly. She put her elbows on her knees and propped her head with her hand. Like she had no energy left for anything, even to hold up her head.

CHAPTER 47

I knew she was having side effects from Rx, but I didn't think they were anything serious. And I think she didn't tell me everything because she knew Dad was working for the company and helping to develop and market Rx. She didn't want me to feel bad about it. And she didn't want to have to give it up."

"It was that important to her."

Rain nodded. "Of course it was. You don't know how much it meant to her."

"I need to find a way to get into TrimProGenix, Rain. I need to see what information is on their servers about Kristin. That watch recorded her heart rhythm and other important statistics. It could be the proof we need of what killed her—or didn't kill her."

Rain rubbed at her eyes with the palms of her hands. “Get you into TrimProGenix? How am I supposed to do that?”

“I don’t know.” Zachary had been thinking about it all night, but hadn’t been able to come up with the perfect solution. “If I could get a temporary job there. Or get your dad’s computer login to their servers. Or maybe physical access through their parking garage or something like that. What’s their security system like? Passcodes? Swipe cards?”

“I don’t know any of that stuff.”

“You must know whether he has an access card or not.”

“Yeah, I think he does. But I don’t know what it gets him through. And… I can’t get it for you. That would be stealing, and if he found out what I did…”

“But it would be to help Kristin. To prove what it really was that killed her. You want to know, don’t you?”

"No. I just want you to leave it alone. I want you to leave me in peace. Let Kristin be at peace. How are we supposed to rest when you keep coming back here and asking questions? And when you won't let her go? I just want you to stop."

"I will soon. When I know what happened to her. I just need a look at her health records at TrimProGenix. I need to get on to their computer system."

"You're crazy."

"Where does your dad keep his passwords? Does he use the same password on everything, or does he write them down?"

Rain's face twisted this way and that as she tried to come up with an acceptable solution. "He writes them down," she admitted finally. "He did use to have the same password for everything. Pluviophile. But everyone started cracking down on not being able to use the same password everywhere, and you had to add numbers and symbols, and he started writing them down in his little book. It's really stupid. They should be using biometrics."

"What?" Zachary asked stupidly.

"Biometrics. Fingerprints, facial recognition, all of that kind of thing."

"No. I know that. But the word that he used to use for his password?"

Rain laughed. "Pluviophile." She cocked her head at him. "Someone who loves rain."

"Oh. That's very sweet."

She nodded. "Yeah. Science geeks. Believe me; I know all of the words for all of the precipitation..."

"I'll bet."

"And do you want to know how many times I heard 'rain, rain, go away' on the playground?" She rolled her eyes. "It isn't exactly the most normal name."

"People can be cruel."

"Uh-huh."

"So, where does your dad keep his notebook? Can you get it to me? Or snap pictures of the pages to send to me?"

"I can't," she protested immediately.

"You can. Kristin's mom has a right to that data. She has the right to know what happened to her daughter. If you can do this for me... I can put this case to rest. I'll be finished."

"You'll stop asking me questions? And you'll know it wasn't anything to do with Rx?"

"Exactly."

Rain shook her head. “I don’t know,” she complained. “I’m just a kid. I shouldn’t even be involved in this. Why don’t you find another way to get in?”

“Because you already hold the key. I don’t know how long it will take me to find a way to get the information another way. If you want this wrapped up quickly, helping me is in your best interest.”

* * *

Kenzie noticed Zachary yawning and rubbing his dry, gritty eyes.

“You look like your body is ready for bed.”

“Maybe.” Zachary yawned again. “But my brain is still going a mile a minute.”

“Take a sleep aid to slow it down. You need to get your rest.”

Zachary clenched his teeth to keep from arguing. He had promised Kenzie that he would, and he had told Dr. B that he would. So there was no point in voicing his complaints again about how he would feel in the morning. Everybody was in agreement on the fact that he needed to take a pill to make sure that he got enough sleep tonight. So he would.

Kenzie was giving him an odd look. Zachary nodded. “I will,” he agreed, in as flat and neutral a voice as he could.

Kenzie opened her mouth and then closed it. Then she nodded again as if this was the answer she had been expecting and nothing out of the ordinary. “Great. I’m sure it will help. Do you want me to get it for you now?”

“Uh... sure. Why not.”

Kenzie looked even more surprised at this. She went to the main bathroom and he heard her open the medicine cabinet to get one out for him. The mirrored cabinet door clicked back into place and Kenzie brought him the pill and a glass of water to wash it down. He knew she hated it when he dry-swallowed pills, so he washed it down with plenty of water. He was very dry anyway. He handed the glass back to Kenzie.

"I'll need a little time for it to kick in."

"Sure. Of course. You want to put on a sitcom for a few minutes and we'll relax before bed?"

"Yeah."

Zachary had already closed his computer, but he pressed the lid down anyway in case it wasn't closed all of the way.

CHAPTER 48

By the time the sitcom was over, Zachary could feel the sleep aid kicking in. His thoughts were slowing down, and he was getting the distant, removed feeling it brought on. He rubbed his eyes and pushed himself up off the couch once the show was over. He tripped over his feet on the way out of the living room.

"Do you need a hand there?" Kenzie asked with a laugh.

"No, I'm okay," he assured her. His whole body seemed to be bigger and more difficult to control than usual. His fingers were, he was sure, swollen to twice the size they usually were, but they were numb, so he couldn't really be sure of anything. Going through his nighttime routine was difficult. Brushing his teeth was bad enough; he wasn't going to attempt flossing. He swished an extra mouthful of water around his mouth, hoping that would clear away any remaining bits of food, and opened his pill organizer to dump his night meds out into his hand.

He made it to the bed before Kenzie, as usual, since her nighttime routine took longer than his and she did take the time to floss. When she climbed into bed, he was struggling to keep his eyes open.

"You're really tired," Kenzie observed.

"I know."

It had been a long few days and he knew his body was starved for sleep. Kenzie was right to get him to take a sleep aid so that he could get several hours of sleep and not lie awake all night. Maybe it would give him a full eight hours of sleep for once.

Kenzie snuggled comfortably against him. "Go to sleep now," she advised. "See you in the morning."

* * *

Zachary was trapped in a nightmare he couldn't get out of.

A loud siren wailed close by. He reached out his hand and tried to shut it off, but he didn't know where he was or what he was doing, so he just felt around him blindly for a button to make the noise stop.

Was it a fire alarm? Was the house on fire? Despite his usual anxiety over fires and alarms, he didn't feel the usual panic at the thought of the house burning around him. It was like he was locked on the other side of a wall of ice.

Someone grasped his arm, shaking him, shouting at him to wake up. Zachary just turned his head away from her, and tried to figure out how to get out of the nightmare into normal sleep. He wanted to rest. His brain wasn't working. A series of hard pinches down his arm roused him slightly. He pulled away from her, complaining.

"Is it a fire?" he asked, but wasn't sure whether the words came out right.

"Zachary!"

“Go to sleep.”

He tried to take his own advice and return to the dark cocoon he had been in before the nightmare had started.

“See you in the morning,” he tried to tell her.

There were more sirens, blinding lights, and other voices. Zachary put his arm over his eyes and tried to block them all out.

A grinding pain in his chest roused him more. Zachary yelped and tried to push it away. There were more hands there. More arms to fight against.

“Sit him up. Sir! Sir, can you hear me?”

Forced to sit up, Zachary tried to gain control of his head, which was bobbing around like a newborn’s.

“Zachary!” He finally identified Kenzie’s voice.

Kenzie. He was in Kenzie's house. He had been asleep, but who was there? Had someone broken in? He remembered the siren. The burglar alarm.

He tried to pry his eyes open. He physically pulled down his bottom lids with his fingers and tried to peer out at the uniformed men around him. His brain was starting to ramp up, trying to process what was happening, but it was still not moving the way it was supposed to. He had been drugged. Who had drugged him? And if he had been drugged, why was he at Kenzie's house sleeping?

"He's not usually like this," Kenzie's voice was worried. "I don't know what's wrong."

"Try getting him up and walking him around," a gruff voice advised. "That should wake him up. Give him a cup of coffee."

Zachary didn't have control of his own limbs as other hands moved his legs to the edge of the bed and then off. He was hauled to a standing position, arms wrapped around the thick necks of two men who were larger than he was. They walked him across the room, back and forth, then down the hallway. Zachary tried to regain some control, moving his feet to keep up with them, but they were much too fast for him.

There were other men there. The house seemed to be filled with men in uniforms. They kept asking him questions in urgent tones, but he couldn't process their words.

He smelled the fresh coffee and took it eagerly. He thought that he had pretty good control of the coffee cup, but when he opened his eyes a crack, he saw hands on it other than his own. He drank one coffee, and then another. Another walk around the house.

He was standing on the cool tile floor of the kitchen, supported on one side by a man who was either a paramedic or a cop, but Zachary couldn't figure out which.

“What happened?” The words were difficult to force out, his tongue thick and brain still trying to return to a peaceful sleep state.

“There was an attempted break-in,” the man told him. “Your security system was tripped.”

“He must have taken more than one pill.” Kenzie’s voice floated to him from somewhere far away. “I’ve never seen him like this.”

“Sometimes people forget and take another one. Though this looks more like half a bottle. Do you want him to be taken to the hospital to have his stomach pumped?”

“No, I don’t think so. His prescription is very strong. If he took more than one, that would explain why he is so dopey. But it should wear off. One pill doesn’t usually keep him asleep for more than a few hours.”

"You might want to have him under a doctor's care. Just to make sure his breathing doesn't get too depressed."

"I am a doctor. I can monitor him. Call an ambulance if it slows down too much."

"Sir? How are you feeling?" The man holding on to Zachary shook his arm as if still trying to wake him up. "Can you talk to me now?"

"I'm fine," Zachary told him. "It's okay." His words came out slurred, but he thought they were recognizable.

"Can you tell me your name?"

"Zachary. Goldman."

"Do you know what day it is?"

"Sunday night. Or Monday."

"What's your wife's name?"

"Kenzie. Not married."

He was suddenly concerned. Would she be upset that he had stayed over when they were not married? Should he go back to his apartment?

"Should I go home?" he asked Kenzie. "Is it okay?"

"You are home."

There was a chuckle from the man. "You're not in any shape to go anywhere, Mr. Goldman. It's here or to the hospital, my friend."

"No. No, I'm okay."

"I think he'll be fine," Kenzie confirmed. "I was a little concerned when I couldn't rouse him, but he's on his feet and talking. He's oriented. Mostly. A little confusion is understandable."

"We've checked everything out." A higher, nasally voice spoke from the other side of the room. "Everything seems to be secure. No sign of your intruders. Just re-arm the burglar alarm when we leave, and you should be fine."

"What intruders?" Zachary asked. The word felt foreign in his mouth. Like it was too big or had too many syllables. He grimaced, repeating it under his breath to analyze whether he had made a mistake.

"We'll talk about it in the morning," Kenzie assured him. "I guess... we may as well go back to bed. I won't be able to go back to sleep. I'll just keep an eye on Zachary, make sure he doesn't get any worse."

"We can take him to the hospital if you want. It would just be overnight. They would release him in the morning. But they could put him on a monitor. Then you wouldn't have to stay up."

"It's okay. We'll be fine here."

CHAPTER 49

When Zachary woke up next, he was in bed where he expected to be. He sat up, his back against the wall, but he had a throbbing headache. He pressed the heel of his hand to his forehead, groaning.

“What happened?”

Kenzie was at his side. “How are you feeling?”

He moaned. “Like crap. You run over me with a truck last night?”

She moved around, and then was pressing a cool glass into his hand. “Drink water. It will help you over the hangover faster. And with the coffee last night, you’re probably even more dehydrated than you would normally be.”

Zachary had a few swallows of water, then pressed the glass to his head. “What happened last night?” He tried to break through the fog and figure it out.

"The burglar alarm went off. I tried to wake you up, but you were out like a light. The security company came by and made sure everything was secure. The paramedics checked you out."

"The burglar alarm went off?"

"Yes."

"Why did it go off? Was it a mistake?"

She didn't answer right away. Zachary lowered his glass and looked at her, even though his head was pounding and he preferred to keep his eyes shut.

"Was it a malfunction?" he persisted.

Kenzie shook her head. "No. Somebody tried to break in."

Zachary sat forward, sending his head spinning. "What?"

Kenzie's eyes were wide and her face pale, though she was trying to mask her expression. "It was hours ago. We're safe."

“Who tried to break in? Did we get them on the surveillance camera?”

“I don’t know how to work that thing. You’ll have to check. The security guy who came around would have done it, but he doesn’t know your password, and neither do I.”

Zachary would have to rectify that situation immediately. A lot of good it was to have a surveillance camera that no one could access if someone broke into the house and killed Zachary. They could have a full facial view of him and never know it.

“I’ll take a look. And I’ll show you how to do it if something happens and... I wasn’t here to do it sometime.”

“Okay.”

“We’ll set it up on your computer. There’s no reason for the access to be limited to mine.”

“That would be good. I have to file a police report today.”

"Were the police here?"

"A couple of them, yes. But I couldn't give them much. The intruders were gone by the time they got here. Even the security company's team didn't get a look at them, and they were here in about two minutes.."

"Are you okay?"

Kenzie raised her hands with her palms up and dropped them again. "Neither of us was hurt. They didn't get into the house. Everything functioned the way it was supposed to. But... I'm pretty freaked out. I jumped at every noise last night. Even made myself jump a couple of times when I dropped something or made a noise."

"Do you want to sleep? I'm up now, so you can have a rest."

"No, I don't think I can. I have work." She looked at the clock beside the table. "In a couple of hours."

"You could have an hour or two of sleep. You could tell Dr. Wiltshire what happened and that you can't make it today."

"I can, though, and I'd rather not be here listening to the house creak anymore."

"Are you sure? Will you come home early if you're too tired? I don't want you driving if you're tired. I can come and pick you up."

"I'll let you know if it's a problem. I slept a few hours before, so I did get some sleep. Just not in the last couple of hours."

Zachary rubbed his head and took another drink of water. "Why... did I wake up at all? I think... I was in the kitchen."

"Yes. The paramedics helped to get you up and walk you around to make sure that you were okay." Kenzie hesitated, not sure what to say next. She shook her head slightly. "You never sleep that soundly. Did you take something last night? Besides your sleep aid? It's never affected you that way before."

"No. Nothing out of the ordinary. I guess... I was just tired."

"No." She shook her head adamantly. "That was not 'just tired.' You were stoned. Barely able to function."

"Just the sleep aid."

"Just one pill?"

"Yes."

"Because you've never had this happen before, right? You've been on that same prescription since you got out of the hospital. And while you were in the hospital."

"I've had it happen... I guess... once before. When I was investigating Jose's disappearance, and I combined the sleeping pills and painkillers. They said I took more than one dose, but I don't remember doing that."

"So it isn't the first time."

"And... when I was younger, I guess they had me on too high of a dose. I couldn't wake up when somebody came by to talk to me. My social worker made sure it got straightened out after that, so I could still go to sleep, but be able to function if something woke me up. That's where I've tried to keep it since then. Never so much that I can't wake up when I want to."

"Then what happened last night?"

"I don't know. No one could have gotten into the house to drug me."

"No. The only other person here was me. And believe me; I didn't want you to be in the state you were in last night."

"I just had the pill you gave me."

"You were really tired when I got into bed. Almost asleep."

"Yeah. I don't know why I was so tired last night."

"You didn't take another pill before bed, right?"

"No, I just took—" Zachary cut himself off.

Kenzie looked at him, waiting.

"When you brought me a pill, you took it out of my med organizer, right?"

"No, out of the bottle."

"Oh. Then… I guess there was another one in with my night meds. I don't remember checking. I just took everything in the organizer. Didn't even think about it."

Kenzie rolled her eyes and hit her forehead with the heel of her hand. "Stupid. I didn't even think about you doing that. I'm sorry. I ended up double-dosing you."

Zachary let out his breath, relieved. "Okay. That makes sense. I couldn't figure out what was wrong. I don't remember being that dopey before. Except… for those two times. And I don't even remember the first time. I just remember my social worker talking to me about it, saying that I needed to be able to wake up at night if there was an emergency."

He tried to block himself from remembering her actual words, knowing that they had sent him into flashbacks at the time and would again if he let them.

"Next time, if you get me a pill, just take it out of the organizer. I'll try to remember to double-check before I take my night meds. But if I'm as tired as last night, I might forget..."

Kenzie leaned over and hugged him. "I'm sorry. I never meant to do that."

Zachary tried to pull back too soon. She clung to him. He patted her on the back, reassuring her. "It's okay, Kenz."

"I'm just... really glad that you didn't take extra pills yourself. When one of the paramedics said you were acting like you'd taken half a bottle..."

"No." Zachary tightened his grip on her. "I didn't take that many. I didn't do this on purpose. It was just an oversight. Neither of us thought about it."

"I didn't think so, but...I was just really worried. I kept an eye on you the rest of the night and made sure you weren't in any danger. If you had intentionally overdosed and I didn't know everything you were on, that could be a really dangerous situation."

"I didn't. You can put that right out of your mind. I'm not suicidal. That was the farthest thing from my mind when I went to bed last night."

Kenzie took a long, shuddering breath. "Okay."

CHAPTER 50

They both stayed home for a while, but Zachary knew he wouldn't be able to go back to sleep and, after Kenzie lay down once and was not able to settle in, she knew she wasn't going to get any more sleep in and might as well go to work. She was anxious about Zachary and his health and state of mind, but she was much calmer since they had figured out how Zachary had accidentally double-dosed. She would be better off at work, where she could distract herself with dead people, than staying home jumping every time Zachary moved and checking in on him every few minutes.

And he would feel better about it if she were at work and didn't keep hovering over him and interrupting the work he was trying to do.

So she was a few minutes late getting off to work, but Zachary knew she would be fine once she got there.

Neither of them focused on the fact that they had both been followed recently and then intruders had tried to break into the house. It was easier to focus on Zachary's mishap with the meds than the fact that they could be in danger from an outside source.

Kenzie couldn't be much safer than she would be working in the police building. There was plenty of security to make sure she wasn't bothered, as well as law enforcement officers coming and going. She could work without Zachary feeling like she was in danger. She would be careful arriving and leaving the parking garage. She wouldn't roll her window down and talk to anyone and would keep an eye out for anyone following her. And Zachary could check on her location with his phone app, ensuring she was where she was supposed to be.

They said lighthearted goodbyes, each doing their best to sound carefree and not worry the other. Zachary sat back down at his laptop desk in the living room, his phone placed on the table beside him, with the friends app open, watching Kenzie's progress from the house to the office. There were no unexpected stops or changes in her route, and he could relax once he knew she was at her destination.

He wanted to call Campbell to see if he had made any progress on having the autoinjector tested. But he knew that lab testing took time, longer than it should, and he didn't want to have to listen to another lecture from Campbell on how he should stay away from Bridget.

He had promised to call Dr. B to report back that he had taken his sleep aids as he was supposed to. The details could wait. He didn't feel like explaining the goof-up with the overdose to her over the phone.

As it turned out, she was in a session, so he just left a message with her receptionist, Elizabeth. That was easier. There was nothing to explain, just confirmation that he had called in as he was supposed to and had followed Dr. B's instructions. By the time he got to his next session, he would have several days behind him and be able to confirm to her that everything was going just fine, with only that one mistake.

He checked Kenzie's location again and wondered whether he should call her. While he wanted reassurance that everything was fine, a call might not be taken as one concerned partner checking in on another, but as Zachary smothering her and not trusting her to tell him if she needed something from him. He did trust her; it was only for himself that he wanted the reassurance. And if it was only for him, then he should leave her alone and not interrupt her workday.

He checked the social media on Kristin's phone and then the fake accounts he had set up to check on Rx in social media. He looked for any messages from Brittany and found a couple of body positive messages from her that he upvoted. There were no private messages from her. There were a few more from people who reported side effects while taking Rx. For the first time, there were also two messages from people who thought that Rx might have had something to do with the deaths of their loved ones. He studied each account carefully, noting any similarities to Kristin's case in his notebook, before composing messages back to them. He was careful not to say that Kristin's death might have had something to do with Rx or that he believed Rx had anything to do with the deaths that they reported, but instead asked for more information. His heart beat fast as he sent the messages out. Was he finally getting somewhere? Even if Kristin's data wasn't accessible, maybe one of these contacts would have readings from another Rx-related death. And maybe they would show a pattern. A risk factor or side effect that could help them anticipate who Rx would be dangerous to.

His phone blipped and he looked over at it. It was just a reminder to call Dr. B, which he had already done, so he ignored it and continued his work.

A minute later, it buzzed, and he reached over to dismiss the alert, then realized that it was a message, not a repetition of the reminder to call Dr. B.

He stared at the screen.

Do you really think you can keep them safe from us?

Zachary blinked and tried to compute the message. The jumble of characters told him it was from a blocked call or burner phone. Replying would probably not get him anywhere; the words would just float off into the ether. And what would he say?

His first thought was of Kenzie. But she was safe in the police building, and the message clearly said "they," not "her."

Could "they" mean all of the kids who had been prescribed Rx? It couldn't be. TrimProGenix wasn't trying to kill its customers. Even if Zachary thought that the drug was dangerous, that didn't mean that it was and the company certainly wouldn't be selling it if they knew there was a problem with it.

They could only mean one thing.

CHAPTER 51

Kenzie's phone buzzed and flashed, but she was in the middle of cross-referencing all of the reports on a drowning victim and couldn't take her eyes off of what she was doing, or she would have to start again. She took the time to ensure that all appropriate reports had been printed, filed, and saved to the proper digital folder. Once she was sure everything had been properly documented, she put the file in her outbox and looked at her phone. A quick press of the home button brought up her notifications screen, and she saw that a text had come in from Zachary. She unlocked it and tapped the message. The message was brief and incomplete.

I am

Kenzie put her phone back down on the desk. A pocket dial. She'd done it herself. Everyone had. She went on with her filing and collating reports.

When she took her next break, she looked at it again and decided to give Zachary a call. He had been very good about not interrupting her, which she had not expected after all that had happened the night before. She knew that her anxiety level was high. It was hard to concentrate on her work, but she also reveled in her work focus because it was the only way to distract herself from that feeling. If she was anxious, she could bet that Zachary was doubly so.

She had been able to see the wheels turning that morning as he realized that he had failed to protect her. Failed to wake up when the burglar alarm had gone off. Left her lying awake, keeping watch over him, while he went back to sleep, oblivious to the danger. She had seen the flash of fear as he realized that anything could have happened during the night, and he would not have been able to wake up. A home invasion. A fire. Anything.

She had expected at least one anxious check-in—probably more.

But maybe he'd been able to throw himself into his work too. His ADHD could result in hyperfocus if he were interested enough in what he was working on. And in a hyper focused state, hours could pass without his even realizing it.

Kenzie tapped Zachary's picture on her favorite contacts list and waited for him to pick up.

He didn't answer right away. She waited and, eventually, the call went through to his voicemail. Kenzie rolled her eyes. Hopefully, he was focused on the Rx case. She wanted to see that one put to bed as soon as possible.

She didn't know who was behind the attempted break-in during the night or in trying to scare her after work, but she had dealt with threats from big pharma companies before, and that was who her brain went to as the culprit. Someone at TrimProGenix wanted them off of the case. Both Zachary and Kenzie. Some loose cannon had decided to see to it personally.

Kenzie didn't bother to leave a message. Zachary would see that she had called and would call her back once he surfaced again from his work.

Before she put her phone back down, she tapped the friends app to see where Zachary was. While it was possible that he was at home, staring at his computer screen, he might also have gone out to meet with someone and wasn't answering because he was in the middle of a conference.

It took half a minute for the program to locate Zachary and zoom in on his phone signal, and the map moved to show his location.

Kenzie swore.

He was in front of Bridget's house.

She swore several times, venting her anger at Bridget for how she had twisted Zachary around while they had been together and even since they had broken up. And at Gordon for calling Zachary in to investigate the twins' kidnapping when he knew what it would likely do to Zachary's mental health. Gordon knew how hard Zachary had worked to overcome his compulsion to check on Bridget. They had all been through it before, and he had to throw all that work away and call Zachary in again.

She dialed Zachary's number again. She didn't wait patiently for the call to ring through to voicemail this time.

"Answer the dang phone, Zachary," she muttered.

He didn't. It went through to voicemail a second time.

She knew better than to try again. Whether he was avoiding her call or oblivious to it, calling multiple times would make absolutely no difference. She picked up her desk phone and punched Dr. Wiltshire's line.

"Kenzie," Dr. Wiltshire answered. "What's up?"

"I have to go out. A bit of a family emergency. I'm sorry."

"Is everything okay?"

"Uh… probably. But I have to go check. I'll get Julie to come down and sit on the phones when she's able to. I'm not sure what her schedule is like today."

"No problem. Just forward it to voicemail for now."

"Thanks. Sorry to leave you in the lurch. I'll get back as soon as I can."

"We have to take care of our families. Go ahead."

Kenzie hung up and picked up her cell phone and her purse from the drawer. She quickly forwarded the desk phone. She could call Julie from the car.

She was steaming mad as she drove out of the parking garage and waited for the call to connect to Julie, who was hopefully on site today and would be able to watch her desk for a while. Kenzie looked around and didn't see anyone suspicious hanging around where they shouldn't be. No sign of the man who had assaulted her the day before,

When she reached Bridget's street, she expected to find Zachary's anonymous white compact car parked along the curb somewhere, but it wasn't obvious. She drove once around the block. Of course Zachary had decided to park farther away this time to try to avoid the surveillance cameras that had captured his presence there the last time. She didn't know how close he had to get to satisfy his need, but he could walk closer if he wanted to, carefully staying out of range of the cameras. There would be some corners that they didn't cover. He didn't usually look in windows or do anything intrusive. But he had escalated to leaving notes in Bridget's mailbox, which was pretty disturbing.

She didn't find him in any of the streets surrounding the house. More than likely, he had come and gone already. He had maybe only been there for a few minutes, just long enough to satisfy himself that Bridget and the twins were still okay, and then he had gone on with his day.

Kenzie pulled over and took out her phone to check his updated position. His location marker was still there where she had seen it. But he wasn't parked on the street. It must have been a malfunction. She had flipped out over a stuck location pin. Kenzie closed the app and opened it again, then waited for Zachary's location pin to come up. It was still in the same place. There must be something wrong with it, maybe on Zachary's end. She tried calling him again without any luck.

Eventually, she drove her car slowly down the street until her signal and Zachary's were right on top of each other. She looked around again for his car. It wasn't there. She looked in the undergrowth of a stand of trees to see if he were hiding there. She tried phoning him once more, and this time her eyes caught a flash of light. She walked up to Zachary's phone, lying in the gutter against the curb.

CHAPTER 52

Zachary awoke groggily once more. He tried to rouse himself properly to figure out where he was and what was happening, but he couldn't break free of the sedative. He was vaguely aware that he had been at home. There had been people in his house. There had been an emergency. He knew that he was no longer at home. It didn't feel right. The sounds and smells were not right. The bed did not feel like Kenzie's bed. He could remember her talking about his taking an ambulance. There had been sirens. Had there been a fire?

The thought didn't send him into a panic attack as it normally would. The drugs he was on were too strong. He only wondered briefly, curiously, as if it were someone else's life. Maybe there had been a fire, and he had been sent to the hospital to recover. He wasn't in pain.

The thoughts passed through his brain slowly and he drifted out of consciousness between them. A very long time had passed before he could start evaluating his state. If there had been a fire, he didn't seem to have been hurt in it this time. His throat was not raw. His skin was not burning. In a moment of stronger consciousness, he ran his fingers over his arms and could not feel an IV. So his lack of pain was not due to a morphine drip. That was good. He allowed himself to rest.

As the sedatives gradually wore off, he knew he was in a hospital. So something must have happened. He could vaguely remember talking to Kenzie about overdosing and suicide, but he couldn't make it fit into a timeline that made any sense. Had he intentionally taken too many pills? He was pretty sure that he hadn't. It was summer, and his deep depressive cycle always happened in the winter as Christmas approached. Unless something else had triggered it, like when Bridget had kicked him out. He had walked around in a fog for months after that.

The thought of Bridget made him open his eyes and he tried to hold on to conscious, logical thought. Had something happened to Bridget? He was worried about her. And the twins. Not just his usual uneasiness and compulsion to go see her, but a directed, immediate concern. What had happened? Where was she? Had he left the house to find her? Had she been kidnapped?

He could remember hands holding him back. He was sure he had gone to the house. And then he had done something stupid. He could picture himself banging on her front door, demanding she open it and talk to him. He could feel hands on his body, pulling him back, forcing him into restraints. Handcuffs. She'd called the police. What had made him go there? Maybe that was why he was in the hospital. He had shown up at Bridget's house, a raving lunatic, demanding to see her, and the police had decided to invoke Title 18 to put him on an involuntary psychiatric hold. He had still been out of control when he got to the hospital, so they had sedated him.

Zachary looked around the room, but something was wrong. He was still too groggy to get out of bed or call a nurse. He just lay in the bed looking around him, trying to make sense of it.

He wasn't in the psych ward at the hospital. He had been there enough times to recognize it immediately. The walls were a pale green instead of white. There was wood trim around the doors. Instead of acoustic tile overhead, there was a flat ceiling. But it still looked like a hospital. Metal hospital bed. Small side table. A rolling table for meals. A call button for the nurse and a pull chain for the light over his bed. It was light outside, so he didn't need to turn it on. He looked out the window. He was too low to see anything but a piece of the sky and some treetops. Not the view from the psych ward.

He wanted to get up and investigate further, but he was still too doped up. He closed his eyes and drifted for a while longer.

CHAPTER 53

Kenzie was barely holding on to her panic. If she had to endure it for much longer, she was going to lose her mind. She stood there with Zachary's phone in one hand and her own phone in the other, waiting for the police to arrive.

The first person she had thought to call was Mario Bowman. He was a good friend of Zachary's and knew him well. He wouldn't just brush something like this off. If Kenzie had called 9-1-1, the dispatcher might have decided it was a lower priority. A man having dropped his phone and left the scene was not an emergency. Adult missing persons were not a priority unless there was some sign of struggle or evidence of violence. Kenzie could not see any blood on the pavement. There were no signs of a struggle other than the dropped cell phone with a cracked screen. It could have been dropped accidentally, even driven over by the car. There was nothing to indicate that Zachary hadn't left voluntarily. He could be at home. He could be at the grocery store. Most adult missing persons showed up within 48 hours, none the worse for wear.

But she knew that Mario would understand. Zachary had lived with him for several months after the apartment fire, when he'd had nowhere else to go. He and Kenzie had not been together yet. They had gone on a couple of dates, but she wasn't about to invite a mentally ill person she barely knew to live with her for an indefinite period of time until he managed to replace all of his ID, get access to his bank account, get the payout from his insurance company, and find an apartment of his own. Instead, she had called Mario, and he had agreed to put Zachary up for a few days. Mario knew that if Zachary didn't have his phone with him, something was wrong. Whether Zachary had suffered a psychotic break or someone had kidnapped him, Kenzie didn't know. But she needed to find him. The police needed to investigate immediately, not put it off until it was too late.

She felt strangled. She couldn't get enough oxygen. Every time she let herself wonder what could possibly have happened to Zachary, her mind returned to her own kidnapping. Men jumping out of a van, grabbing her, manhandling her, throwing her into a van with a bag over her head. The utter panic and loss of control. She had been terrified. Hurt and helpless and unable to do anything to help herself. Remembering all of the van's turns and what kinds of roads they had passed over like in TV shows? No way. She had no idea what direction they had gone or what turns they had taken. There was no cobbled road, no ringing church bell or railway crossing. Nothing that she could use to orient herself to place. She felt displaced, lost in space. She was out of control of her own body, unable to make any decisions for herself.

A siren started in the distance and got gradually closer. Kenzie didn't dare hope that it was in response to her call to Mario, but the wail grew louder and louder until the squad car pulled onto the street and she waved it down.

The two uniformed officers were not much help. They were there to secure the scene, to evaluate whether there was a need for an emergency response. Still, they were not the ones who would be investigating Zachary's disappearance and making a decision about what response to take. They nodded gravely as they looked at Zachary's cell phone and walked around looking at the ground for any other clues. They took down the information about Zachary's missing car and put out a BOLO for it. They repeatedly asked what evidence Kenzie had that something had happened to Zachary, unwilling to accept a dropped cell phone as evidence of anything malevolent.

About half an hour had passed when Gordon showed up. Kenzie assumed that he had been at the office, since it was the middle of the day, and that Bridget had called him when she saw the police car arrive. She knew Kenzie by sight. She would know that it had something to do with Zachary. But since Zachary himself wasn't there to yell at and abuse, she hadn't come out of the house herself. She was in frail health and had twin girls to worry about. She wouldn't want anything to do with the police.

Gordon parked his car in the garage of the big house and emerged. He crossed the street to talk to Kenzie. The police officers did not keep him from walking up to her. They hadn't put up any yellow tape to keep people away from any evidence that might have been left behind. Though Kenzie had to admit that if there was any evidence, it was certainly not obvious. No black tire tracks. No blood. No footprints.

"Kenzie. What's going on?" Gordon asked, putting out both hands to take hers in what was half a handshake, half a comforting squeeze.

"Zachary has disappeared. His phone was here. On the road. In the gutter." Kenzie showed it to him. "I don't know what happened. But something... I can't get ahold of him if he doesn't have his phone. I don't know where he would go. I'm afraid... something might have happened to him."

Gordon looked around, as if Zachary might be hiding in the trees or watching from somewhere nearby. His eyes were sharp and calculating. He gave a nod. "I'll check the security feed."

Kenzie squeezed his hand in response, grateful that he didn't see a need to stand there and argue about whether it might or might not be an emergency. He was a practical man, and seeing whether his surveillance cameras had picked anything up was the best way to figure out what had happened. He motioned to one of the police officers. "With me," he ordered.

There was no question in his mind that the officer would obey. The uniformed policeman looked startled, then offended at being ordered around, and then had fallen into step with him. Gordon's attitude and the wealthy neighborhood they were in suggested he would do well to just do as he was told. If he didn't, there would be complaints, and complaints from citizens like Gordon could mean an officer's job.

The other cop looked at Kenzie. “Who was that?”

“Gordon Drake. He owns the house over there.” She indicated Gordon’s big white mansion across the street from where they stood. “He owns a very successful investment banking firm.”

“Drake Chase Gould?” The officer said the firm name almost reverently.

“Yes.”

He looked at the house and gave a low whistle. “And he’s friends with your missing man? Goldman?”

“They’re not friends, exactly. Zachary has done work for Gordon. Gordon is married to Zachary’s ex-wife.”

After saying it, Kenzie wasn’t sure whether Gordon and Bridget were married or whether it was a common-law relationship. Not that it mattered. The cop didn’t need to know the legal details.

"I'd better follow up on this," the officer muttered, walking away from Kenzie to make an additional report on his radio. The connection to Gordon Drake had obviously made a difference. No one wanted to do anything that would result in bad press for the police, for suggestions that they had just stood around and done nothing when a prominent community member had been kidnapped. Zachary's complex relationship with Gordon Drake at least raised his importance in their minds.

Kenzie paced back and forth, trying to keep herself under control. The flashbacks to her own kidnapping were bad. Not like Zachary's flashbacks, where he actually relived the fire of his childhood, but she remembered everything vividly, and her thoughts and breathing raced as though she had run a race. She leaned against her car, counting out her breaths, trying to extend them long enough that she did not hyperventilate. Passing out would not move things forward.

Eventually, Gordon came back out of the house. The cop was not with him. He touched Kenzie's shoulder. "Are you okay?"

"Not doing very well," Kenzie admitted. "Was there anything on the tape?"

He nodded. He opened the door to Kenzie's car and motioned for her to sit. Kenzie gathered that the news was not good. Her knees folded and she sat on the seat sideways, feet hanging out the door.

"What is it? What happened?"

Gordon nodded slowly, confirming all of Kenzie's fears. He bit his lip, trying to decide how to break it to Kenzie, before releasing the words. "He was abducted."

CHAPTER 54

A nurse entered the room. Zachary watched her through mostly-closed eyelids, lying still so as not to give away the fact that he was awake. His automatic reaction on finding himself in such a situation was to hide, to play possum and not give away to anyone what he was thinking. He still couldn't remember exactly what had happened. It was all jumbled up in his head and he couldn't work the timeline out. He still thought that it must have been Kenzie who had sent him to the hospital, but he couldn't figure out why or in what order things had happened.

"How are you feeling, Mr. Goldman?" the nurse asked him briskly.

Zachary didn't answer. She studied his face, then shook his arm. "Mr. Goldman. I need you to talk to me, please. Wake up."

Zachary reluctantly opened his eyes. If he didn't at least put on some show, she wouldn't leave him alone.

“That’s better,” she approved. “How are you feeling?”

Zachary looked around the room slowly. He weighed his answer, wishing he understood more about what he was doing there. “Little groggy,” he told her eventually.

“That’s to be expected. Are you thirsty?” She picked up a cup from the side table and held the straw to his mouth.

Zachary’s mouth was parched, so he sipped the water eagerly. A number of meds had dry mouth as a common side effect, so she probably knew he would be thirsty. And if he’d been deeply under, as he thought, he had probably been sleeping with his mouth open.

“Thank you,” he whispered as she put it back on the side table.

She nodded and took his wrist, checking his pulse. There was still enough sedative in his system that Zachary didn’t have to worry about a racing pulse giving away his anxiety over the situation. His body felt very slow and sluggish.

"Nice and strong," she told him with a smile. "And how are you feeling? Emotionally? You were quite distressed when you were brought in."

"I don't remember. Why... why was I brought here?"

"You were having some emotional difficulties." She picked up a paper chart and flipped through it. "You have a history of psychiatric admissions. So I don't imagine that comes as a surprise to you."

"Well... a little. I usually admit myself."

She nodded and made a note on the front page. "Have you been taking your meds?"

"Yes."

"Are you sure? You haven't been skipping doses? Leaving something off because you don't like how it makes you feel?"

"Well... not lately. The last few days. I've been taking everything for... the last week."

She raised her brows at him and made another note on his chart. "It can take a few weeks for some of the medications to reach full efficacy. Though I wouldn't have expected you to be as unstable as you were if you've been taking everything for a week. Are you sure about that?"

"Yes."

She didn't believe him. But Zachary supposed that patients probably often lied about whether they were med-compliant. They would have to test his blood to see what the various chemical levels were to determine the truth.

"Where am I?" Zachary asked. He looked around the room again. "This isn't the hospital."

"It is a private facility."

"Where? Who put me here? I don't understand what happened."

"I'm sure it will all come back to you as we get you stabilized again. In the meantime, just know that your loved ones care for you and want you to get better."

"I was stable," Zachary insisted. "What happened?"

"You had a psychotic break."

Zachary shook his head. He'd had breakdowns before. Meltdowns. Physical collapse. Panic attacks. Depressions that left him unable to do anything for himself. But a psychotic break? That didn't fit his profile. He didn't suffer from psychosis, unless he was put on a med that caused a reaction, which hadn't happened for a long time. He had been stable when he'd been released from the hospital. And the only meds he'd taken were the ones he'd been on for over six months. It didn't make sense that he would suddenly go off the rails.

"I don't have psychosis."

She chuckled. "I think you know that's not true."

"I don't. I have depression. Anxiety. PTSD. But not psychosis."

"You were raving when they brought you in. Paranoid. Sure that you were being attacked and abducted. Abducted by who?" She shook her head, eyes twinkling. "Little green men, maybe?"

"No." Zachary was stung. "I don't have delusions about aliens. About anything. Just what I said. Depression. When I've been admitted to the hospital, it has been for depression."

"Okay. Well, I will leave the diagnoses and a discussion of your patient history to the doctors. It's not my place. My job is to ensure you are comfortable here and have everything you need. Is there anything I can get you? I don't imagine you're ready to eat anything yet."

"Where's my phone? I need to call Kenzie. My partner."

"Your personal belongings have been safely stored. Your partner knows where you are. When you have stabilized, I'm sure she'll be in to see you. Right now, we don't want any visitors. You need to be focused on yourself. Your mental health."

"Kenzie needs to know—"

"I told you, your family has been filled in. What you need right now is rest." She looked at her watch. "And you are due for a refill." She placed a paper pill cup on the table and counted various pills into it. They were not familiar to Zachary. He felt panic rising. He knew what the meds he was supposed to be on looked like. He knew what all of them looked like, his regular meds and any emergency rescue doses. And the ones she was dispensing were not right.

"Those aren't my pills."

She picked up his chart and looked at it, her eyes flicking back and forth between the pill cup and whatever was written on his chart. “No, that’s all good. Down the hatch.”

“Somebody wrote them down wrong. That’s not right.”

“Well,” she smiled sweetly, “Why don’t you go ahead and take them anyway, and you can talk to the doctor about them when he does his rounds? You’re doing much better than you were. We don’t want you to lose ground.”

Zachary looked at the cup of pills and then at the nurse. While she smiled and used a pleasant, encouraging voice—and not that “talking to a child” voice that some people adopted when dealing with the mentally ill—there was a certain hardness to her eyes. She might be softly encouraging now but, if he refused to follow her orders, he could see that there would be consequences. If they put him on an IV, he wouldn’t be able to see or control what they put into his body.

Zachary slowly reached for the dosing cup and emptied the pills into his mouth. The nurse picked up the cup of water again and offered it to him. Zachary washed the pills down.

“Let’s see,” she said briskly, obviously having been trained in compliance. “Mouth open. Stick out your tongue.”

Zachary obeyed her instructions to prove he had swallowed the pills—nothing in his cheeks or under his tongue.

“Thank you,” she told him sincerely. “I’m glad you are cooperating with your treatment. You will feel a lot better.”

Zachary nodded. “I think… I still need to sleep.”

“Yes, you do. Lie down and close your eyes. Get some more rest. Being short on sleep can exacerbate mental health problems.”

Zachary settled back into his pillow and closed his eyes. The nurse spent a minute writing something down on the chart, still watching him, and eventually hung the clipboard at the end of the bed and left the room.

It was rare to see a paper chart anymore. Most of the hospitals were using electronic records and tablets. Another clue that this was not the hospital Zachary was used to, as if he needed any more proof.

He counted to sixty after the nurse was gone to make sure that she wasn't going to peek in on him again or come back for something that she had "forgotten." Then he opened his eyes and slid his feet out of bed. He was still feeling very unsteady, but he needed to make it to the little bathroom across the room, and he needed to do it quickly.

He ended up walking around the room's perimeter so he could keep his hands on the wall and not fall over. The solidity of the wall helped him to feel more grounded and connected to his body, as did the cold tile under his bare feet. He was lightheaded and weak and it took a long time to get around the room.

He reached the bathroom and entered, shutting and locking the door behind him. He was sure the nurses could open it anyway, but it would slow them down a few more seconds.

He hovered over the toilet and threw up.

CHAPTER 55

The detective who had shown up to spearhead the kidnapping investigation was El Garcia, who Kenzie really didn't want to work with. Garcia had been helping Zachary with his investigation into John Godfrey's murder, and Kenzie hadn't appreciated how closely she had worked with him. They had spent too much time too close together.

Maybe nothing had happened, but that wasn't the point. Garcia should have kept her distance. Cops didn't work with private investigators. She could have gotten the information she needed from Zachary and pursued it independently.

To top it off, Garcia didn't think that Kenzie should see the recording that Gordon had queued up.

"It is going to be too upsetting," Garcia told him. "We don't show family footage like this."

"I can handle it. I want to see what happened. I want to know if I recognize the... people."

"Leave it to the police."

"Gordon," Kenzie turned and appealed to him. "Please. Show it to me now or send a copy to my phone. I want to see it."

Gordon's eyes flicked from Garcia to Kenzie. "I don't want to be guilty of interfering in a police investigation."

"That's your own private recording, taken on your own equipment. You are sharing it with the police. You can share it with whoever else you like."

He looked at Garcia, who nodded.

"I may as well show it to you both now, then," Gordon said. "If neither of you has any objection."

Garcia had the grace to back off. She knew when she was beaten. Kenzie was going to see that recording one way or another. There was no point in wasting time arguing about it.

Gordon pressed play, and they all watched the large screen he had displayed it on. Zachary pulled up to the road in front of the house. Looked out his window for a moment, his pale face barely distinguishable through the glass. Then he parked and stepped out of the car. He looked all around, up and down the street, checking to see if anyone was watching him, Kenzie assumed.

He looked at the house again. His face was grim and determined. Not relieved that he had been able to get another glimpse of Bridget's house without being caught. Not the hit of dopamine from feeding his addiction. He was still tense, waiting, worried about something.

After another look, he leaned back against his car and started to type something on his phone.

A dark figure moved out of the trees beside the car and leveled a gun at Zachary's head before he finished turning to see what was going on. Zachary's mouth was open in a wide 'O.' Despite the gun pointed an inch from his face, he still tried to run. He twisted around and tried to sprint in the other direction. But another man was coming up from behind and, between the two large, solidly-built men, they managed to subdue Zachary and wrestle him into a pair of flexicuffs that held his wrists in place and wouldn't allow any twisting.

Kenzie was relieved that they hadn't used the gun. There was hope that Zachary was still alive and well. A van pulled up, and one of the men threw Zachary into it and climbed in behind him. Kenzie rubbed her forehead, the place she had hit her head when she was abducted, which suddenly flared with pain so startling it made her gasp. She knew it had healed months before, but it still hurt. Knowing it was psychological pain did not make it any less.

Gordon looked at her with concern. Garcia glanced over, but said nothing, not pointing out that she had warned Kenzie that the video would be too distressing for her. Kenzie watched the final few seconds as the one kidnapper shut the side door of the van and it sped away. The other man climbed into

Zachary's car, keys still in the ignition, moved the seat back to accommodate his taller form, and drove away. Leaving behind the phone, which had flown from Zachary's hand during the struggle.

Kenzie thought about the final text from Zachary. The moment he had started typing into his phone before the two men had appeared.

I am

He had started to send her a message. What? "I am at Bridget's"? Why would he tell her that? "I am going to be late getting home"? That didn't make much more sense. But he had been about to tell her something, seconds before the abduction.

"Why was he here?" Kenzie burst out.

Gordon just shook his head. They both knew why Zachary had been there. Because he was obsessed with Bridget and couldn't help himself.

But how had the abductors known that he would be there?

Why had he been taken?

None of it made any sense.

* * *

Zachary slept little. He dozed off a couple of times, his body still trying to shake the effects of whatever sedative and antipsychotics they had given him. And maybe another small dose that he had absorbed before managing to rid his stomach of the pills the nurse had given him.

They would expect him to sleep for several hours, which was good, because it gave him more time to shake the effects of the earlier dose and figure out what he was doing there and how to get out.

As he came out of the drug-induced fog, he became more and more sure that Kenzie had not sent him there. It might be the kind of thing that she would have done if he'd had a psychotic break. Taking him to a private clinic for treatment instead of to the hospital. She had paid for Tyrrell's stay in the recovery retreat where he had dried out and gotten back on the wagon after his latest binge. It had been better than the public programs and would, Zachary hoped, "stick" this time so that Tyrrell continued to get better and was able to stay on track.

But he hadn't had a psychotic break.

He could only remember bits and pieces of the night before, when he had overdosed on the sleeping pills. Those memories, while fragmented, made sense. They fit in with the rest of the mental narrative. What he was sure had happened. Kenzie hadn't taken him to the hospital or a clinic, but had stayed with him, watching over him to make sure that he didn't stop breathing. He had woken up in the morning. They had talked, had spent time together. All of that made sense.

After that, it fell apart. He couldn't remember for sure anything that had happened after that. He remembered being grabbed, forced into the clinic against his will, and shouting that he was being kidnapped. Of course, anyone watching would think he was having an episode. That he was paranoid or delusional. That he had broken with reality. And then they had injected him with whatever had put him to sleep, and who knew how long that had lasted.

Had he only slept for a few hours? For a full day? Did Kenzie realize he was gone or was she still at work, finishing her day at the morgue? He knew it was getting late in the day because the sun was getting lower in the sky.

But which day was it?

CHAPTER 56

Can you unlock that?" Garcia indicated Zachary's phone.

Kenzie looked at it. She and Zachary had never shared their passwords. Did couples do that, or did they keep their passcodes secret from each other too?

It probably depended on how close they were and whether they kept confidential information on their phones. It was not something she had ever talked to her friends about. Maybe it was just something that everybody assumed. Like that everyone had a joint bank account if they were living together. Or at least if they were married. But there had to be people who still kept their finances separate and never intended to share accounts with each other.

Or passwords.

"Uh... I don't know." Kenzie tried to remember Zachary's thumb movements whenever he unlocked his phone with his number code instead of his fingerprint. She could vaguely see the pattern in her mind, and she worked through their birthdates and phone numbers to see whether she could find the digits he had typed. She made a couple of guesses, but they were rejected, and she knew that if she entered too many, she would get locked out of the phone for a short period of time. And it would keep locking for longer each time she guessed wrong. She wasn't sure if it would ever lock down and erase permanently. Zachary might just have set something like that up, bricking the phone in case someone made a serious attempt to break into it.

"Let me find out whether Heather knows," Kenzie told Garcia, who was waiting for Kenzie to guess the right code.

Kenzie found Heather's number on her own phone.

"Who is Heather?" Garcia asked. "I know about you and Bridget. Is Heather another ex?"

"No. His older sister. And she helps out with the business, so she would be more likely to know his passcodes. If he uses the same one across different accounts or devices, she might know..."

"He's a private investigator. He would know that doing that would leave him more open to a security breach."

"I know. But sometimes people aren't worried about that. Or if he doesn't have anything on his phone that he cares about, just some personal contact numbers and chats..."

"He uses it for work. He had those Godfrey documents scanned into it," Garcia reminded her.

"Well... yes. But Heather might know. She's in business with him."

Garcia turned and took a couple of steps away. She didn't go to talk to one of the other law enforcement officers or to look at the kidnap scene again, she was just giving Kenzie a small semblance of privacy while she placed the call.

“Hi, Kenzie.” Heather’s voice was pleasant and friendly, as always.

“Heather. I have sort of a situation here. I have Zachary’s phone, and he’s not here, and I need to unlock it. Do you know his code?”

There was not an immediate answer from Heather. Kenzie could imagine her thinking this through, trying to understand how Kenzie had Zachary’s phone and why she needed to get into it.

“What’s going on?” she asked finally.

“I don’t want to worry you, but…” Kenzie couldn’t think of any way to soften it or pretend it wasn’t as serious as it was. How could she not worry Heather? Did she think she could call and ask for private information and not tell Heather what was happening? “Zachary has… well, he’s been abducted.” Kenzie’s guts tied in knots, fighting her own visceral reaction to the word. She could still hardly even say it without being flooded with memories and emotions she could not control.

Heather gasped and swore. “What? When did this happen? Do you know who it was? Why?”

At least she didn’t say, “Are you kidding?” which seemed to be the default when people were told bad or shocking news. Kenzie couldn’t count the number of times that she’d listened to police make a notification of a death, and the first words out of the friend or family member’s mouth always seemed to be, “Are you kidding?” As if someone would make a joke about a tragic death.

Or a kidnapping.

“It was a few hours ago. The police are here and investigating it now. I’m sure they’ll get it sorted out and Zachary will be fine. But it would be helpful if we could get into his phone.”

Heather recited a string of numbers, and Kenzie tapped them in. The phone unlocked. Kenzie tried to place the numbers, but they didn't match up to anything she was aware of in Zachary's life. No birthday, anniversary, address, phone number, or pattern. Did anyone actually use random numbers? Did Zachary?

"Thank you." Kenzie turned to hand the phone to Garcia, to find her right there at her elbow, already snatching the phone from her hand. "Do the numbers mean anything?"

Heather chuckled. "An old junior high locker combination."

"Zachary's?"

"Mine. He just memorized it. He wanted something that wasn't related to him, that no one could guess."

"Well, that certainly fits the bill."

"What can I do, Kenzie? Do we know if this is related to a case? What information do you need? I can drop everything and do research for you."

"I don't know. I don't have a clue what to do at this point. If it is related to a case..." Kenzie gazed at Gordon's house, trying to imagine how Gordon had become involved in it. Had the kidnappers just followed Zachary and picked him up when he had stopped? No, they had been there already, lying in wait. They had known that he would be there. "I guess if it is related to a case, then it is probably the one he is working on for that old school friend. Jennifer. Her daughter's death. He's looking into the biotech company that developed LipoSlayerRx. And... well, I've dealt with big pharma before, and they are very cutthroat."

"You're talking about TrimProGenix?" Heather asked promptly.

"Yes. That's right. Did he have you do any work on them?"

"Some background. I'll pull up everything that I gathered for him and dive into it a bit deeper. What do you need?"

"From the research I did," Kenzie told Heather, "The product testing was... not very complete. I would say it was rushed to market. We don't know how dangerous it might be or what the risk factors for an adverse reaction are. Or if it is safe for kids."

"Big surprise there," Heather said cynically. "I guess I'll start with the financial end. Follow the money. See if I can tell who had the best financial motive to get Zachary out of the way. There hasn't been a ransom demand...?"

"No. Nothing like that. They haven't been in contact. The only way we know that it was an abduction and not just... Zachary wandering off and leaving his phone behind is because we have it on video."

"That's good. It was at the house, then?"

"No." Kenzie swallowed. She hated sharing the intimate details with Heather, feeling like doing so might be breaking her trust with Zachary. But if anyone could help with the investigation and possibly point them in the right direction, it was Zachary's business partner. "It was outside of Bridget's house."

"Bridget's?" Heather's voice rose. "Oh, Zachary! What was he doing there? Actually, you don't need to tell me. I know exactly what he was doing there."

"No. It was an ambush. The abductors were there ahead of him."

"And you're sure Gordon Drake didn't sic them on him? If he was tired of Zachary showing up and bothering Bridget, Drake certainly has the money to hire someone to remove him. Maybe he figures if he throws a big enough scare into Zachary, he'll stop."

CHAPTER 57

Kenzie hadn't considered anything along these lines. She shook her head. "No... I can't see him having anything to do with it, and he seemed very shocked by it all. He was at work at the time and, when he returned, he checked the video and found the footage of the kidnapping."

"That doesn't mean he wasn't involved, just that he's a good actor."

"Well... I suppose so." Gordon had always struck Kenzie as being too smooth, too mild and considerate. Particularly concerning Zachary. What kind of person was that patient with his wife's stalker? And would actually hire her ex for a job? There had to be something wrong with someone like that. Gordon Drake had more secrets than most people would ever accumulate in a lifetime. "I don't get that feeling, but I'll think about it. We'll consider it."

"Tell me if there is anything else you need. I'll be by the phone. Call or text me and I'll be right on it."

"Thanks, Heather. I really appreciate it. I'll let you know if we make any progress."

Kenzie hung up the phone. There wasn't any easy way to end that conversation. But talking to Heather wasn't going to tell Kenzie where Zachary was. She looked at Garcia.

"We'll consider what?" Garcia asked immediately, not even pretending she hadn't listened in on the conversation.

"Uh—whether he might have been involved," Kenzie jerked her head slightly toward Gordon's house. She didn't want anyone to overhear her accusing such a wealthy and influential person of kidnapping. She didn't have any desire to face a lawsuit for defamation.

“Oh.” Garcia nodded. “Yeah, we’re already on to that possibility. He’s married to the ex and the kidnapping goes down in front of his house? Of course we’re all over it.”

“Okay. I don’t think it was Gordon.”

“You think it was to do with a case.”

“That’s the best that I can come up with, yes. He was working a case that... could have caused trouble for a big pharma corporation. And I know from dealing with that kind of company before what the culture is like. A kidnapping wouldn’t be beyond the realm of possibility if they thought it was the only way to shut Zachary up.”

Of course, there were much more permanent ways to shut someone up. She had seen those implemented before too. But she took comfort in the fact that if they had wanted to kill Zachary, they could have shot him down in the street more easily than kidnapping him. By snatching him, they signaled that they didn’t want to kill him. That they thought they could get what they wanted with just a warning, or if they kept him off of the scene for long enough.

“Give me that information too,” Garcia ordered. She wasn’t really a people person, Kenzie noted to herself. She made no attempt to soften her words by making them sound like a polite request instead of an order. She didn’t try to calm Kenzie or tell her that she was sure they would find Zachary alive and well.

“Is there anyone else?” Garcia asked. “What about the ex herself? Could she have arranged something like this without her husband’s knowledge or involvement? I understand the woman is unstable.”

Garcia had been involved in the investigation when the twins had been snatched. As far as Kenzie knew, she hadn’t had the chance to interview Bridget in that case, since she had already been sedated by the time the detective had gotten there. She had been quite hysterical when the police arrived on the scene, which aggravated her Huntington's symptoms. She hadn't been much help during that investigation.

"I don't think that Bridget would have done anything like this. Not after having had to go through it herself."

"You never know. That might have been exactly what triggered the idea. She wanted Zachary out of the picture, so why not just have him removed?"

"I just... don't think she would have had anything to do with it. You can talk to her, but..."

"Of course I will. If he was harassing her... She might have gotten to the end of her rope."

Kenzie nodded her agreement.

Garcia handed Zachary's phone back to Kenzie. "I don't see anything on this. See if you see anything that doesn't belong or raises alarm bells. It might be something completely different, unrelated to the case or Bridget."

“Thanks.” Kenzie took the still-unlocked phone back. She brought up the list of most recently used applications. She would go through each of them individually to backtrack what he had been doing. If something he had done had triggered the kidnapping, then maybe she could figure out what it was. And more importantly, who it was.

CHAPTER 58

Zachary's mind grew more and more clear as the sun went down and the room dimmed. He was still unsure what to do about it or who had brought him there, but things were becoming clearer. If he managed to fool them into thinking that he was still under the influence of the strong sedatives, maybe he could escape from the facility. He hadn't yet tried the door to see whether he was locked in or only under chemical restraints. He hadn't heard the nurse unlock the door, but he had still been pretty groggy and some door locks were almost silent, and were just unlocked with a proximity card rather than an old-fashioned door key. He wouldn't necessarily be able to hear it unlocking or locking.

There were more voices outside his room than he had heard during the time he had been awake. Not just the nurses calling back and forth to each other or gossiping as they performed their duties, but strong male voices, which Zachary couldn't help noticing did not sound too happy.

The door handle turned and visitors entered. Zachary was pretty sure that it wasn't going to be Kenzie or Tyrrell. They didn't know where he was. Someone else had taken him and was keeping him hidden while they decided what to do with him. He didn't delude himself into thinking that they would keep him there indefinitely. It was a temporary measure. And when they had made a decision, it probably would not mean good things for him.

The two men who entered would not be able to see him clearly in the dimness. They would be able to see him lying still in the bed, but they would not be able to see his eyelids cracked open just a little. Just enough to see them through the fringes of his eyelashes.

Two men in lab coats. Larger than he was. Most men were, especially the younger generations, who seemed to grow like weeds, topping their own parents by inches.

"He's been quiet," one of the men said. "Hasn't caused any trouble. The nurse said that he was awake earlier. She gave him the meds and he has been down the rest of the day."

"How much does she know about what's going on?"

"Nothing." The first man, his voice slightly younger and higher, shrugged. "All she knows is that he was brought here in a state of emotional turmoil and needed to be sedated. He has a long psychiatric history, so we didn't need to fake anything there. Maybe an admission or two," he temporized, "but the guy is a nut without us having to make him out to be one. She's used to dealing with people like that."

"We still won't be able to keep him here for long."

"Have you decided, then? What you're going to do with him?"

The other man was silent, thinking about it or unwilling to share his conclusion. Zachary admitted to himself that he didn't really want to hear what had been decided. It wasn't likely to be anything good. They wouldn't brush him off and say that it had all been a mistake and he was free to return to his own business.

"There are others who need to be consulted. This is turning into a mess. Everything was supposed to be so carefully planned out, and now it's all getting out of hand. It's only a matter of time until they decide to pull Rx. They'll say it is just for further testing, but you know it will never hit the market again."

"It's been so lucrative," the higher-voiced man protested, as if that would change anything. "It's miraculous. If it didn't work, that would be one thing, but it does! It could be the answer to obesity in America."

"It's had a good run, but it will go the same way all other miraculous cures have gone," the older said gruffly, "An initial run, changing lives, the whole way society looks at disease, and then... it will be discarded as far as the public is concerned. We will use it as the starting point for other drugs with other names, some of them for completely different things. But this heyday... this pay day, will be gone."

"And Goldman?"

"People like our Mr. Goldman, who get in the way of a runaway cart... get run over. He chose to dig into things that were none of his business. One death. Do you know how many people die from obesity-related diseases every day? How important is one child dying in surgery from an unrelated condition? And why should it prevent every other porker from being able to get her hands on the miracle cure if she's willing to pay the price? Why isn't every responsible parent trying to get this prescription for their little fatties? We've barely touched the market."

"How long can we keep it going? If Goldman hadn't stumbled onto this and started to make noise in the wrong places, how much longer would we have had? Is there any way we could extend it longer if... he is silenced?"

"You're still after your nice fat bonuses?" the deeper voice mocked. "You haven't been paid enough?"

"I just see that there's so much of a larger target market out there. We've barely scratched the surface. It's viral and still pulls in thousands of new customers daily, legitimate and aftermarket. We don't want to lose that."

"If Goldman is silenced," the deeper voice got deeper and quieter still, so Zachary had to strain to make it out. "If his voice can be silenced and no one else takes up the torch... we could still have months left. Billions of dollars."

"He's just one person. He's not that well-known. It should be easy."

"Yes," the other agreed. "It should be."

There was silence as they both considered this.

"But didn't you say... you had to consult with others?"

"And I do," the bass acknowledged. "That takes time, and we must be very careful how we go about this, who is part of the discussion. But if something were to happen to him before a decision was made?" Zachary could see the man shrug. "That would be out of my hands."

The two of them stood there and finally withdrew, letting the door shut behind them. Zachary listened for a click or whir, but it was impossible to tell whether the door was automatically locked or not.

But it didn't sound like the men were taking any chances.

They had confirmed it was to do with Rx and his investigation into Kristin's death. At least he knew that much.

He had attracted too much attention, made too much noise, and not figured out that word of his questions would get back to management of TrimProGenix. Had Rain talked to her father about it? Had Dr. Race contacted the company to let them know what was happening? Or had it been somebody else that he hadn't even thought of? He had to wonder whether the medical examiner's office in Burlington had anything to do with it, losing Kristin's smartwatch as they had. Lost? Or intentionally thrown out or destroyed? Had they really assumed that Kristin had been injecting insulin without checking with the next of kin? Or had they known all along it was Rx?

Everybody had been happy to go with the medical examiner's report that Kristin had died from natural causes, until Jennifer had hired Zachary. Once they knew the report was being questioned, TrimProGenix had started to target Zachary and Kenzie. And who was in a better position to know that there was a relationship between Zachary and Kenzie than another branch of the medical examiner's office?

CHAPTER 59

Kenzie worked on Zachary's phone, hoping to find something that would lead them to the kidnappers. She quickly discovered she was right about Zachary being lured to Bridget's house. Just one brief text.

Do you really think you can keep them safe from us?

Zachary had concluded that "them" referred to Bridget and the twins. Or maybe just the twins. They had been kidnapped before, so of course he was protective of them. Anyone would be, not just someone with an obsession with Bridget. His concern for the babies was different. Not just an offshoot of his obsession with Bridget, but also of her refusal to have children with him and the way that he had taken care of his younger siblings for those first years of life until the fire that had destroyed the family home. Take a caring person, trained to take care of children from an early age, add an obsession with and multiple rejections from the mother, and could there be any doubt that he would rush immediately to the aid of the babies when they were threatened?

And someone had known enough about him to know that he would go.

But that probably included anyone who had read the news stories when he had rescued the twins after they were snatched just weeks before. The press had included as much information as possible about Zachary's and Bridget's connection and their relationship. They hadn't gone so far as to accuse Zachary of stalking her, but it had certainly been implied.

And for sure, much of the Roxboro police department knew about Zachary and Bridget, had known them while they were together, and were aware of how broken up he had been about the divorce. Bridget had a knack for drawing people to her, and she had quickly become a favorite of the cops Zachary knew.

Even those who were not well-disposed toward him. They still knew Bridget.

Garcia had already grabbed the information about where the text had come from. A burner phone that they would not be able to trace the ownership of, Kenzie was sure. It would be a dead end. Garcia had also ordered the footage from traffic cams in the surrounding streets to see how far they could track the van that had taken Zachary and his car as it was removed from the scene. If they were lucky, they might be able to follow it to its destination. But there was a lot of footage to check and, while they did that, Zachary was still locked in some hole somewhere, wondering if anybody were going to find him.

A text banner zipped across the top of the screen, and Kenzie tapped to open it. With her luck, it would just be a pizza delivery coupon.

She read through the message, and then read through it again.

There was no name attached to the phone number. Would Zachary have known who it was? Of course he would.

999 inset

mmurdoch@TrimProGenix.com

Pluviophile2!

Login at:

Followed by a string of numbers.

Kenzie stared at it for a few minutes. She needed to get to a computer. Whoever was helping Zachary out was expecting him to follow up on the information. She had no idea who Zachary had managed to contact who knew how to log in to the TrimProGenix system, but she wasn't going to let the information go to waste.

She could find her way around a company server, medical reports, and financial statements. After logging in, Zachary would probably have called Kenzie for her help and expertise anyway. She was the one who would be able to sift through and interpret the medical information he found.

Kenzie waved at Garcia, who was still directing the crime techs on the scene, hopefully collecting evidence that would help lead them to where the kidnappers had taken Zachary.

Garcia raised her brows questioningly and approached Kenzie. “What can I do for you, Dr. Kirsch? Did you find anything?”

Kenzie held up the phone. “I’m going to take this home and recharge it. Plug it into his computer and see if I’m missing anything. And I’ll check his laptop to see if there is any information there that might help us...”

Garcia nodded. “Sounds good. You have my information. Call me as soon as you find anything out. I’ll keep doing everything I can from here and then will move back to the police station to coordinate from there. We’re doing everything we can. The minute we find out where that van went from here, we will follow up on it.”

"I just can't believe this is happening. I appreciate you working on it."

"Of course. Adult missing persons don't always get the attention they deserve, but when you have clear evidence that it was an abduction and not just someone going off for a hike without their phone..."

"Yes. I guess we should be grateful for Gordon's surveillance."

Garcia gave a curt nod. "Give me a call anytime."

Dismissed, Kenzie walked back to her car. It seemed like a long time since she had left the medical examiner's office to find Zachary, thinking she would find him sitting in his car outside of Bridget's house. She hadn't noticed how dark it had grown, outside the pool of brightly illuminated crime scene. But it was night, only a streak of light left in the sky.

* * *

Spreading out Zachary's phone and laptop and Rain's phone and laptop around her on the living room floor, Kenzie could jump from one device to another to coordinate her investigation and get up to speed. Thanks to Heather, who had supplied her with Zachary's laptop login. Zachary had been diligently photographing the pages in his small notepad daily so that she could look at everything he had written down during the investigation. Which was actually very little. And even less of it was legible or made any sense to her. The case notes typed on the computer were better, a more complete record. Using Kristin's phone, she confirmed that Rain's last name was Murdoch. She had to be the person who had texted the login information to Zachary.

Kenzie logged in as soon as she could, hoping that Zachary's laptop would not be identified as an intruder. A username and password were not always all it took to log on anymore. There might be security questions, two-factor verification, biometrics, or a critical program or cookie that had to be present on the computer logging in.

But everything appeared to work without setting off any alarms.

Kenzie logged in to the server and started looking through the directory structure. Rain's father appeared to be high enough up in the organization to have rated access to all of the medical and financial information.

Kenzie performed a search for Kristin's name.

CHAPTER 60

Zachary allowed himself to be shaken awake by the nurse, making appropriate sleep noises and confused queries when she turned on the light and insisted on waking him up from his drug-induced stupor.

It wasn't the same nurse as before. Of course. That nurse would be at home, having supper, watching TV, and getting ready for bed. The night nurse was on in her place. They probably had three or four shifts.

"Mr. Goldman. You need to take your meds," she told him briskly, furnishing him with another cup full of pills.

Zachary rubbed his eyes. "What are these? What time is it?"

"Time for meds."

He picked them up and put them down. "These aren't right."

Not only were they not his prescriptions, but they were also not the pills he had been given earlier in the day either. What were they up to now? It didn't make sense to keep changing what he was given. There was too much risk of interactions, of giving two things that would cause a dangerous reaction. Three different sets of prescriptions in one day were more likely to cause psychosis than to cure it.

"Those are your night meds. They will help you to sleep," the nurse told him firmly.

"You woke me up to put me to sleep?"

She smiled at him. "That's what we do here. It might not seem very productive, but we want to get you back on your feet, don't we?"

"Not at night."

"No, not at night. These will help you sleep through, and you should feel calmer in the morning."

"I am calm." Zachary rubbed his forehead. "Any more, and I'll be catatonic."

The nurse gave a sympathetic grimace and shrugged. "You do seem to be doing much better now. I'm just following the doctor's orders. You will get a chance to talk to him tomorrow and can discuss any concerns with him then."

"Why didn't he come by today?"

"He did. You were sleeping at the time."

Zachary indicated the pills. "And if I take these, won't I be sleeping when he comes by tomorrow, too? I want to be able to be awake to talk to him."

"You won't still be sleeping tomorrow. These will just help you to get through the night."

"Do you know… what all of these are? I don't recognize them. Can you tell me what I'm taking?"

She looked hesitant, as if this weren't something she had anticipated his asking and she wasn't sure whether she was allowed to share this information with him.

“I’m the patient,” Zachary said, “I have a right to know what I’m taking.”

“Well... okay.” She spilled the pills onto his table and indicated each one with the point of her pen while she ran through a spiel about each one. Some of them he recognized, but there were a few chemical names he wasn’t familiar with. Which seemed strange, considering he had tried practically everything on the market. But then, he was familiar with the medications used to treat depression, anxiety, ADHD, and the other symptoms that he experienced. He didn’t take antipsychotics and might only recognize the biggest names on the market. And probably by their brand names, not their generic chemical names.

“I haven’t taken most of these before. Is it safe to start me on so many new meds at once? I’ve had reactions when I’ve started too many at the same time before.”

She thought about this, chewing on the inside of her cheek. “That’s what the doctor has prescribed, so it is safe,” she assured him. “If you have any problems, you can give me a call.” She indicated the call button within reach of the bed. “And, of course, you can discuss these concerns with the doctor tomorrow.”

“If I take them tonight.”

“I’m sure that you’ll be fine.”

Zachary wasn’t so sure. He gathered the pills together and dumped them back into the cup. “I’m going to need more water,” he advised. “I have trouble getting them down if I don’t have enough water.”

She nodded her agreement. She picked up the cup from his side table and went into the bathroom to refill it. Zachary jumped when the door opened and another nurse came into the room. He spilled the pills on his table and sheets. It was a male nurse this time. He was young and ruggedly handsome and had a prox card on a lanyard around his neck, confirming Zachary’s suspicions that the door was locked and probably had to be unlocked by the electronic proximity key before it was opened from either side. When he had visited Summit Living Center, they had a similar system where everyone wore a bracelet with an RFID chip embedded in it to unlock the door whenever a staff member reached for the doorknob.

Zachary swore and started to pick up the pills he had spilled. "You startled me. Don't you have rules about knocking before you enter a room? Patient privacy?"

The nurse looked embarrassed. "I'm sorry. Yes, we do. I wasn't thinking. I was in a hurry. I need to talk to nurse—" The young man looked around for the other nurse, just as she came out of the bathroom with Zachary's cup of water. "Oh, there you are. Do you have—"

"Can you help me?" Zachary demanded in a petulant tone, dropping one of the pills he had just picked up and missing the dosing cup. "My fingers just aren't working today..."

The new nurse stepped up to Zachary's bed and helped gather the pills together and put them back into the cup, chattering away with the female nurse as he did so about another patient's care. Another breach of privacy. Was it something they frequently did, or they just did it in this case because they knew Zachary wouldn't be there for long or that they wouldn't need to worry about him keeping his mouth shut? Were any of the nurses in on what was going on or were they oblivious, just following the instructions on Zachary's chart as if he were any other patient?

"Wait," Zachary insisted, as he downed a pill or two at a time with copious gulps of the water. His command kept both nurses there, waiting to see what he wanted.

"Can you call my doctor?" Zachary requested. "I don't know if she's been talking to the doctor here. She can give him more of my history and what has and hasn't worked before..."

"I'm sure the doctor has been in contact with your regular practitioner," the female nurse assured him. "We have your latest medical records here. Everything is in order."

"I have... a fairly lengthy history. You might need more than you have there," Zachary told her, eyeing the fairly thin stack of papers on the clipboard. "Can you just call her? Make sure she knows I'm here and what for? I'd feel a lot better." He lay back against his pillow. "I don't know if I'll be able to sleep if I'm worrying about whether she's been told. If you could bring me a phone, I could call her myself..."

"It's after hours now," the woman pointed out. "We'd better wait until morning. She won't be in her office right now."

"She always says to call anytime, night or day, if I have an admission. It's very important that she be kept informed. If she hasn't already been called... I'd feel much better if you could..."

The woman finally conceded. "Okay, what is her name?"

Zachary kept his hand on the male nurse's arm to keep him there until the first nurse was ready to leave. He recited Dr. Boyle's name and phone number, which he had previously taken care to memorize in case he was ever separated from his phone or in a situation like this.

"You'll call her tonight? Right now?"

The nurse looked at her companion, shaking her head slightly in impatience. "I have another urgent patient matter to look after," she told him, nodding to the male nurse. "And then I will call her."

"Do you promise?"

She chuckled. "I promise, Mr. Goldman. You can rest easy. You do not need to worry."

"Okay. But please don't forget. She'll be quite upset with the hospital if you don't call her. There have been problems in the past..." He left the sentence hanging, as if he didn't want to get into just what those problems were. She could conjure them up herself. Lawsuits. Accusations of negligence or malpractice. Media coverage. Anything that would help her remember and call Dr. B after she had dealt with the other patient. He didn't want her to put it off and forget until the next day.

He let himself be soothed; then the two nurses walked out together.

CHAPTER 61

Kenzie had rarely called Dr. Wiltshire after hours, so his voice was understandably concerned when he answered her call, especially since she had left work early due to a family emergency.

"Kenzie. Hello! How are you doing? Is everything okay?"

"Well, things are quite a mess right now, actually. I... don't want to get into it because it will just distract me from the questions I want to ask you. And it is kind of urgent."

"Of course. How can I be of service?"

"I have some records to send to you. A patient—well, a deceased patient—who passed away suddenly during surgery. I have data on her heart function in the days before she died, and I want to know your take on it."

"Is this to do with one of our cases?"

“No, a case that I am looking at for Zachary, that he’s been hired to investigate.”

“We really can’t be crossing lines. You should deal with the medical examiner on that case. And it should be on a formal basis. We can’t be accused of improperly prying into cases that are not our jurisdiction.”

“I don’t have the private phone number of the medical examiner in Burlington who handled it, and I need to talk to someone urgently.”

“What is the urgency?”

Most of their cases were not urgent. Once someone was dead, there wasn’t anything they could do about it. Whether the autopsy took one day or one week, the victim wasn’t going to get any more dead. It wasn’t like working in emergency medicine.

"The urgency is... that Zachary has been abducted and whether I can help him or not may depend on the answers in this case."

Dr. Wiltshire gasped and then was silent momentarily, gathering his thoughts.

"Kenzie! He's been abducted?"

"That's the matter I said I didn't want to get into. I need to stay focused on the monitoring done before the victim died. That's the only way I can move this case forward for Zachary and hopefully find a way to... get him back safely."

"Have the police been informed?"

"Yes. They're on it. A detective is doing everything she can. I'm sure that they'll eventually be able to trace him, but... I have information we can act on now."

"Okay." He refocused. "Tell me what you have, then. EKG traces?"

"No. Smartwatch. So it doesn't give as much detail about the rhythms as an EKG would."

"No. That's too bad. But something is better than nothing. You are going to forward it to me?"

Kenzie was already saving the data to Zachary's hard drive, and would then forward it to Dr. Wiltshire from there.

"Yes. I'll email, if that's okay? Do you have access from home?"

"Of course. I'm not quite as old a fogy as all that," Dr. Wiltshire teased. "I am able to check my email remotely."

"Good. I'm sending it from Zachary's computer, so it will have his name in the sender field."

She quickly typed an email to Dr. Wiltshire and attached the files showing Kristin's smartwatch health tracking in the days before her death. She clicked Send.

"You should have it in a few seconds."

"Okay, wait just one moment. I need to get re-situated at my computer."

Kenzie waited for several minutes before Dr. Wiltshire came back onto the phone.

"This is more detailed than I had expected," he observed. "I wasn't aware that the smart watch technology was to this level yet."

"It is probably experimental," Kenzie said. "It was done as part of the monitoring for patients taking a new drug."

"Which one?"

"Something they are calling LipoSlayerRx."

Dr. Wiltshire cleared his throat. "I see. You know, I was asked previously if you had been assigned any cases involving that prescription, and I told them no..."

"Well, you were telling the truth. I haven't been assigned to it. But I am looking into it. Who asked you?"

"Someone who is rather prominent in the industry." He cleared his throat again. "You know what some of these companies are like, Kenzie. It's not wise to be poking around on something that isn't your job."

Or sometimes, even with something that was her job, as she had discovered in the past.

"I know. But Zachary has been kidnapped," she said in a voice that she hoped could be called "steely." She needed to keep Dr. Wiltshire on her side, willing to help her out.

"Right." Dr. Wiltshire agreed. "Zachary. Is this... the patient's terminal report?"

"The last date is, yes."

Dr. Wiltshire was quiet as he looked at the information on his screen. “That is very tragic. And yes, it looks like the patient was experiencing heart problems before her death.”

“How would you interpret the data? I know it isn’t an EKG. We don’t have the information that we would from multiple leads. But based on just what we have... what do you think?”

“I would speculate that this patient had a series of cardiac events before her death.”

“Since the company was monitoring this information live, they should have responded to those events,” Kenzie suggested.

Dr. Wiltshire didn’t respond immediately. “I would be reluctant to say what the company or whatever doctor was in charge of her care should have done.”

Of course.

“But it was probably something they should have looked into further,” she prompted.

Dr. Wiltshire couldn't deny that if they were getting live data from a patient in order to monitor their health and be advised of any concerns, they should follow up on any anomalous or unexpected readings as quickly as possible.

"Yes," he admitted slowly. "It would have been important data to follow up on."

"This was a young girl. Who died within a couple of days. Somebody should have followed up on it."

"It's not our place to make those judgments. We just report the facts and our assessment and, if there is blame to be placed or a crime has occurred, it is up to the police to follow up on that."

"I'm not even officially on this case. I'm not making any recommendations. Just trying to find out the truth."

"Yes. Well, I hope that my feedback is helpful. It isn't very much."

"It is. I just needed to know that I wasn't looking at it all wrong, seeing what I wanted to see because I'm worried about Zachary."

"You'll take this to the police now? Will it help them to find him?"

"I hope it will help," Kenzie agreed, though she didn't say she would go to the police with the information. She needed to find the right way to deal with the information now that she had it. Knowledge was power. It was the only asset she had. She didn't want to throw it away.

Even as she considered what to do after hanging up, she was aware of how she would have responded if Zachary had been in the same position and she had been talking to him. She would have told him that his responsibility was to turn the matter over to the police, not to use it himself like some vigilante. There was a proper procedure to follow, and he should avail himself of all of the resources of the police department. He wasn't some fictional hard-boiled detective with a gun and a quick trigger finger, lurking in the shadows and exercising his own brand of justice. He was just Zachary Goldman, private investigator. Her Zachary, who did what he did because he cared about other people and the truth.

She decided to reach out to Brittany Blake. Brittany would have a better idea of how Kenzie could use the information to the best advantage.

CHAPTER 62

Zachary knew that leaving the room was a huge risk. By leaving, he would be exposed. Other people might see him. He wouldn't know who was on his side and who was against him. And who was just an innocent bystander. He would have to avoid the doctors, nurses, staff, and probably the other patients too. He couldn't have any of them giving him away.

His best bet was to act immediately while both nurses were occupied following up on the patient that the male nurse had come into Zachary's room to talk about. He couldn't hear any conversations in the area outside his door where he assumed the nursing station would be, but that didn't mean there was no one there. Any number of nurses could be working quietly away, focused on their own jobs.

He used the prox card he had managed to snag from the male nurse as he had leaned over Zachary helping to pick up the spilled pills. Zachary tried the door and the lever turned without a sound. He pulled the door open a crack to look out into the hallway and common area.

He didn't see anyone or hear the clacking of computer keys. All seemed to be quiet, the unit shut down for the night. Just a couple of nurses left to watch the unit and ensure everyone took their night meds?

Zachary opened the door farther. His heart was pumping hard and fast, drumming in his chest. But that was good. Earlier, he had been unable to react emotionally to anything. His reactions had been shut down by the meds, so he hadn't felt any anxiety or worry.

He didn't like that muffled feeling. He didn't like not being in charge of his own reactions, even if he didn't always handle them very well. At least he had some choice in the matter, which he didn't if he let a drug control him.

It was the first time he could remember being grateful for feeling anxious.

He opened the door just far enough to slip through it, then slowly closed it, not letting it slam shut or make a loud noise as it clicked back into place.

The ward extended down the hall to his right, so he turned left. Out. Toward exits, somewhere.

He hoped that he was still inside the city so that once he escaped, he could make his way home, but he could be hours from Roxboro and not know it, since he had been dosed with a sedative after they had spirited him away in the van. He didn't even know if he was still in Vermont.

CHAPTER 63

Kenzie looked up Rain's number on Kristin's cellphone, but she didn't call from that phone. Rain might get a little freaked out by receiving a call from beyond the grave. But she might also ignore Kenzie's number, since she didn't know it. Decades before, people had answered the phone blind every time it rang, with no way of knowing who it was. Now, it had become the norm to only answer the phone if she knew who was on the other end. An unknown number, and she would just let it go to voicemail. And who knew if the younger generation even checked their voicemail? Kenzie strongly suspected that most of them did not. Not unless they were dealing with "old" people about things like employment and the only way that those people would deal with them was by phone.

After a few rings, Rain did, in fact, pick it up. Maybe she accepted it because Kenzie had a local number. Or maybe Rain was feeling generous. Or lonely, with no one to talk to about the loss of her friend.

"Hello?"

"Hello, Rain. You don't know me, but I'm a friend of Zachary Goldman, the man you've been talking to about Kristin Jones?"

"I told him I wasn't going to talk to him anymore. That doesn't mean I want to talk to someone else about it instead."

"I don't expect you to talk to me for long. I just need one thing from you. I discovered that Kristin was having heart problems before she died. It's possible that was a reaction to the LipoSlayerRx. I was hoping to talk to your dad about it."

"My dad?"

"He works at TrimProGenix, right?"

"Well... yes."

"That's why I was hoping I could talk to him."

"He isn't going to talk to you. He doesn't talk to anyone. He isn't allowed to."

"Don't you want justice for Kristin?"

"I… I don't know what I want. I don't want to get my dad in trouble. That's all this is doing."

"Is your dad aware of the lack of testing of LipoSlayerRx? Especially on minors?"

Of course he knew. Kenzie wouldn't have been able to see that information if the files hadn't been accessible to Rain's dad.

"Rx is safe," Rain asserted. "I wish you guys would just leave it alone. You aren't going to find anything. My dad wouldn't be working there if they weren't doing the testing they're supposed to."

"Maybe he thinks that it was the right thing to do. To get Rx out to as many people as possible to prevent any deaths due to obesity. Sometimes they shortcut the process because the need is so great and they believe that the results will dramatically improve people's lives and prevent unnecessary deaths."

Rain made a noise, but didn't argue with this. She couldn't very well say that they had rushed it to market for another reason. Kenzie was giving her an "out."

"Could I get your dad's phone number, and then I could talk to him and see what he has to say? You don't need to have anything else to do with it."

"No. I don't give his number out."

"Then have him call me."

That was also a non-starter.

"Rain, I think you want the best for people like your friend. You don't want other people's lives being cut short or others having to deal with a loss like this."

"Leave me and my dad alone. We don't want to talk to you."

Kenzie considered telling Rain that Zachary had been kidnapped due to his questions about Rx. Possibly by her father's company. But that would probably make Rain withdraw further. She wouldn't want to be blamed for whatever had happened to Zachary. She wouldn't want to believe that her father or his company could have had anything to do with his abduction.

"You won't even give me his number? I won't say anything to him about you. He can decide for himself whether he wants to have anything to do with me."

"No." Rain stuck stubbornly to her guns.

"I was really hoping that you could help me out."

She could picture Rain on the other end of the phone, as Zachary had described her. Arms folded, scowling. She had drawn her line in the sand, and she wouldn't cross it. She would continue to dig in her heels and not budge.

That meant Kenzie needed to find another way to talk to Dr. Murdoch or someone else from TrimProGenix. And Dr. Murdoch was the one they would have the most leverage over, since it was his daughter's friend who had died. He had to feel guilty over that, even if he hadn't looked at her medical records and realized that she'd been having heart problems before she had died. He had to suspect that her death could have something to do with Rx, no matter how remote the possibility.

Kenzie knew doctors. Mostly pathologists and mental health professionals. Some other doctors she had known in school who had gone into other specialties. But she was looking for something else; a doctor or scientist who was used to looking at research studies and making evaluations as to the safety of a product and what the risks and other considerations were.

That was very different from someone who went into medicine to treat patients.

As she scrolled through the contacts in her phone, Kenzie's mind was drawn to Eddie Godfrey, one of the siblings who had hired Zachary to investigate his father's death recently. Zachary had done well, sorting out what had happened and who the culprits were. And Eddie Godfrey was a scientist. A chemist and an inventor, precisely the type of person who would be trained to dissect a dataset and decide what was and was not significant. It was a long shot, but Kenzie decided to take the chance.

CHAPTER 64

Eddie was a geek, taking great delight in his numbers and chemistry and in the joy of analyzing all of the data Kenzie could find for him. She was amazed at how quickly he was able to consume what she sent him and asked for more, looking for specific data and results that she had to search the server for. Most of it was over her head, she had to admit. She had done well in both biology and chemistry, and reasonably well in mathematics and statistics, but he took it to a whole new level. They worked in tandem for several hours, with Kenzie feeding him the numbers and Eddie analyzing them and asking for more.

But the next problem would be getting Eddie and Rain's father, Dr. Murdoch, to talk to one another. Rain wasn't giving up her father's number. The number on the TrimProGenix servers was an internal number that went to voicemail. He didn't appear to have shared his cell number or landline with the company. Maybe he had given it to a select few who recorded it in their phone contacts, but it wasn't listed on the internal contacts sheets or HR file. A private man. Someone who didn't like to be interrupted from his work.

She started to explain the circumstances to Eddie, thinking that maybe she would call Heather to see if she could track down another number for Dr. Murdoch using the databases at her disposal. It was too late to call Heather, but she would want to be woken up. She wouldn't want Kenzie to just wait until morning, being polite, when she needed the information now.

"Dr. Murdoch?" Eddie asked. "Sure, I know him."

"You know him?"

"Yeah. We were in some classes together way back when. We don't talk much, but I have a number for him."

"Do you think you can make him see what you've discovered with the Rx data?"

Eddie made a clicking noise with his tongue. “I can share it. I can’t guarantee he’ll see it the same way. But I am right. My conclusions will be proven sooner or later.”

“Well, hopefully sooner, because we need him to get on board with us now. Zachary’s life could be riding on this. And so many other people whose lives could be in danger if they keep taking Rx.”

“I’ll take him through the data,” Eddie assured her. “But I can’t promise that he’ll agree. People can get pretty possessive about their pet drugs, be blinded by their pride in what they’ve helped to create. It’s hard to shut down something that you thought was the answer. It often takes companies a while to pull a drug, even when it’s obvious that it is causing harm.”

“And you’ll call me and let me know what he says? If you’re able to get anywhere with him?”

“I’ll let you know as soon as I can.”

Kenzie tried to put the matter aside and wait patiently. There wasn't even any guarantee that Eddie would be able to get ahold of his old friend that late. His phone was probably already on Do Not Disturb for the night and Eddie wouldn't be able to get through to him until the morning.

Kenzie herself should take the opportunity to sleep while she could. Currently, everything was quiet. As the rest of the city went to sleep, she should too. Garcia would call her if there were any break in the case. Her eyes were tired and sore from spending so much time on the computer.

But she wasn't going to be able to sleep. She already knew that.

Not while Zachary was out there, suffering at the hands of his captors. She knew what it was like to be kidnapped, even if they treated him well and only kept him for a short period of time. Her own imprisonment had been very brief, and then her father had managed to get her released by cooperating with her captors. But no one had received any demands from Zachary's kidnappers. There was nothing to give them.

Kenzie's phone rang. She supposed it was Eddie, calling back to tell her that he had left a message for Mr. Murdoch but would not be able to meet with him until the morning. It was nice of him to let her know, so she didn't sit up waiting for his response.

"Hello?"

"Kenzie, I'm sorry to call you so late."

It took a minute for Kenzie to place the voice. She looked at the caller ID and then put the phone back to her ear. "Dr. Boyle. Hi."

"I had a strange call tonight. I'm not sure what to think of it."

Kenzie frowned. Maybe Zachary had called her before his abduction. To talk through what he should do about the text from the kidnappers. To give Dr. B the opportunity to talk him out of going over to Bridget's house to check on the twins.

"Okay...?"

"Is Zachary with you? Or has something happened?"

"Um... well, yes, something happened."

"He had a psychotic break?"

"No." Kenzie frowned at the phone, trying to understand what was going on. "He didn't have a psychotic break... he was abdu... he was... kidna... someone took him."

"Took him? He was attacked? Kidnapped? I don't understand."

"Yes. He was lured and ambushed. The police are trying to find him."

"Oh, dear. Well, maybe I can help, then."

"You can?" Kenzie sat up straighter. "Do you mean it? How can you help?"

"This call I got... was from a private facility that said Zachary was a patient there."

"He's a patient? Where?"

"As I said, it was a very strange call. A nurse was asking me about his medical history. She said they had his most recent records, but Zachary had asked her to call me. That he said he had no history of psychosis and they were mis-treating him. Giving him the wrong meds."

"Psychosis?" Kenzie tried to reconcile this with what she already knew. Zachary had been kidnapped. That was what they had seen on the video recording. It wasn't an apprehension by the police or paramedics under Title 19. He had definitely been kidnapped. She had seen it with her own eyes.

"Zachary has no history of psychosis," Dr. Boyle said. "I'm not allowed to tell you that under confidentiality laws, but you already know that. Psychosis is not one of the issues that we've been treating. That I've ever dealt with Zachary on."

"Then why would they say that he did?"

"The only thing I can think of is that they are trying to get it on record as a Title 19 commitment for psychosis, so they have a reason to hold him, for some reason."

"And to sedate him," Kenzie said. "They're using the medical system to keep him locked down and drugged up."

"I don't think that would work," Dr. Boyle protested. "Too many people would know that it's not true."

"But none of them are there. They only have to convince whoever is at the medical facility that it is true. To get them to hold him, until they're ready to let him go or... something else."

“That’s not the way the system is designed to work. There are checks and balances.”

“And whoever is behind this has found ways around them, at least temporarily.”

“Do you think so?”

“I know he was thrown in a van by masked men. Grabbed off the street and...” Kenzie choked up, unable to go on any further.

“It’s okay,” Dr. B soothed, understanding that this scenario would trigger Kenzie’s own memories. “We can talk about that another time. Right now... who do I talk to about sending the police over there and getting him out?”

CHAPTER 65

Kenzie was getting ready to go and had to keep stopping to remind herself of what she was doing. Her head was whirling and her emotions so out of control that she couldn't hold one thought in her head for thirty seconds as she ran across the house to pick up her phone or her purse or some other item that she needed as she went to meet Garcia at the facility where Zachary was possibly being held prisoner.

Her phone rang as she picked it up. Kenzie glanced down at it, then put it to her ear. "Hello?"

There was no answer. Kenzie lowered it again to swipe the call, but there was no call. There was a message on one of her social networks. Not something that she needed to answer right away. But Kenzie saw Brittany's name and hesitated. It wasn't as important as getting to Zachary and making sure he was safe, but Zachary would want to know that the case was on track and that Kenzie had been handling things while he was gone, moving them forward in order to save him and to deal with the data she had discovered on Kristin.

She stopped and tapped on the social network, feeling anxious about standing still. She needed to get in her car and go to Zachary. Nothing else. Anything else was in the way of her accomplishing her goal.

She had been tagged in a video posted by Brittany.

Thanks to my friends, Zachary and Kenzie, we are finally going to be able to bring this giant down.

Kenzie started the video playing and listened, her mouth dry, as Brittany introduced the topic of undisclosed side effects and deaths related to LipoSlayerRx. Then the picture split and Brittany's face was on one side of the screen and an unfamiliar man on the other. The name under the face was Dr. M. Murdoch, TrimProGenix.

Dr. Murdoch outlined in a dry, unemotional tone how one of his daughter's friends had been on LipoSlayerRx and had died suddenly in the middle of an unrelated medical procedure. In looking at the live data that her smartwatch had been transmitting, he had seen that she'd had a series of cardiac events in the days preceding her death. Events that, under the testing and monitoring protocols for Rx, should have been followed up on by the company immediately. But rather than being dealt with, the data had been pushed into another silo of data to be reviewed at a later date.

On reviewing the data from other Rx users and the studies that had been done before Rx's release, he had found that there was a pattern of data being ignored or deemed unimportant. Information that should have been closely monitored and possibly resulted in warnings on the Rx prescribing information sheet, if not in the drug being pulled until further research could be completed.

Brittany asked some follow-up questions, adding emotion to the doctor's dry, clinical report. Kenzie detected changes in Dr. Murdoch's tone. He was not unaffected by the news. Just the opposite. He was blowing the whistle on his own company, something that would have serious consequences for himself, his daughter, and the company. Words that he would never be able to take back. He was distancing himself from his emotion by using dry facts and statistics, but he would not have stepped forward and spoken out, agreeing to be interviewed by Brittany, if he hadn't been convinced that the company was doing something inexcusable.

Kenzie glanced at the stats on the video. It had gone viral. Despite being late at night, it was getting views all over the world. It was not a recording, but a live feed, but Kenzie didn't have the time to keep watching it. She had another job to do.

CHAPTER 66

Zachary had escaped from his room, but that was as far as he had gotten. Almost as soon as he had stepped out the door, he had been able to hear an alarm ringing at the nursing station and had barely had time to duck into the next open doorway upon hearing the approach of footsteps as someone moved in to see what was going on. He ducked into a supply area with a curtain pulled across it. Not a secure room or a very good place to hide, since they would be able to see his feet under the curtain if they looked for him.

“What’s going on?” a young female voice asked.

“Just an alert.” An older, gravelly voice that could have been a man or a woman. There were some clicking keys and the alarm stopped. “Goldman, the new admission. He’s out of bed again.”

“Again?”

"He's been up a few times. Not quite as far under as you would expect him to be with the cocktail they've put him on."

"Do you want me to check on him?"

"Give it a minute. He might just be up to the john and go back on his own. And he's supposed to be Collins's patient. If she doesn't get back, we'll go check."

Zachary hadn't realized when he'd been alone in the room that there was a bed sensor, like at a nursing home. They didn't use them in the psych ward at the hospital, though he imagined they might use them in the unit for dementia patients. The nurses would want to know if people with dementia were out of their beds and wandering around. The psych patients were not as closely supervised.

The alarm must have gone off before when he'd gone to the bathroom to throw up the pills. But he'd returned to his bed, so they hadn't been back in to check on him. The gravelly-voiced nurse said that he had been out of bed several times, so he must have been restless even when sedated. He couldn't remember getting up any other times.

Zachary looked around the small supply room. It was dim, the light from the hallway mostly blocked by the curtain, with no light on inside. There were shelves of linens, paper towel rolls, toilet paper for the bathrooms, and other odds and ends needed by the nursing or cleaning staff. There was a small rolling step stool that he could stand on if he didn't want them to see his feet under the curtain, but he wouldn't be able to withstand a thorough search. All they had to do was pull back the curtain, exposing him to view.

He waited, listening to the idle talk of the nurses at the desk, who were joined a few minutes later by the two nurses who had been in Zachary's room.

"Goldman is up again. His bed alarm went off," the gravelly-voiced nurse advised the new arrivals.

“I’ll check on him,” the woman, who must be Nurse Collins, sighed. Zachary looked for a way out of the supply closet. The best time for him to move was while they were distracted, looking toward the room he had just vacated, but it wasn’t far enough away from him to be sure that they wouldn’t catch the movement in their peripheral vision, even if they were distracted.

The nurse moved on quiet-soled shoes over to his room door. There was a faint beep as the prox card sensor unlocked the door, and she opened it. She didn’t go into the room, but stood there for a minute.

“Must be in the bathroom. He was pretty wide awake when we were in there, so it might take him a while to settle again. But those pills should put him under pretty quickly.”

Zachary’s stomach writhed, partially due to his anxiety and partly to the mixture of pills that he had downed. He hadn’t taken all of them. Particularly not the ones he had not recognized or the sedative. He had swallowed the rest, knowing he could do so without ill effects. It wasn't ideal, because they weren't part of his current protocol, but he had taken most of the drugs on the market before and knew that he at least wouldn't react to them and that they could be taken together. And he hadn't had his own night meds, so there shouldn't be any conflict with what he had already taken. Though who knew what he'd been given earlier after being snatched off the street?

Collins let the door to Zachary's room shut again, and the four nurses continued to chat with each other while they kept an eye on whatever monitors were in his room. Zachary hadn't noticed a security camera, but a covert spy cam could be very hard to spot if you didn't know exactly where it was and didn't know what to look for. A random screw in the wall. A lens camouflaged by a mirror that reflected the blank wall, making it invisible unless you got just the right angle or something other than blank wall reflected in the mirror. He'd hidden them himself. He knew how hard they could be to spot.

He peered out the crack between the doorframe and the curtain, watching for an opportunity to sneak out. If he got out of the closet, where would he go? How far was it to the unit exit? Was there a security door, or were all the security measures in the individual bedrooms?

If there was a locked door, the stolen prox card should get him past it. But it could also set off alerts at the nursing station.

The young nurse started an animated discussion on what was apparently their favorite series on TV. Zachary figured it was the best time for him to make his move. They weren't watching his door. They were focused on each other, and they were distracted. If he waited too long, they would realize he was missing and begin a search, and he would be quickly discovered.

CHAPTER 67

When Kenzie arrived at the private psychiatric facility, there was a single police car in the parking lot with its light flashing. There was no crime scene tape, no crowd of cops and techs coming and going as they gathered the information they needed. And no sign of Zachary.

She had no idea whether the police who were already there were even there about Zachary. It could have been something else. Something routine. She hurried from her car to the big front doors, hoping she could get in, or at least get some information.

Four sets of eyes turned to her as she walked in. Two uniformed cops, looking casual and unworried. A security guard for the facility, overweight, hitching his duty belt up on his bulging belly and trying to look competent and official. And a doctor or nurse in scrubs, female, the only one who seemed at all worried.

“Can I help you, ma’am?” The security guard asked, intercepting Kenzie. “Visiting hours are not until ten in the morning.”

“My name is Kenzie Kirsch. I’m here about Zachary Goldman.”

They looked at her and then at each other. The law enforcement officers looked Kenzie over. “You’re the next of kin?”

Kenzie nodded. That was a stretch, but she was the only one who could take on that role at the moment, and it might get her somewhere.

“The facility is currently on lockdown.” The two cops looked at each other. “We’re just waiting to get in and have a look around.”

“Why is it on lockdown?”

They all looked at each other. The security guard and the nurse seemed reluctant to give her any information. Kenzie drew herself up and looked the nurse in the eye.

“Why are you on lockdown?”

“We have a patient who has wandered. We need to make sure that they can’t leave the facility before we find them.”

“Is it Zachary?”

She did not look at all happy to answer this question. She looked at the guard as if hoping he would jump in and tell Kenzie that it was none of her business, but he didn’t. He just hooked his thumbs into his duty belt, weighing it back down, trying to look as official and important as the two cops standing by.

“I don’t have that information,” the nurse said hesitantly. Kenzie looked at her name badge. Nurse Ford.

“You don’t know who got out of their room?”

“Well… I don’t have the authority to share it.”

“Is it Zachary Goldman?”

She looked at the police officers and then back at Kenzie, hoping for a reprieve. She looked at her watch. She took out her phone and examined it for messages from the other staff who were presumably conducting the search.

“It… might be,” she admitted finally.

“Is it Goldman or not?” One of the cops demanded. His badge gave his name as Morrison.

Nurse Ford cleared her throat, then finally nodded. “Yes.”

“He has been reported kidnapped. This is not something that we treat lightly. We need to see him and talk to him to verify his welfare.”

"Well, I would be happy to let you, but we don't know exactly where he is right now. When we have located him, we will let you know."

The cops looked at each other as if they weren't sure what to do with this. Wait for the facility to handle it? Insist on going in and doing a room-to-room search, which could be tedious and fruitless?

"I want to get in there," Kenzie said. "I want to see where he was being held. I want to see his medical chart and what he has been given today. He got a message to his doctor that he's being treated for a psychotic break when he isn't psychotic." She looked at the officers. "He could be knocked out. Restrained. Killed. This is someone who was kidnapped and brought here against his will. Not for medical treatment, but because he has been making problems for a drug company that is implicated in a number of deaths. What if he is in there right now in need of medical treatment and this 'lockdown' is just a means of keeping you from finding him?"

Morrison drew himself taller, finally looking serious instead of bored with the whole thing. Kenzie wondered where Detective Garcia was. Where the rest of the department that should have been there was. She felt like there should be arc lights pointing at the building, black-jacketed SWAT cops assembled outside with a battering ram to get into Zachary's unit and room if they were not granted full access. A big to-do like there would have been on TV. Instead, she had two bored cops who didn't seem to know what was happening.

"I'm afraid we're going to have to get in to look at his room," Morrison announced, using his "tough cop" voice.

His partner, Stone, backed him up, looking serious and putting his hand on his sidearm. He gave a firm nod of agreement.

Nurse Ford looked at them, and then appealed to the security guard, who was in way over his head. "We're on lockdown. We're not supposed to let anyone in or out."

"You can let us in. Don't let anyone out without us approving it."

"I'm not supposed to..."

"We have reason to believe you are holding a man hostage here. That gives us the right to enter and search before he is hurt or killed. Please step aside, open the doors, and take us to his room."

"This is just a mistake. No one is being held hostage. This is a patient with psychosis. They can be very convincing. Of course he would tell you he's not supposed to be here, because he wants to go home. But people are not admitted here after being kidnapped. That's ridiculous."

"Then there shouldn't be any problem in us looking at the paperwork or talking to Mr. Goldman once he has been found. And to his doctor, of course."

"This really is out of the ordinary—"

“Nurse Ford. Are you going to ignore the lawful order of a law enforcement officer?”

She dithered a bit more, looking for a way out, but unable to find any way to refuse him. She scowled at Kenzie and clearly wanted to tell her to stay where she was, but Kenzie aligned herself with the cops and tried to make it obvious from her body language that she was going up with them no matter what they said. She was the next of kin. She had medical training. She was the one who knew what was going on and could explain to them that Zachary had been snatched off the street, not admitted to the facility through the usual procedures.

Nurse Ford sighed again, continued to scowl, but gave in. She turned her back to lead them to the elevator. The cops followed, and Kenzie stayed close behind them. Nurse Ford stepped through the open elevator doors and turned to the button panel. She inserted a key, turned it to unlock the elevator, and pressed the button for the second floor. The doors closed and Kenzie's stomach lurched as it started to rise. She tried to ignore the anxiety about what she would find when they arrived at the unit. She wasn't going to find Zachary well in his room. She was sure of that. Either he had escaped and would not be there, or he would be under restraints, chemical or physical. She didn't know which to hope for.

As long as he was still alive and well, she would take either one.

CHAPTER 68

A grim Nurse Ford led them off the elevator on the second floor and through the corridors. Everything was quiet, with the patients down for the night. Those who didn't sleep well would be sedated. Nighttime at a facility like this should be pretty quiet.

A janitor worked down one of the hallways, his back to them and cleaning cart nearby, swabbing the tile floor in a slow, rhythmic, side-to-side swipe with his mop. He was a small man, dressed in cleaning scrubs, and Kenzie's eyes caught on him for a moment before she hurried after Nurse Ford and the cops as Ford swiped her card and they entered the unit.

"What is this?" another nurse demanded, looking at the visitors. "We are on lockdown. You aren't supposed to be letting anyone in here!"

"They're here about Goldman," Ford said. "Some convoluted tale about how he isn't supposed to be here and he was not being treated properly. The police are involved, and his regular doctor…"

The new nurse rolled her eyes. Kenzie looked at her name badge. Collins.

"He's been telling stories," Collins said, "I don't know how he managed to get the police here, but…"

"We need to see him," Morrison insisted firmly.

"Well, that's sort of hard, since he isn't in his room. We're looking for him."

"We'd like to see his room."

Collins looked at Kenzie. "You don't look like law enforcement."

"I'm not. I'm his partner. And a medical doctor. I'd like to see his chart and what he was being treated with. He was stable on the cocktail he was on before coming here."

Collins snorted. “Not so stable, if he was paranoid and delusional. If you’re his partner, why aren’t you the one who admitted him?”

“That’s a good question, isn’t it?” Kenzie asked, looking at the cops.

“His room?” Morrison prompted.

Collins reluctantly led them to a private room and opened the door. Kenzie looked around, still half-expecting to see Zachary. Unconscious in the bed, hiding in a corner, handcuffed—something. But he wasn’t there. There was no sign of him.

Kenzie looked into the bathroom, but it was neat and clean. No sign of blood or of Zachary’s presence. There was no sign at all that he was hurt. Kenzie let her breath out slowly.

He had escaped. He was safe.

Or they had secreted him somewhere else where the police wouldn't find him. Maybe to be thrown off the roof once they were out of the way.

Kenzie turned back toward the bed and Nurse Collins. "Where is his chart? How was he being treated?"

Collins silently removed the clipboard from the end of the bed and handed it to her. She didn't demand any identification or proof that Kenzie was really Zachary's next of kin. Maybe she had some idea that what was being done there was illegal and hoped to get out of any charges by cooperated fully.

Kenzie scanned the doctor's orders. If Zachary had been on such heavy sedation, she had no idea how he had managed to escape. There were antipsychotics in the mix, as well as drugs she didn't recognize the names of.

"What are these? Experimental drugs?"

“This facility is working with the manufacturer of some leading-edge psychiatric drugs currently under trial,” Collins told them. “So... yes, Mr. Goldman was added to the trials.”

“Who authorized that?”

“His doctor.”

Kenzie shook her head. “I talked to his doctor less than an hour ago. She did not authorize any experimental protocols. She knew he was stable on the cocktail he’s on right now.”

A bit of an exaggeration, since Dr. Boyle had recently upped Zachary’s meds due to his increasingly obsessive behavior. But that wasn’t psychosis, and she knew Dr. Boyle would not have authorized any experimental drugs without reviewing them thoroughly with Zachary first. And even then, she would be unlikely to jump into a new drug unless it were in the final stages of its trials and had been proven safe and effective.

“Mr. Goldman’s doctor is a man, not a woman,” Collins asserted. “Dr. Evans.”

Kenzie shuddered as if chilled. “Dr. Evans? Is that the same Dr. Evans as works for TrimProGenix?”

Collins looked puzzled and shook her head. “I don’t know anything about TrimProGenix. He is a well-known and regarded doctor. He is the one who admitted Mr. Goldman and added him to the trials.”

“He is not Zachary’s doctor. He’s never treated him.”

Collins gave a shake of her head. “He has been treating Mr. Goldman for some time.”

“He has not,” Kenzie disagreed. She flipped through the pages on the clipboard, which briefly documented Zachary’s psychiatric history going back a few years, and found that several entries had been added which included Dr. Evans’s name. “This is wrong. These records have been falsified. Dr. Evans has never treated Zachary.”

“Whether he has or not, Mr. Goldman does not appear to be here,” Morrison pointed out. “What is being done to find him?”

“We’re conducting a room-by-room search. We don’t have a lot of staff on at night and can’t spare a lot of people, so it is slow going, but we are confident that he was not able to make it out of the facility.”

“How long will that take?”

“I’m sure he will be found quickly. But… if not, it could take a few hours to do a thorough search.”

Stone, the other cop, had been looking down at his phone. He put it away and squared his shoulders. “Detective Garcia is on her way over. And the whole crew, I expect. You can expect to have all the help you need within the hour.”

“This is all unnecessary,” Collins insisted. “He probably wandered into another room and fell asleep when the sedatives kicked in. We’ll find him curled up on a bed or a couch somewhere, snoring away peacefully. There is no need for police and detectives and all of this...”

“He was snatched off the street,” Kenzie told her. “Grabbed by masked men and thrown into a van. We’re not talking about a patient who had a psychotic break, like you have been told. This man was k-kidnapped.”

Collins was shaking her head. “No...”

“Yes. He was. We have a video of it. So if you don’t cooperate fully, you’re aiding these kidnappers and you could be charged too.”

“I am cooperating,” Collins said hotly. “You are here, aren’t you? Someone who doesn’t have any legal standing to even look at these documents? You can’t say that we are not doing everything in our power to help to sort this situation out.”

As a group, they moved out of the room into the hallway. There was no discussion of the next steps, but it was clear that Zachary was not in his room and they should not touch anything until the detective and crime tech guys had been through there. Kenzie looked around, trying to imagine how Zachary had escaped and what steps he would have taken. He wasn't stupid. He was pretty good in an emergency, although he was very impulsive, which could have either good or bad results in a dangerous situation. He might be the first one to spot an escape route or understand what was going on, or he might say something incredibly stupid to a potential killer while she had him under her power. One just never knew.

There was a utility closet a little way down from Zachary's hospital room. The curtain that normally covered it had been pulled back. There was a variety of linens and cleaning equipment lining the shelves.

Kenzie suddenly straightened.

"Zachary!"

CHAPTER 69

The cops looked at Kenzie as if she had flipped her lid. Morrison looked around to see if she had seen Zachary and was talking to him.

“Ma’am?”

“We walked right by him.”

Kenzie headed toward the door that led out of the unit. She made an impatient motion to Nurse Collins. “Unlock the door.”

“I don’t see what—”

“Just do it!”

Kenzie waited impatiently while Collins walked over and pulled out her prox card to unlock the security door. Kenzie pushed it open.

“We walked right by him. I didn’t even see him.”

She looked down the adjoining hallway where the janitor had been. It was empty, though the tiles still shone wetly.

“This way.” Kenzie led the cops across the glistening tiles and around the corner.

She could hear other footsteps and voices. Other people who were searching for Zachary, she assumed. They would have enlisted everyone they could. And no one would even see him.

“Zachary!” Kenzie called out.

The janitor down the corridor turned to look at her. A smile blossomed on his face. He turned around and opened his mouth to call out a greeting to her. Two doctors who had been opening doors as they searched for the missing patient turned around to see what was going on.

One of the doctors dashed over to Zachary. Happy to have found him, Kenzie thought. Right there in front of him, in plain view.

He grabbed Zachary roughly, knocking the mop out of his hands. He twisted Zachary's arm up behind his back as if he were a dangerous criminal. Kenzie shouted out a protest. There was no need for them to treat him so roughly. He was a small man, unarmed, and not violent by nature.

"Hey! Let him go!"

It would probably take a while to convince them that Zachary wasn't a danger to anyone. Everyone there had been told that he was on a psychotic break, that he was a potentially dangerous patient who needed to be heavily sedated and had just escaped. Kenzie marched toward them to give the doctors a piece of her mind. She didn't even stop to think about whether one of them might be Dr. Evans, or someone else who might be involved in the conspiracy. Dr. Evans might not even be involved, but just be the patsy they had chosen in case anything went wrong.

But what were the chances that the medical facility and TrimProGenix would both have a Dr. Evans who was involved in developing and trialing new drugs? Even if they were in completely different industries. You never knew what off-label uses might be found for a new drug. Psychiatric medicines frequently caused weight gain. Maybe LipoSlayerRx had started out as a psychiatric medicine with the welcome effect of weight loss.

“Let Zachary go. He isn’t a danger to anyone,” she insisted, closing in.

The doctor who had put Zachary into a hammerlock put his beefy arm around Zachary’s neck and squeezed. Kenzie saw Zachary’s eyes bulge. What was he doing? As a doctor, he should know how dangerous choke holds were. The police were not allowed to use them. Bouncers and security guards were taught other methods of subduing people. Doctors surely knew how dangerous it was.

“Everyone can just stay back,” the doctor yelled. “Just go back the way you came.”

The cops had both drawn their guns but were looking confused. The world was turned upside down. It was supposed to be the patient who was a danger, not the doctor.

Where was Detective Garcia? Kenzie felt a lot more sure of her education and training than she was of these two cops.

“Just calm down,” Kenzie told him. “No one is going to do anything to hurt you. Let Zachary go. You’re holding on to him too tight.”

“He’s not going anywhere,” the doctor snapped back. He said something in a lower voice to his companion, who looked at him uncertainly, then back at Kenzie and the cops. “Now!” the doctor holding on to Zachary ordered.

The other one reluctantly pulled something from the pocket of his lab jacket and handed it over to the first.

“You want to know what this is?” the doctor demanded, one-handedly popping the lid off of an autoinjector and releasing the injection mechanism. “Do you want to know what this will do to him if I stab it into his carotid?”

Kenzie looked at the two cops, holding their guns steadily on the doctor. Zachary’s hands were prying at the doctor’s arm, trying to escape the choke hold. The doctor clenched the autoinjector tightly near his throat.

“You don’t need to do anything to hurt him,” Kenzie said. “Look, I know that he went too far. He should have just kept his nose out of your business and let you do what you’re doing. It’s important work, developing drugs like Rx that can make such a difference to society. Vital. I appreciate what you’re doing.”

He didn’t look too convinced by her words.

“LipoSlayerRx is revolutionary,” Kenzie said, trying to remember as many words as possible from the leaflets she had read. “It’s the first advancement in battling obesity in decades. Until now, no one has really understood the mechanisms of weight gain and how to combat it. In today’s society, when we have so many temptations, food with such high caloric density… It's a totally different world than it was when our grandparents were still working on farms, eating fresh, unprocessed whole foods."

"Goldman should just have left it alone," the doctor sneered. "Who does he think he is, waltzing in and making judgments without understanding how it works? How many people need this solution? It's not up to some lone private investigator to decide whether a drug is safe and effective or not. He doesn't understand the nuances."

"How many people's lives it could be saving," Kenzie agreed. "Lots of drugs have side effects. Look at chemo. Obesity is a much bigger problem than cancer now. Obesity raises the cancer risk. Why do they think cancer rates have been rising like they have?"

"We are saving people's lives," the doctor declared. "This is the only effective solution available to us right now. The only effective solution that is available to everyone. Kids, adults, pregnant women, whatever. It is safe and effective."

"We'll explain that," Kenzie promised. "I know how hard it is to reach people, but I can explain it to Zachary. He'll see reason. There's no need to go to these extreme measures. Nothing has been done that cannot be undone."

But she knew it wasn't true. She had seen the live video that Brittany Blake was doing before coming to the facility to find Zachary. She knew that there was no way to take that back. Brittany had a huge following, and they would believe her and the scientist from TrimProGenix who told everyone with cold, calm certitude that Rx needed to be pulled. That it had been responsible for Kristin's death and others and needed to be removed from the market.

The doctor was watching her. His anger had dissipated slightly, but he was still a time bomb. He could explode at any moment. Especially if he became aware of the firestorm that was exploding—or about to explode—on social media channels.

Once it hit the tipping point, his phone was going to start buzzing. Notifications from his apps, calls from other people at the company. Shareholders. Directors. People that he was responsible to. They would all want an explanation as to what was going on and what he was going to do about it. And there was no easy answer. He wasn't going to be able to fix it.

"Let Zachary go," Kenzie urged. "We'll take care of it. He can make a statement to the public. Make sure people see that he has endorsed it."

The doctor looked down at Zachary's face, his arm pulling tight against Zachary's throat once more. Zachary's eyes were glazed. Kenzie wasn't sure that he was even able to comprehend what was going on now, let alone engineer a way to get away from his captor.

The doctor finally pulled the autoinjector back and considered his options. There was no sign that any additional police had arrived. Just the two officers down the hall from him, their guns trained in his direction. And they would have been taught not to shoot down an unarmed man. He let the autoinjector clatter to the floor and removed his arm from Zachary's neck, though he still kept a hold on his arm. He backed away from the cops.

CHAPTER 70

All at once, Zachary went down.

He went limp in the doctor's grip, his eyes rolling up. Startled, the doctor let him collapse to the floor, following him down and cushioning the impact as much as possible. His training kicked in and he immediately started to examine Zachary before thinking about his position. His back was to the police.

"Hands up!" Morrison shouted. "Back away from Mr. Goldman!"

The doctor turned to look at him, face white and frozen. His companion, who had been standing there frozen during the hostage-taking, raised his hands immediately. Unlike Dr. Evans, he obviously had no taste for violence. He didn't have the same desperation.

Evans looked from the other doctor back to the cops again. He looked down at Zachary, who was moving sluggishly.

"Move away from Zachary, and I can take care of him," Kenzie told him.

Slowly, Evans put his hands up. Rising from his crouching position, he took a couple of steps back from Zachary.

"Hands behind your head, lace your fingers together," Morrison instructed. As he obeyed, Morrison and Stone moved in to frisk and handcuff him.

* * *

Zachary closed his eyes for a moment to center himself and regain his equilibrium. He took a deep breath and slowly sat up. Kenzie was there, talking to him and pressing his shoulder back to the floor.

"Don't sit up too quickly. Just rest for a minute and let me check you over."

"I'm fine," Zachary protested, though his throat hurt from the compression.

"You're fine when I say you are," she said in a firm, no-nonsense voice. Zachary knew that voice from countless foster moms, caregivers, and supervisors. So he stayed there, lying on the floor, while the police activity went on around them.

Kenzie's hands were reassuring, checking his pulse and other vital signs. "How does your throat feel?"

"Sore."

"Is it swelling?" Her fingers probed gently.

"No. Just... achy."

"Are you dizzy? How does your head feel?"

"Headache. But I've had that all day."

"Do you know what day it is?" she challenged.

"Tuesday. Unless they kept me unconscious longer than I thought."

"It's Tuesday," she agreed.

"Tuesday night," he told her, to confirm that he knew what time of day it was too. He was fully oriented. No need to worry that he didn't know what was going on.

"They gave you some pretty heavy sedatives. How are you still awake?"

Zachary muffled a laugh. "The last dose is in my pocket."

"You palmed them?"

"I was too dopey from the previous dose," he advised, grinning. "Spilled them all over. The nurse helped me pick them up and take them... but some didn't make it that far."

"And what happened to the previous dose?"

"Threw them up."

"And they didn't re-administer them?"

"They didn't know."

She laid a hand on the side of his face. "You're pretty sneaky, aren't you?"

"I've had lots of practice."

"They should have kept you on an IV if they wanted to keep you under. That wasn't very smart of them."

"Where is this?" Zachary asked. He tried again to sit up, and this time Kenzie let him, though her eyes were sharp and she kept a close eye on him for any unsteadiness. "I don't think they're very used to noncompliant patients."

"It's a private clinic. One of those places you might send Auntie Sue when she was off her meds or Cousin Frank to dry out. Tell people they're on a retreat or at the spa. And they are discreet about any comings and goings."

Zachary nodded slowly. He rubbed the back of his neck, which was throbbing. Not from his fall to the floor. Just a hangover from the drugs he had initially been given, or maybe from something that had happened during the abduction, which was only a vague, blurry memory.

“Are you okay?” Zachary searched Kenzie’s face for clues as to her anxiety level. She had been unable to even talk about kidnapping since her own experience at Christmas, and her PTSD wasn’t getting any better, despite her assurances. “This whole thing must have... been really hard.”

“It has been hard,” she agreed. She touched him again, her fingers resting on the back of his head and neck for a moment. Not checking vital signs this time, just reassuring herself and him. “But not because of me. I was worried about you. Worried about what had happened to you and whether...” She swallowed, trying to keep her emotions under control.

Zachary nodded. He reached over to give her a hug and pulled her close against him.

“It’s okay. I’m fine. Everything is okay.”

She nodded, but he could feel her sobbing silently against him. He held her firmly and rubbed her back, hoping to calm her down.

CHAPTER 71

There were footsteps and Zachary looked around, slowly taking in the activity around him instead of just Kenzie. Detective El Garcia was arriving with a bevy of uniformed and plainclothes law enforcement officers. She looked down at Zachary and Kenzie.

“Well, I guess you found him,” she observed dryly. “Mr. Goldman, I will need to talk to you. Are you okay?”

Zachary nodded. “I’m fine.”

“We’ve been looking for you. I didn’t expect to find you somewhere like this. Not after being taken off the street.”

“Maybe tied up in a warehouse?” Zachary suggested, stroking the back of Kenzie’s head and waiting for her to regain control.

“Yes. Best case scenario,” Garcia agreed.

The worst case being that she would find his body in a dumpster somewhere. Or maybe never. Zachary was lucky that whoever had coordinated the kidnapping had been unsure what to do with him and had decided to keep him incapacitated long enough to make that decision.

“I heard them talking. When they thought I was unconscious. They were… from TrimProGenix?”

“I’ve been hearing a lot about that. I haven’t been able to confirm it yet.”

“They were,” Kenzie agreed, her face still pressed against Zachary.

“What did they say?” Garcia asked.

“I think… they decided to kill me. I don’t know what all the pills they gave me were… I kept the ones I didn’t recognize.”

“You think that they were trying to poison you? To cause an adverse reaction?”

"Yeah. I think so. They said they wanted me silenced. So I couldn't cause them any more problems and Rx could bring in a few billion dollars more before it got pulled."

Kenzie sniffled. She pulled her face back from Zachary. "Well, they're going to have to rethink that now. I don't think they'll be able to keep Rx on the market any longer."

"No?" Zachary studied her face, wondering what the details were.

"When I was coming here, Brittany Blake was interviewing Rain Murdoch's father."

Zachary was floored. "How did that happen?"

He hadn't hoped in a million years that someone within the company would blow the whistle on them. Rain's father was particularly well-positioned to do so, but Zachary had not asked him to and couldn't imagine being able to convince him to do so.

"I used his login to pull information from the TrimProGenix servers. Kristin's smartwatch data and the results of some of the studies they did that were not published or where the data was manipulated, showing an alarming rate of cardiac events in the Rx users."

"And you black—" Zachary cut himself off and looked at Kenzie. "And you convinced him that he should talk to Brittany?"

"I talked to Eddie Godfrey. And he talked to Dr. Murdoch and convinced him to talk to Brittany. With Brittany's fan base..." Kenzie trailed off and patted her pockets, looking for her phone. "She was broadcasting live when I left home. Millions of people listening to her and Dr. Murdoch talking about the problems with Rx."

Zachary blew out his breath, relieved. "Well then... we've done everything we can. If they don't pull it, and no one investigates it, and people keep buying it, there's nothing we can do about that."

Kenzie nodded, looking amused at his analysis. "We've done everything we can," she agreed.

"How did you get Rain's father's login?" Zachary blinked at her, trying to pull together the different pieces of the puzzle.

"From Rain. She sent them to your phone."

He opened his mouth, but didn't ask. Kenzie smiled.

"And I got your unlock code from Heather. We should call her, by the way. I didn't call people to let them know what had happened to you, but I did talk to her and we should let her know as soon as we can that you are okay."

"Yeah." Zachary patted the pockets of his smock before his brain caught up to the fact that he didn't have his phone anymore. "You found my phone?"

"Yes. Sorry, I didn't bring it. It's at home. And the screen is cracked. It needs to be repaired."

"But it still works."

"Yes. It is still in working order."

Zachary took a deep breath in and let it out. Everything had worked out okay. He had not been sure, when he had been lying in that hospital bed, if there was any way he was going to get out of there alive. But he was out, he was okay, and they had succeeded in figuring out what had happened to Kristin.

"You got Kristin's data?"

"Yes."

"And that convinced Rain's father to talk to Brittany about it? To go public?"

"That, when presented by Eddie Godfrey. I figured if I could find someone who spoke the same language..."

"Good call. I would never have thought of calling Eddie about it. What did Kristin's data show? Was the Rx causing health problems for her?"

Kenzie's brows drew down and she nodded. "Yes. We don't have really great data, because to get the more nuanced data, you need multiple leads. But even with just the smartwatch, you can see that she was having cardiac events for a few days before her death."

"Heart attacks?"

"Most likely, yes."

"Why didn't the medical examiner find that in the autopsy?"

"There isn't always visible scarring. He might have looked but not been able to see anything pathological. Sudden cardiac death is really difficult to attribute to a particular cause. Even in Kristin's case, we can't say absolutely that it was caused by

Rx. We know it happened while she was taking Rx, but would it have happened anyway?"

"You can't tell from the data?"

"I only looked at the last few days of data. We might be able to look all the way back over the months she was using it and see if there are changes that showed up in that time. But I don't know if it is all on the server. Or if they did any testing before she started on the Rx. We really should have a baseline to compare it to. And preferably, a standard EKG rather than just the smartwatch data."

"You won't be the ones investigating that," Garcia warned, looking down at Zachary and Kenzie where they were still sitting on the floor. "Computer hacking is a crime. I wouldn't want to find out that you had been poking around places you shouldn't be, and have to charge you with something."

Zachary couldn't help grinning. Obviously, she knew very well that they had hacked their way into a server where they were not authorized to be. She was willing to look the other way on that. But she wouldn't let them pursue it any further.

Not that she would know about it. He didn't plan on telling her.

"I will need a statement from you about the kidnapping," Garcia said, changing the subject. "Especially if you saw any faces and can tell me some of the players involved."

Zachary rubbed his temples, thinking about it. It was all still very foggy. He knew that he had been lured to Bridget's house. And he could vaguely remember fighting people off, being dragged away against his will, and then into the private facility, where everyone had pretended that he was having a psychotic break rather than a perfectly natural reaction to a kidnapping. But it was all very fractured and he was missing chunks of time. He didn't know if he had been knocked out or drugged, or if he had dissociated during those periods. But there was very little he could actually remember from the kidnapping.

"Not sure if I can help. I was drugged… and most of it is a blank."

Garcia's gaze slipped over to Kenzie, asking her silently for more details or verification.

"From what was on his chart, I wouldn't expect him to be able to remember anything," Kenzie advised, shaking her head.

Did she really think that, or was she just being supportive and trying to keep Garcia from pushing him too hard? Zachary decided he didn't care. The result was the same either way. He was going home. There wasn't anything he wanted more than that right now.

CHAPTER 72

Garcia's eyes stayed on Kenzie. "Not so long ago, we were both lecturing Zachary on rushing into an investigation on his own when he should have gone to the police. Do you and I now need to have that same conversation?"

"I came in with your police officers." Kenzie shrugged innocently. "I didn't come here on my own. And I helped them to get up here to find Zachary and to talk that doctor down." She looked at him, sitting on the floor scowling, with his hands cuffed behind his back. He didn't look at her. "Is that Dr. Evans? That's the name that was on all of Zachary's papers."

Garcia gave a brief nod. "Apparently, he works at TrimProGenix."

"And here. Prescribing psychogenic drugs. And apparently, trialing experimental drugs."

“Like LipoSlayerRx?” Zachary asked, trying to get a handle on the connections.

“It would be strange for him to work in both weight loss and psychosis,” Kenzie said, shaking her head. “I wondered whether he discovered the weight loss aspect of Rx while testing it for something else. That happens sometimes, you know.”

A lot of scientific discoveries had been accidents.

Zachary rubbed his eyes. He put his hands down on the floor to shift his position and get his feet under him. “I’m getting up now,” he informed Kenzie, in case she had any ideas about keeping him down or tackling him to the floor once he made it to his feet. He didn’t like all of the cops towering over him. He felt small and vulnerable.

Kenzie stood up right after him. She kept one hand behind him for a moment, obviously expecting him to be lightheaded or unsteady. After he managed to stay on his feet without any obvious swaying, she figured out that he wasn't going to fall down and withdrew her hand.

* * *

It took longer than it should have to finish at the clinic so they could go home. But checking out of the hospital always felt like it took way too long too, so Zachary supposed he didn't have anything to complain about. As far as the clinic was concerned, he had been admitted under Title 19, so he should have had to stay there for a couple more days being observed and evaluated. But Garcia repeated the assertion that Zachary had been kidnapped and not lawfully admitted under Title 19 and, eventually, the staff had agreed to let him go home.

There was no way he would be able to go to sleep right away, and he figured Kenzie was probably pretty keyed up too. She had dark circles under her eyes, but didn't look or act sleepy. Maybe they were caused more by worry than by lack of sleep. Eventually, her physical fatigue would catch up with her and she would be able to sleep, but that was probably at least a couple of hours away. Neither of them was a tea drinker, but he brewed some anyway, hoping Kenzie would find it comforting.

“How are you?” he pressed. “This must have been really hard for you, considering... what happened to you.” He shook his head. “I can’t believe you watched it on video. You’re very brave.”

“Or stupid,” she said with a shrug. “Maybe watching it happen to someone else is a pretty dumb idea.” She stared off for a minute, and Zachary watched her closely for signs of distress or dissociation. But she seemed to be okay. “It was actually cathartic. I can even say the word kidna—” The word caught in her throat, surprising her. She tried again. “K-k-kidna—” She stopped trying. “Well, I was able to say it. That word.”

Zachary smiled as reassuringly as possible and nodded. “I’m sure you will again. You’re just thinking about it too much right now.”

She nodded her agreement, stirred her teabag around gently, and pressed it to the side of her cup to squeeze out the juices.

Looking at his cracked but still functional phone, Zachary tapped through his various notifications and messages. He followed a mention to Brittany Blake's profile and saw that she was still broadcasting live. She must have been hoarse after talking for hours. He tapped the Like button, and she must have gotten a notification on her side, because she gave a bright smile and greeted him by name.

"For those of you who have just arrived, we are waiting for an announcement by TrimProGenix, which they said would be made this morning." She looked at her watch.

While it was technically the next day, the workday hadn't started yet and Zachary would be surprised if they were ready to issue a formal statement until late morning or early afternoon. After their lawyers had a look at it.

"They should be on any minute now," Brittany assured her audience.

He kept an eye on his phone while he and Kenzie talked. Then a banner came up on Brittany's live video and he turned his volume back up to watch it. Coverage switched to a man in a suit reading a prepared statement, looking appropriately grave.

"Due to rumors of negative side effects and out of an abundance of caution, the board of directors of TrimProGenix has decided to temporarily suspend sales of LipoSlayerRx while an investigation into these allegations is conducted."

The written statement went on, but that was really all that Zachary needed to hear. The rest was just puffery about the company and its history and what a difference LipoSlayerRx had made in the world during the time it had been in distribution. They didn't answer questions. Eventually, the feed reverted to Brittany. She smiled broadly.

"Well, there you have it. This is a huge step for society. Sales of Rx have been suspended and, with any luck, they will never resume. Thank you to everybody who has had something to do with this. Especially my friends Zachary Goldman and Kenzie Kirsch. You guys rock."

Zachary grinned at Kenzie. "We rock."

"Apparently, we do."

CHAPTER 73

So, how are you feeling now that it's all over and life has returned to normal?" Dr. Boyle asked Zachary, uncrossing her legs and crossing them in the other direction. "About the kidnapping, I mean. I'd like to know how you're handling things. If we need to work on your meds. Extra therapy sessions."

"I'm doing pretty good," Zachary protested. "I don't remember much of what happened because of how they drugged me."

"But that doesn't mean that it didn't happen or that your body and brain don't react to triggers that bring it back. Look at Kenzie and the difficulty she has had. Things don't just snap back to normal after a traumatic experience like that."

Maybe it was because he'd been through so many traumatic things in the past that Zachary couldn't really see it. It wasn't like when he'd been captured by Archuro, paralyzed, tortured, and abused.

Dr. B studied him closely for a few seconds before nodding. “Okay. But I want to hear as things bubble up to the surface. If you start having new triggers or thoughts, I need to be aware of them.”

“Okay.”

“And how about your obsessive thoughts? We should discuss whether that is any worse and what we need to work on. Did you get to your OCDA group?”

“Yeah, once. But I didn’t really… feel like I belonged there. It’s not the same…”

“It’s enough the same that I think your association with them, talking to others who have obsessive thoughts, will help you.”

Zachary shrugged. He would see. He wasn’t sure that it was worth his while to keep going.

“Have you been over to Bridget’s house?”’

Zachary gave an involuntary shudder when he thought of the street in front of Bridget's house, where he had pulled over so many times to watch the house, hoping for a glimpse of Bridget or the twins, even just a shadow passing over the window.

"What was that?" Dr. B asked.

"Umm..." Zachary tried to put it into words. "Just... I don't want to go back there."

"You don't want to? But you feel compelled to?"

"No. I don't want to go anywhere near there. Where I was abducted." Zachary shuddered again, though he tried to control his reaction. He no more wanted to go back there than he did the cabin where he had been held by Archuro. He wanted to put as much space and time as possible between himself and that experience.

"The memories of the abduction bother you," Dr. B suggested.

“Yes. I don’t... want to be where that happened.”

She sat back in her chair, observing him with a half smile.

“What?”

“I wouldn’t have expected a kidnapping to have a positive effect on your mental health. But if it has made you averse to going to Bridget’s house... that’s not a bad thing.”

“No...” Zachary laughed. “I guess it’s not.”

* * *

Kenzie had been talking on the phone when Zachary got home. She finished saying goodbye and hung up, then looked at him with an expression he had difficulty interpreting.

“What?” Zachary asked uneasily, immediately casting his mind back to identify what he might have done wrong. Not anything serious. He hadn’t gone to Bridget’s and didn’t see himself going there again any time in the near future. He had just been at his therapy appointment, so it wasn’t because he had missed it. Was he supposed to run an errand for her while he was out? Bring something home for dinner? Or maybe he wasn't supposed to, but she had expected him to anyway. One of those spontaneous things couples did for each other. Unplanned, but expected. "Is something wrong?"

"That was Detective Garcia."

Zachary hadn't seen El since the clinic, so it wasn't anything he had done. Why would she be calling Kenzie instead of Zachary? He was the one who had a previous professional relationship with her. He was the one who had been abducted and held hostage. Not Kenzie.

"They got results back on the pills that you didn't take at the clinic."

His chest got tight and he found it hard to breathe normally. "They were supposed to kill me, weren't they?"

He remembered the low conversation of the two doctors when they had checked in on him, believing he was doped up. He had been an obstacle to Dr. Evans and to billions of dollars of earnings for TrimProGenix. Evans had been able to think of only one way to remove that obstacle permanently.

Kenzie nodded her head. Her expression was grim. “A very strong opioid, combined with the Benzodiazepines the doctor had prescribed... you would never have woken up.”

Zachary swallowed. His mouth and throat were suddenly very dry. “Could it have been a mistake? An oversight?”

She shook her head. “There was no reason to give you an opioid. And opioids mixed with benzos are a big no-no. If he had prescribed both, the nurses would have flagged it. But I guess someone just slipped it in.”

He remembered the nurse patiently telling him what each pill was. She hadn’t said any of them were opioids. And then the other nurse had helped him to pick up the spilled pills. Was that when he had slipped an extra one in, thinking Zachary was too dopey to notice the difference?

Zachary shook his head. He thought of the night he had taken two of his sleep aids and been so groggy, unable to wake up. If he'd been sedated and given the opioid, he never would have known there was anything wrong. He would just have ceased to exist, leaving Kenzie and his family behind. He had fought so hard against his depression and suicidal thoughts over the years, the idea of dying from an accidental—or intentional—overdose hit him like a punch in the gut. He couldn't let that happen.

Kenzie hugged him. "You stopped them. You knew you weren't supposed to take whatever it was, and you didn't let them succeed."

Zachary gripped her firmly and pressed his cheek against hers. He could feel her heart pounding. Both of their hearts together, strong and fast.

CHAPTER 74

It had taken some work for Zachary to get Jennifer to meet with him somewhere other than in her office. He wanted to avoid the corporate atmosphere, the pretty shades of pink and chrome, and everything being perfectly arranged and decorated. For some reason, he couldn't put himself back into that setting and didn't want to see Jennifer in it either. She was a different Jennifer from the one he had known as a teen. Not just because she was grown up and grieving Kristin. She had become something different. He couldn't put his finger on it or put it into words, but he didn't like what he saw. The corporate veneer was false. It didn't suit her.

He found a coffee shop near her office. Not in her building, because she would still have the advantage there. She had probably met many people there over coffee, so it was just an extension of her office. The shop he picked was independent, not one of the big chains. The type of place they might have gone to as teens, skipping out of classes or going somewhere over lunch. Finding a place they would make "theirs" and use as a home base. Or a touchstone.

He got there first, and then Jennifer arrived. She looked around the cafe uncertainly. Then she met his eyes and smiled at him. Her expression said she was still grieving, but her slight smile acknowledged their shared history.

Jennifer went to the counter to place her order and joined Zachary at his table a minute later, steaming cup in hand.

"This is nice," she commented. "It has real atmosphere."

"Yeah, it does," Zachary agreed.

Jennifer sat down.

"So... I guess you know about the company taking Rx off the market," Zachary said.

"Suspending it."

"Yes. But no one thinks it will be coming back in any form."

"It will be back. For something else, next time, and maybe with warnings on it and better monitoring. But these drugs don't disappear forever. They just tweak it, rebrand it, and sell it to another segment of patients. This time it isn't for weight loss, but weight loss is a known side effect."

"They were initially testing it as a psychoactive drug."

"Well, there you go." She shrugged. "They can go back to that. Maybe you'll take it someday. Although, you can't stand to lose much weight."

"This is the heaviest I've been in a few years. My doctor is happy that I'm finally well into the 'healthy' bracket."

"So maybe you'd better not take it when it comes back as BeHappyRx."

"Yeah. I don't think so," Zachary agreed.

"I appreciate you looking into it. The medical examiner has

agreed to reopen the investigation and look at Kristin's autopsy in light of the new data… but he said that probably nothing would change. They don't have any proof that it was the Rx rather than the anesthetic. Or a combination of the two."

"There were others who had cardiac issues with Rx."

"Yeah. But not enough to be able to identify it as the cause of death."

"You couldn't have known it would cause her problems. Even if you had known that she was on it, you would have had no way of knowing that it was potentially dangerous. The company was holding back any information about it being related to cardiac issues and death. The surgery would have gone ahead anyway. The results would have been the same."

"I knew she was on it."

Zachary opened his mouth and stared at her, stunned by the

admission.

“Or I suspected,” Jennifer amended. “She never came out and said it, but she had asked me about it, and then she was losing weight, and I didn’t think it was anything to worry about. I was proud that she was losing weight. Glad that she was getting into better shape and would be healthier and fit in with her peers.”

Zachary wondered if Kristin would ever have reached the level where she blended in with the rest of the school population. Not a cheerleader, but someone who didn’t stick out as being fat. And if she did, would she be more acceptable to her peers? Or would she just be an ex-fat girl to them?

But it was Jennifer’s dream, not his. In her mind, Kristin succeeded. She became the girl she had wanted to be. Not the girl who stayed an outcast forever. The girl in Jennifer’s dream had a nice body and straight teeth and friends.

Zachary looked toward the door as the tinkling of bells

announced a new customer. Jennifer followed his eyes.

“Oh, I know her,” Jennifer said, standing partway up to wave to the girl. Rain approached the table with her father, and then both sat down, looking awkward and uncomfortable. “Rain!” Jennifer took the girl’s hands in her own. “I’m so glad to see you.”

Rain nodded. “You too, Mrs. Jones.” She sniffled and swallowed. “It’s been really hard,” she confessed. “I miss her.”

Jennifer nodded. “I do too.”

Jennifer’s corporate woman persona was fading. She was a mom. A person. Zachary’s old friend. Something that she had lost was returning in this setting, with Rain there. She let go of Rain’s hands and sipped her coffee, nodding to Rain’s dad.

“Mr. Murdoch.”

“Doctor,” Rain corrected.

Zachary looked at her. It wasn’t exactly the time to remind

Jennifer that her father was a doctor, one of the scientists who had killed Kristin with their experiments, holding back the truth that Rx could kill, and did so all too often. But Rain didn't look away or back down.

Jennifer nodded. "Dr. Murdoch. It's nice to see you again."

"I'm so sorry about what happened to your daughter. It was a terrible tragedy."

Jennifer nodded her agreement.

"Dr. Murdoch was instrumental in getting Rx pulled from the market," Zachary reminded her. "At the risk of his job."

Dr. Murdoch nodded. "I will be looking for employment elsewhere," he acknowledged.

Rain looked both angry and proud at this information, her chin coming up slightly.

"You did the right thing," Zachary said. "I'm sorry you lost your job over it."

"Better my job than my integrity. It was wrong to hold back information about the risks of Rx. More people would have died. Deaths that were preventable."

It had taken some convincing for him to get to that point, but it seemed like he was now very solid in the position.

"Are they allowed to fire you for that?" Zachary looked at Dr. Murdoch. "For speaking up about information they should have released to the public? It isn't like you told lies about the company."

"I had a contract. I broke it."

They all nodded understandingly.

"We'll never forget Kristin," Rain promised. "Me and Ala. She was our friend, and we won't forget what happened to her."

Jennifer looked briefly at Zachary. Maybe balancing just how important school friendships were later in life. How much Rain and Ala would think about Kristin a year in the future. A decade. Twenty or thirty years. Would anyone even remember her name? Zachary wasn't in touch with anyone he had known in high school. Maybe he was an anomaly, because he had never really had a best friend, never been allowed to stay in one place long enough to create a solid bond of friendship. He had counted himself lucky if people were reasonably nice to him, or he could blend into the background with the other students and not be bothered.

"We'll keep in touch, Zachary," Jennifer said later as they prepared to go their separate ways. "It was nice reestablishing contact with you. You're... just the same as you were as a kid."

"I hope not." The life he had lived then was not one he would ever wish to go back to. He was glad to be away from the abusers and the bullies. Not to have to do homework or study anything he didn't want to. To give Heather the work responsibilities he didn't want to have to do.

"But you are," Jennifer said. She picked up her purse and

pulled the strap over her shoulder. “You’re kind and thoughtful, and you care about people.”

“Of course I care about you and what happened to Kristin.”

“Not everybody would. Plenty of people just turned their backs on me, even before... it happened. They weren’t friends because they were too busy, or they didn’t socialize with people with kids, or we just didn’t have anything in common.” She met his eyes. “The only thing you and I had in common was Ptarmigan House. But that didn’t matter to you.”

People were so much more than their circumstances, what they looked like, or where they worked. Zachary shook hands with Jennifer when she put out her hand, and then she pulled him into a hug and held him tightly.

Did you enjoy this book? Reviews and recommendations are vital to making a book successful.

Please leave a review at your favorite book store or review site and share it with your friends.

ABOUT THE AUTHOR

Award-winning and USA Today bestselling author P.D. (Pamela) Workman writes riveting mystery/suspense and young adult books dealing with mental illness, addiction, abuse, and other real-life issues. For as long as she can remember, the blank page has held an incredible allure and from a very young age she was trying to write her own books.

Workman wrote her first complete novel at the age of twelve and continued to write as a hobby for many years. She started publishing in 2013. She has won several literary awards from Library Services for Youth in Custody for her young adult fiction. She currently has over 100 published titles and can be found at pdworkman.com.

Born and raised in Alberta, Workman has been married for over 25 years and has one son.

* * *

Please visit P.D. Workman at pdworkman.com to see what else

she is working on, to join her mailing list, and to link to her social networks.

* * *

If you enjoyed this book, please take the time to recommend it to other purchasers with a review or star rating and share it with your friends!

www.ingramcontent.com/pod-product-compliance
Lightning Source LLC
Chambersburg PA
CBHW081133300726
48982CB00005B/952

* 9 7 8 1 7 7 4 6 8 5 3 7 2 *